The Greatest Trick
The Devil Ever Pulled

Anonymous

Books by Anonymous –

The Book With No Name
The Eye of the Moon
The Devil's Graveyard
The Book of Death
The Red Mohawk
Sanchez: A Christmas Carol
The Plot to Kill the Pope
The Day It Rained Blood
The Greatest Trick the Devil Ever Pulled
Showdown With the Devil

"The path you choose will matter not, for you, my dear, will always arrive at the same destination. All roads lead back to what feels like home for you. Under the light of a sleepless moon, that boy will be with you always."

Annabel de Frugyn speaking to Beth Lansbury in

The Eye of the Moon.

One

When Rodeo Rex was a young man

"RANDALL'S STEAKS AND BURGERS"

It was exactly the sort of place Rodeo Rex was looking for. He'd been on the road for over an hour, and for most of that time he'd been thinking about steaks and burgers. And fries. Chicken wings too. Barbecue sauce. Ribs. Beer. Bacon. Eggs. Melted cheese.

He was so busy visualising all the things that might be on the menu that he nearly rode his Harley Davidson right past the diner. He swung a sharp turn off the road and parked up next to a red pickup truck on the forecourt. There were no other vehicles in sight, which was a good sign because Rex wasn't in the mood for waiting a long time to get his mid-morning breakfast.

The diner looked like a giant log cabin, built from the deceased brothers and sisters of the enormous trees that surrounded the place. Rex liked the look of it from the outside, but the lack of any windows meant there was no way of knowing if the inside was as good.

He had taken only three steps towards breakfast when the diner's front door flew open and a young dark-haired girl in a bright yellow dress ran out, screaming. Rex wasn't great at guessing the ages of kids, but this girl had to be eight or nine years old. Something had her really spooked because she sprinted towards the red pickup without even throwing a glance his way. As she ran past him he reached out and grabbed her by the arm. Her legs kept pumping, so Rex inadvertently lifted her off her feet for a moment. He lowered her back down, but she responded by kicking him in the shins and trying to wriggle free from his grip. Her terrified face was covered in freckles and spots of blood.

'You okay?' Rex asked her.

The girl looked him up and down, and he hoped she saw a friendly face. She screamed again, which suggested she saw Rex the way most people did. He was after all, a giant, heavily tattooed Hell's Angel in his early twenties, with shoulder-length brown hair, wearing ripped jeans and a sleeveless leather waistcoat that showed off a set of biceps the size of balloons.

She didn't even scream any words, like "Let go of me" or "fuck off pervert". She just screamed that annoying "Aaaaaaagh" sound that kids love so much. Rex didn't love it at all. It made his bones tighten.

'Are your parents here?' he asked, raising his voice so she would hear it over the nightmarish pitch of her own.

The girl continued to writhe and scream, so desperate was she to break free of his grip and get as far away from the diner as possible. Rex was just about to release her, for the sake of his ears as much as anything, when a woman walked out of the diner. She was exactly Rex's type, and could have been a biker herself. She was wearing black leather pants and a matching waistcoat that didn't cover much of her ghostly white skin. And she had long flowing red hair. Her lipstick hadn't been applied well though. It looked like a clown's lipstick. Or did it? On closer inspection it was something else, like ketchup. *Or blood.* It was all around her mouth and dripping down her chin.

'You okay, lady?' Rex asked.

The woman ignored him. She had eyes only for the young girl who had stopped screaming and was now cowering behind Rex.

'Is this your daughter?' Rex asked.

Still no reply. Rude bitch.

The redhead suddenly sprinted across the forecourt towards the young girl. The girl screamed again. Rex gritted his teeth as the piercing sound cut through his ears. But the screams were the least of his problems. There were razor sharp fangs in the mouth of the onrushing redhead. *Vampire fangs.*

Somewhere deep inside, Rex had always had impeccable instincts, in particular, a bloodhound's nose for danger. He knew exactly what needed to happen next. As the woman charged towards him and the girl, he let go of the child and unleashed a sweet sucker-punch into the face of the fanged woman. It knocked her off her feet and she landed on her back, spraying up dirt and dust all around her.

'I'm sorry I had to do that....' Rex said.

The woman had no interest in his apology. She bounced back to her feet as if the ground beneath her was a trampoline. Her eyes were fixed on Rex now. Specifically, his throat.

She leapt up into the air and twisted sideways, aiming a flying kick at his head. Rex had seen similar moves before in his many wrestling bouts. He'd just never seen one done at such high speed. He ducked down and threw an uppercut punch. It was usually the best way to deal with such a move. Typically the punch would land somewhere in the midriff, making it more of a gut-punch than an uppercut. But due to the speed of the redhead's move, on this occasion his punch landed between her legs. One might call it a cunt-punch. It sent the woman spinning over Rex's shoulder onto the ground. But by the time he turned to face her, she was already back on her feet. He didn't want to hit her again and was about to try and reason with her when the high-pitched voice of the young girl shouted out from behind the red pickup.

'SHE KILLED MY MOM AND DAD!'

Rex and the redhead looked into each other's eyes. He raised his fists, ready for her to launch another attack. But the vampire woman had other ideas. She turned and sprinted towards the young girl who was cowering behind the truck. More screaming ensued. And Rex had to act quick. Fucking quick.

Like a gunslinger, he reached down to his hip and unhooked a lasso that he used as his novelty weapon from time to time in some of his more colourful wrestling bouts. With one flick of his wrist he snapped it out at full stretch. It wrapped around the redhead's neck and Rex yanked her back towards him, spinning her around until she was facing him.

CRUNCH!

He timed his head-butt to perfection. The sound it made was like a bite into a thick-ridged potato chip. Blood spurted from the woman's nose, but once again, she recovered instantly. As her head bounced back she grabbed at the rope around her neck with her clawed hands and ripped it away. A somersault later and she was behind Rex. He spun around ready to defend himself but the vampire bitch was already sprinting back to the diner. She ran up the wall of wooden logs and leapt up onto the roof, raced across it and vanished into the woodland, all in the space of about two seconds.

Rex took a moment to process what he'd seen, and then turned back to the young girl. Tears were streaming down her face.

'Are your parents inside?' Rex asked her.

She didn't respond. She didn't scream either, which was a positive thing.

'Wait there a second. I'll be right back,' said Rex.

He hurried up to the front entrance of the diner, keeping an eye out for any cartwheeling vampire women. He pulled the door of the diner open and stepped inside. The walls and tables in the eating area were covered in blood. The first body Rex saw was on the floor near the counter. It was a man in a red and black lumberjack shirt, most likely the father of the young girl and owner of the red pickup. The man's throat had been ripped out and a pool of thick black blood surrounded his head. A few steps further into the diner Rex saw another body on the floor. It was the headless corpse of a woman in a pink dress. He covered his mouth and nose. The smell was nasty.

There was a huge splatter of blood on the wall behind the counter, and there was plenty more sprayed across a row of mugs and glasses. If there was a staff member in Randall's diner, he or she was probably in pieces behind the counter. Rex had seen enough.

He exited the diner, backing away from the horror inside.

BANG!

Rex ducked down and spun around. He needn't have bothered ducking because the gunfire wasn't aimed at him. The passenger door of the truck was open. Blood was spattered across the window and the wing mirror. The young girl fell back against the side of the truck and then dropped to the ground. A shotgun bounced off the ground at her feet.

'NOOOO!'

Rex had never heard of kids shooting themselves. It was something that wasn't supposed to happen, not in any kind of universe. He sprinted over to the girl and knelt down beside her. Blood was pulsing out of her neck. He cradled her head and pressed his hand over the gaping wound. Blood oozed out between his fingers. The fear and terror that he'd seen in the girl's eyes earlier was replaced by a brief look of relief before she died in his arms.

Rex closed his eyes. His face filled up with mucus and snot like he had the flu. He didn't want to open his eyes again and look upon the lifeless child.

'Her name was Tabitha,' said a man's voice. 'She's gone to a better place now.'

Rex looked up and saw a man dressed in a long white dress standing over him.

'What the fuck's happened here?' Rex asked him.

'My name is Levian,' the man replied. 'And I have a proposition for you.'

Rex was staring up into the sun and it was making his eyes fill with water. He wiped them so that he could get a better look at Levian. He was a black man with blonde hair, which was certainly a striking look.

'Where did you come from?' Rex asked.

'I've been sent by the Almighty.'

'The what?'

'Tabitha cannot be saved Rex, but maybe the next girl can.'

'How do you know my name?'

'I know everything about you. I know that you're looking for a purpose, a noble cause, a way to live a virtuous life.'

Rex laid the girl down on the ground and wiped his hand in the dirt to get rid of some of the sticky blood on his fingers. 'Listen, buddy.

I'm not in the mood for this shit,' he said, resting on his haunches. 'Look what's happened here!'

Levian offered Rex a hand and helped him to his feet. 'The woman that you just fought with, she wasn't human was she?' he said.

Rex dusted himself down. 'Yeah, no shit.'

'She was a vampire. There are thousands of others like her, hiding all over the world,' Levian continued. 'Not many people meet one and live to tell the tale like you've just done.'

'What do you want, man?'

'I'm offering you an opportunity, Rex. A job offer, something you're perfect for.'

'And what's that?'

'God would like you to become his personal bounty hunter, finding vampires and killing them for him.'

Rex looked Levian up and down. A blonde haired, black dude dressed as an angel. Could this day get any weirder?

'What the fuck are you talking about?' he snapped.

'Don't you want to prevent more little girls like Tabitha from seeing their parents murdered? Or being murdered themselves?'

Rex reached out and grabbed Levian by the collar of his dress or nightgown or robe—whatever the fuck it was. Except that it wasn't there. His hand passed right through it, and through Levian, as if he were an apparition. It made no sense. Levian had helped him to his feet a moment earlier, yet now he was just a hologram, or some shit like that.

'Who the fuck are you?' Rex asked, growing more impatient by the second. *'What* the fuck are you?'

'I am Levian, an Angel sent by God to give your life purpose.'

Rex attempted to prod Levian in the chest. His hand went right through the white robe again.

'I am real,' said Levian. 'All of this is real.'

A lot of crazy shit had happened in the last ten minutes, including this dude in the dress. But at least he wasn't trying to make Rex a mid-afternoon snack. If there were vampires, maybe there were angels too?

'Okay, I'll play along,' said Rex. 'What do you want me to do?'

'You must head to a city called Santa Mondega. Find La Iglesia dela Santísima Santa Ursula y las Once Mil Virgenasthe.'

Rex wasn't impressed. 'What the fuck is that?'

'The Church of the Blessed Saint Ursula and the Eleven Thousand Virgins. It is in the centre of Santa Mondega. There you will find a preacher named Father Papshmir. He will show you where to find more of the undead. And he will show you how to kill them.'

'Santa Mondega? Never heard of it. Where the fuck is it?'

'It's not on any maps,' said Levian. 'But you will find it. God will show you the way. Just get on your bike and ride.'

Two

Hotel Pasadena: The Devil's Graveyard - many years ago.

Annabel de Frugyn had travelled hundreds of miles to attend the *Back From The Dead* talent show. The singing contest was held in the Hotel Pasadena, a luxurious building situated in an area of desert known as the Devil's Graveyard.

Unfortunately for Annabel, her bus journey there had been an unpleasant one. She had been nervous about some important stuff she had to do when she arrived at the hotel, and in an attempt to calm her nerves she had accepted a drink from the gentleman seated next to her, a tubby Mexican bartender named Sanchez Garcia. She should have known better than to trust him, but it had never crossed her mind that someone might carry around a hip flask full of his own piss. The last part of the journey was spent throwing up in the toilets on the bus.

Shortly after arriving at the hotel she was escorted to the office of the hotel manager, Nigel Powell. Powell had heard all about her ability to see the future and wanted to know if she could tell him the identity of an assassin who had been hired to kill some of the contestants in his talent show.

After giving Powell some bogus information she left his office and headed up to her hotel room to do something she'd been planning for a long time. A meeting with The Devil. A man named Scratch. It was to be her first meeting with him. And she was nervous about it. Fucking nervous. Really, really fucking nervous.

If what she'd heard about summoning the Devil was true, she had to find a mirror, preferably a tall one. The bathroom in her hotel room had that very thing. On the wall next to the walk-in shower was a mirror that would serve as her entry point to the other side. She stood in front of it and stared at her reflection. The face of an old woman stared back at her. She looked terrible, partly because she was old and partly because she'd recently drunk a hip flask full of piss and thrown up a bunch of times. She spotted some puke on her green cardigan so she took the cardy off and tossed it into the shower. Lucky for her she always wore two cardigans, so she buttoned the second one up to hide another vomit stain on her black dress. But rearranging her clothes was only delaying the inevitable. Her heart was pounding louder than ever, creating a strange pulsing sensation in her ears. This was to be one of the key moments in her life. She closed her eyes.

'Scratch, are you there?' she asked.

'I'm here.'

She opened her eyes. In the mirror she saw the reflection of a large, well-built black man in a red suit standing behind her. He had a goatee beard and a bowler hat that matched his suit. This was real. She was in the company of the man in charge of Hell. She turned around to face him, only to find he was no longer there. She turned back to the mirror and saw him behind her once more, grinning.

'What can I do for you, Annabel?' he asked.

'I've come here with a proposition for you,' she said. Her entire body was trembling and it was hard to hide it.

'So proposition me.'

'I'm a psychic.'

'That's not a proposition, that's a statement.'

'It's true though.'

'I'm sure it is. To have found me you must be either psychic or very lucky. Or should that be *unlucky?*'

Annabel didn't have time to banter with him. She'd rehearsed everything she had to say a million times and she just wanted to get it off her chest. She suspected that he knew that, which was why he was being a dick.

'I've seen the future,' she continued. 'And I know that a few years from now I'm going to be murdered in Santa Mondega, the night before a very important eclipse.'

'You want my advice?'

'Not exactly...'

'Well my advice,' said Scratch, his grin widening, 'is don't be in Santa Mondega on the night you're due to be murdered.' He obviously found himself very funny because he laughed for an inappropriately long time. Annabel waited for him to finish and answered him seriously.

'That's a nice idea,' she said. 'But it's vitally important that I be in Santa Mondega that night.'

Scratch stroked his beard and eyed her with suspicion. 'It can't be that important?' he said. 'Worth dying for?'

'It's my destiny to borrow a book with no name from the local library. It contains the identity of the Dark Lord of Vampires, Archibald Somers.'

'Also known as Armand Xavier,' Scratch added.

'That's right. Somers will come to my trailer and kill me before I finish reading the book. But the next day the Bourbon Kid will find the book, and while flicking through it he will discover Somers's true identity. The Kid will then use the book to destroy Somers, which in turn will save Santa Mondega from ruin.'

Scratch took a step closer to Annabel, close enough that she could feel his breath on her shoulder. 'That's quite a noble sacrifice you'd be making.'

'And I'm happy to make it.'

Scratch retreated back to his original position. 'The Bourbon Kid, eh?' he said. 'So, you being psychic and all, you must know that he's in the hotel right now?'

'Yes I do.'

'So why don't you just go up to him and tell him that Archie Somers is the Dark Lord? Save you getting murdered, eh?'

Scratch was more annoying than Annabel had expected, but she couldn't rise to his baiting.

'I can't tell the Bourbon Kid,' she said, 'because the fates are telling me he wouldn't believe me. He needs to find out this information for himself just before the eclipse.'

Scratch seemed to tire of winding her up. 'Okay. Cut to the chase,' he said with a sigh. 'What do you want from me?'

'I want to sign a contract with you, so that when I die, after my head is ripped off by Armand Xavier, I can come and work for you in Purgatory, predicting the future for you.'

'Work for me?' Scratch laughed heartily for an inappropriately long time again, before abruptly pulling himself together. 'What do I need with a psychic?' he asked.

'We have a common goal. I want the world to be rid of the undead and I know you do too. I can help with that.'

'*You* can help *me?* How so?'

'There is an Elvis impersonator in this hotel. He's also a hitman.'

'Aaah yes, I know who you mean. I like him.'

'Everybody does. Anyway, you see Elvis has a friend named Rodeo Rex. Rex works for God hunting down the undead.'

'Yes I know this too. You're not telling me anything I don't know.'

'Well, around the same time I die at the hands of Archie Somers, Elvis and Rex will also both be killed by him. I understand that you cannot reveal yourself to anyone that is not looking for you, but, if you like, I can persuade both Elvis and Rex to sign contracts with you, selling you their souls.'

'Pah,' Scratch scoffed. 'Why would they do that?'

'So that when they die, they can come and work for you, hunting down the undead, with me as the guide, locating the undead for them.'

Scratch was intrigued. 'You could get Rodeo Rex, God's own bounty hunter, to come and work for me?'

'That's what I'm offering.'

Scratch stroked his chin and pondered the offer for a moment before his usual smug grin reappeared. 'God would be livid if Rex worked for me,' he said, his eyes glowing yellow.

'So we've got a deal?'

'Yes, we've got a deal.'

Annabel turned around to face him again. This time Scratch didn't disappear.

'Meet me back here in one hour,' he said. 'I'll have a contract for you.'

'There's a couple of other, very tiny little things I would like to iron out in this contract,' said Annabel, tensing up.

'Go on.'

'This hotel is going to plummet into the depths of Hell later tonight because Robert Johnson is going to win Nigel Powell's singing contest.'

Scratch raised a curious eyebrow. 'Robert Johnson's going to win the show? How exactly is *that* going to happen?'

'He will enter the competition under a different name, posing as a Blues Brother impersonator.'

'And he'll win the show? You're sure of this?'

'Positive. And because you *already* own his soul, he cannot sign the winner's contract, can he?'

'Oh you're good,' said Scratch. 'How on earth do you know all this?'

'Like I said, I'm psychic. Are you impressed yet?'

Scratch nodded. 'I am actually. So you also know that if Nigel Powell doesn't get the winner of the show to sign a contract then *he* has broken *his* contract with me.'

Annabel was growing in confidence. 'And you get *Nigel's* soul, and the hotel sinks back into Hell, yes?' she said, smiling.

'I like it!' Scratch said rubbing his hands together. 'Powell's a smug little fucker who's had it coming for years.'

'So, with all that in mind,' Annabel continued. 'I would like a camper van, a big one, almost as big as a bus.'

'What for?'

'I need to make my escape later on when your army of zombies arrive and the hotel sinks into the depths of hell.'

'You know about the zombies too?'

'I do.'

'Okay, but why a camper van? Wouldn't you rather have a sports car?'

Annabel shrugged. 'I would, but I don't intend to travel alone. I'll need you to arrange for Elvis to make it out alive too.'

'Okay, I'll make it clear to the zombies that Elvis is off limits. And I'll get them to steal a van for you and leave it in the parking lot with the keys inside.'

Annabel was amazed at how well everything was going. 'Thank you,' she said. 'I'd also like for Elvis's friend Sanchez to escape with us too.'

Scratch groaned. 'Why?'

'Because in spite of the fact he's disgusting, I quite like him. It's hard to explain.'

Scratch nodded. 'I know what you mean. I find him amusing too, especially his toilet humour. I don't imagine I'll ever get tired of that.'

'You might.'

'I doubt it. So you, Elvis and Sanchez will be the first people to ever escape from the Devil's Graveyard. It's a deal.'

'Oh, umm, can you arrange for the Bourbon Kid to escape too?'

'Ugh. For goodness sake. Why?'

'Well, because of that thing in Santa Mondega I was telling you about. He's going to kill the Dark Lord Archie Somers, remember?'

Scratch rolled his head from side to side before making a decision. 'Okay, yes that makes sense. You, Elvis, Sanchez and the Bourbon Kid will be the first people to ever escape from the Devil's Graveyard.'

'And Janis Joplin too,' Annabel spluttered.

Scratch frowned. 'Janis Joplin? Why Janis Joplin?'

'I just like her. She's funny.'

'Funny how?'

'She's got Tourette's. She'll make it to the final and ruin the show, which will help Robert Johnson to win.'

Scratch took another moment for some deep thought, as he was prone to do. Then he nodded. 'Okay. I like the sound of that. So you,

Elvis, Sanchez, the Bourbon Kid and Janis Joplin will be the first people....'

'To ever escape from the Devil's Graveyard on Halloween!' said Annabel, finishing the sentence for him.

Scratch looked bemused by her finishing his sentence.

'Sorry about that,' she said.

'No problem. Be back here in an hour. I'll have a contract for you to sign.'

And with that, Scratch vanished.

Three

The Deathbed

'She's got one week. I'm sorry to say, that's the best you can hope for.'

One week. Dr Simpson was the one who said the words, yet they were stuck in Vincent's throat. He wanted to repeat them but saying them out loud was too hard. He had known the day would eventually come. And more recently he'd known it was close, but even so, hearing the words that his mother would be dead in a week, maybe less, these were tough times.

Vincent was outside his mother's bedroom, discussing her situation with the doctor in hushed voices so that she wouldn't hear. Doctor Herbert Simpson had been the family doctor ever since Vincent was a small boy, so the two men had known each other for over thirty years. The doctor had been making house calls for even the most trivial illnesses and injuries throughout that time. When Vincent was younger he had secretly hoped that Dr Simpson would one day marry his mother. The two of them had lots in common. They were both caring and generous, and always putting other people first.

The cotton-haired doctor placed a comforting hand on Vincent's shoulder 'I'm sorry I don't have better news for you,' he said. 'But I can stay a while if you like?'

'No, you've done more than enough, thanks,' Vincent replied. 'You should go. I don't want your wife blaming me if you're late for your dinner again.'

Dr Simpson took hold of Vincent's hand and clasped it between his. 'Your mother's generous donations to the hospital over the years have been greatly appreciated,' he said. 'I'll make sure there's always a nurse here to take care of her. And I'll drop by here again in the morning.'

'She's okay to stay here then?'

Dr Simpson nodded. 'Of course. Anything she wants or needs, you just let me know.'

'Thanks, doc.'

Dr Simpson shook Vincent's hand and went on his way. Vincent watched from the window as the doctor drove away in a shiny new car. He hoped that one day he could be like him. Dr Simpson was always so calm and seemed to know exactly the right thing to say. That took some serious talent. Vincent was going to have to show some similar skill. He knocked on his mother's bedroom door and spoke through it.

'Mom, It's Vince. You still alive?'

She called through the door. 'Come in.' Her voice was weak.

Vincent entered the room. His mother was sitting up in bed in her nightdress. The early morning sun was shining in through the window onto the side of her pale face. Her cheekbones were too sharp, and her greying hair unusually messy. But her eyes lit up when she saw him.

'Herbert just told me the news,' Vincent said.

'It had to happen,' said his mother, patting the bed and gesturing for him to sit down beside her. He took a deep breath and held in the urge to cry. A dry pain wormed its way into his throat. This was hard, and over the next few days it would get worse. His mother was going to die in this bed. He sat down beside her and took hold of her hand. It was cold and bony, not like the warm, soft hand he had held so often as a child.

'Are you in pain?' he asked.

She shrugged. 'I've been through worse.'

'Worse than dying?'

She forced a smile. 'You have such a way with words, my boy.'

'Sorry, I… you know…'

'I know. You're just like your father, he was very blunt, not intentionally. He just told the truth *all the time.*'

Vincent forced a smile of his own. She had raised a subject he had wanted to broach himself. 'Is now a good time?' he asked.

'You want to know about your father?'

He'd wanted to know since he was old enough to know what a father was. But his mother never wanted to talk about it, always telling him the time wasn't right. And even though pestering her for details about it on her deathbed seemed a bit selfish, it was now or never.

'You're going to tell me then?' he said, desperately.

She nodded. 'I want you to know, I only kept it a secret for your protection. It wasn't safe for anyone to know. Not even you.'

'Why?'

'I've not uttered your father's name since before you were born. The mere mention of him could lead evil people here. I wanted to protect you.'

'I'm thirty-four years old, mother. I can take care of myself.'

'I know you can, my boy. Now listen carefully, because what I'm going to tell you is very important. And it's kind of a long story. Did you want to get a drink before I start?'

'I'm not going anywhere 'til you've finished telling me everything.'

She reached up and stroked his cheek. In her eyes he saw a sadness that had always been there. The truth behind those eyes was finally about to come out.

'First of all,' she said, squeezing his hand. 'There's a lot of bad news here, which is another reason why I never wanted to tell you.'

'I wasn't expecting it to be all sunshine and rainbows, mom, but I can cope, don't worry.'

'Okay.' She stared down at her hand. Half a smile broke out on her face as if she had remembered something wonderful. 'Your father and I were never married.'

It wasn't the huge revelation he was expecting, so he pretended to gasp in shock. His mother gave him the same look she always gave him when he was making fun of her. It was a playful look that said, *"Grow up, you dick"*.

'When I met your father my name wasn't Ruth Palmer,' she said, tightening her grip on his hand. 'Back then I was called Beth Lansbury.'

'Beth Lansbury? Does that make me a Lansbury as well?'

She shook her head. 'Never *ever* call yourself by that name. And never mention it again. There are ears everywhere.'

Vincent wondered if a mix of old age and ill-health was making her a touch melodramatic. She was definitely quite paranoid about something. It was possible she was overreacting and the big reveal was that his father had been married to someone else. His mother had always been a bit of a prude and probably would have struggled to live with that kind of shame.

'What was his name?'

'His name was JD.'

'JD. What's that short for?'

'It was short for Jack Daniels. But I usually just called him JD, unless we were arguing about something.'

'Is he still alive?'

She stroked a crease away on the bed sheet, stalling as if she didn't want to reply.

'Mom?'

She looked into his eyes and shook her head. 'He's dead. I never lied to you about that. He died before you were born.'

Vincent's heart sank. He had secretly hoped his father was still alive, and that they would one day be reunited and everything would be awesome. He'd always known it was unlikely, now he knew it was impossible.

'We were on the run,' his mother continued.

That came as a surprise. 'On the run? From what?'

'From the Devil.'

Vincent waited for her to laugh and say she was joking. She didn't.

'Who's the Devil?' he asked.

'Your father did some bad things.'

'Like what?'

'He was a mass murderer.'

Vincent laughed, although only for a second. His mother's face showed that she was deadly serious.

'WHAT?'

'Hey, I loved him, okay. He was never bad to me. But it's complicated. He had a good heart, but there were a lot of people trying to kill him. We came up with a plan. We decided that if we were ever going to be together we would have to fake our own deaths. So we did. And we moved around the country for a while, making a new life for ourselves as Luke and Ruth Palmer.'

'This is so *not* what I was expecting.'

'I know. But whether you want to hear this or not, I'm telling you everything now. I should have done this sooner, I'm sorry. You see, we had a big problem. Your father had signed a deal with the Devil. A contract. And one of the clauses in the contract was that if JD were to ever have children, they would be handed over to the Devil for execution. When I found out I was pregnant with you, we knew that if the Devil ever found out about your existence, you'd be taken from us and killed.' She clicked her fingers. *'Just like that.'*

Vincent felt uneasy. His mother had never been a liar, but this was a mountain of a story, the kind usually known as bullshit.

'Can you prove any of this?'

She nodded. 'Let me start at the beginning. When we were teenagers, JD and me, we met on a pier in a town called Santa Mondega. It was Halloween night. He was dressed as a scarecrow and I was Dorothy.'

'Dorothy who?'

'Never mind, it's not important. But that Halloween night was one of the most eventful nights in the history of Santa Mondega.'

'Santa Mondega? Where is that?'

'It's an evil place, not on any maps. But it has this lovely promenade and a pier where you can stand and stare out at the ocean. It's where your father and I kissed for the first time. It was just after he'd saved me from a vampire that attacked me.'

'A what?'

Vincent couldn't mask his surprise or his dismay. His shoulders slumped at the conclusion that his mother was delusional. Talking shit. He started to get up from the bed but her bony hand held him firm.

'Son, just hear me out. After we parted, JD went to fetch his brother from the church of Saint Ursula. But when he got there the church had also been attacked by vampires. They were everywhere that night. JD's mother was turned into one and he had to kill her.'

'He killed *his own mother?*'

She squeezed his hand some more. 'It's what made him into a killer. He drank a bottle of bourbon to give him the courage to kill her, and after that, every time he drank any bourbon, it brought back the memories of killing his mom, so he would go on these killing sprees.'

'Where he killed vampires?' Vincent added, inadvertently making it sound like he was starting to believe the story.

His mother winced. 'Kind of. Sometimes he killed regular folk too.'

'Jesus Christ, mom!'

'I told you it was a lot to take in. But he wasn't the only one who killed people. I did once too. On the night he killed his mother, I was set on by Devil worshippers when I got home.'

'This is too much, mom, *too much.*'

She ignored him and carried on. 'One of the Devil worshippers was my stepmother. I hated her anyway, but when she attacked me, I stabbed her in the neck and killed her....'

Vincent groaned. 'Okay, hold on, I'm gonna go get that drink now. And a pen and paper because I think I might wanna write this down.'

'Wait.' She clasped his hand tighter. 'It's already written down. In my bedside drawer, there's a book.'

Vincent reached over to the bedside drawer and pulled it open. There was a thick black hardback book inside. He pulled it out and opened it.

'You wrote this?' he asked.

'Yes, in case I died before I could tell you everything,' she replied.

Vincent flicked through to halfway and stopped to read some of it. A name jumped out at him. 'Who is Ryan Miller?' he asked.

'Ryan Miller?'

'Yes, there's a chapter here with the title, Ryan Miller.'

'Oh, him. Yes, he was an FBI agent. He tracked us down when we were living in a place called Wissmore. It was about six months before you were born. Just before your father died.'

Four

Ryan Miller

Six o'clock in the evening was a busy time in Wissmore city centre. To an out-of-towner like Ryan Miller it was chaotic. The pavements were barely wide enough to cope with the swarm of human traffic. And with everyone walking at different speeds it was hard to get anywhere fast. If Ryan ducked past one person, he was soon stuck behind another walking even slower, or even worse, crowded out by a family coming the other way.

The man Ryan was following was one of those freakish types who breezed effortlessly through the swarms of people without anyone so much as brushing up against him.

All of the buildings in the city centre were lit up with bright neon lights and glitzy videos that played on their sides. Like all modern cities with large populations, everywhere you looked there were adverts weaving their way into your subconscious.

Drink this fizzy drink.

Watch this movie.

Drive this car.

Vote for this prick.

Buy this watch.

Eat this burger.

Spend. Your. Fucking. Money. On. Shit. You. Don't. Need.

None of the advertising blitz had any effect on Ryan Miller, not today anyway. It remained in his peripheral vision, ignored, unnoticed. His entire focus was on the man with the shaggy dark hair in the brown suede jacket gliding through the crowd ahead of him, untouched by everyone else.

A bald man in a yellow tunic, holding out a flyer promoting some kind of religion, made a beeline for Ryan. What was the deal with these people anyway? They seemed to be drawn to anyone who made an extra-special effort not to make eye contact with them. Shitheads.

'Excuse me, sir. Can I interest you in the…..'

'Get fucked.'

The bald man looked crestfallen, as if no one had ever told him to get fucked before. It must have been his first day on the job. Ryan shook off any thought of the man. His focus had to remain one hundred percent on the guy he was following, because *that guy* was a mass murderer. If what he'd heard about the Bourbon Kid was true, then all it would take was one second, one momentary lapse of concentration and the Kid would vanish, gone forever. This chance might never come around again. He had to take it.

The man he believed to be the Bourbon Kid, took a turn away from the main streets, ducking into a side road just past an Olé Au Lait coffee shop. Ryan acted as if he was going to continue past the side road, but really he was checking out of the corner of his eye to make sure the Bourbon Kid wasn't lying in wait for him. When he knew everything was okay, he made a late detour and carried on his pursuit.

The new street wasn't as well lit. The neon lights and shiny adverts were gone, replaced by crappy posters and graffiti on the walls. But there were still a million people hustling and bustling along the street, making it hard to keep the suspect in sight. The Bourbon Kid and his effortless walk came dangerously close to losing Ryan completely. Ryan sped up into a jog that didn't help him one bit. If anything, it hindered him further, making him magnetic to anyone coming the other way.

Bzzzzz.

Bzzzzz.

He reached down into the hip pocket on his grey trench coat and answered a call on his cell phone, still keeping his eyes on his prize. He already had an earpiece tucked discreetly in his ear, and he'd been waiting for this call. It was his boss returning a call from earlier.

'What's up Ryan?'

'Hey, Captain. I've found him.'

'Found him? You mean.....'

'Yeah, the man we're looking for. I'm tailing him through the streets of Wissmore right now. Can you get a fix on me?'

People were throwing strange glances Ryan's way. He had to admit, it did look like he was talking to himself. But that shouldn't make him stand out. Half the nutters in the world spent their time talking to hidden mouthpieces, or to themselves.

'You're sure it's him?' said Captain Moranis.

'He looked right at me.'

'Right at you?'

'Yeah.'

'Did he see you?'

'If he had, I wouldn't be talking to you, would I?'

'I guess not.'

A gentle splash of rain dropped down from above and landed on the peak of Ryan's baseball cap. In Wissmore, when you feel one drop of rain, it's a sign that a major downpour is imminent. People everywhere started ducking inside shop doorways or hailing taxicabs. It was like a scene from a Godzilla movie. And sure enough, a torrential downpour of rain followed that first drop. Ryan was thankful he was wearing a cap. He hunched his shoulders, pulled up the lapels on his coat and carried on, only now he was fighting his way through the rain instead of the crowds of people.

'Where is he now?' asked the Captain, his voice almost drowned out by the rain.

'He's right in front of me.'

'What? I can't hear you.'

'He's just turned a corner.'

'Okay, I got your location on the map. You're heading down Hannover Way. Keep him in your line of sight. I'm sending the whole unit down there right now.'

'You got it boss.'

'I'm gonna hand you over to Stacy. Stay on the line. And Ryan, be careful.'

The line went quiet, which often meant the Captain had cut himself off. Hopefully he'd put Ryan on hold while he located Stacy, one of the senior agents. Ryan wasn't concerned though. His focus was on the Bourbon Kid.

He watched from a safe distance as the Kid ducked into an alleyway to get out of the rain. Ryan scurried along the street after him, the rain already soaking into his socks and shoes. He stayed hunched over to stop his cap from blowing off and turned into the alley the Kid had disappeared into. Ryan hissed in annoyance. The rain had brought with it a darkened sky making it hard to see anything. The sound of rain pattering on his cap and the shoulders of his coat began to drown out the distant sounds of beeping cars and chattering shoppers. The alley was empty, save for a few dumpsters, puddles, discarded coffee cups, and backstreet shops that may or may not be open.

Ryan stood in the rain, thinking through the situation piece by piece. He was halfway down the alleyway. The Bourbon Kid had vanished. Maybe he'd seen Ryan following him and made a hasty escape? But there was another possibility. Ryan had owned a suede jacket once, just like the Bourbon Kid's, and when it rained, the best thing to do was to find shelter, or prepare to buy a new jacket. However, there were no shop doorways in which a person could hide. No alcoves, nothing. Just dumpsters, and who in their right mind would hide in a dumpster to get out of the rain?

'You lookin' for me?'

The voice came from behind him. And it was gravelly in tone. Ryan spun around in surprise. Through the heavy rain that was dripping off the peak of his cap, he saw the outline of the man he had been following. *The Bourbon Kid*, this man who could move through crowds without being touched, could also disappear in a dark alley and then reappear a matter of inches behind an FBI agent who was tailing him. Ryan looked into the eyes of the renowned killer. And he didn't like what he saw. Some bluffing was required.

'Oh, hey, I was just....'

The words got stuck and turned into gurgling sounds. The Bourbon Kid had plunged a sharp hunting knife into Ryan's throat.

Five

Maggie's Farm was the nicest place Beth had ever stayed in. From her kitchen window she could see nothing but green fields, tall trees, blue skies and the beautiful lake. It was the third home she and JD had rented in the last six months, and she hoped it would be the last. Now that she was four months pregnant she dreamed of family days on the farm, of seeing her child grow up surrounded by gorgeous countryside and friendly creatures. But as farms go, it was somewhat light on animals. These days Maggie's Farm was a former farm, where no crops were harvested and no animals roamed. She had suggested to JD that they buy some chickens, but he'd been quick to remind her that they would probably be moving on again in the near future.

They moved home regularly because they were on the run, not just from the law, but also from the Devil. If he found out they were both still alive, his revenge would be malicious, spiteful, violent and most likely drawn out. It had been six months since they had faked their deaths in the Black Forest on Blue Corn Island. And in that time there had been no indication that the Devil knew they still existed, but even so, JD didn't like staying in one place for too long. These days they didn't even use their own names. Beth was Ruth Palmer and JD was her husband Luke. It was about as close as they were ever likely to get to being married. But they were having a baby. She looked down at the beginnings of a bump showing through her apron as she prepared some sausages for dinner. There were times in the past when she feared she might never have a child. Now she feared having one and seeing it snatched away by the Devil. JD's contract with Scratch had a clause in it, stating that if he ever had any offspring it had to be handed over to the Devil for execution. The last thing Scratch wanted was another living person with holy blood. JD was the son of Ishmael Taos, one of two men who drank the blood of Christ from the Holy Grail, granting them immortality and a long life. Immortality only went so far of course, because Taos and his fellow blood drinker Armand Xavier were both dead. And that had left JD as the last person alive with the blood of God in his veins. The baby in Beth's womb would have that blood too, and that made the child a threat to the Devil. It was a sobering thought that crossed Beth's mind every time she thought of her unborn child.

JD arrived home just before seven o'clock. As soon as he walked through the door Beth knew something was wrong. He had blood on his hands and specks of it on his face and neck.

'Oh no,' she said, her shoulders drooping. 'What have you done?'

'We need to move again. Start packing.'

'Do we always have to move right when I'm in the middle of making dinner?'

'Okay, we've got a little time. I'll start packing. You finish what you're doing.'

Beth normally heard him arrive. The roar of his black Ford Mustang always announced he was returning home. But today it hadn't. 'I didn't hear you pull up,' she said, looking out of the window. 'Where's the car?'

'I parked it in the woods.'

'Why?'

'So no one will see it.'

He approached her and put his arms around her and tenderly kissed her. 'I killed someone,' he said, ruining the moment.

'What did you do that for?' she asked, pushing him away.

'I had an FBI guy tailing me around town.'

'How did you know he was FBI?'

'Gut instinct.'

'Gut instinct?'

'Yeah.'

'You were right about him though? You saw his ID before you killed him, didn't you? Please tell me you did.'

'Okay, I did.'

'You didn't though did you?'

'No.' JD shook his head. 'He was undercover, those guys don't carry ID, but he had the name Ryan Miller engraved on his phone.'

'Did you ask him how he found you?'

'I killed him before I had time to question him.'

Beth put her hands on her hips. 'If you didn't question him and he had no ID on him, then how the Hell did you know he was FBI?'

'Like I told you, he was tailing me. And he was wearing a trench coat.'

'You killed someone for wearing a trench coat while he was walking behind you?'

'Yeah.'

Beth picked up an uncooked sausage and lobbed it at his head. *'I liked it here!'* she groaned.

JD caught the sausage and smiled at her. 'You know how I caught this?' he asked.

'With your hand, dickhead,' she replied, a smile breaking out on her face too. JD was such a dick sometimes, but when he smiled at her, it completely disarmed her, even when he'd just admitted to killing what might have been an innocent man.

'Gut instinct,' said JD. 'I knew you were going to throw it, just like I knew that guy was FBI.'

Beth held out her hand. 'Give me back that sausage.'

He threw it at her and it hit her in the face and bounced onto the floor. Beth raised her eyebrows. 'That one is yours,' she said.

'So *get cooking*. I'll start packing.'

JD headed past her into the back rooms to start packing things up. Beth picked up the sausage from the floor and put it on a tray with the others. 'How do you think this guy found you?' she shouted out.

'I don't know. All I can think is that someone recognised us somewhere. Maybe the old man who rented us this place, but it could be anyone who's seen us since we moved here.'

Beth couldn't recall anyone looking at them in a funny way. Maybe JD really had just killed a random stranger and convinced himself it was an FBI agent in order to justify it? She knew he missed killing people. He never said it, but she could tell living the quiet life was harder for him to adjust to than it was for her. Sometimes she wondered if he was secretly enjoying being on the run from the FBI and the Devil.

'What if it wasn't an FBI agent, and it was someone who was working for the Devil?' she called out.

JD reappeared in the kitchen doorway. 'If it was, Scratch would be here already.'

'You think?'

'I know. If Scratch ever finds out we're alive, then one day he's just gonna come walking out of the bathroom with a fucking pitchfork in his hand or something.'

Beth gently pressed her hand to her stomach. 'Okay, no more questions,' she said. 'Get packing.'

Six

Sanchez hated taking a dump in the ladies toilets in Purgatory. But he'd already been banned from using the men's toilets *and* the disabled toilets. Purgatory was a strange place. The main area was decked out like an old saloon from the Wild West, complete with the stupid flapping doors at the front, and a circular bar in the centre of the room where the bartender (usually the Devil himself) could see everything that was going on.

And on top of that, the men's toilets were fake. The door to the men's was actually a portal that could transport its user to any bathroom in the world. The only person who was supposed to know how to operate it was Scratch (aka the Devil), but one quiet afternoon when no one was around, Annabel the Mystic Lady had shown Sanchez how to use it. For the next few months he'd had a great time using the portal to travel to different toilets all over the world. Unfortunately, when he still had seventeen countries to visit in order to complete the full set, the Devil found out what he'd been up to. To say Scratch went ballistic would be an understatement. Sanchez shuddered when he thought about it.

Scratch explained to him that no one was supposed to use the portal without him overseeing it. Apparently it was something to do with security, because if an ordinary member of the public were to discover the portal and walk through it into Purgatory they might discover its secrets, like the fact that it was situated above the pits of Hell. According to Scratch it would be bad if that happened. Or something. Sanchez couldn't remember exactly because Scratch had been blowing fire out of his ears at the time. All he remembered was that Scratch had called his mistake "Strike One". Three strikes and you're out.

After that Sanchez had tried using the disabled toilets, which were his preferred destination anyway. But unlike most disabled toilets, the ones in Purgatory actually led directly down to Hell. When taking a particularly sloppy dump in there one morning, Sanchez had unknowingly been shitting into a bottomless toilet. He should have realised something was amiss when he didn't feel any splash-back. His foul smelling turds ended up falling hundreds of miles down into the pits of Hell, and one of them had landed on Scratch's face while he was in the middle of giving a speech to some new inmates. That became known as Strike Two. Or as Sanchez had unwisely called it, *"Strike of the Big Number Two"*. Scratch hadn't found that funny at all. So Sanchez was left with only one alternative when he wanted to take a shit. He had to start using the ladies toilets. That option wasn't popular with anyone. Since he'd started using them, an abundance of different air fresheners had appeared hanging from all corners of the washroom. It made everything smell like Fruits of the Forest, mixed with lavender. And poo.

And so it was that on a Tuesday morning Sanchez rose at six a.m. in order to "sneak one out" before anyone else was up and about in Purgatory. He headed straight for "trap one" in the ladies toilets. Everything went smoothly at first, but when he finished crapping he discovered that "trap one" had no toilet paper. So at six forty-five a.m. he attempted to do a "Penguin walk". With his pants around his ankles he waddled out of "trap one" and headed for the next stall along. His timing was terrible. The first thing he noticed was a cold draft blowing up his ass. Then he heard a voice.

'YOU DIRTY BASTARD!'

Sanchez looked over his shoulder and saw a black man in a red suit standing in the doorway of the ladies toilets. The man in red was known by many names. Sanchez called him Scratch, to his face anyway. And right now, Scratch was in such a position that he was looking right up Sanchez's butthole. And he looked really fucking angry.

'THAT'S IT. YOU'RE OUT OF HERE! I'M SENDING YOU BACK TO THE TAPIOCA!'

Scratch's insane ranting drew the attention of everyone else who lived in Purgatory. The faces of Jasmine, Rodeo Rex, Elvis, Annabel de Frugyn and Flake all appeared in the doorway behind Scratch. And they all got a good view of what was occurring. And judging by their initial reactions, they got a good waft of it too, because all of them (apart from Sanchez's girlfriend Flake, who was used to it) covered their noses and turned away.

'Did I do something wrong?' Sanchez asked, pulling his pants up and clenching his butt cheeks to avoid leaving any new skids in his underpants.

'THAT'S STRIKE THREE!' Scratch yelled. He then turned on Flake. The petite brunette girlfriend of Sanchez, was wearing a pair of *Hong Kong Phooey* pyjamas. 'That's it. You and him are going back to the Tapioca. I don't care how much it costs.'

'It'll cost about two hundred grand,' said Flake, winking at Sanchez.

'DONE!' said Scratch. 'Now get him out of here before I shove a red hot poker up his butt.'

****

It took less than an hour for Scratch to get rid of Sanchez and Flake. He even gave the rest of the Dead Hunters the day off to help them move back into the Tapioca. He'd naively thought it would be fun to have Sanchez and Flake working for him. But Purgatory smelled like a pig sty all the fucking time, so he was glad to be rid of them. That is to say, he was glad to be rid of Sanchez. Flake was fucking awesome, but she came in a package with Sanchez so she had to go too. The only positive thing about losing Flake was that Scratch got his *Hong Kong Phooey* pyjamas back.

After sending everyone to the Tapioca via the portal in the men's toilets, Scratch finally had some time to himself. The first thing he did was change his clothes. He'd been wearing cheap suits for months because of the smell from the toilets. So it was a relief to be able to put on one of his best red suits, knowing that it wouldn't smell like Sanchez's ass. He checked himself out in front of his own personal full-length mirror in the bar area. The great thing about his mirror was that it showed only his reflection, so no one else could see anything in it. He tilted his red bowler hat to one side and sucked in a breath of air. The air didn't smell that great yet, but it would in a few days. Anyway, he looked good, which was something to be happy about.

He poured himself a glass of vodka from behind the bar and sat down on a stool to watch the news on the big television screen on the wall. It was pure bliss to finally have some time to himself.

A voice from behind him called out. 'Excuse me, boss.'

It was Zilas Brockett, a mass murderer who had been in Hell for centuries. To the ordinary person there wasn't much to like about him. He had a hunch on his back and he walked with a limp. His face was covered in sores and he had one eye a couple of inches higher than the other. He stank too. Not of shit, but of something like feet, mixed with onions. Scratch liked him though, because watching him waddle around crashing into furniture provided some much needed amusement from time to time.

'What do you want?' Scratch replied, without looking around.

'There's a new inmate downstairs.'

One of the things about Zilas that got on Scratch's nerves was that he never got to the point. When asked a question he would give part of the answer and then wait for permission to continue.

'And?' Scratch sighed.

'He had something interesting to say.'

Scratch swivelled around on his stool and glared at Zilas. The hunchback was wearing a green tweed waistcoat over a grey shirt, and a pair of black pants that looked sticky, as if he'd been wearing them for years without ever washing them.

'Who is this new inmate?' Scratch asked.

'His name's not really important,' Zilas replied. 'It's what he *told me* that was so interesting.'

Scratch rubbed his head in frustration, knocking his hat out of place, which irritated him further. 'Go on. What did he say?'

'He said he was murdered.'

'And?'

Zilas looked at the floor and mumbled his next words. 'It's *who* he was murdered *by*. That's what I'm here about.'

'SO SPIT IT OUT MAN, FOR FUCK'S SAKE! WHO KILLED HIM?'

'Well he says, and you know, it's just what he says, so it might not be true….'

'JUST FUCKING TELL ME FOR FUCK'S SAKE!'

'Okay, so he says he was working for the secret service, or was it the FBI?' Zilas scratched his chin and tried to remember. He soon caught sight of Scratch's eyes turning a violent yellow colour, so he carried on. 'Anyway, this *government agent* had been tracking this fella for months. And he found him. He thought he was going to get a medal of honour or something like that.'

Scratch pulled a cigar from his top pocket and started chewing on it to take his mind of the urge to do something medieval to Zilas. The hunchback stared at him blankly and stopped relating his story.

'Have you got a spare one of those?' Zilas asked.

'No.'

'Oh yeah, right, okay, just checking. I should probably just get to the point shouldn't I? Because you don't like it when I ramble, do you?'

'JEEEEEZUSSSS FUCKING CHRIST! GET ON WITH IT!'

Zilas panicked, and shook as he replied, spitting out words at a hundred miles an hour. 'The man downstairs is called Ryan Miller and he was murdered by this other man while he was following him.'

Scratch sighed. 'What's the name of the man who killed Ryan Miller?'

'Umm, well, that's just it, you see. Ryan Miller claims he was killed by the Bourbon Kid.'

Without meaning to, Scratch squeezed his glass of vodka so hard it shattered in his hand. 'This had better not be a joke,' he hissed.

'It's not a joke,' Zilas replied. 'If I was telling a joke I would have told you that one about the Lone Ranger and Tonto.'

'You told me that one last week. Why would you tell it again?'

'Because it was funny.'

'ENOUGH!' Scratch launched himself up off his stool. 'Bring this Ryan Miller fellow up here now.'

'Yes sir.'

Zilas took a few steps backwards towards the disabled toilets, bowing and smiling as he went, like a fucking idiot.

'Wait a second,' said Scratch, thinking on his feet. 'This Bourbon Kid thing, you keep it between us, right. Don't tell anyone else about this.'

'Yes, boss.'

It had been a very long time since someone had broken a contract with Scratch. The Bourbon Kid had signed a contract promising to work for Scratch until every last undead creature on earth was dead and in Hell. And at last count there were still over a hundred thousand undead fuckers walking the earth, many of them high up in politics.

A broken contract was a serious offence. Scratch rubbed his hands together to flick away a few specks of broken glass and sticky vodka. He'd been tricked. The Bourbon Kid had faked his death. It had been six months, *six fucking months* since the Kid and Beth had been killed in the Black Forest on Blue Corn Island. And that useless witch, Annabel de Frugyn had used her crystal ball to confirm they were dead. Bloody fortune-teller. Scratch should have known she'd get it wrong. She only ever got half of her predictions right anyway. The stupid fucking cow.

After inwardly ranting for a few minutes, Scratch eventually calmed down and allowed himself a wry smile. The law of God that forbid the Devil from involving himself in the matters of the human race didn't apply when someone broke a contract with him. Revenge would be fun. And bloody.

Seven

Death Row was really boring. There was no one to speak to apart from the guards, and they wouldn't speak to Melvin Melt anyway. Even when he threw his own faeces at them they wouldn't engage in conversation. They beat the crap out of him with their batons instead, and the sneaky fuckers were careful never to hit him in the face. It wouldn't go down well with the Human Rights folks if it became apparent he was being beaten up by prison guards every day. He was a fifty-three-year-old former doctor who hadn't lifted weights since he was a teen. So, with just two days left until his scheduled execution, he had some badly bruised ribs, his legs were black and blue and his testicles were swollen beyond all recognition. And none of the injuries could be seen through the bright orange onesie he was forced to wear day and night. He had only three things left to look forward to, his execution, the special meal of choice he was entitled to on the day of the execution, and a visit from a preacher who might absolve him of his sins before he was put to sleep. Not that it would do him any good. He was going straight to Hell, and everyone in Santa Mondega knew it.

Melt was to be the first person executed in Santa Mondega in over a hundred years. It was just his rotten luck that the new Mayor was a bastard, elected purely on the promise that he would bring back the death penalty for Melvin Melt. What a bastard indeed.

Melt's crimes had affected just about everyone in town. He had been a respected local doctor for twenty years, until one day, inspired by a serial killer movie he had seen, he took it upon himself to administer a lethal poison to any of his patients who he believed had broken any of the Ten Commandments. The poison he'd used was virtually untraceable, like the drugs used by cyclists when they want to win important races. The people who suffered from the effects of Melt's poison weren't in a bike race, they were in a race to die. All of them were winners, or losers depending on your point of view. Each death looked like it had been the result of a heart attack or seizure. Like many serial killers, Melt had gotten carried away with his work and was finding just about any reason to administer his poison. After all, the Ten Commandments were open to interpretation. He didn't even know what half of them meant, so after ridding the town of most of the adulterers, he set about killing off those that missed church on a Sunday, or muttered the words, "Oh God".

He amassed fifty-two victims in less than a year.

Even the dumbass cops in Santa Mondega were smart enough to put two and two together and figure out he was responsible. And in a cruel twist of irony, the judge in Santa Mondega's High Court decided that Melt's execution should be by lethal injection from the same poison he had used on his patients. That meant a slow and painful death involving forty-eight hours of flu-like symptoms followed by a massive heart attack.

Of the three things Melt had left to look forward to, the first was the visit from the local preacher. A pair of mute guards who had given him a good kicking the day before (and rammed a Cactus plant up his ass) slapped a pair of cuffs on him and escorted him to a private visiting room. The room consisted of one plastic table with a chair on either side. The preacher was already there, seated on the opposite side. Melt took his seat and the two guards exited the room leaving him alone with the holy man. Melt recognised the elderly man opposite him. Father Papshmir was dressed in black and had wispy grey hair and a saggy face. He was holding a red hardback copy of The Holy Bible.

'Good day to you Melvin,' Papshmir said.

'What's good about it?' Melt replied. 'Are all the sinners dead?'

'No, but I have come to hear your confession and offer you counselling, should you wish to receive it.'

'Did you bring any jazz mags?'

'I'm sorry no, I didn't know you liked jazz.'

'I meant pornos. There's nothing to look at in here.'

Papshmir slid the Bible across the table to him. 'I knew what you meant,' he said. 'But no, I didn't bring any pornos. I thought a Bible would be more useful.'

Melt picked up the book with both hands, which wasn't an easy thing to do in handcuffs. 'Any pictures in here?' he asked, turning the book over.

'No. Are they treating you well?'

Melt looked around to double-check that the guards weren't loitering anywhere. 'Aside from the occasional Cactus rape, it's not too bad.'

'Ah yes, the cactus up the anus. It used to be very popular,' said Papshmir. 'Aside from that, how are you feeling?'

'Regretful father.'

'For your sins?'

'For getting caught.'

'Well, you did make it easy for them, didn't you? I mean, fifty-two victims in one year? How the fuck did you think you would get away with that? You know, you deserve to be executed just for being so fucking dumb. How did you ever become a doctor?'

'I wasn't concerned about getting away with it. I was doing God's work.'

'And you think God wanted you to induce heart attacks in innocent people?'

'They were sinners, Father. All of them broke the sacred Ten Commandments.'

Papshmir leaned across the table and spoke softly. 'That's not a good reason for murdering them. Sins can be forgiven, you know?'

'Got a cigarette?'

'No. I didn't know you were a smoker.'

'I'm not, but you're supposed to bring a prisoner cigarettes! Haven't you ever seen any prison movies or TV shows?'

'I have, but you're in solitary, so you wouldn't be able to trade them with anyone anyway, would you?'

'No,' said Melt, tutting. 'But that's not the point. It's etiquette.'

'You know what else is good etiquette?' said Papshmir. 'Not killing your patients when you're a doctor!'

'Very funny.' Melt took a puff on an imaginary cigarette and blew some invisible smoke at Papshmir. 'Don't you see the hypocrisy in all this?' he asked.

'In what?'

'Me being sentenced to death for my sins? That's what sickens me about this city. Everyone preaches about forgiveness and following The Bible, and then they condemn me for murdering sinners, while demanding that I be murdered for *my* sins. Don't you see how fucking bullshit that is?'

Papshmir nodded. 'It is bullshit.'

'You agree?'

'Fuck yeah.'

'So you can have a word with the authorities on my behalf and get me a pardon?'

'No.'

'Then what fucking good are you?'

Papshmir rolled his eyes. 'Oh come on. If you were pardoned by the judge and somehow miraculously set free, the minute you re-entered society, there would be a thousand angry relatives of the people you murdered, lining the streets, queuing up for the chance to kill you for what you've done to them.'

Melt made a dismissive gesture with his hands, even though he knew Papshmir was right. 'You might as well go then,' he grumbled. 'This is a waste of my time. You've brought no porn and no cigarettes. Christ, what a shambles.'

Papshmir looked around the room, checking for any listening devices, then he leaned forward and lowered his voice. 'What if I could make you a deal?'

Those were the exact words Melt was hoping to hear. He'd daydreamed about a fantasy situation where Papshmir broke him out of prison, ridiculous though it might seem. A man on Death Row can get pretty creative with his daydreams. 'What kind of deal?' he asked, his palms sweating with anticipation.

'I can get you out of this place, and in return you can do me a favour.'

'You can get me out of here?'

'I can. But only if you will do something for me in return.'

'Anything, name it?'

'It's a one-week job. I get you out of here and in return, you'll do everything I ask of you for one week. After that, I'll get you a new identity and fix you up in a place where no one will know you. But if you commit any murders after that, or tell anyone about what I've done for you, you'll be history. I'll see to that.'

Melt's heart was racing. But there was the possibility that this was a cruel joke. 'Are you serious?' he asked.

'Deadly.'

'Okay, you got yourself a deal, Father. How are you getting me out of here?'

'When the time is right, I will send someone to break you out of here. But you must be ready, because time will not be on your side. Your escape will have to be done quickly and quietly.'

'Yeah, sure. Whatever you say.'

'And I shouldn't need to tell you this, but you mustn't speak a word about this to anyone.'

'Who the fuck am I gonna tell in here? I'm in Solitary for Chrissakes!'

'Right. But remember, you have to do exactly as I tell you, or you'll be back in here before you know it.'

Melt leaned as far across the table as he could. 'Just so I know, this thing I gotta do for you, is it sex?'

Papshmir tutted. 'No it's not. But it is complicated, so listen very carefully to what I have to say.....'

Eight

FBI Agent Michael Tipper had been in the job for fifteen years. And ninety-nine percent of the time, the job was boring. Hour upon hour was spent listening in on wire-taps, analysing data and participating in endless conference calls with boring idiots. Unlike all the phoney FBI agents on TV shows, Tipper had never even fired his gun in public. That was about to change. He had a handgun strapped to his thigh, a rifle in his hands and a serial killer in his sights. The home of a serial killer anyway. It was the dead of night and the Bourbon Kid was cornered in a farmhouse just outside Wissmore, surrounded by Tipper and forty agents, all armed to the teeth, itching for some action.

The dense woodland around the farm provided excellent cover for the operation. The agents were concealed behind trees, dressed from head to toe in dark blue body armour. They looked the shit. Tipper thought about that for a moment *"Looked the shit"*. It was a phrase he'd never really understood. It meant they looked cool, looked like they meant business, but yet the word "shit" when used in any other context was always a bad thing. *There was nothing good about shit.* Unless perhaps you've been constipated for a few days. Tipper had been constipated once for three days.

"What the fuck are you doing?" he asked himself. *"Thinking about shit? And constipation? This isn't the time! Fuck me, if the other guys knew the fucking nonsense that goes on in your head, they'd never do a thing you asked. You'd be a laughing stock."* He suddenly realised he was having a bonkers conversation with himself in his own head. *"Shut up for Chrissakes!"*

He shook himself as if he was trying to get a spider off his shoulder. He needed a clear head. He was behind a large tree, his M16 rifle aimed at the farmhouse in the clearing up ahead. There was only one way the Bourbon Kid was coming out of that building and that was in a body bag. As for the woman he supposedly had with him, Beth Lansbury, she was expendable. No one gave a shit about her. If she ended up as collateral damage, shot by a stray bullet or ten, no one would give a fuck. She had no family. And since she was allegedly dating the Bourbon Kid, she probably had no friends either. Talk about being in the shit. He gave himself another mental shake.

"Stop stalling you idiot. This is your moment. Everybody's waiting!"

He twisted the mouthpiece on his headset into position and cleared his throat, ready to speak into it. Everyone was ready, and probably had been for quite some time while he'd been thinking about constipation, the various meanings of shit, and other stuff. They were all itching for him to give the signal.

'Okay, this is Tipper, Blue Unit make your move.'

The thirty agents of Blue Unit all set off in unison, silently weaving their way through the trees towards the target. Tipper and the ten members of the elite Gold Unit kept their positions in the woods. All he had to do now was hang back and wait for the Blue guys to carry out the mission. It ought to be straightforward. *Ought to be.*

As the agents closed in on the target, a flashing red light came on inside the farmhouse, and some ear-shatteringly loud music blared out, not just from inside the house, but also from some high-powered speakers hidden in the surrounding trees. Tipper recognised the song as "Bob George" by Prince. The sensation of hearing it from all directions was disorientating. Tipper's surprise ambush wasn't a surprise after all.

A handful of the advancing agents panicked and stopped in their tracks, thrown off by the loud music and flashing red light coming from the farmhouse. They were waiting for a second order. Tipper saw one of the agents put his hand to his ear, checking to see if his headset was still working.

This was no time for indecision. Tipper shouted into his mouthpiece, 'GO, GO, GO!'

'Nice ambush!'

Tipper couldn't tell if the words *"Nice ambush"* were part of the song that was fucking up his mission. It sounded like someone with a gravelly voice had shouted it in his ear.

There was a dumb phrase often used in the armed forces about how *"You never hear the bullet that kills you"*. Tipper hated the phrase and had argued many times that it was fucking bullshit. You could get shot in the leg and hear the bullet but not die for a few hours, or even days. The phrase only worked if the shot killed you instantly, like a headshot. But there was also another lesser-known phrase that was used about the Bourbon Kid. It went something like, *"If you hear a gravelly voice behind you, it will be the last thing you ever hear"*.

And in Tipper's case, it was.

He only saw a flash of silver as the point of the knife swung up towards his face. The blade cut through the soft blubbery flesh under his chin and then ripped through his tongue and the roof of his mouth, into his brain. It was one big fucking knife.

Tipper was dead long before the hooded man in the long black coat gently lowered his body to the ground and stalked through the woods towards the next agent, Tipper's friend of twenty years, Bobby Stoneman.

The Bourbon Kid snuck up behind Stoneman, his hunting knife concealed behind his back, ensuring that the agent never saw a glint of light from the blade as he closed in on him. The knife was still dripping with Tipper's blood and a few bits of his brain and tongue. In one lightning quick swipe the Kid ripped open Stoneman's throat with the jagged side of the blade. The FBI agent's body turned "rag doll", and the Kid stepped away, leaving the corpse to crumple to the ground as he moved faster towards his next victim.

Three agents had their throats slit before the Kid switched to the miniature crossbow concealed in his sleeve. Two silver darts took down the next two agents, each dart hitting the target in the side of the neck.

Five down, thirty-five to go.

Thirty of them were dispatched in one deadly move.

BOOM!

A bundle of explosives inside the farmhouse went off all at once. A mountain of fire blew up into the sky, decorated with arms, legs, torsos and the occasional head. No amount of body armour was going to save those poor fuckers. Even the ones who hadn't yet entered the building felt the full force of the explosion. Bodies smashed into trees, and balls of fire burst from the house in all directions.

The Kid ducked out of the way of a flying boot and weaved his way back through the trees towards a pile of mud and leaves that covered a trapdoor in the ground. He flicked a severed hand out of the way and lifted the trapdoor. It led down into an underground tunnel that had only recently been created. The tunnel led from a bedroom in the farmhouse, all the way out to the area in the woods where the Kid had come out and snuck up behind the FBI agents.

He reached down into the tunnel and Beth handed him two suitcases containing all their worldly possessions. He set them down on the ground and helped her out of the hole.

Beth turned and stared at the fire, her eyes wide and mouth agape. 'Oh my God,' she said. 'Did we really just do that?'

'Nothing to see here,' said JD. 'Let's move.' He grabbed the suitcases and headed for the spot where he'd parked his car behind some bushes.

Beth hurried after him, finally appreciating the bonkers paranoia behind her lover's insistence on digging escape tunnels out of every property they rented. And parking the car half a mile from home suddenly seemed sensible too. JD was a complex man. Aside from being a paranoid, mass-murdering psychopath, he was also the love of her life, the man of her dreams and the man of most people's nightmares.

They bundled into his black Ford Mustang and within a minute of their house exploding, they were speeding along a dirt track that led out of town. JD drove with the lights off to avoid drawing attention to them. Beth took one last look back at the burning mess that had once been her dream home.

'I don't believe it,' she said, shaking her head. *'You and your tunnels!'*

'You know what they say,' JD replied, as he swung the car around a bend. 'If you love someone, you dig them a tunnel.'

Beth slapped him on the arm. 'No one says that. It's not a catchphrase!'

'It is. Lots of people say it.'

'Name one.'

'Me.'

'Idiot. Can you put some headlights on? I keep thinking we're going to crash.'

'In a minute, when we can't see the fire anymore.'

'So where are we going?'

'Texas.'

'Why Texas?'

'Because that's where we're headed.'

'You know, you can be really annoying sometimes.'

Beth switched on the car stereo. Some classical music came on. 'What's this?' she asked.

'Young Guns 2 soundtrack.'

'Is that the one where they all die at the end?'

'Yeah.'

Beth turned off the CD player and switched over to radio. The song "I've Lost You" by Elvis Presley came on.

Beth knew the words, so she sang along as loudly as she could. A curious oddity of her relationship with JD was that they enjoyed annoying each other. She knew he hated her singing along to songs on the radio, so for the next fifteen minutes she did just that while they headed to Texas. It was the last place they would ever visit together.

Nine

Scratch was behind the bar in Purgatory watching the television on the wall. A female news reporter named Sasha Miller was standing in front of a burned-out farmhouse in Wissmore, reporting on an explosion which had cost the lives of a number of FBI agents. So far there was no information about what the FBI had been doing there, but Scratch had a pretty good idea.

A pinging sound behind him indicated that someone had come up to Purgatory via the elevator at the back of the disabled toilets. A moment later Zilas shoved a timid young man through the toilet door into the bar area.

'This is Ryan Miller,' said Zilas.

Scratch looked Miller up and down. The young man was stark naked, with his hands and feet in chains. Like most new inmates he was somewhat modest, using his hands to cover his genitals while simultaneously avoiding Scratch's gaze. He looked terrified, which was good. He hadn't developed much of a tan yet either, his skin still white and freckly. Scratch looked forward to watching him burn. Miller shifted from foot to foot, the chains clanking in the process.

Scratch had expected Miller to be physically imposing. But this guy was a wimp. Average height, barely any muscles on his arms and a terrible centre-parting haircut. It was no wonder the Bourbon Kid had killed him. Miller was no match for the Kid. Whoever it was in the FBI who had sent him to track down the Bourbon Kid must not have liked him very much because it was obvious he would get killed. Obvious to Scratch anyway.

'You wanted to see me?' said Miller, his voice trembling.

Zilas shoved Miller in the back again, pushing him closer to the bar.

'Would you like a drink?' Scratch asked him.

'Umm, er, water?'

'One water coming up.' Scratch grabbed a drinks dispenser and used it to fill a tall glass with water. No one had ordered water in Purgatory for months. It was a surprise that the water dispenser still worked. It sprayed liquid out in all directions, and some of it went over Scratch's fingers. That was when he noticed it was a lot warmer than it should have been. And it was a suspicious yellow colour.

'GODDAMMIT! FUCKING SANCHEZ!' he cursed. He threw the water dispenser onto the floor and hurled the glass of piss across the bar at Ryan Miller. It zipped past Miller's ear and hit Zilas in the face, adding both a new cut to his already hideous face and some extra piss into his sticky hair. Zilas wiped some of the liquid from his face and sniffed it. The smell didn't seem to bother him. He poked his tongue out and licked the tips of his fingers. He then nodded approvingly and started wiping all the piss out of his hair and face so he could sample some more of it.

Scratch shook his head and muttered under his breath before turning back to Miller. 'How about a beer?' he asked, noticing that Ryan Miller was bewildered and probably in need of something to calm him down.

'You know what, I think I'm okay,' said Miller. 'I'm not that thirsty anyway.'

'Fine. So you're probably wondering why you're here?'

'In Hell?'

Scratch hadn't expected that response. He looked over at Zilas. 'Why is he in Hell?'

'Cruelty to animals and self-righteousness.'

'Oh, what did you do?'

Miller looked surprised. 'I really have no idea. I don't think I'm supposed to be here.'

Zilas chimed in. 'He suffocated a hamster once when he was twelve, and in the last few years he's spent an abundance of time on social media judging other people and telling them how to behave.'

Scratch shook his head and tutted. 'I fucking love hamsters. How could you?'

'I don't remember it,' Miller replied.

'That's even worse. But anyway,' Scratch went on, 'you've been called up to see me because you're claiming you were killed by the Bourbon Kid. Is that correct?'

'Yes sir.'

'Well, if you'd like to be moved to a nicer area of Hell, one where you can wear underpants, then you could do yourself a favour and tell me what happened.'

'I tracked him down to a town called Wissmore.'

'That's what I thought.' Scratch pointed up at the television. 'A farmhouse in Wissmore has just been blown up, causing the death of a number of your FBI colleagues.'

Miller looked up at the screen. 'That's the farmhouse he was staying at. I passed the information on to my department about an hour before I actually saw him. They must have followed up my lead.'

'Yes, and now they're all dead because of you.' Scratch said, shaking his head, before quickly returning to the matter in hand. 'How do you know it was definitely the Bourbon Kid you saw?'

'I looked him right in the face just before he stabbed me in the throat.'

Scratch opened up a bag of peanuts and flicked one up in the air. He caught it in his mouth and winked at Ryan Miller. 'And how did you know the Bourbon Kid was in Wissmore?' he asked.

'I received an anonymous tip off.'

'From who?'

Miller frowned. 'I don't know. Isn't that the whole point of it being anonymous though, so that you don't know who it is?'

Scratch hurled his bag of peanuts at Miller. The bag hit him in the face and the peanuts bounced off in all directions. A couple of them got stuck in Zilas's hair, glued to all the piss. The hunchback accepted the gift and started picking them out and eating them. It rattled Scratch further but he kept his anger focussed on Miller, who looked like he might cry, which was pleasing.

'Listen numbnuts, you're dead, and you're in Hell. So, unless you like having red hot pitchforks rammed into your eyes every ten seconds for all eternity, TELL ME WHO YOUR FUCKING SOURCE WAS, YOU FUCKWIT!'

Miller turned even paler. Scratch recognised that he may have overreacted. The last thing he needed was an inmate shitting himself and making a mess on the floor in Purgatory, especially as the place was just beginning to smell normal again.

'The tip off came from someone who worked in the Wissmore General hospital,' said Miller. 'A worker there submitted the sighting online anonymously. We get about a hundred sightings of the Kid every week since the news reported he was dead. But the guy who filters through all the sightings thought this one looked credible.'

'Why?'

'Because it wasn't just the Kid. He was with a woman who fitted the description of Beth Lansbury. She's the Bourbon Kid's girlfriend.'

'I know who she is,' Scratch sneered. 'What were they doing in the hospital?'

Miller swallowed hard, like he thought Scratch was going to throw something else at him. 'She had a scan.'

'What kind of scan?'

'An ultra-scan.'

'She's pregnant?'

'Yes sir.'

'You're sure?'

'Yeah, I did some follow up work and that's when I found the address she gave the hospital.' He pointed up at the farmhouse on the news. 'I staked it out to see who was really living there.'

'But, the Bourbon Kid spotted you, and killed you?'

'Well, not at first. Within an hour of me staking the place out, he left the house and drove into town. I tailed him, and when he left his car I followed him, you know, keeping my distance. But he knew I was there.'

Scratch snorted a laugh. 'Of course he did, you retard. And that's when he killed you, yes?'

'Yes. He disappeared, and the next thing I knew he was behind me.'

'I could have told you he'd kill you. If I gave you another hundred lives you couldn't follow him without getting killed.'

Miller cleared his throat. 'Does this information mean that I can get a transfer, up to Heaven?'

'Heaven? Pffft, absolutely not!'

'Okay, so to a better part of Hell then?'

'Do we have a contract?' Scratch replied, frowning.

'Err, umm, a verbal one, I guess.'

Scratch laughed out loud for a ridiculously long time, holding his hip and pointing at Miller as if he'd heard the best joke in the history of the world. When he eventually finished guffawing, the smile vanished from his face. 'Verbal contracts aren't worth dick,' he said. 'It needs to be a written contract. That's a valuable lesson you've learned today, isn't it?'

'Seriously?'

'Yes, seriously. Now fuck off. I've got no time for snitches. Zilas, have him put in a cell with one of those randy giant hamsters.'

Ryan Miller didn't know which way to turn, and suddenly Scratch became aware of a dripping sound. He leaned over the bar and looked down at the floor. Miller had lost control of his bodily functions and was pissing himself. He still had his hands over his genitals but piss was seeping through his fingers. Scratch closed his eyes and tried to remain calm. He'd enjoyed intimidating the Hamster killer, but now it was backfiring.

'Zilas,' he said in his calmest voice. 'Get this asshole out of here.'

'Yes sir, and should I get the mop and bucket?' Zilas asked, pointing at the pool of piss on the floor.

'No, you won't need to clean that up,' said Scratch. 'Annabel de Frugyn can do it.'

'The Mystic Lady?'

'Yes. That useless old hag told me the Bourbon Kid was dead.' Scratch screwed his face up and hissed at Zilas. 'Her and *her useless crystal ball!*'

'Do you want me to go get her?'

'No, I'll do that myself.'

Ten

When the gang of Dead Hunters travelled through the portal in Purgatory into the Tapioca they found it in a state of disrepair. It had been left unattended for six months, and as a consequence, looters had ransacked the place. Most of the furniture was gone and the local council had boarded all the windows up.

Jasmine, Flake and Elvis had taken the suitcase with the two hundred thousand bucks in it that Scratch had given Flake, and gone out shopping for new furniture. Rex, Annabel and Sanchez slung on some overalls and set about cleaning the place up and redecorating it.

By nine o'clock in the evening, after a hard days work from everyone, the place was beginning to look like a shit-hole again, much to Sanchez's delight. And so with the bar stocked up with alcohol, Flake and Sanchez threw a private party for everyone, where the drinks were free.

By this point everyone was in overalls. Elvis looked particularly strange because he normally wore a suit, whether it be a jumpsuit or a leather two-piece. But even in a set of overalls he still looked like a dead ringer for Elvis Presley. The only person who made the overalls look good was Jasmine. She normally wore a catsuit that showed off ample amounts of her smooth brown skin. The overalls were a looser fit but still shaped well around her slim, athletic figure.

Seeing as how all the booze was paid for with Scratch's money, there was a real sense of camaraderie. It was particularly nice to have Annabel with the gang for a change. The Mystic Lady was not allowed out of Purgatory very often so she was trying out all of the free drinks. By the time she'd had her fourth drink she was "away with the fairies" and had to have a sit down. She plonked herself down at a table opposite Jasmine and Elvis, who were snuggled up on a comfy sofa underneath a window that was partly boarded up.

In her drunkenness Annabel was enjoying telling old stories. Elvis knew most of them already but Jasmine loved hearing about the singing contest in the Hotel Pasadena, and the story of how Annabel had witnessed JD and Beth kiss for the first time when they were teenagers. On that occasion she had been in her trailer on the promenade in Santa Mondega, and had offered them shelter and given Beth a hot drink after she had been attacked by a vampire.

Rex came over with a tray of drinks and joined them. By now Annabel was wearing a cardigan on top of her overalls and had moved onto the famous story of how she was murdered by Archie Somers.

'So I was reading this book with no name,' she said, gesticulating wildly with her hands. 'And I heard a knock at the door.'

'Oh for Chrissakes, not this again,' said Rex. 'Give it a rest will you.'

'Hey!' said Jasmine. 'She was in the middle of a story.'

'Yeah and it ends with her being beheaded and having her eyes and tongue ripped out!' said Rex. 'Same thing happened to me and Elvis that week. Then we all went to work for Scratch. The end. Shit story.'

'I think it's so weird that you all got killed,' said Jasmine, running her hand through her long dark hair.

'I knew I was going to be killed,' said Annabel.

'Bullshit!' said Rex. 'If you'd known you were gonna be killed, you wouldn't have been there. What a crock of shit.'

Annabel pulled a face at Rex and then grabbed a bottle of red wine that was on the table. She poured some into her glass and filled it almost to the top. Her hands were a little unsteady and she managed to spill some of the wine on the brand new table.

Sensing that Annabel's stories were over for a while, Jasmine tackled Rex about another subject. 'Hey, Rex, did you speak to Alexis Calhoon yet?'

He nodded. 'Yeah. She's fixed everything for you. Every website that had the footage of you and Sanchez murdering that bartender has had to take it down. She's cleared both of your records. So Sanchez should be able to reopen this place without being arrested.'

'What about Flake?'

'Believe it or not, Flake has absolutely no criminal record.'

'Really?' Jasmine was surprised. 'How come I have a record and she doesn't?'

Elvis squeezed Jasmine tight and kissed her on the cheek. 'You murdered the Pope, remember?'

'Oh, does that stay on my record then?'

Rex nodded. 'Yeah. You ain't never getting rid of that one.'

'That seems so harsh,' said Jasmine. 'Is there not a points system in place, like when you get caught speeding and the points get wiped after a few years?'

'I asked Calhoon about that,' said Rex. 'And she said it's the dumbest fucking idea ever.'

'She did?'

'No! Of course she didn't, because I didn't ask her! *You killed the Pope.* You carry that shit with you for life. Everyone knows that.'

'But Calhoon got rid of my porno video, and that was everywhere,' Jasmine protested. 'I even found it on your phone.'

Rex recoiled in horror. 'What are you doing looking at my phone?'

Annabel sat up. 'You were in a porno?' she said, her eyes struggling to focus on anything.

'It wasn't a real porno,' said Jasmine. 'It was just CCTV footage of the time I was doing naked somersaults in that bar on Blue Corn Island, while Sanchez poured poison into the bartender's asshole.'

'Oh that,' said Annabel. 'Yeah, I saw that on Rex's phone.'

Rex furrowed his brow. 'Why the fuck is everybody looking at my phone?'

Elvis answered, 'Because your PIN code is 1-2-3-4.'

'You've been on my phone too?'

'Only when I make long distance calls.'

Rex took a swig of his beer. 'Christ almighty. Nothing's sacred around here is it?'

'Not even my porno,' said Jasmine, shaking her head at Rex. 'Have you been jerking off to it with your metal hand?'

'NO!'

Jasmine leaned across the table and tapped Annabel on the arm. 'I bet he has. I can tell by the look on his face.'

Annabel agreed. 'I saw it in my crystal ball. Horrible image.'

Rex stood up and kicked his chair back. 'If you're all gonna be immature, I'm gonna go sit at the bar and talk to Sanchez.' He picked up his beer and stormed off to the bar, where he grabbed a stool and sat down with his back to everyone.

Elvis squeezed Jasmine's thigh. 'I'd better go sit with Rex. I think he's in a mood.'

'Okay, honey. I'll listen to some more of Annabel's stories.'

'Good luck with that,' Elvis muttered. He left the two women by themselves and pulled up a stool at the bar next to Rex.

'Just us girls then?' said Jasmine, raising her wine glass.

Annabel didn't acknowledge her. She was busy staring at the window behind Jasmine, and it looked like she was struggling to focus. Jasmine had never seen her so drunk before. Some stimulating conversation would be required to keep the fortune-teller awake.

'Hey, Annabel, this place sure needs a lot of refurbishment, doesn't it?' she said.

The Mystic Lady snapped out of her drunken gaze and nodded.

'Are you feeling okay?' Jasmine asked.

Annabel grinned like only drunk people can. 'Someone is gonna knock on the front door any second now.'

Three booming knocks on the door drew a hush over the bar. Everyone looked around.

'Who the fuck is that?' Rex asked.

'It's okay,' said Annabel. 'It's only Papshmir.'

Jasmine was impressed. 'How do you know that?'

'He just walked past the window.'

'Oh.'

Rex opened the front doors and greeted the preacher with a broad smile. 'Papshmir! How you doin'? Come on in!'

Father Papshmir walked in and waved to everyone. He was dressed in black with a silver crucifix hanging from his neck on a chain. He joined Rex and Elvis at the bar and ordered a glass of wine.

Jasmine's jaw dropped and she gazed at him like he was a rock star. 'So that's Papshmir,' she said. 'I've heard a lot about him, but never actually met him. He's the one who recommended us to that Amish priest who lived by the haunted Black Forest, isn't he?'

'That's right,' said Annabel. 'He met the Amish priest at the Pope's funeral and gave him a card with details of how to contact you guys.'

'Is it true he swears a lot?'

'No more than anyone else round here. But yeah, for a preacher he sure does love a good cuss.'

'I should go introduce myself,' said Jasmine. 'He probably doesn't know who I am.'

'He knows who you are.'

'He does?'

Papshmir looked over at them and pointed at Jasmine, a big smile on his face. Then he waved at her. 'I'm a big fan,' he called out.

'Cool!' said Jasmine. 'He *really* does know me!'

Papshmir walked over to the table and stood beside Annabel. Jasmine leapt up from her seat and gave him a big kiss on the lips. 'So nice to meet you!' she beamed.

'You too!' said Papshmir, his face burning up red. 'I've seen your video hundreds of times. You're some athlete.'

'My video?'

'Yeah, the one on Rex's phone.'

'Oh that one. It's just been taken down from the internet for legal reasons or something.'

Papshmir's face dropped. 'It has? Awwww.'

'Oh no, don't be sad,' said Jasmine, rummaging around in a pocket on her overalls, trying to find her phone. 'I can send you some photos if you like? I know how you preachers don't get much action.'

'Action?'

'Did you know I killed the Pope?'

Papshmir nodded. 'Uh, yes, I heard that. I was at his funeral. Apparently you shot the fucker six times, is that right?'

'All in the chest.'

Jasmine fired six imaginary shots from her fingers at Papshmir's chest to demonstrate how it happened.

'Wow, that's awesome,' said Papshmir. 'I can see why you're such a good assassin. You can disarm a man just with your good looks. You know you're even prettier in person.'

'Awww, thanks,' said Jasmine.

Annabel elbowed Papshmir in the stomach. 'Hey, Paps, was there something you wanted?' she asked, her voice suddenly not so slurred.

Papshmir placed his hand on Annabel's shoulder and rubbed his stomach. 'Not particularly,' he said. 'I was just keen to meet Jasmine in the flesh.'

'Christ, why don't you just ask her to show you her tits?' said Annabel.

'I beg your pardon?' said Papshmir, blushing even more.

'I don't mind showing you my tits,' said Jasmine, unzipping her overalls.

'He doesn't need to see them right now!' said Annabel, reaching over the table to stop Jasmine from unzipping any further.

'I'm sure they're lovely,' said Papshmir politely.

'Don't worry,' said Jasmine. 'I'll get your number from Annabel later and send you a text.'

'Really?'

Annabel elbowed Papshmir in the stomach again. 'Go on, get lost,' she said.

'Err, right,' said Papshmir. 'Well, it was nice to meet you Jasmine. And, always a pleasure Annabel.'

'Yeah, yeah,' Annabel said, waving him away.

Pasphmir retreated to the bar to rejoin Rex and Elvis. Jasmine watched him walking away, and decided he was quite hot for a really old preacher man. Then she caught sight of Annabel, scowling and muttering to herself. She pieced things together in her head.

'Oh my God, you like Papshmir, don't you?' she said.

Annabel scoffed. 'Don't be daft.'

'He's looking over at you.'

'Nah, he's probably looking at you Jasmine. All guys do.'

'Well you're a psychic, you should know.'

Annabel picked up her glass of wine. 'He'll have a heart attack if he gets a text from you later,' she said before taking a large swig.

Jasmine gasped. 'Oh no. Is that one of your visions? You know, like when you see the future?'

'No, but if you want me to predict the future, I can tell you what he's about to do now,' said Annabel.

Jasmine's eyes lit up. 'Oh go on, do tell.'

'He and Elvis and Rex are going to get up and go sit at a table on the other side of the bar.'

'Why?'

'They just are.'

Jasmine looked over Annabel's shoulder. Sure enough, all three men picked up their drinks and walked over to the furthest table away from everyone else.

'That's a bit rude,' said Jasmine.

'What's worse is, when you ask them later what they were talking about, they won't tell you.'

'Elvis will tell me.'

'I promise you he won't.'

'He will when I suck his dick.'

Annabel laughed politely, unsure whether it really was a joke or not.

'Just to be clear though,' said Jasmine. 'Papshmir won't really have a heart attack if I send him some nudes, will he?'

Annabel sighed. 'No, but he might end up with a sore wrist.'

Jasmine couldn't hide how impressed she was with Annabel's amazing visions of the future. The fortune-teller had predicted many events correctly, most notably the exact time and date that the Pope would be killed, so she was obviously very good, even though no one other than Jasmine and Flake really appreciated her.

'So how *do* you see the future?' Jasmine asked. 'Can you teach me?'

'You wanna know how I do it?'

'Fuck yeah.'

Annabel leaned forward and whispered quietly so that no one else could hear. Her breath smelled like garlic and stale wine. 'I'm not really psychic,' she said. 'It's a trick.'

Jasmine covered her mouth to stop herself from screaming something obscene, like "GET THE FUCK OUT, YOU OLD HAG!".

She took a few seconds to regain her composure, then spoke quietly. 'Oh my God, Annabel, how? You've got to tell me.'

Annabel took another swig from her glass of red wine. 'I can't,' she said.

'Why not?'

The Mystic Lady pointed over at the toilets. 'Scratch has just showed up.'

Scratch had walked into the Tapioca through the disabled toilets. He was wearing one of his best red suits and a matching bowler hat, but he wasn't grinning like he usually did when he made a grand entrance. His eyes were a dark yellow colour, which usually signified he was in an evil mood.

'Annabel,' he said in a serious voice. 'I need you back in Purgatory, *right now.'*

Eleven

'ZILAS! Make this drunken bitch some fucking coffee!'

The "drunken bitch" Scratch was referring to was Annabel de Frugyn. He was hoping that she would be of some use to him. But as was often the case, she was more annoying than she was useful, hence the coffee order. While Zilas the hunchback was busy behind the bar, Scratch sat down at a small round table with Annabel. She was so drunk her head kept rolling around, so Scratch was slapping her across the face every few seconds to keep her awake.

'You useless old crone,' he hissed at her. 'You told me the Bourbon Kid was dead. Some Mystic Lady you are!'

'He was,' said Annabel, turning cross-eyed as she tried to focus on Scratch's face.

'Well he and his bitch, Beth are still alive. I want you to use your crystal ball to find where they are.'

'Bitchessssss,' said Annabel with a dopy grin.

Scratch gritted his teeth and called out to Zilas. 'Hurry up with the coffee. And make it Hell strength. I want her sobered up, quick sharp!'

One of the marvellous things about the coffee in Hell was that it was so damn potent it could sober up the drunkest person in the world after just one sip.

'Nearly done,' said Zilas. 'Milk and sugar?'

'FUCK THE MILK AND SUGAR! LOOK AT THE STATE OF HER. JUST BRING THE FUCKING COFFEE YOU HUNCHBACKED CUNT!

Annabel reached across the table and with one of her wrinkly old hands she stroked Scratch's goatee beard, which pissed him right off. He slapped her hand away. 'What do you think you're doing?' he said, glaring at her.

'Are you using Soul Glo on your hair?' she asked, chuckling to herself.

It was a blessing really that Zilas showed up with the coffee as quickly as he did because it probably prevented Scratch from setting fire to Annabel's favourite cardigan.

'There you go,' said Zilas, placing a mug of coffee in front of Annabel. 'Drink up. It's not too hot.'

Annabel took an age to get her fingers through the handle on the mug, and she spilled quite a bit of coffee onto the table. She took a sip and almost immediately the life raced back into her eyes. By the time she put the mug back down she was sobered up. She looked around the bar area, as if she was surprised to be there. When her eyes eventually settled on Scratch sitting opposite her, she jumped like she'd seen a ghost.

'Hello Scratch,' she said. 'What can I do for you?'

'I want you to get your fucking crystal ball out and tell me where the Bourbon Kid is. You told me him and his bitch, Beth Lansbury were dead, but now I'm hearing they're not. They're alive and well.'

'I'm sure they're dead….. *aren't they?*'

'No they're alive. And they've got an unborn child that belongs to me.'

Annabel gasped. 'You got Beth pregnant?'

Scratch raised his fist above his head and slammed it down on the table, smashing it in half. Annabel's mug of coffee flew up in the air, spun over and splashed all over Scratch's suit and hat.

'YOU FUCKIN' MORON!' he yelled, jumping to his feet. He took his hat off and tried to shake away some drops of coffee.

'Don't blame me,' said Annabel. 'You're the one who smashed the table.'

Scratch grabbed Annabel by her cardigan and hauled her off her seat. 'Listen you old fluffer. I did not get Beth pregnant. *The Bourbon Kid did.* But the child *belongs to me!*'

'How does it belong to you?'

'Sacred law. The Kid signed a contract making me the owner of any offspring he might have. And Annabel, *I want that child*, and I want it now.'

'When is it due?'

Scratch loosened his grip on her cardigan. 'I don't know,' he said. 'Zilas, when's that baby due?'

Zilas was chewing on his fingernails. 'What's a fluffer?' he asked.

'JUST ANSWER THE GODDAMNED QUESTION!'

'Oh, erm, about when the baby is due?'

'YES!'

'Well, based on what Ryan Miller told us, I was assuming it was about six months before the child would be born.'

'Six months?' said Scratch. 'That's ages.' He grabbed Annabel and dragged her over to the bar and pushed her onto a stool. 'Get your crystal ball out and tell me where they are,' he said.

Annabel reached into a pocket on her cardigan and pulled out her crystal ball. She placed it down on the bar top and did her usual routine of waving her hands over it.

Scratch and Zilas stood either side of her, watching intently as she tried to conjure up some information.

'What do you see?' Scratch asked.

'I see a monastery.'

'Where?' said Zilas, peering into the ball. 'I can't see anything. Just white liquid.'

Annabel picked up the crystal ball and shook it, generating a white mist within it. She placed it back down on the bar surface and used her hands to shield it from the light.

'It's her new crystal ball,' said Scratch. 'This one is not as good as the last one. Only Annabel can see anything in it.'

'What happened to the last one?' Zilas asked.

'It broke,' said Annabel, peering closely into the mist inside the new ball. 'I dropped it about six months ago and it smashed into a million pieces. But this new one works just fine. I'm seeing JD and Beth in here. They're heading to a monastery where they're going to rent a cottage.'

Scratch slapped Annabel on the arm. 'Tell me where the monastery is.'

Annabel moved her head around, looking at the crystal ball from different angles. 'It's called Coldworm Abbey, and it's in a small village in Texas.'

'Coldworm Abbey?' said Zilas. 'I thought you said it was a monastery?'

'Abbey, monastery, same thing,' said Annabel.

'Hmm, Coldworm?' said Scratch, stroking his beard. 'That name sounds familiar.'

Annabel ignored him. 'I'm getting visions of something bad that happened there.'

Scratch's eyes lit up a fluorescent yellow colour. 'YESSS!' he said, jumping back away from the bar. He did a strange moonwalk back across the bar area, before pulling off a quick spin move that almost burned a hole in the floor. A huge grin had spread across his face. 'Something terrible did happen there!' he said, boogying to some imaginary disco music.

'What happened there?' asked Zilas, his face showing how impressed he was by Scratch's dance moves.

'A lot of people were murdered there,' Scratch replied. 'Annabel, are you're sure that's where they're headed?'

The Mystic Lady nodded. 'I'm positive. They're going to rent a small cottage in the middle of a graveyard on the grounds of the monastery.'

'I thought it was an abbey?' said Zilas.

'This is perfect,' said Scratch. 'Now all I need is some really evil people to execute a magnificent idea I just had.'

Zilas clapped excitedly. 'Who are you gonna use?'

Scratch mulled over his options for a moment until the answer came to him. 'Perfect,' he said. 'Let's head downstairs. This is a job for that cunt Dracula.'

'You mean Count Dracula?' said Zilas.

'That's what I said isn't it?'

'Is it?'

'Just find out where his cell is. You and I are going to meet with him.'

Annabel put her hand over her mouth. 'Oh, no, wait a minute,' she said. A thick snow was forming in her crystal ball. She rubbed it and moved her head closer to it, studying something deep within the snow.

'What? What is it?' said Scratch.

'The monastery is not really used as a monastery anymore,' she replied. 'There are only two people living there, a monk named Brother Loomis and his housemaid, an old lady called Mavis.'

Scratch shrugged. 'So what?'

'This is why they call it an abbey now,' said Annabel. 'As a monastery, in the past it took in lots of homeless people, and sick people. But now the guestrooms are all filled with junk. The place has fallen on hard times financially, so they've decided to rent out the cottage in the graveyard outside the abbey.'

'I don't care about any of this,' said Scratch.

'But you should,' said Annabel, her eyes widening as she gazed into her ball. 'The abbey is haunted by its evil past. There is a room on the ground floor that has been locked for over a hundred years. Brother Loomis has the only key to it secured on a chain around his neck.'

'I'm not bothered about that,' said Scratch, his irritation growing. 'I only want to know if you can see what will happen to the Bourbon Kid?'

Annabel leaned back and pressed her hand against her chest. 'Oh my God,' she whispered.

Scratch knew that Annabel liked to put on a show for effect when she was using her crystal ball, so he remained calm and resisted the urge to throttle her to death. 'What have you seen now?' he sighed.

'The monk that runs the abbey, Brother Loomis.'

'What about him?'

Annabel turned ghostly white. 'He belongs in Hell.'

Scratch raised both eyebrows. 'Why? What has he done?'

Annabel looked like she was going to faint. It was hard to tell if she was genuinely troubled or just being annoying. After a few deep breaths she looked Scratch in the eye and said, 'You're not going to believe this....'

Twelve

Rex and Elvis were huddled over a small table in the corner of the Tapioca, discussing a rather unusual request from Father Papshmir.

'How the fuck are we supposed to break someone out of a maximum security prison with less than a days' notice?' Rex complained, unable to hide the scorn in his voice.

Papshmir looked disappointed. 'I figured you would know how to do it. You two are very resourceful people, right? Oh, and by the way, it's not just a maximum-security prison. It's *Death Row* in a maximum-security prison.'

'That's mental,' said Elvis. 'Have you ever seen that show *Prison Break?* It took them a whole series to break out of prison. And you want us to break someone out tonight! There's no fucking way it can be done without a shitload of planning. The guy in *Prison Break* had the whole prison infrastructure tattooed on his body. It'll take us months just to get the tattoos done.'

'You don't need tattoos,' said Papshmir, rolling his eyes.

'I've got too many already,' said Rex. 'There's no room on my upper body for a prison map.'

Papshmir clenched his fists in frustration. 'How do you guys ever get anything done? Forget the tattoos and the TV shows and think like a fucking convict with twenty-four hours to live.'

'I'd want a steak dinner,' said Elvis.

Rex nodded in agreement. 'I think I'd have a burger, and some beers. I wonder if they let you have a hooker with your last meal?'

'For fuckssake!' Papshmir hissed through gritted teeth. 'I came to you guys because I know you broke your friend Baby out of prison a while back. And you did that in less than a day, didn't you?'

Rex and Elvis high-fived each other and then both grinned at Papshmir.

'Chill out, Paps,' said Elvis. 'We'll think of something.'

'You *can* do it then?'

Rex grimaced. 'Look, Paps, getting Baby out was a different story. We broke her out while she was in a prison truck on *her way* to prison. This doctor you want broken out, he's already *in* prison. Even if we could get him out, the prison is on Hubal Island, so we'd need a helicopter or a plane to make our escape before the cops showed up.'

'He's right,' said Elvis. 'And you can't just hide a helicopter behind a tree, trust me, I've tried it.'

Papshmir looked around the bar and checked to see if anyone was within earshot. Then he spoke in a hushed tone. 'I actually had an idea myself,' he said.

'Hallelujah!' said Rex. 'Why didn't you just say that to begin with?'

'Because I was hoping you two idiots would have thought of it already.'

Elvis tutted. 'Rex isn't an idiot.'

'What's the plan, preacher man?' said Rex.

Papshmir lowered his voice even more. 'I can still vividly remember a time, some years ago, when a group of vampire clowns broke into the church. One of them had a knife to the throat of that nice girl, Kacy.'

'What's that got to do with anything?' said Rex, failing to see the relevance of the story.

'The clowns didn't see me,' Papshmir continued, ignoring Rex's frustration. 'See, I was hiding in the bathroom.' He looked at Rex and Elvis, as if he thought they understood what he was getting at. They didn't, so he carried on. 'I'd only been in the bathroom for about ten seconds when the Bourbon Kid appeared out of thin air. He'd come through a hole in the wall, like a magic portal. He was armed to the teeth with guns and knives. He'd come directly from Purgatory.'

'Oh right, yeah I remember that,' said Elvis. 'We gave him all the weapons and stuff. He had to kill that Mummy, Rameses Gaius.'

'That's it!' said Papshmir. 'But before he killed the Mummy he took down all the vampires in my church, while I hid in the toilet. I remember it well because one of the Sunflower Girls in the church took a dump in my Confessional box.'

'Pah,' said Elvis. 'Everyone's taken a dump in your Confessional box. It's a rite of passage for teenagers.'

Papshmir looked incredulous. 'Fucking hell! Is that what that is?' For a moment he seemed to forget he was in the company of others, because he began shaking his fist and muttering to himself.

Rex clicked his fingers in front of Papshmir's face. 'Yo, Paps, what's your point?'

Papshmir snapped out of his fist-shaking trance. 'Oh, well I was thinking you could use the portal to break into Melvin Melt's cell on Death Row.'

Rex blew his cheeks out. He didn't look keen on the idea.

'Is there a toilet in this Melt fella's cell?' Elvis asked.

'Yeah.'

'Then yeah, I suppose we can do it. The portal only works if the destination is a room with a toilet in.'

'Really?' said Papshmir. 'That's weird isn't it?'

Rex took a sip of his beer and swilled it around like mouthwash before swallowing it and giving his response. 'It is,' he said, 'but the guy who designed it, I think his name was Einstein, he thought it was a good fail-safe. It was either toilets or closets, and he opted for toilets, thankfully. You walk in on someone on the toilet, they don't have time to react, so you can duck back into Purgatory before they know what happened.'

Elvis nodded in agreement. 'Imagine the shock someone would get if they saw Rex coming out of the closet.'

Papshmir looked baffled. 'Are you saying you can do it?' he asked. 'You can break Melt out of his cell?'

'Yeah we can,' said Elvis, elbowing Rex. 'Can't we?'

Rex nodded. 'I suppose so. I mean it's a better idea than the whole tattoo thing.'

'Okay, hold on,' said Elvis. 'Even if this does work and we grab Melt out of his prison cell and take him back through the portal. Where do we take him *then?*'

A low buzzing sound came from Papshmir's pocket indicating he had a text message. Instead of answering Elvis's question, he checked his phone. His eyes lit up when he saw the message. He quickly put the phone back in his pocket, his cheeks burning red.

'You okay?' Rex asked.

'Uh huh,' said Papshmir. The preacher looked over his shoulder. On the other side of the bar, Jasmine was waving at him. Papshmir turned back to face Rex and Elvis. 'I'm sorry, what were you saying?' he said.

'Okay, listen Paps,' said Rex. 'This is important. If Scratch sees this Death Row prisoner Melvin Melt hanging around in Purgatory, he'll go fucking mental. We're not even supposed to use the portal without Scratch's permission.'

Papshmir looked over his shoulder again and waved at Sanchez. 'Sanchez! Another round!' he called out. Then instead of turning back to Rex and Elvis, he waved at Jasmine, who gave him a "thumb-up" sign in return.

'What's that all about?' Elvis asked.

'Just wanted some more drinks,' said Papshmir, turning back to face them. 'Anyway, in answer to your question, once you've got Melt out of prison, I need you to redirect the portal to my bathroom at the church, like you did that time you sent the Bourbon Kid through. Once Melt is in the church, he'll be my responsibility.'

'I don't know, man,' said Elvis, shaking his head. 'If Scratch finds out about this, he'll do more than just shit in your Confession box.'

'Good point,' said Rex.

'What will he do?' Papshmir asked.

'I dunno,' said Elvis. 'But it'll be some nasty shit involving pitchforks and buttholes probably.'

'He's big into his pitchfork torture at the moment,' said Rex.

Papshmir nodded to show he understood. 'But you can do it, so long as Scratch isn't there?'

Rex and Elvis shared a concerned look. The two old friends had a fairly telepathic understanding when it came to dealing with danger. Eventually, Rex spoke up. 'Yeah, we can do it, but if we get caught, we'll be dead, and then you'll be even deader.'

Flake came over to their table with a tray of drinks. She placed two bottles of Shitting Monkey down for Rex and Elvis and topped up Papshmir's glass with more wine. 'There you go guys,' she said. 'Anyone want anything else?'

'We're fine, thanks Flake,' said Rex.

Flake returned to the bar, leaving the three men to finish their conversation.

Papshmir took a sip of his wine and then held his glass up to the others. 'So you'll do it, yes?' Neither of them chinked their bottles against his glass, so he was left hanging.

Rex leaned across the table. 'You're gonna have to tell us what we're breaking this guy out for, because as far as I can see, this fucker deserves the death penalty more than most.'

Papshmir put his glass back down. 'Listen fellas, I've never *ever* asked you to do anything that wasn't for the good of mankind, have I? But on this occasion I can't tell you what's going on. If you knew why you were doing this, it would put your lives in danger.'

'That doesn't make any sense,' said Elvis. 'We're putting our lives in danger just by agreeing to do it, because you're asking us to do something behind the Devil's back.'

'I understand,' said Papshmir. 'But when this is all over, I suspect you'll figure out all the answers for yourselves. And you'll understand why this is so important, and why I can't tell you about it.'

'Are you sure?' said Elvis. 'Because I still can't figure out what Blade Runner is about. And I've seen it like twenty times.'

'Really?' said Papshmir. 'It's about the meaning of life, and death and shit like that. Look, are you two gonna do this job for me or what?' He held his wine glass up again to try to toast the moment. 'Come on, don't leave me hanging.'

Elvis picked up his beer bottle and chinked it against Papshmir's glass. Rex let out a frustrated sigh, but then did likewise.

'Sure, we'll do it,' said Rex. 'But one day you're gonna have to explain this to me. And if this Melt fucker goes on another killing spree once he's free, it's on you.'

Papshmir finished off his glass of wine in one quick gulp. 'Thank you,' he said, standing up. 'And may God go with you.'

Thirteen

Scratch hadn't seen Dracula in decades. The once notorious vampire had been rotting away in Hell for so long that Scratch couldn't even remember what his personal Hell was like. Back when the Count had first arrived, his personalised punishment involved witches and imps taking turns to shove pineapples up his butt all day. And seeing as how all punishments in Hell are supposed to be for eternity, it was considered to be a marvellous act of retribution, and one that was laced with irony, what with him impaling things up people's rectums during his time on earth. The torture had gone on for centuries, until someone eventually noticed that he was enjoying it.

When Scratch entered Dracula's cell in the lower levels of Hell, he was pleased to find him hanging upside down with no clothes on, listening to an old witch scraping her fingernails on a chalkboard while a group of midgets threw flaming tennis balls at him. The cell walls had a never-ending stream of blood running down them into a set of drains on the ground. The blood was meant as an extra torment for Dracula, to keep him thirsty while he was tortured.

At the sight of Scratch entering the room, the witch and the midgets stopped what they were doing and exited in a hurry. When they were gone, Zilas stepped inside the cell behind Scratch and immediately trod on a tennis ball, lost his balance and fell over.

While Zilas climbed back to his feet, Scratch circled Dracula, checking if the old bloodsucking bastard was still in good shape. Dracula was dashingly handsome and he'd picked up a sharp tan while roasting in Hell. His jet-black hair had grown long enough to be touching the floor.

'Hello Dracula, old buddy,' said Scratch, leaning down and turning his head so he could look his prisoner in the eye. 'You look a little down.'

'Is that supposed to be funny?' Dracula replied.

'Not really,' said Scratch. 'But it's as close as you'll get to a laugh down here.'

'What do you want?'

Scratch clicked his fingers again. 'Zilas, cut him down.'

Zilas pulled a lever on the wall. It loosened the rope holding Dracula, causing him to hit his head on the stone floor. The vampire didn't complain, he merely rolled over and sat up, his expression impassive.

'I have a proposition for you,' said Scratch.

'Is it more fun than this?'

'I think so. You remember the contract I got you to sign all those years ago?'

'Yes, I do. You screwed me over. How could I forget that?'

'You should have used a lawyer,' Scratch said nonchalantly. 'But never mind, you live and learn. Anyway, fortunately for you, I've decided to exercise a clause in the contract. I'm offering you your freedom in return for a small favour.'

Dracula stood up and dusted himself down. 'Will I be killing someone?' he asked.

'Of course you will. I'm not pulling you out of Hell to cut people's hair am I?'

'I suppose not. I can cut hair though.'

Scratch sighed. 'You'll do it, yes? Murder someone in return for your freedom?'

'Eternal freedom?'

'Freedom until you get yourself killed again. So if you're smart enough not to get staked through the heart again, then yes, it will be eternal freedom.'

'Can I have a castle too?'

'No, but you can have a brothel.'

Dracula wasn't in a position to drive a hard bargain, so he accepted the offer. 'You've got a deal,' he said. 'I'm going to need some clothes though.'

'Obviously. Zilas will arrange all of that for you. And when you're kitted out with all your new gear, you will meet up with another prisoner, a man named Eric Einstein.'

'Eric who?'

'Einstein. He's the brother of a famous German.'

'Hitler?'

Scratch closed his eyes and counted to three to calm himself down. 'No, not Hitler, someone else.'

'Who?'

'Never mind, it's not important. Zilas, the door please.'

Zilas held the cell door open so that Scratch and Dracula could exit into the corridor, the walls of which were made of a boiling hot red rock. Screams came from all directions because lots of other prisoners were suffering eternal tortures.

'Will I get my powers back?' Dracula asked, looking around.

'Now that you have been freed, all of your supernatural abilities will return. Try hitting Zilas and see what happens.'

Dracula shoved Zilas in the chest with one hand. The hunchback bounced back into the wall behind him as if he'd been hit by a train. Dracula then kicked him in the face, which almost knocked his head off.

'Marvellous!' said Scratch, clapping his hands together boisterously. 'Now show Zilas your party trick.'

Zilas held up his hands to protect his face from whatever was coming his way. But he needn't have bothered. Dracula vanished into thin air leaving Zilas and Scratch alone in the corridor together.

'Impressive, huh?' said Scratch.

Zilas climbed to his feet and looked both ways along the corridor. 'Where did he go?' he asked.

Scratch pointed at the ceiling. 'He's up there.'

Zilas was hindered somewhat by his hunched back and lack of a neck, so in order to see where Scratch was pointing he angled his head one way and then the other, trying to focus on what was up there.

'See him?' said Scratch.

'No.'

'He's turned into a bat, up there.'

Scratch pointed at a bat hanging upside down from the ceiling with its wings down by its side. It was about six inches in length and was concealed well by the shadows.

Eventually Zilas spotted the bat and tried to jump up to flick it, but it was too high for him to reach. He soon gave up.

'Pretty cool, huh?' said Scratch.

'I suppose. How does he do it?'

'It's ancient witchcraft.'

The bat transformed back into the naked figure of Dracula and landed on his feet behind Zilas. He crouched down and threw a hard punch right into the hunchback's nut-sack. Zilas crumpled to the floor in a heap again, groaning and holding his aching balls.

'Good work!' said Scratch, kicking Zilas in the ribs for good measure. 'Hey you, get up. I'm not paying you to lie down on the job.'

Zilas stood up gingerly and tried to make sense of what had happened. 'My balls hurt,' he whined.

'No one cares,' Scratch reminded him. 'I want you to take Dracula upstairs and find him some clothes and a sharp spear. A big one.'

'Yes sir.'

Zilas held his hand up like he wanted to ask a question.

'What now?' said Scratch.

'Can he still do that bat thing when he's wearing clothes?'

Dracula answered the question. 'No I can't,' he said. 'In order to transform into a bat I must first shed my clothes, otherwise it won't work. A bat cannot wear pants, surely that's obvious?'

'Have you tried it?' Zilas inquired.

'SHUT UP!' Scratch yelled.

It wasn't just Zilas's inane banter that made Scratch call for silence. He'd also heard something, some music, specifically someone playing a harmonica nearby.

'Jacko?' he called out. 'Is that you?'

The harmonica stopped and a few seconds later a young black man in his twenties, wearing a brown pin-stripe suit with a fedora hat, walked around the corner. He had a guitar strapped across his back and a harmonica tied around his neck.

'You called?' he said.

'What are you doing down here?' said Scratch. 'You should be up by the crossroads.'

'It's my morning off,' said Jacko. 'It's in my contract.'

Scratch sneered at him. 'That doesn't mean you can loiter down here playing that fucking harmonica!'

Jacko shrugged. 'Some of the chicks down here dig the music. What can I say?'

'Were you listening into anything we were saying?'

'No. Why? What were you talking about?'

'None of your fucking business. Now listen, I want you back outside manning the crossroads within an hour. I'm expecting a group of people to show up later. I want you to be there to open the secret road to Purgatory for them.'

'Okay. Who are they?'

'You'll know when you see them.'

'Are you sure?'

Scratch grinned. 'Yes, you'll recognise them from lots of movies.'

Jacko's eyes lit up. 'It's Ninjas isn't it?'

'How did you know that?'

'I noticed you've been watching a lot of Ninja movies lately.'

Scratch was livid that Jacko had worked it out so easily. It was supposed to be a surprise. 'Yes, okay, it's Ninjas,' he said. 'Happy with yourself?'

'A little.'

'Good. NOW FUCK OFF!'

Jacko backtracked down the hallway and vanished in a hurry. As soon as he was out of sight the light tones of his harmonica floated back down the corridor, much to Scratch's chagrin.

'Who was that guy?' Dracula asked.

'Jacko,' Scratch replied. 'His real name is Robert Johnson. Best guitar player that ever lived.'

'What's he doing down here?'

'He works for me. He sits at a crossroads a few miles away and controls who gets access to the secret road that leads to Purgatory. If I want someone to find me, he opens up the secret road and allows them in.'

Zilas nudged Dracula. 'I like him. He plays me a song every year on my birthday.'

Scratch slapped Zilas across the face, which knocked him back into one of the raging hot red walls. 'Would you just take Dracula to get some clothes, like I asked?' he hissed at the hunchback.

Zilas straightened up and rubbed his ass, which was raging hot. 'Yes boss,' he said. 'Anything else?'

'Yes, whatever you do, don't let any of the Dead Hunters see Dracula. They mustn't know anything of this.'

'Yes boss.'

Scratch looked around the corridor. 'What happened to Annabel?' he asked.

'She's still upstairs,' said Zilas. 'You never told her to come down here with us.'

'Well, from now on, don't let her leave Purgatory. I don't want her mingling with anyone, especially the Dead Hunters. She knows too much already.'

Fourteen

'I've got a bad feeling about this,' said Elvis.

'Me too,' said Rex. 'This is one of the worst ideas we've ever had.'

'Technically, it's not our idea. It's Papshmir's.'

Rex and Elvis were still wearing paint-covered overalls from earlier in the day when they'd helped redecorate the Tapioca, so they looked like a couple of drunk janitors. They were in the disabled customers washroom in the Tapioca, looking at a hole in the wall that led back into Purgatory. Scratch and Annabel had gone through it a few minutes earlier and had left the portal open. Elvis poked his head through the hole and checked to see who was in the bar at Purgatory.

'I can't see Scratch anywhere,' he whispered. 'It's now or never.'

Rex poked his head through the portal to see for himself. Elvis was right. Purgatory was empty.

'Fuck. Okay, let's do it,' he said.

Elvis went first, stepping through the portal into the bar area. He didn't make a sound, but almost immediately Annabel poked her head up from behind the bar.

'Evening Elvis,' she said.

Elvis froze and Rex bumped into the back of him.

'What did you stop for?' Rex complained.

'Annabel's here.'

'Oh.'

'What are you two up to?' Annabel asked, eyeing them suspiciously as she uncorked a bottle of Scratch's favourite red wine.

'Nothing,' said Elvis. 'We just wanted to use the portal to go somewhere.'

'Where do you wanna go?' Annabel asked, walking up to the till behind the bar.

'It's a secret,' said Rex.

'I'm sure it is,' Annabel replied. 'But I'm guessing neither of you two knows how to change the destination on the portal?'

She had a point. Neither of them had ever used the control panel on the till to change the portal's destination.

'Okay,' said Elvis. 'Can you do it?'

Annabel poured herself a glass of wine and placed it next to the till. 'Who do you think was helping Sanchez in his quest to take a dump in every country of the world?' she asked.

'You'll keep this secret then?' said Elvis.

'Of course I will. But you'd better hurry. Scratch has gone downstairs, but he'll be back any minute.'

'Great,' said Rex. 'Change the location to the Santa Mondega maximum security prison, cell number six on Death Row.'

'Shut the door then,' said Annabel.

Rex attempted to close the portal door, only to be confronted by Jasmine who had followed them into the Tapioca's toilets.

'What are you two up to?' she asked, stepping into Purgatory. She looked a little worse for wear, like she'd drunk more than she usually would. Her overalls were unzipped halfway down at the front, showing off a lot of skin.

'Hey honey,' Elvis said, cheerily. 'We were just having fun with Annabel. Why don't you grab us some more beers. We'll be back in a minute.'

'No way,' said Jasmine. 'You two are up to something and I want in on it.'

Rex stepped around Jasmine and closed the portal door. He ushered her away towards a jukebox.

'I know how you can help,' he said. 'We're just going to use the portal for something. It would be a real help if you could hang out by the disabled toilets to keep an eye out in case Scratch comes back up from downstairs.'

Jasmine's face lit up. 'Am I the lookout person?'

'Yeah, really important in this mission.'

Annabel finished typing location details into the keypad on the till. 'It's done!' she called out.

It was now or never. Rex re-joined Elvis by the portal entrance. They exchanged a look. Both of them wanted the job over with as soon as possible.

'Come on then,' said Rex. 'Let's do this.'

He opened the portal door. The destination had already been altered. The Tapioca toilets were gone, replaced by a prison cell. It was bigger than any cell Elvis or Rex had ever been in. A grey-haired man in orange prison scrubs was lying on a bed, reading a porno mag. There was nothing much else to see other than a shitty metal toilet and a sink on the opposite wall.

'See any guards?' Elvis asked.

Rex shook his head. 'Just that old guy. Is that Melvin Melt?'

'I dunno,' said Elvis. 'What does Melvin Melt look like?'

'I don't know. I thought you knew?'

'Shit.' Elvis cupped his hands around his mouth and whispered as loudly as he could to the man on the bed. 'PSSST, you over there. What's your name?'

The man looked up and immediately snapped shut the porno mag. 'What the fuck?' he said, panic spreading across his face.

Rex poked his head through the portal and asked the man, 'Are you Melvin Melt?'

'I am, but who in God's name are you? And how did you come to be here? What skulduggery is this?'

Elvis frowned. 'What the fuck is skull buggery?'

Rex budged him aside and took over. 'Listen, I'm Rex and this is my buddy Elvis. We've come to get you outta here. Papshmir sent us.'

'Papshmir? Good Lord, it's a miracle!'

Elvis waved Melt towards the portal. 'Just get your ass over here, dickhead, before anyone sees us!'

Melvin Melt rolled into a seated position, but didn't climb off the bed. 'Can you just give me a minute?' he said, taking a few deep breaths.

'What? No!' Rex hissed at him. 'Get a fucking move on!'

Jasmine poked her head between Elvis and Rex. 'He's got a boner,' she said. 'So he doesn't want to stand up yet.'

'For Chrissakes!' said Rex, glaring at Melt. 'We're on a deadline here. Get your ass up, you piece of shit!'

'I can jerk him off if it'll speed things up?' Jasmine offered.

Elvis ushered her away from the portal. 'That's a real sweet offer Jas, but no. We haven't got time. Aren't you supposed to be keeping watch?'

'It'll only take me a few seconds,' she replied. 'Prison guys are usually ready to pop at the slightest thing.'

'Oh, fuck this!' said Rex. He stormed into the prison cell and grabbed Melvin Melt by his collar. He hauled the convict up from the bed and dragged him back through the portal into Purgatory. Melt was too scared to protest.

As soon as they were back in Purgatory, Elvis pulled the portal door shut and yelled at the Mystic Lady. 'Yo, Annabel. Can you switch the destination again?'

'Where to?'

'The downstairs bathroom in the church of Saint Ursula!'

'Papshmir's church?'

'That's the one.'

'Why is he going there?'

'Would you just do it already! We're on a tight schedule here.'

'Fine.'

Annabel typed in some information on the keypad on the till.

Melvin Melt stared in wonder at his new location. 'What is this place?' he asked.

'None of your fucking business,' said Rex. 'Are you done yet, Annabel?'

'Almost.'

Jasmine tapped Rex on the shoulder. 'Are you sure you don't need me to jerk this guy off?'

'NO!'

Annabel shouted, 'DONE!'

Elvis reopened the portal door. Annabel had worked her magic again. The destination had changed. The prison cell was gone, replaced by a small bathroom in the church of Saint Ursula. There was just a toilet, a washbasin and a towel rail with a blue towel hung on it. The door on the opposite side of the room was closed, and there was no sign of Father Papshmir.

Elvis held the door open and Rex pushed Melt towards it, but the recently escaped prisoner resisted.

'Who's the nice lady in the overalls?' he asked, trying to get a look over Rex's shoulder at Jasmine.

'Never you mind,' said Rex.

Elvis leaned through the portal and called out, 'Papshmir are you there?'

The holy man did not reply.

Elvis tugged his hair in frustration. 'Where is he for fuckssake?'

Annabel shouted. 'Hurry up, Scratch is coming back!'

Neither Elvis nor Rex saw any need to drag this shit-storm out any longer. Rex shoved Melvin Melt through the portal and into Papshmir's bathroom.

'Go find Papshmir,' he bellowed at Melt. 'And if you ever tell anyone you were here, I'll find you and rip your fucking nuts off, you understand?'

Melt looked back at them. 'Uh, yeah, sure.' A smile broke out on his face, as it dawned on him that he was free from Death Row. 'Thanks guys,' he said. Then he shouted out, 'Bye Jasmine!'

Rex slammed the door shut and wiped some sweat from his brow. 'I've got a feeling we might regret this,' he said.

Elvis nodded. 'Me too.'

Fifteen

Detective Sally Diamond awoke with a start and reached over to her bedside table. The display on her phone was lit up. She grabbed it and saw the incoming call from Captain Raymond Wilson. Just above his name on the phone's display was the time, 04:25. She did the maths. Three hours sleep. Three hours sleep after a bottle and a half of wine. She'd been binge-watching an old TV show called *It's Your Move*. It had been better than she expected, hence the one o'clock bedtime. Boy, was she regretting it now.

'Hi, Captain,' she said, trying to sound like she was awake.

'Sally, get your ass down to the alley behind the Swamp nightclub in Pumpkin Street. There's been a murder down there. It's the third one of the night, so you're up. You've got ten minutes.'

'I'm on it, boss.'

She put her phone back on the bedside table and closed her eyes. The temptation to grab five more minutes of sleep was immense. But she knew five minutes would turn into forty minutes, followed by a massive panic. And she couldn't afford to get on the wrong side of Captain Wilson. He was the latest in a long line of captains who spoke fast and short. Diamond couldn't tell if he liked her or not. The guy showed no emotion, just barked out orders. Orders that needed to be obeyed.

She rolled out of bed and staggered into her bathroom. Her early morning routine was something she could do with her eyes closed, giving the false impression that she was getting that extra five minutes of sleep. She brushed her teeth, slung on a pair of black pants, a white blouse, some ankle boots and a slim brown leather jacket, grabbed an apple from a basket in the kitchen and took one look in the mirror. She looked shitty, like someone who'd just gotten dressed with her eyes closed. Her bright red hair was in its usual morning style known as "bed head". She tied it back into a ponytail, giving her the just-barely-acceptable look that was usually greeted by her colleagues with the words, *"rough night?"*

She drove across town in her "hangover car", a crappy blue Chevy Impala that had hit more trashcans than Frank Drebbin's Plymouth Satellite. She arrived at the crime scene at 04:37. Twelve minutes from "bed to crime scene" was pretty epic, all things considered. She parked up behind a squad car with two "boys in blue" leaning against it. The older of the two, a forty-something lazy fucker called Ched Chepstow was smoking a cigarette and scratching his butt. His younger, much more likeable and handsome partner, Tony

Romano, a twenty-five-year-old Latino cop, was eating a donut and holding a plastic cup of coffee. As soon as Diamond stepped out of her car, Romano held out the coffee.

'Got this for you, white no sugar, right?'

'You're a star Tony, a fuckin' star,' she replied.

Ched Chepstow dropped his cigarette on the ground and stubbed it out under his shoe. He took one look at Diamond and shook his head. 'Rough night, Sally?'

'Fuck you.'

She breezed past Chepstow and accepted her coffee from Romano. 'What have we got here?' she asked him.

'It's over there,' Romano replied, pointing to a dead body propped up against a fence further down the alley. The morning sun was blinding Diamond's view, so she snagged a pair of sunglasses from Romano's breast pocket and slipped them on. Everything suddenly became much clearer. The victim was a man, naked from the waist down. His shirt was covered in blood that had poured down from his mouth and also from a pair of holes in his face where his eyes ought to be.

'Are forensics on their way?' she asked, peering over the sunglasses at Romano.

'They should be. But they'll be late. There's been two other murders tonight. So there's still no fucking ambulance crew either.'

'This town, huh? What time was the body discovered?'

'About four-fifteen. We happened to be a few blocks away so we got here first.' Romano nodded at the corpse. 'He's really fucked up. This is some proper biblical shit.'

'Any idea of the murder weapon?' She took a sip of the coffee. It was a Nicaraguan blend. Her favourite. Romano sure did know how to spoil a girl at 4.40 in the morning.

'I ain't no expert,' said Romano, 'but it kinda looks like he was ravaged by a wild animal. You should take a closer look, coz, I'll be honest, I ain't seen nothing like it before.'

Diamond handed him back the coffee and picked a pair of rubber gloves out of her jacket pocket. She put them on and walked over to inspect the dead body. Romano followed behind her, while his dickhead partner hung back by the car, muttering snide comments under his breath.

Diamond crouched down next to the body. 'Are his eyes anywhere around here?' she asked, scouring the ground nearby.

'I don't think so.'

'What about his tongue?'

'I'll be honest with you,' said Romano. 'I don't know what a tongue would look like when it's not in your mouth.'

'Just have a look around, see if you can find anything.'

'We have looked,' said Romano. 'We've been pretty thorough.'

Diamond tapped the side of the corpse's neck. 'Did you notice this?' she asked.

'What?'

'This guy has recently been injected with something.'

There was a red spot on the victim's neck, but Romano and Chepstow obviously hadn't seen it.

'How did you see that?' asked Romano, disappointment etched on his face.

'Not my first day on the job,' Diamond replied. 'You know it's easier to cut someone's eyes and tongue out if you paralyse them first.'

'Are you sure that's not a spot.'

'Yes. This guy's only been dead an hour or so. Any idea who he is?'

'We think it's Nick Manning,' said Romano. 'There's no ID on him though. No wallet, nothing.'

'Does he have any family? Have they been informed?'

The questions were greeted by shrugs from Romano. 'We clock off in ten,' he said.

'Come on Tony, tell me you did more than just grab me a coffee while you were waiting?'

Diamond stood up and covered her nose with her hand to stifle the smell of death while she sucked in some air.

Romano finally offered a useful insight. 'If it *is* Nick Manning, then his mom is Harriet Manning,' he said. 'She's a big church-goer.'

'And his father?'

'Not sure he ever knew who his father was.'

Diamond took another look at the corpse. It was an undignified way to die. 'This is before your time, Tony,' she said.

'What's that?'

'I've seen this before.'

'What, in a dream or something?'

She snatched her coffee back from him and took another sip. The caffeine was helping her to concentrate. Images flooded into her mind, photos she'd seen of other murder victims that had been killed the same way as the semi-naked man on the ground. She made a call on her cell-phone to a senior, murder detective called Bob Muncher. If there were two other murders this morning, then Muncher would be awake and investigating one of them. He answered the call straight away.

'Sally, what's up?'

'Hey, Bob. Have you picked up one of the murders from last night?'

'Yeah, I got one just outside the church. Local idiot, a guy named Mark Hasell.'

'Mark Hasell? Shit! I know him,' said Diamond. 'He's an ugly bastard, dated my sister for a while in high school. He was into threesomes and stuff, so she dumped him.'

'Thanks for that *vital* information, Sally,' Muncher replied sarcastically. 'That could really help crack the case.'

Sally didn't bite. 'Has your victim had his eyes and tongue ripped out?' she asked.

'Yep. Yours too, huh?

'Yeah, I got a guy in the alley behind the Swamp, naked from the waist down. Do you know if the other murder is the same as ours?'

'Yup, McNulty's got a John Doe three blocks away, exactly the same thing. Have you ID'd yours yet?'

Diamond glanced across at the victim again. 'Romano thinks it's a guy called Nick Manning.'

'Never heard of him.' Muncher's voice turned sour. 'I thought this shit was finished five years ago.'

Diamond knew all too well what he was referring to. Five years ago, in the lead up to the last eclipse in Santa Mondega, a very famous series of killings had been committed. All of the victims had their eyes and tongues ripped out. And the killer turned out to be Archibald Somers, the cop who was investigating the murders. It was a total embarrassment for the Santa Mondega Police Force.

'Bob, does this mean Archie Somers has come back from the dead?'

'I fucking hope not,' said Muncher. 'But, if it's not him, then we've got ourselves a copycat killer.'

Sixteen

There was something about a red sky in the morning that JD had always liked. A red sky could be interpreted a million ways. To some people it might be peaceful, to others it might be scary, or pretty, or symbolic of something personal to them. JD liked to think of it as a reflection of his mood. If he'd been in a murderous mood, it might signify the forthcoming bloodshed. As it happened, he wasn't in a murderous mood. He was filling his car up in a gas station on a deserted highway. Beth was in the gas station's store, picking out groceries and supplies for the next part of their journey.

The only blot on the horizon was a set of pylons. Apart from those metal monstrosities everything looked just as God intended. Big green fields as far as the eye could see. No big cities, no millions of people moving from A to B in their cars, honking their horns at each other.

Some days he wondered what it would be like to be part of the nameless hordes of people who lived in a constant fight to make their existence as ordinary as possible. It was hard to comprehend how in almost every civilisation, whether rich or poor, most people were trying to make their lives the same as their neighbours, their parents, their co-workers or their favourite celebrities, all in the name of "fitting in". JD had never fitted in, and he knew Beth hadn't either, for different reasons. Their lives had been hard, but they *had been lived.* He had no idea where their journey together would take them, but that's what made his blood flow, what made a life worthwhile and exciting. That, and the knowledge that if the Devil ever found out they were alive, he and Beth would be hunted until their dying days, as would their *yet-to-be-born* child.

The fear that the Devil would find out he'd been tricked was what made JD check his rear-view mirror every five seconds when he was driving. It was also why he dug tunnels and planned escape routes from every place they stayed in. It was all worth the trouble because *Beth was worth it.*

He finished filling up the tank and got back into the driver's side of the car. He switched on the radio to look for some music to complement the horizon. The first thing to come on was a local news station reporting on the explosion and the carnage he had left behind in Wissmore. There was no mention that he was involved, not yet anyway. Maybe the FBI were keeping it under wraps.

He checked on Beth and saw she was at the counter paying for the groceries and gas. He switched the radio to a music station so she wouldn't hear the news when she returned. The first decent song he found was "Dream Baby Dream" by Bruce Springsteen. He turned up the volume and for just a few seconds he was able to lose himself in the music.

The passenger side door opened and Beth set a brown bag full of groceries down on the floor. Rather than take her seat, she walked away from the car and took out her phone to grab a photo of the horizon.

'Beautiful isn't it?' said JD.

'It's how I imagine Heaven would be,' she replied. 'Wouldn't it be great to wake up to this view every day?'

'Shame about the pylons.'

Beth turned around. 'You know what they say about pylons?'

'Are we still playing this game?'

'You started it. They say pylons can grant wishes.'

JD laughed. 'That's a good one. I like that. It's the stupidest one yet.'

'Try it. Wish upon a pylon.'

'Okay. I wish you would get back in the fucking car. Come on, get in.'

Beth took one last look at the horizon, before jumping into the passenger seat. 'See, it worked,' she said. 'Your wish came true.'

He started up the engine. 'Yeah, those pylons are something else. Let's see where this road takes us.'

'I've actually just found us the perfect place to stay,' Beth replied.

'Where?'

'Coldworm Abbey.'

'Cold what?' said JD, steering the car off the forecourt and onto the highway.

'Coldworm Abbey.' She held up a postcard. It was a promotional postcard featuring a picture of Rowdy Roddy Piper from the movie *They Live*.

'Why am I looking at a postcard?'

'I wrote the address down on the back of it,' said Beth.

'You found the address in the store?'

'While I was in there I used my phone to look for places to rent nearby.'

'Okay, but an abbey, seriously?'

'Don't knock it. It's a cottage in the grounds of the abbey. The advert says it's only fifty dollars a week rent, they prefer cash, and there's no deposit required.' She slapped JD on the arm. 'What do you think?'

JD steered the car around a bend and thought for a moment before replying. 'I guess it could be what we're looking for. Where is it?'

'About forty miles away. And the advert was only posted yesterday, so we've got a real good chance of getting it.'

'Okay, let's check it out.'

Beth did a fist pump. 'Yesss! I'll give them a call now and let them know we're interested. This is such a lucky break, almost too good to be true.'

Seventeen

The party at the Tapioca officially came to an end at 2 a.m. when Jasmine, Rex and Elvis left and headed for the local motel to get some sleep. Sanchez and Flake retired to bed shortly after, leaving the bar in quite a mess.

Sanchez woke early in the morning and had a good stretch. He left Flake asleep in bed and sneaked downstairs in just his underpants. It was great to be back home, somewhere where no one would be on his case every time he took a dump. And it was such a joy to see the bar area again first thing in the morning. There was still lots of work to be done cleaning the place up, but there was plenty of money left from the two-hundred grand Scratch had given them to buy new furniture.

Sanchez opened the front door and a few windows to let some fresh air in while he brewed some coffee. When the coffee was ready he poured himself a mug and stood behind the bar, soaking in the wonderful sight of his old home. It was a feeling of pure bliss, and as an added bonus the smell of the coffee overpowered the stench of stale booze from the night before. As was often the way for Sanchez though, his good fortune didn't last. He was about to take his first sip when he heard Flake call his name.

'Sanchez!'

Her voice went through him like a razor blade. He could tell from the sharp tone that he was in trouble for something. She marched down the stairs behind the bar, carrying a thick hardback book. She was wearing a pink bathrobe and a pair of fluffy slippers.

'What the hell is this?' she asked, slamming the book down on the bar top.

'I'm guessing it's a book,' Sanchez replied, hoping to take the sting out of the situation, whatever it was.

'Why have you got it?' Flake asked, tapping the book cover.

Sanchez leaned forward to get a look at the book. He needn't have bothered looking because deep down he knew exactly what it was anyway. *The Gay Man's Guide to Anal Sex.*

'Oh that,' he said. 'It's a long story.'

'I found it hidden under the floorboards in our bedroom.'

'Typical,' Sanchez groaned. 'The only thing the looters didn't take.'

'Fuck the looters! I wanna know why you've got this book. And why is it under the floorboards?'

'Well I didn't want anyone to see it, did I?'

'Sanchez, are you gay?'

Sanchez recoiled in shock. 'What? No, of course not. Like I said, it's a complicated story.'

'You said long story.'

'That too.'

'Well I've got time, and I'm not stupid, so start telling it!'

Sanchez's ass was beginning to perspire under the pressure of Flake's interrogation, so he reached back and prised his underpants out of his butt crack to provide some relief.

'It was a misunderstanding,' he said, sniffing his fingers. 'You remember that librarian Ulrika Price?'

'The one I melted with The Book With No Name?'

'Yeah, that's her.'

'She gave you this?'

'Not exactly. But you see, there was this one day when I was in the library and I was looking for The Book With No Name, but I actually found The Book of Death. You remember The Book of Death?'

'Yes. Get on with it.'

'Well, I stole The Book of Death from the library, by hiding it down the back of my pants.'

Flake didn't look convinced. 'There's room for a book down the back of your pants?'

'Yeah. Look, I'll show you,' Sanchez said, reaching out for the copy of *The Gay Man's Guide to Anal Sex.*

Flake slapped his hand away. 'That book is not going anywhere near your ass! Get on with the story.'

'Well, Ulrika Price told me to borrow a book or get out, so I grabbed the nearest book from the shelves and took it up to the counter, but when I got there I saw it was *The Gay Man's Guide to Anal Sex.*'

'And you still borrowed it?'

Sanchez flicked some fluff out of his belly-button. 'I didn't want her to think I was a weirdo, did I?'

'She already *knew* you were a weirdo!'

'You think?'

'Everyone knows!'

''Well, it distracted Ulrika, so I was able to escape with The Book of Death and she didn't suspect a thing.'

Flake picked up Sanchez's mug of coffee and took a sip, while she contemplated the story. 'Okay then,' she said. 'Let's say I believe that ridiculous story for a minute. Ulrika's been dead for years, so why have you *still* got this book? Why haven't you returned it to the library yet?'

'Well, I can't very well take it back, can I?'

'Why not?'

Sanchez grimaced. 'Because of the title. I don't want the librarians thinking I've been doing all the stuff in that book, do I?'

'So throw the book away!'

'I tried that too.'

'*Then why the fuck is it still here?*' she hissed before taking another sip of his coffee, this time a long one. He sensed she was going to drink the whole mug, but he didn't dare ask for it back.

By this time, he was sweating all over, so he grabbed a soft-drink dispenser from under the bar and pulled his underpants open at the front. He squirted some water over his crotch to cool things down a little. He was just about to spray some down the back when Flake snatched the dispenser away and put it back on its hook beneath the bar.

'Stop washing yourself with the water gun,' she said, glaring at him. 'I want to know how come you've still got this book. If you threw it away it wouldn't be here anymore, would it!'

'It's the darndest thing,' said Sanchez.

'I bet it's not.'

'Well, you know the garbage men?'

'Yes.'

'They rummage through our trash for stuff they can steal.'

'No they don't.'

'They do. See, I put the book right at the bottom of the dumpster. But when the garbage-men came to empty it, the skinny one, Pete, he brought the book back in and told me it was a federal offence to destroy a library book. Can you believe that?'

'Not really, no. When you say Pete, do you mean the gay one?'

'He's not gay is he?' Sanchez asked, surprised.

'Pete the Pansy? Yeah, of course he's gay. *Jesus*, Sanchez it was you that gave him his nickname!'

'Shit. I didn't even know he was queer. I just thought he walked funny, and he was kinda camp, and a bit touchy feely.'

'Well he's gay,' said Flake. 'And that reminds me, he dropped by yesterday with a card for you. You were in the toilet at the time and I forgot to give it to you.'

'A card?'

'Yeah, a *"Welcome back to Santa Mondega"*, card. He said he made it specially for you.'

Sanchez scratched his backside. 'For me? You mean for *us*, don't you?'

Flake scowled at him. 'He forgot to put my name in the card.'

'You opened it?'

'I did.' She drank some more of his coffee to emphasise her bad mood.

Sanchez shuddered. 'Maybe that's why he's going through our bins. He's looking for stuff.'

'Stuff?'

'Yeah, y'know. My used underpants and stuff.'

Flake grabbed the water gun and pulled Sanchez's underpants open again. She sprayed some seriously cold water all over his gear, then let go of the underpants so they slapped back against his stomach. 'Stop changing the subject,' she said. 'What are you going to do about this book?'

'Can you spray some down the back?' Sanchez asked, turning around. 'My cheeks are a bit sweaty.'

Flake sighed and duly obliged, spraying water all over his ass, which he took as a sign she was calming down a bit.

'Aaah that's much better,' he said, feeling his butt cheeks cooling off. 'You're the best Flake.'

She switched off the water gun and put it back under the bar. 'So what are we going to do with this book?' she said, her voice softening a little.

Sanchez turned back around and stretched his underpants out. They were soaking wet and liable to fall down if he wasn't careful. 'You know, there's a section in chapter twelve of that book that's quite interesting,' he said, rearranging his junk. 'It's not just for gays. I think we could try it?'

Flake didn't reply, choosing instead to drink some more coffee.

'It was a section about something called *Golden Showers*,' he continued. 'I thought it looked like fun. It's something we could both have a go at.'

Flake put the mug of coffee down on the bar, and after a sustained period of silence, during which her eyes narrowed like she was doing the "Superman laser eyes" thing, Sanchez backtracked on the suggestion.

'Or not,' he said. 'It was just a thought I had.'

Flake shook her head. 'I can't believe you've actually read this thing.'

'Only once,' Sanchez replied. 'There were some very graphic photos in there. They'll make your eyes water. There's even a fella on page sixty-four that....'

'Enough already!' She pulled Sanchez's underpants open again and held the mug of coffee over them. 'If that book is still here tomorrow…'

The sound of a man clearing his throat interrupted her. 'Good morning,' he said.

Neither Flake nor Sanchez had noticed the man standing at the bar watching what was going on. Flake let go of Sanchez's underpants and acted like nothing unusual was happening.

'Can I help you?' she asked.

The man at the bar was a heavy set, tubby, balding gentleman in his mid-fifties with a thick grey moustache. He was wearing a musty old beige suit and a green kipper tie. He reached into his jacket and pulled out a wallet, flipping it open to reveal a police badge. 'Bob Muncher,' he said. 'SMPD. How are you both doing on this fine morning?'

Sanchez felt a rush of panic. Had General Calhoon forgotten to clear his criminal record?

'I'm fine, thanks,' said Flake, calmly taking another sip of coffee.

'I hope I haven't called at a bad time,' said Muncher, staring over the bar at Sanchez's soggy underpants.

'It's not what it looks like,' said Sanchez, covering up.

'Yeah,' said Flake. 'I was just washing his balls.'

Bob Muncher replaced his wallet inside his jacket. 'Well, I'm just here to see if either of you heard anything going on round here late last night?'

'Like what?' asked Flake.

'There's been a murder outside the church of Saint Ursula. I'm asking around the neighbourhood to see if anyone saw anything last night. I saw your door open and thought I'd drop in to see if you'd witnessed anything unusual.'

'We both had a fairly early night,' said Flake. 'Certainly didn't hear any murders.'

'Who's dead?' Sanchez asked.

'A man named Mark Hasell. I'm hoping to ask Father Papshmir if he heard anything, but he's nowhere to be found at the moment.'

'Have you tried the church?' Sanchez asked.

Muncher sighed. 'I'm not a rookie, you know. Of course I've tried the church, but it's not open and I can't get hold of Papshmir. Don't suppose either of you has seen him lately?'

'Nope,' said Flake.

'You know, we're kind of busy,' said Sanchez.

'Okay, well I'll keep asking around,' said Muncher. He glanced down at the book on the bar top, then looked suspiciously at both Flake and Sanchez. 'Maybe I should come back later when you're both dressed?' he suggested.

'You can,' said Sanchez. 'But we still won't know anything.'

'Riiii-iight,' said Muncher. 'Nice to have you both back in town anyway. Will you be open during the eclipse on Friday? Hear you had a big shootout in here last time.'

At the mention of the big shootout, Sanchez felt a sudden cold chill all over, not just in his underwear. 'We might be closed during the eclipse this time,' he said.

'I don't blame you,' said Muncher. 'You know every five years is the same. The week leading up to the eclipse we get a bunch of murders.'

'I'm aware of that,' said Sanchez. 'My brother and his wife were murdered last time, by that asshole Archie Somers.'

Muncher took a moment to take the information on board. Eventually his eyes lit up. 'Thomas and Audrey Garcia?' he said. 'Thomas was your brother!'

'Nice detective work,' said Sanchez.

'I never would have guessed,' said Muncher. 'Thomas was good-looking.'

'Just like Sanchez then,' said Flake, defending her man.

Muncher looked puzzled. 'Er, okay. Well, anyway I'd best be going. If you see Papshmir, tell him to give the police a call.'

Muncher turned to leave, but Sanchez called after him. 'Wait a second, Bob. Seeing as how we're reopening, we're giving a free hip flask of my special homebrew to all customers, and you being a cop an' all, I think you should get one.'

'Really?' Muncher's dour expression vanished, replaced by a look of excitement. 'Wow, thanks. I haven't had a drink for hours.'

Sanchez reached under the bar for a hip flask he'd filled up with piss the night before. He handed it over to Muncher.

'Happy Lunar Festival, officer.'

'Why, thank you. You have yourselves a good day.'

Eighteen

After a long road trip, JD and Beth arrived at Coldworm Abbey in the late afternoon. JD drove the car through a set of large metal gates at the entrance and cruised up a long driveway to the main building. Coldworm was much bigger than either of them expected. A ten-metre high brick wall surrounded the estate, which was big enough to fit a small village inside. The main building looked a little worse for wear. The red brickwork was covered in ivy and moss that stretched up to the top of the towers on each of the four corners. There was a densely packed graveyard in front of the main building, with a sign explaining that it was the last resting ground of many of the abbey's previous residents.

'Wow, look at this place,' said Beth. 'I think we may have gotten lucky here. It's huge.'

'Don't get too excited,' said JD. 'My guess is we'll be living in that tiny cottage in the middle of the graveyard.'

Beth hadn't noticed the small cottage. It was situated eighty metres from the main building at the end of a narrow winding path.

'I think I still like it,' she said, her enthusiasm waning only a little.

'You're okay with sleeping in a place surrounded by dead bodies?' asked JD. 'I bet there's some buried under the cottage.'

'Don't be a dick.'

JD slowed the car so they could both get a good look at their new surroundings. 'You know what?' he said. 'I think I like it. It's creepy as fuck.'

'Creepy? How is creepy a good thing when you're looking for a home?'

'It keeps people away.'

'Your logic is undeniable.'

JD pointed through the windshield at something up ahead. 'Look at this,' he said, the enthusiasm draining from his voice.

'What's the matter now?'

'The old lady, look at the state of her.'

An elderly woman was standing outside a pair of large red, arched wooden doors at the front of the main building. She had puffed up blue hair and was wearing a blue dress with a white apron. She waved to them as they approached.

'She must have seen us coming,' said JD. 'Did you see any CCTV cameras anywhere? Because I didn't.'

'No,' Beth replied. 'But she looks nice.'

'She looks like Mrs Doubtfire.'

'Well, I liked Mrs Doubtfire.'

'Mrs Doubtfire was a dude.'

'I don't care. I think she looks friendly.'

JD parked the car up near the entrance and turned off the engine. 'Okay, you're doing the talking,' he said, 'because I can't even look at this woman. Have you seen the size of her face?'

'Shut up,' Beth whispered out of the side of her mouth. 'She'll hear you.'

'Good. I'll grab our stuff out of the trunk. You do the pleasantries.'

Beth climbed out of the car and headed over to greet Mrs Doubtfire, while JD grabbed the luggage.

'Hi, I'm Ruth,' Beth said, shaking the woman's hand. 'And that's my husband, Luke.'

The woman smiled and looked at Beth's hand. 'No wedding ring?' she said.

'Err, no. We sold our rings and gave the money to charity.'

'Oh, that's so nice,' said the woman. 'I'm Mavis. We spoke on the phone earlier. It's a pleasure to meet you.'

JD walked over from the car, carrying two suitcases. He set them down on the ground next to Beth and grunted a barely audible *"hello"* at Mavis.

'Good morning, Luke,' Mavis replied. She reached out to offer a handshake, but then inexplicably, her arm started shaking. She retracted it and turned her head away. She muttered something under her breath that Beth didn't quite catch.

'You okay?' JD asked the old lady.

Mavis stopped twitching and regained her composure. 'Do excuse me,' she said. 'It's an old condition I have.' Her neck twitched a little, and then as if to draw attention away from herself she pointed at the cottage in the graveyard. 'Your new home is over there. I'll show you around.'

She gestured for them to follow her, then led them along a path through the graveyard to the front of the cottage.

'No one's lived here for years,' she said. 'But Master Loomis recently decided that we should rent it out, so your timing is excellent. I think lots of people would have wanted it. It's such a nice little home, especially for a young couple like you.'

'Are cottages in the middle of graveyards popular then?' JD asked.

Mavis's face twitched as if she wanted to hurl an insult at him, but she held it in.

Beth stepped in to smooth things over. 'I think it's gorgeous,' she said.

Mavis stopped twitching. 'So do I,' she said. 'And don't worry about all the graves. The people in them are all dead, honest!' She laughed rather heartily at her own joke, slapping herself on the thigh a few times before switching suddenly back into normal behaviour again. 'I'll open up for you.'

JD certainly had no fucking idea what to make of it. Maybe the old woman had a nervous twitch and a dark sense of humour? Or maybe she was just a cunt? Time would tell.

Mavis pulled a large metal key from her apron and unlocked a big purple door at the front of the cottage.

'Would you like me to give you a guided tour?' she asked.

'No,' JD replied. 'Just the keys.'

'Oh.'

Mavis handed the key to Beth.

'Is that it? One key?' said JD.

Mavis covered her mouth and sneezed. It was a much louder sneeze than was necessary, the kind of sneeze that was a begging for someone to comment on it.

'Bless you,' said Beth.

'Thank you,' said Mavis. 'It's the hay fever this time of year. Anyway, about the key, there's only one door, so just the one key. But I have a spare in the house if you ever lose it.'

'No back door?' JD asked.

'No,' Mavis replied. 'That's why I said there's only one door.'

'I love this purple door,' said Beth, changing the subject.

'So do I,' said Mavis. 'There's more purple inside. Take a look.'

Beth grabbed JD's hand and pulled him into the cottage with her. The first room inside was the kitchen. Beth liked it straight away. It was a little old fashioned, but exactly how she would have wanted it. There was a vase of purple flowers on a wooden table in the middle of the room and a purple kettle on the sideboard. Beth had never seen a purple kettle before.

'I love it,' she announced. 'What do you think, Luke?'

JD put the suitcases down on the floor and stopped in the doorway, preventing Mavis from entering. He took a quick look at the surroundings. 'It seems okay.'

'He's enthusiastic isn't he?' said Mavis, sarcastically.

'Thanks for showing us to the door,' said JD, turning around to face the old lady. 'When we're done, I'll come find you and sort out the paperwork, *if* we like it.'

'No need to do that,' Mavis said. 'I know you're going to like it. Master Loomis will drop by later to sort out the financial side of things. Have a lovely stay.'

Before leaving, Mavis covered her face with both hands and sneezed again. It caused her whole body to shudder like she'd had an electric shock. She brought it to an end by stamping her foot on the ground twice. JD closed the door in her face before she could spread any germs their way.

'She was annoying,' he said.

'*You* were annoying,' Beth replied. 'She was perfectly friendly.'

'Are you kidding? Commenting on your lack of wedding ring before she even introduced herself! And what's with the twitching and sneezing? I bet she's one of those judgemental old hags, and she's probably got a load of cats.'

'She's obviously got a medical condition. You shouldn't make fun of her.'

'A medical condition? You mean she's mental.'

'You're mental.'

'At least I don't have blue hair. Anyway, forget her. Let's check this place out. If it's shit we're only staying one night.'

'I like it already.'

In spite of the surrounding graveyard, Beth did love everything about the cottage. It was snug and spotlessly clean. And the layout felt like it was designed just for her.

'This place is perfect,' she said. 'Mavis must have given it a good spring clean. I wouldn't change anything about it.'

JD ignored her and went on a quick tour, poking his head around every door and corner, checking the windows and knocking on the walls with his knuckles, which he did with every new place they stayed in. When he was done checking everything he joined Beth in the main bedroom, which was a decent size and had a double bed with a predictably purple quilt on it.

'Okay, we can stay,' he said. 'We've got windows on all four sides and a good view of the estate. If anyone approaches, we should see them coming. Did you notice we even have security lights outside?'

'No I didn't see that.'

'All we need now is an escape route. The lack of a back door is probably a good thing. But I'll have to start work on a tunnel tonight.'

Beth sighed and rolled her eyes. 'Will we really need one here? Like you said, we can see anyone coming from miles away.'

'And anyone can see us leave. We need an escape route. Always.'

Beth knew there was no point in arguing, but she enjoyed teasing anyway. 'Just make sure you don't tunnel your way into somebody's coffin,' she reminded him.

JD wasn't paying any attention to her. He was staring at the floor. 'There,' he said, pointing at a red and black patterned rug next to the bed. 'Under that rug is the perfect place.'

'I hope you're not intending to spend all night digging while I'm trying to sleep,' said Beth.

He ignored her and lifted up the rug. 'Look, it would....,' he paused.

'What is it?' Beth asked.

JD rolled the rug over and Beth saw what had made him stop talking in mid-sentence. There was a trap door built into the floor. JD knelt down beside it and grabbed a small metal ring-pull on the hatch. The trapdoor opened easily and he poked his head down to see what was underneath it.

'What's down there?' Beth asked.

JD leaned further in and looked around for a while. When he resurfaced his face was red where it had been upside down. 'This is weird,' he said. 'Someone's already dug a tunnel here.'

'That *is* weird. Where does it go?'

'That's what I'm going to find out.'

Nineteen

Bob Muncher left the Tapioca in a relatively jovial mood. Armed with a hip flask containing a mystery drink, he felt like his day was getting better. He'd been working through the night so he was looking forward to sitting in front of the TV at home and getting drunk.

The streets of Santa Mondega were still quiet with the rush hour almost an hour away. It made Muncher feel like he was in a zombie movie, where he was the last person alive. Old sheets of newspaper and pieces of litter blew across the street, and there was a funky stale smell in the air. As Muncher walked along the main street back to his station wagon, a few spots of rain landed on his face. He was about to break into a jog to get away from the rain, when Sally Diamond called him on his cell again. His heart sank. Much as he liked Diamond, she was a little too keen on the job for his liking. He answered the call anyway.

'Hey Sally, what now?'

'Have you spoken to the Captain yet?'

'No. Why?'

'I'm back at HQ. Wilson just called McNulty and me into his office to say we're not allowed to investigate the three murders from this morning.'

'Huh?'

'He said he's going to call you and tell you the same thing. I wanted to give you a heads up.'

'Who's picking up these cases then?'

'No one.'

Muncher ducked into a shop doorway as the rain came down heavier than before. 'What do you mean no one?'

'Wilson says he called the Mayor to inform him about the murders. Mayor Shepherd has told him to hold fire on investigating these cases until the Lunar Festival is over.'

Muncher fumed. 'What the fuck's it got to do with the Mayor?'

'You know what he's like. That asswipe has been on TV for the last month promoting this festival. It's expected to be a big shot in the arm for the local economy. I guess a serial killer would screw the whole thing up for him.'

Muncher tutted. 'And what the fuck are we supposed to tell the families of these victims?'

'I asked Captain Wilson that very thing. He says we tell them we're working on the case, but that we've got no leads.'

'Fuck that. I'm still working the case.'

'Wilson told me anyone who disobeys this order will be suspended without pay.'

'Shit,' Muncher groaned. 'I need the overtime!'

Sally Diamond said something else but Muncher didn't hear it because the roar of a garbage truck cruising down the street drowned her out. The garbage truck drove close to the sidewalk and went right through a puddle, splashing water all over Bob Muncher, ruining his suit and spraying over his face. He was going to have to shower when he got home today, something he usually avoided.

'Fucking hell!'

He wiped some muck off his suit and regretted it instantly when he looked at all the shit on his hand. He looked up at the garbage truck and was about to yell some abuse at it when he saw one of the garbage men hanging off the back of the truck, laughing at him.

'JERKOFF!' Muncher yelled at him.

'You okay?' Diamond asked.

'Yeah, fucking garbage truck splashed me again.'

'Oh okay, I thought you were shouting at me for a minute.'

'No, I wouldn't do that Sally.'

'Well listen, Bob, do you remember Richard Williams from Phantom Ops?'

'No.'

'He was posted here a few years ago after the Bourbon Kid massacred most of the Police Department.'

'Oh, that guy. What about him?'

Diamond lowered her voice. 'I'm going to give him a call. I figure he'll be interested when he hears these murders have started up again.'

Muncher winced. 'Sally, if the Captain's telling us not to work this case, it's one thing to ignore the order. It's another thing altogether to go over his head to Phantom Ops.'

'I don't care. People are dying, Bob. And the next victim could be your wife, or my brother. How would you feel then?'

'Pissed, I guess.'

'Exactly. So when the Captain calls you and tells you to back off the case, just go along with it. Let him think we're not working it, and I'll get Phantom Ops on the case. They can overrule the Mayor and make him look like a chump.'

'He is a chump,' said Muncher. 'But if you do this, and you get found out, you're gonna get yourself fired.'

'I signed up to protect and serve. That's what I'm doing.'

'Good for you. I'm going home. My suit is fucked.'

'What?'

'That garbage truck fucked up my suit. Motherfuckers.'

'Okay. Well, have a good day Bob, and remember, do as the Captain says.'

'Yeah, right.'

He hung up and slipped his phone back into his pocket, which by now was soaked through with dirty rainwater. Fuck it, this had been a shitty day all round, and it was still morning. Muncher reached into one of his other soggy pockets and pulled out his new hip flask. He opened it and took a big swig.

FUCK!

He swallowed a mouthful of Sanchez's piss and knew straight away he was going to vomit it back up. But being a cop and a respected member of the community he couldn't just puke in a shop doorway, or on the sidewalk. He ran out into the rain and ducked into an alleyway. With his jacket pulled up over his head he hurried down the alley to a dumpster, desperately fighting the urge to blow chunks. He hid behind the dumpster so no one passing by would see him, then he threw up all over the wall.

The smell from the dumpster was already bad, but with Muncher's vomit added into the mix it was borderline unbearable. He wiped some puke from his chin and tried to catch his breath. Puking was a tiring business, especially for someone like Bob Muncher who was physically unfit.

Fucking Sanchez.

Muncher was going to have to buy some alcohol now. But first of all he was going to give Sanchez a piece of his mind. He straightened up and turned around to head back to the Tapioca.

'OWWW!'

He felt a sharp prick in his neck and spun around to see where it had come from. A gloved hand holding a syringe was the cause of the prick. The tall shadow of a man loomed over him. Muncher blinked a few times and stared at the man's face. It was concealed behind a black mask.

'Who the fuck....'

The liquid that had been injected into Bob Muncher's neck kicked in before he could finish the sentence. His vision blurred and his legs wobbled. As his knees gave way and he fell forward, the man who had injected him, caught him in his arms.

After that, things got nasty.

Twenty

JD slung on a leather jacket, tucked a pistol inside it in case he ran into any trouble, and then lowered himself into the hole he'd just found in the floor of the bedroom in the cottage. A set of metal rungs had been built into the side of the tunnel, making it easier to descend to the bottom. When he touched down on the ground below, he saw a battery torch clipped onto the wall next to the metal rungs. He unhooked it and switched it on. It worked like new. He shone it up at Beth, who was poking her head down through the trapdoor.

'I found a torch in the wall down here,' he called up to her. 'Looks fairly new.'

The light shone in her eyes, so she shielded them with her hand. 'I can see that,' she said. 'What's down there?'

'It looks like it's just a tunnel. I think it goes on quite a long way. I'm gonna follow it to the end. Don't answer the door to anyone until I get back.'

'What if the master of the house shows up? Remember Mavis said he would drop by at some point?'

'Just hide.'

'Hide?'

'Yeah hide.'

'Fantastic,' said Beth. 'I'll just have a party up here on my own while you're crawling around underneath a graveyard.'

'I'll be five minutes.'

'I'm counting. One… two… three….'

JD shone the torch along the tunnel and started walking. The air was cold and damp, and the floor was littered with small stones. Wooden support beams lined the walls of the tunnel every few metres. Someone had taken great care in building this underground passage. But what for?

He reached the end in just under a minute, where he was faced with another set of metal rungs on the wall leading up to the exit. He shone the torch up and saw another hatch. Where the one in the floor of the cottage had been square-shaped, this one was round and made of metal, like a manhole cover. He tucked the torch into a pocket on his jeans and climbed up the ladder. He slid aside a locking mechanism on the underside of the hatch and pushed it up so he could peer out. A sliver of daylight seeped in. He was still in the graveyard, but he was near the red arched doors at the abbey's entrance. He listened carefully for any sound of people moving around but heard nothing. No voices, not even the chirp of a bird. He pushed the cover up a little further and poked his head out. He was surrounded by gravestones, which provided the perfect cover for him to exit the tunnel without being seen. Once he was out he dusted himself down and replaced the cover over the hole.

The main building loomed over the graveyard, casting a long shadow where it shielded the afternoon sun. JD scoped out his surroundings and tried to figure out the purpose for having the tunnel. Nothing obvious came to him, but his intuition told him something was amiss. He had a gift for sniffing out danger. In particular, he could sense when he was being watched. He looked up at the main building. In one of the windows on the second floor he saw the pale face of an old man staring down at him. When the man realised JD had rumbled him he backed away into the shadows.

"Time to go pay Master Loomis a visit," JD decided.

He entered the main building and walked straight into a long corridor with a floor made up of black and white chessboard tiles. He walked along the corridor, taking a look in all the rooms he passed. There was a kitchen, a cloakroom and several other rooms with nothing in them.

Halfway down the corridor he came to a staircase that led up to the second floor. A balcony ran all around the upper floor so that anyone up there could watch what was going on below. But as there was no one up there, JD carried on inspecting the ground floor. In the wall opposite the staircase there was a door with a name plaque on it. It was called THE VIOLET ROOM.

JD tried the door handle. It was locked.

'Excuse me, sir? Can I help you?' said a woman's voice.

Mavis the housemaid had appeared out of nowhere and was walking towards him from the front entrance.

'Hello again,' said JD. 'I was just showing myself around. What are you doing?'

Mavis hurried over and wedged herself between JD and the Violet room. 'You can't go in there,' she said.

'Why not? What's in there?'

'I've no idea,' she said, leaning in close and lowering her voice. 'I've been here fourteen years and I've never seen what's in there. Master Loomis says it's haunted.' She shuddered as if a blast of cold air had rushed through her.

'Haunted? By what?'

'Oh, I don't really know anything about it. And I'm not supposed to talk about it.'

'I bet you've tried to get in though, haven't you?'

Mavis glanced both ways to check no one was within earshot. 'Me and Lenny the gardener tried to get in there once when the master was away,' she said. 'But it's locked real good. There's only one key and Master Loomis keeps it on a chain around his neck at all times. I don't think I've ever seen him take it off.'

'Lenny the gardener? I thought you and Loomis were the only people living here?'

'That's right,' said Mavis, her shoulder twitching. 'Just me and Master Loomis… Lenny the gardener just works here. He doesn't stay. He lives miles away.'

Mavis was an oddball. JD couldn't decide if she was just quirky or someone to be wary of. 'Are there any other rooms that are off limits?' he asked her.

'No, just this one. Don't let Master Loomis see you trying to get in here. He's very secretive about it.'

'He's probably just got a stash of porn in there.'

Mavis pressed her hand against her chest like she was having a mild stroke. 'I don't think Master Loomis is into that sort of thing.'

'It was a joke.'

'Oh, HAHAHAHAHA!' Mavis doubled over with laughter and pressed her hand on JD's arm to steady herself. 'We don't hear many jokes round here,' she said wheezing like she'd heard the funniest joke in the history of the world.

JD ignored the inclination to kill her for grabbing his arm and forced a fake smile. 'So what goes on in this place? How does it stay open?'

Mavis straightened up and stopped laughing. She stamped her right foot twice on the ground and shivered like she was cold. When she steadied herself, she pondered JD's question. 'Stay open?'

'Yeah, who's paying the bills? It looks like an expensive place to run.'

Mavis did her sideways double-take again before leaning in and answering in a whisper. 'It's been in the master's family for centuries. It used to be a monastery, with a mix of monks and nuns. But something bad happened here a long time ago. After that, the Loomis family took over the place and have owned it ever since.' Suddenly in mid-sentence she had a weird spasm and covered her mouth. It soon passed and she regained her composure. 'Pardon me,' she said. 'I've got a bad nerve in my neck. Keeps playing up.' She twitched again briefly before asking him, 'Did you meet Master Loomis yet?'

'No. I think he's upstairs though. I saw an old bastard at the window and assumed it was him.'

Before Mavis could reproach him, the sound of a door closing upstairs made both of them stop and look up.

'That's him,' Mavis whispered.

An old man in a long brown robe with a hood hanging down at the back walked along the landing above them towards the stairs. When he reached the top of the staircase he made his way down. He walked carefully so as not to trip on his robe, which was held together by a string belt. JD noticed that he was wearing sandals. A sure sign he was not to be trusted.

'Hello, I am Brother Loomis,' he said in a surprisingly jovial, possibly drunken voice. 'How lovely to meet you. You must be Mr Palmer.'

Loomis hopped off the stairs, missing the last two steps entirely. He walked up to JD and shook his hand, beaming a big smile the whole time, like he was meeting his favourite celebrity.

'What are you?' JD asked. 'Friar Tuck reincarnated?'

The grey-haired monk looked surprised for a moment before letting out a deep bellowing laugh and slapping JD on the shoulder. 'HAHAHA! Friar Tuck! Good one!'

JD was well aware that his *Friar Tuck* joke wasn't funny. But now the monk was pulling out a fake laugh not unlike the one Mavis had demonstrated moments earlier. Either these two weirdoes never heard jokes, or they were a pair of disingenuous fuckers.

'I saw you up in the window just now,' JD said.

Loomis scratched the back of his head. 'Uh, Mavis, could you give us a minute, please?' he said.

Mavis bowed her head like Loomis was the fucking Queen or something. 'I'll go make some of those nice cinnamon buns you like, sir,' she said.

'Wonderful,' said Loomis. 'Coffee wouldn't go amiss either.'

'Of course.' Mavis patted JD on the arm. 'See you again.'

'Yeah.'

The blue-haired housemaid wandered back the way she had come, leaving JD alone with the old monk. When she was a safe distance away, Loomis unwittingly did an impersonation of her. He looked both ways, leaned forwards and spoke to JD in a hushed tone. 'You found the tunnel then?'

'I did. What's it for?'

Loomis looked both ways again, which was really starting to grate on JD's nerves. 'There was some trouble here many, many years ago,' the monk whispered.

'How many years?'

'Oh, like over a hundred.'

'Okay, carry on.'

'Back when there were monks *and* nuns living here in harmony, the old Mother Superior used to live out there in the cottage. She didn't like it in here apparently, so she had the cottage built specially. And because she was all paranoid and stuff, she had a tunnel put in.'

'What was she afraid of?' JD asked.

Loomis, who smelt like he'd been overindulging on the communal wine, grinned like a baboon. 'I dunno,' he said. 'But I think she was using the tunnel to sneak out at night and meet her lover. Or *he* was sneaking into her bedroom. I'm not sure which, but you know how the old saying goes…'

To JD's annoyance, Loomis didn't finish his sentence, instead he waited for JD to prompt him. Tiresome though it was, JD indulged him. 'No, how does the old saying go?'

Loomis hunched his shoulders together and grinned again before replying. 'If you love someone, you dig them a tunnel!'

What the fuck?

JD knew the catchphrase because it *wasn't a catchphrase*. At least, not to anyone other than him. *"If you love someone, you dig them a tunnel"*. It was a stupid remark he'd made to Beth when they escaped from Maggie's Farm and he was justifying his digging of tunnels. And now this annoying, gurning monk in sandals had recited it back to him.

A loud fluttering noise distracted both men. JD spun around and reached inside his jacket, his hand resting on the handle of his gun. A small winged creature flew up to the ceiling high above them on the second floor.

'What the fuck was that?' said JD, removing his hand from his gun.

Loomis stared at JD's hand, as if he could tell he'd reached for a weapon. It seemed to sober him up, because he stopped grinning.

JD's question was answered by Mavis who reappeared out of nowhere again, carrying a tray with a mug of coffee and a cinnamon bun on it. 'Bats,' she said. 'Don't worry about them. We get them in the belfry all the time, little blighters.'

'Bats, huh?'

Mavis handed the tray to Master Loomis and then stroked JD's arm. 'Won't your wife be wondering where you are?'

'Yeah,' JD agreed. 'I should be getting back.'

Twenty One

Sanchez hated the Mayor. It was a fairly irrational hatred born out of jealousy. Everyone seemed to like and respect Mayor Tim Shepherd, just because he was the Mayor. He swanked around town in fancy cars and expensive clothes, sponging free stuff everywhere he went. He'd been into the Tapioca once and had expected free drinks. Sanchez had attempted to serve him a glass of piss, only for Flake to intervene and give the smug git a free beer on the house.

So when Mayor Shepherd tapped on the window next to the front door of the Tapioca, asking to be let in, he wasn't greeted with much enthusiasm from Sanchez. The bartender hadn't even showered yet and he was only wearing his underpants, so he had no intention of opening the door for anyone. Unfortunately, Flake had obviously seen Shepherd from an upstairs window. She bounded down the stairs in her pink bathrobe and a pair of fluffy slippers, and before Sanchez could tell her not to, she raced over to the front doors, unlocked them and let the Mayor in.

Shepherd strolled in flanked by two burly bodyguards dressed in black suits and dark sunglasses. Shepherd had a sharp silver suit, which matched the streaks in his otherwise brown hair. He'd been a male model in his younger days and still had the chiselled jawline and slim muscular figure. He'd used his charm and good looks to woo the voters when he'd campaigned for office. Sanchez recalled his naff campaign slogan. *"If you want it, I'll make it happen"*. The words fell out of his mouth at every opportunity. And for reasons that made no sense to Sanchez, people cheered like morons every time he said it. And women swooned in the same way they did when Joey Tribbiani said, *"How you doin'?"*.

'You know we're closed?' Sanchez called out.

Shepherd either didn't hear him, or just plain ignored him. He only had eyes for Flake. He threw his arms around her, lifting her up off her feet and swinging her around, which caused her bathrobe to ride up, revealing a little more than she would have liked. Shepherd somehow ended up with one of his hands on her naked ass. It stayed there for about five seconds before he put her back down.

'Flake Munroe,' he beamed. 'Why, I was beginning to think you'd left town forever.'

Flake fanned herself with her hand like she was having a hot flush, which was hardly surprising considering she'd just had the Mayor's hand on her ass, and his two beefy security guards had just had front row seats at the free peep show.

100

'Well, I'm back now,' she said. 'I missed this place too much.'

Shepherd reached forward and rearranged her bathrobe, which had fallen open a little at the front. 'There, that's better,' he said. 'You don't want any perverts getting a look at the goods, do you?'

Flake blushed. 'Oh, er, no.'

'Speaking of which,' said Shepherd, checking out the bar area. 'Is the fat guy with no friends still working here?'

'I'm over here, behind the bar!' said Sanchez.

Shepherd walked up to the bar, leaving his two goons standing by the entrance. 'Aah, good day to you Sandro,' he said, cheerily. 'Have you lost weight?'

Sanchez sucked in his stomach. 'Not particularly,' he replied.

'Didn't think so.'

Flake joined Shepherd at the bar and squeezed his bicep. 'Someone's been working out,' she said. 'Very impressive.'

'Not really,' he replied. 'I've just been eating more porridge in the mornings since you stopped making those breakfasts at the Olé Au Lait. You know, I've yet to meet another woman who knows what to do with my morning sausage.'

Flake turned quite bashful. 'You're just saying that,' she said, leaning her head to one side and fluttering her eyes at him.

Sanchez butted in. 'She does my sausages every morning now. And my bacon, and hash browns, beans, eggs, mushrooms, tomatoes and toast!'

Shepherd laughed. 'Every morning! Haha, yes I can tell.'

Fucker.

'So what brings you to our humble establishment?' Flake asked.

Shepherd stroked her arm. 'I heard you were back in town. I wanted to drop by and welcome you back to the neighbourhood. I've really missed you.' He looked over at Sanchez. 'And your little friend, Sandro.'

Sanchez flipped. 'It's *Sanchez!*'

'Hahaha, of course,' said Shepherd. 'I remember now, you're the fella who was chased through the streets by a troop of Sunflower girls once, weren't you?'

'One of them had a knife,' Sanchez retorted.

'I rescued him,' Flake chimed in. 'I was driving past and saw him being chased so I gave him a ride.'

Shepherd rubbed Flake's arm again, which was really irritating Sanchez. 'Every man needs a woman like you Flake,' he said. 'A

101

fearless woman who comes to the rescue whenever her man is being bullied by a group of young children.'

'Did you want to order something?' Sanchez asked, changing the subject, while reaching down below the bar for a secret bottle of piss he'd stashed down there.

'No, I'm teetotal these days,' said Shepherd, patting his stomach. 'You can't keep in shape like this if you're drinking all the time.' He smiled at Flake again. 'What I want to know is how this young lady keeps in such great shape? What's your secret, Flake?'

Flake blushed some more. 'Oh well, you know I keep myself busy.'

'Cooking his five meals a day?' Shepherd joked.

Flake laughed, so did the two bodyguards, and then Shepherd joined in, laughing at his own wisecrack. *The weasel.*

'Anyway, I didn't just come here to tell you how good you both look,' he said. 'I'm actually here in an official capacity.'

Sanchez groaned. 'How much do you want?'

'Oh nothing,' said Shepherd. 'I've got something rather big for Flake.'

'Me?' Flake gasped.

'Yes, you see it's been brought to my attention that you were responsible for saving the city of Santa Mondega a few years back when we had that terrible vampire incident. I'm told you were the one who killed the head vampire. I believe her name was Jessica?'

'That's right, I did,' said Flake. 'I hit her with a magical book and she burst into flames.'

'Hang on a minute!' Sanchez butted in. 'I lured Jessica into the trap. And it was me that poisoned the Mummy she was in cahoots with.'

'Cahoots?' Shepherd said with a snigger. 'Do people still use that word? And what's this Mummy you're talking about? I've not heard anything about a Mummy.'

'Tell him Flake,' said Sanchez.

'Well, I never actually saw the Mummy,' Flake replied. 'But Sanchez and the Bourbon Kid killed him together. That's right isn't it?'

Sanchez was about to confirm the story when Shepherd butted in and talked over him.

'Oh I see,' said the Mayor. 'We don't have any witnesses for that *amazing* story!'

'Just Sanchez,' said Flake.

Shepherd laughed again, a really*, really* fake laugh this time. 'Thought so,' he said. 'Well, anyway, enough about *him.* I'm here for you, Flake. I want the city to celebrate the fact that Santa Mondega is now a safe place to live. And you are directly responsible for that. I'm having a ceremony at the Town Hall on Friday, where I would like to publicly present you with the key to the city, if you'd be willing to accept it.'

Flake gushed. 'Oh my God, really. *Me?'*

'Of course, *you!*' said Shepherd, rubbing her shoulder and inadvertently pulling her bathrobe open a little again. 'You're a local hero. I want you there to receive your award and add a bit of glamour to what will otherwise be a rather dull and formal event. Oh, and wear a nice dress, something sexy. There'll be TV cameras there and I want everyone to see that heroes can be beautiful and intelligent, as well as brave.'

'I've not got many clothes at the moment,' said Flake. 'We had all our stuff stolen when we left town.'

'I wouldn't worry about that,' said Shepherd with a glint in his eye. 'You'd look good in anything, but what I'll do is have my secretary, Agnes pick out some dresses for you this afternoon. You're a size six, yes?'

'An eight actually.'

Shepherd's jaw dropped. 'No way! Well, I'll get Agnes to pick out five or six dresses for you. You can keep whichever ones fit you.'

Flake beamed. 'Oh my God, thanks.'

'Oh, one other little thing,' said Shepherd. 'We can't actually announce publicly that you killed a vampire, because it's not good for the tourist trade if the rest of the world finds out about our old undead problem. So, when I explain to the world's press how you saved the city I'll actually say you defeated a gang of terrorists. Is that okay with you?'

'Oh yes, that's fine,' said Flake.

'Hang on a minute,' said Sanchez. 'If anyone's saved this city from terrorists, it's me. I single handedly took down a high-rise building full of them on Christmas Eve a few years back.'

Shepherd scoffed. 'You mean the terrorist attack at Waxwork Tower?'

'That's the one. Flake was one of the hostages.'

'I was,' Flake agreed.

'As I understand it, Mister Garcia, you gave a gun to handicapped child and got him to shoot the terrorists for you. And the child was shot during the incident. He now walks with a limp, crippled for life. If anyone deserves a medal it's the poor child you crippled.'

Sanchez couldn't think of a clever response, so Shepherd turned back to Flake.

'Anyway, Flake,' he said. 'Would you be able to find time in your busy schedule to come to my office tomorrow night at about seven o'clock? I'd like to go through a few things with you over dinner, a rehearsal of sorts if you will, just formalities about how I will present you with the key to the city. And I thought perhaps we could prepare an appropriate speech for you. There will be a lot of press at the official event, so it's worth making sure we know what we're doing.'

'Oh wow, yeah. That would be great!' said Flake.

'Perfect. I'll have Agnes leave all those dresses with me, so you can try them on while you're in my office and decide which one you want to wear for the official engagement.'

Flake cooed, 'This is so exciting!'

'What's this big event for anyway?' Sanchez asked.

'It's the Lunar Festival,' said Shepherd, frowning. 'How can you not know that? Surely you haven't forgotten that we have an eclipse every five years? You of all people should remember because your little bar was the scene of a massacre last time.'

'Of course I remember,' said Sanchez. 'I just wasn't aware that your office thought it was worth celebrating the anniversary of a massacre.'

'Oh to hell with the massacre,' said Shepherd. 'This is to celebrate the liberation of Santa Mondega. Thanks to my war on crime, and Flake's bravery destroying the vampires, we can actually have a peaceful festival for once. The world will finally see that Santa Mondega is a place worth visiting.'

'Crap. More tourists,' Sanchez groaned.

Shepherd ignored him. He took hold of Flake's hand and kissed it. 'Until we meet again, *Miss* Munroe. Good day to you, and to you Sandeep.'

'It's Sanchez!'

Shepherd didn't seem to hear him. He patted Flake on the ass and then exited the bar, hastily followed by his bodyguards. One of them rushed past him and opened the door on his Limousine that was parked outside. Shepherd jumped in and the bodyguard shut the door.

Flake turned around and grinned at Sanchez. 'How cool is that?'

'Sounds like a scam to me,' Sanchez said dismissively. 'You should be careful. I bet he's a pervert.' He picked up a water dispenser from under the bar and handed it to Flake.

'What am I doing with this?' she asked, frowning.

Sanchez pulled his underpants open. 'Front and back please.'

Twenty Two

Beth was hanging some clothes up in a wardrobe in the bedroom when JD returned to the cottage via the front door. She ran out into the kitchen to greet him, but the expression on his face indicated that all was not well.

'The tunnel does come out somewhere then?' Beth said.

'It comes out in the graveyard.'

'So what took you so long? I've almost finished unpacking all our stuff.'

'The guy that owns the place, Master Loomis.'

'What about him?'

'He's a bigger weirdo than the housemaid. He was watching me from his window on the second floor. Saw me climb out of the tunnel.'

Beth thought about what he'd said for a moment. 'Does that make him a weirdo?' she asked, unconvinced.

'Yes it does. So, naturally I went into the main building to go meet him.'

'Oh no, what did you do?'

'Nothing. But, something's fucking weird about this place. I can't put my finger on it.'

Beth playfully flicked his arm with the back of her hand. 'You're too quick to judge people.'

Flicking him on the arm didn't amuse him. 'What's with all the slapping today?' he said. 'The fucking maid, what's-her-name, Mavis? She kept slapping me on the arm and the shoulder.'

'She's just being friendly.'

'She's a fucking nutjob. Her twitching and foot-stamping is out of control.'

Beth sighed. 'Come on, lots of people have odd conditions and behavioural issues. If we never stayed in places where people twitched or sneezed, we'd be living in the car for the rest of our days.'

'Yeah. But like I said, Mavis is nowhere near as weird as Loomis. He dresses like a monk and grins like a chimp, and he just said the strangest fucking thing to me.'

Beth sighed. 'Go on, what did he say?'

'I asked him about the tunnel, about where it came from, and you know what he says? He says it belonged to the Mother Superior over a hundred years ago, and she was all paranoid and stuff, so she had a tunnel built so that her lover could get into the cottage without anyone seeing him.'

'I'm still not seeing anything weird in all this.'

'Well, get this, Loomis smirks at me and says, *you know what they say... If you love someone, you dig them a tunnel.*'

Beth frowned. 'What? *He* said that? Or *you* said that?'

'He said it.'

'I'm confused,' she said. 'That's what you said to me the other night when we escaped from the farmhouse.'

'Exactly!' said JD. He took his jacket off and set it on a chair by the kitchen table while he carried on talking. 'And this weird monk fella Loomis, when he said it to me just now, he was fucking grinning at me, like he knew that I knew what he was doing.'

'And what was he doing?'

JD took off the shoulder holster with his gun in it and placed them on the table. 'I don't know,' he said. 'But it's like he's been listening in on our conversations or something. I can't figure it out.'

'It *is* weird,' Beth agreed. 'Did he really say those exact words?'

'Yeah, fucking word for word.'

'Well, I guess it must just be a coincidence?' said Beth. 'Or maybe it really is a catchphrase.'

'This isn't funny.'

A sudden fluttering sound in the next room interrupted them.

'What was that?' said Beth.

'It came from the lounge.'

'It sounded like a bird.'

Beth moved towards the lounge only for JD to block her off and head there first. She followed him out of the kitchen and into the lounge. There was nothing to see in there, just two purple comfy chairs, a coffee table and an old-fashioned fireplace.

JD walked over to the fireplace. He leaned down and twisted his head to look up the chimney.

'What is it?' Beth asked.

'Nothing there,' he said. 'But there was a bat in the abbey when I was in there. Could be an infestation of the fucking things.'

'Bats are pretty harmless, aren't they?' said Beth.

JD stepped away from the fireplace and checked the ceiling. 'That depends on whether they're trying to kill you,' he replied.

'You need to relax,' said Beth. 'You're wound too tight. Let's just stay here tonight and see how we feel about it tomorrow. If you still don't like it, we'll hit the road again. How's that sound?'

JD was deep in thought. 'I just need to drop down into the tunnel again,' he said eventually.

'What for?'

'I left the hatch at the other end unlocked. If we're gonna stay here, I want to make sure no one can get in through it.'

'So we're staying?'

'We stay one night, but tomorrow, I say we go. This place is too weird.'

■■■

A small bat flew out of the chimney in the cottage and made its way back into the abbey. A short while later it travelled through a portal in a downstairs bathroom and arrived back in Purgatory where Scratch was waiting for it.

The bat transformed back into Dracula. The tall naked vampire stood in front of Scratch, a sly grin on his face.

'Your fortune-teller lady was right,' he said. 'They're staying the night in the cottage.'

Scratch rubbed his hands with glee. 'Perfect,' he said. 'We'll put the plan into action at three o'clock in the morning while they're asleep.'

Twenty Three

It was just past midnight and only one apartment in The County Motel in Santa Mondega had its light on. Rodeo Rex was lying on his bed in Apartment 16 watching the movie *Crank* when he received a phone call from Alexis Calhoon, the head of Phantom Ops. She'd given him some quite shocking news.

Rex was going to have to share the news with Elvis, who was asleep in Apartment 17 with Jasmine. Seeing as no one else was up and about, Rex didn't bother getting dressed. He left his apartment wearing nothing but a pair of boxer shorts. He closed the door behind him and hurried across to Apartment 17.

He knocked twice on the door and turned the handle at the same time. To his surprise, the door was unlocked. He stepped inside, his heart pounding in his chest. It was dark in Elvis's room, so Rex felt around on the wall for the light switch. He flicked it on and the bright light that filled the room dazzled him momentarily.

'Rex, what the fuck are you doing?' said Elvis.

Rex wasn't prepared for the sight that greeted him in Room 17. The first thing he saw was Jasmine's naked ass bouncing up and down on the bed in the middle of the room. Elvis was underneath her, also naked, with his hands cupping Jasmine's tits.

'Shit, sorry,' said Rex. 'I'll come back later.'

'Is it important?' Elvis asked, while pulling a strange face.

'Yeah it is, I wouldn't have burst in otherwise.'

'Okay, hang on, I'm nearly finished,' said Elvis.

'We were being quiet too,' said Jasmine, looking around. 'So as not to disturb you.'

Rex didn't know where to look. And he really wished he couldn't hear, either. It was hard to make eye contact with either Jasmine or Elvis because they were both pulling weird faces.

'I'll just wait outside,' said Rex.

'You may as well stay in here,' said Jasmine. She slid her hand around Elvis's neck. 'WHO'S MY BITCH!' she screamed.

'Is it me?' Elvis replied.

'YES IT'S YOU! AND WHO AM I?'

'THE HEADMISTRESS!'

'SO COME ON AND FUCK ME HARDER BITCH!'

Rex shifted his weight, not sure what to do. 'Should I turn the light off?' he asked.

'DON'T YOU DARE!' Jasmine screamed at him. 'AND SHUT THE FUCKING DOOR!'

'Shit, sorry.' Rex closed the door and wished he was on the other side of it. He wasn't sure where to look. He stood in the corner of the room, by the door, looking up at the ceiling, then the floor. He found a quite fascinating chest of drawers to focus on at one point before his eyes settled on the mirror above the drawers and he got another view of Jasmine's ass.

'You know in future you should lock the door, right?' he suggested.

'Jasmine likes it unlocked,' said Elvis. 'She likes the thought that someone might walk in on us.'

'FUCK YEAH I DOOOO!' Jasmine howled. She looked back at Rex. 'Are you just gonna stand there?' she asked.

'I, err…. what?'

'Get over here and stick one of your metal fingers up my butt.'

She turned away and leaned down to kiss Elvis on the mouth. Her ass was looking Rex right in the eye.

'Umm, I'm not sure I'm comfortable with that,' Rex mumbled.

Jasmine slapped Elvis around the face and looked back over her shoulder, glaring at Rex. 'DON'T JUST STAND THERE YOU PUSSY!'

Rex glanced down at his gloved metal hand, then back at Jasmine's ass. 'You know, I, erm, I don't even have any lube.'

Elvis peered around Jasmine. 'She's already lubed,' he said.

'Can't I just tell you what I came here to say?' Rex pleaded.

Jasmine slapped Elvis with her other hand and roared at Rex again. 'YOU CAN TALK WITH YOUR FINGER UP MY BUTT CAN'T YOU?'

'I guess so.'

'SO WHAT ARE YOU WAITING FOR?'

Rex wiped some sweat off his forehead, then removed his leather glove and set it down on the chest of drawers. He wiggled his fingers. It was tough to decide which one to use. Jasmine was hurling all kinds of abuse at Elvis and the sex was becoming ever more violent.

Elvis glanced at Rex. 'Why are you taking your glove off?'

'I don't want to ruin it. It's real leather.'

Jasmine shouted, 'QUIT STALLING, YOU LOSER!'

'Hurry up!' Elvis pleaded.

Rex approached the bed. 'I just had a call from Alexis Calhoon,' he said. 'Something major has happened.'

Jasmine wrapped both her hands around Elvis's throat and started throttling him. He carried on squeezing her tits and the bed creaked like it was ready to break.

'STICK THAT FINGER IN MY ASS!' Jasmine yelled.

Rex whispered a quiet apology to the index finger on his metal hand, and then slowly slid it into Jasmine's ass.

'ALL THE WAY IN!'

Rex took a deep breath and pushed his finger in a bit farther. 'So, anyway,' he continued. 'Calhoon's colleague Richard Williams had a call this afternoon from Sally Diamond in the SMPD, and—'

'WIGGLE IT AROUND!'

'And Diamond says there's been some murders in Santa Mondega. Three victims have all had their eyes and tongues ripped out.'

'FUCK YEAH! THAT'S THE SPOT! KEEP GOING!'

Elvis nodded at Rex. 'Yeah, keep going.'

'The thinking is, it's either a copycat killer, or Archie Somers is back.'

'I CAN TAKE ANOTHER FINGER. DO IT!'

Up to this point Rex had managed to quite successfully zone out on what his index finger was doing. One of the benefits of a metal hand was that it didn't feel things like pain, or hot and cold temperatures, or more importantly, what the inside of Jasmine's butt felt like.

'COME ON!' Jasmine yelled. 'YOU KNOW YOU'VE ALWAYS WANTED THIS!'

And that was the crux of it. The next thirty seconds were a blur, and it was a great relief to Rex when Elvis and Jasmine both finally climaxed, although Rex wished he hadn't been there to see it. On the odd occasion when he'd fantasised about the possibility of a sexual encounter with Jasmine, he'd never imagined it would turn out like this.

'Phew,' said Elvis. 'That was great.'

With the sex over, the whole situation felt even more awkward, so Rex carried on talking. 'Calhoon is arranging a time and place for us to meet with this detective Sally Diamond tomorrow. She's going to call me again later with the details.'

'That's great,' said Elvis. 'Really great.'

Jasmine was panting heavily, but she'd calmed down, and thankfully wasn't hurling abuse at anyone or hitting Elvis in the face anymore. She looked back at Rex, sweat dripping down her face and body. 'That was fun wasn't it?' she said. 'You can take your fingers out now.'

'Uh, yeah, about that,' said Rex. 'I think they're stuck.'

Twenty Four

Three o'clock in the morning and all was quiet in Coldworm abbey. In the darkness of the shadows, three figures moved along a corridor, ready to carry out the first, crucial part of a plan that would wreck the lives of several unsuspecting people.

The tallest of the three figures headed up the main staircase, his movements silent and graceful. Dressed from head to toe in loose black clothing, his face concealed behind a balaclava, Dracula looked like a Ninja. So balletic were his movements that nothing stirred, not even a speck of dust. In a sheath across his back he carried a long, extremely sharp sword, one that would soon be covered in blood.

His two companions waited down below for him to complete his part of the mission. They watched with bated breath as he crept along the landing to the door in the corner. Dracula's gloved hand settled on the doorknob. He twisted it slowly, eliciting the first noise since their arrival in the building via the downstairs washroom. The door opened easily without any further sound. Dracula peered around it into the bedroom. The monk, Brother Loomis was sound asleep in a double bed in the middle of the room. Dracula snuck in and left the door only slightly ajar. He approached the bed and unsheathed his sword, wielding it over his shoulder. He waited at the foot of the bed for a moment, gazing down upon the sleeping monk. Loomis was on his back with the covers pulled up to his chin, and his mouth was open, sucking in air, accompanied by a low hissing sound.

Dracula was light enough of foot to leap onto the bed without waking Loomis. He spread his feet either side of the sleeping monk's waist and used his sword to peel the bed sheets away from the monk's neck. And there it was, the item he had been sent to collect, the necklace with the gold key on it that Loomis wore around his neck. The key rested against Loomis's hairy chest, positioned almost exactly over his heart. Dracula felt a twinge of excitement, something he hadn't felt for centuries. He was about to kill, to see the blood of a mortal spurt out like volcanic lava. He used his sword to flick the key aside, opening up a clean avenue to the monk's heart.

The slight movement woke Loomis up. He opened his eyes and saw Dracula looming over him with a sword, ready to strike a fatal wound. Like someone waking from a nightmare only to find himself in a worse nightmare, the monk took a sharp intake of breath.

THWACK!

Dracula plunged his sword into Loomis's chest before the monk had a chance to scream. It sliced through him like he was already a ghost, stopping only when the tip of the blade touched the floor beneath the bed. Blood spurted in all directions, specks of it spraying over Dracula's balaclava.

He unpeeled his headgear and stared into the dying eyes of Loomis. The monk's mouth was arched open in shock, his eyes wide and white. Death was close. The monk had just enough time to utter one final thing before he died.

'This isn't happening......'

Dracula leaned down closer. 'What's that you say?' he asked.

Loomis's eyes rolled up in his head and he offered nothing further, other than a quiet gurgling sound.

Dracula yanked his sword back out of the dead monk's body and stepped down from the bed onto the floor. Blood was already seeping across the floorboards as it gushed out through the hole in Loomis's back. The sight of all the blood awakened something in Dracula, a thirst for blood that he had not felt for a long time. He gazed upon the thick black blood on his blade. It was peppered with small chunks of flesh, giving it the look of fresh blackcurrant jam. He leaned in and kissed the blade. As soon as the blood touched his lips he stuck out his tongue and took a long lick from the bottom of the blade up to the tip.

Bliss.

He was so exhilarated by the taste of blood he didn't hear Zilas walk through the door behind him. The hunchback was also dressed in black, and carrying a long, heavy spear.

'You did it!' Zilas cried.

Dracula lifted his head back and let the blood slide down his throat for a while before answering. 'Yes, *oh yes!*'

'So he's dead then?'

'Yes, of course he's dead.'

Zilas balanced his spear against a chest of drawers next to a window that overlooked the graveyard, and bounded over to Dracula's side. He looked down in awe at the mess Dracula had made of the unsuspecting monk.

'Ewww, that's fucked up,' he said, wincing, before excitedly adding. 'Go on, now cut his head off. Scratch wants his head off. And give me the necklace with the key on it.'

While Zilas watched on and clapped excitedly, Dracula raised his sword high above his head again, wielding it over the monk's neck. With one swift, brutal swing of his arm he sliced the dead monk across the neck, separating his head from his shoulders. Loomis's head flopped to one side, gawping at the two men as more blood pumped out onto the floor.

Zilas lunged forward and grabbed the thick gold necklace. He yanked it away from Loomis's shoulders, flicking blood across Dracula's face. The vampire gratefully licked it up with a long, luscious flick of his tongue.

Zilas wiped the key clean on the bed. 'Perfect,' he said, gazing upon it with love in his eyes.

'Did you kill the housemaid?' Dracula asked.

Zilas shook his head. 'She's not here. We searched everywhere.'

'And the gardener?'

'He doesn't live here. He's just an employee.'

'Do I need to hunt them down?'

'I don't think so. The boss said we were only supposed to tie them up if we found them anyway. It's better that they're not here.'

'What now then?' Dracula asked.

'You can finish drinking this asshole's blood,' said Zilas heading for the door. 'I've got to go back downstairs to the Violet Room with Einstein. When you're done, make sure you impale Loomis on the spear. Scratch was very clear about that, so don't forget to do it.'

'As you wish.'

Zilas hurried out of the room, holding his new key in his hand like it was the Olympic torch.

Dracula stared down at the decapitated corpse on the bed. It was a bloody, gruesome mess. He reached down and touched the monk's cheek. It was already cold. He slid his finger around the ragged, bloodied edge of Loomis's throat, where he'd made the cut. The blood was thick and he was able to scoop some up underneath his fingernail. He licked it up. The flavour was irresistible. He scooped up more and more, licking it feverishly like a child left alone with a tub of ice cream. The flavour was irresistible, more like Neapolitan than Vanilla.

For a brief time Dracula was oblivious to everything else in the entire universe. The blissful feeling only ended when he caught sight of something on the wall. A woven textile, made from a red material was stretched across the wall above the bed. There was a message sewn across it in black cotton. It said -

REMEMBER MY LAST WORDS TO YOU.

Twenty Five

Ever since Annabel had passed out drunk on a sofa at the back of the lounge bar in Purgatory, Scratch had been drinking on his own, anxiously awaiting the return of Dracula, Zilas and Einstein. He'd polished off two bottles of cherry vodka while watching episodes of *When Animals Attack*. Normally the show had him in hysterics from start to finish, but tonight he'd barely raised a smile. He hadn't been this uptight in a long time.

It was almost four-thirty in the morning when, to his great relief, Dracula walked through the open door of the men's toilets. The vampire's face and clothes were covered in blood, which was a promising sign.

'How did it go?' Scratch asked, trying really hard not to give away how excited he was.

'He's dead. I took his head off and impaled him on the spear, just like you asked. Right up through his asshole and out the hole where his head used to be. Stood him upright. Someone's gonna get a real shock when they find him.'

'Perfect,' Scratch grinned. 'You caught him by surprise then?'

'Sort of. There was one strange moment though. I stabbed him through the heart first, and just before he died he opened his eyes and said something weird.'

'Like what?'

Dracula cringed. 'I'm sure he said, *this isn't happening.*'

'Pfffttt. I wouldn't worry about that,' said Scratch. 'People say all kinds of stupid shit when they're taking their last breath. Where are the others?'

Dracula hopped onto a stool at the bar. 'Einstein's still doing his thing in the Violet room, and Zilas is installing those CCTV cameras you gave him. They should be done soon. I just couldn't stay there any longer. Zilas was getting on my nerves.'

'He can be annoying,' Scratch agreed. 'Can I get you a drink?'

'Red wine, the good stuff.'

Scratch reached under the bar and pulled out a bottle of cheap Merlot. He uncorked it and poured out a glass for Dracula. He sniffed it before sliding it across the bar.

Dracula paid no attention to the wine, or Scratch. He was staring at something over Scratch's right shoulder. Whatever it was, he was totally engrossed in it.

'It's called *When Animals Attack*,' said Scratch. 'It's pretty funny.'

'Huh?' Dracula snapped out of his daze. 'Oh, no not that,' he said. 'I was looking at that photo.'

The photo he was referring to was pinned to a shelf of bottled spirits behind the bar. It was a fairly recent photo of Scratch with the members of the Dead Hunters. It was one of his favourite photos, taken shortly after Flake had killed Cain, the son of Adam and Eve, and Elvis had shot one of the four horsemen of the Apocalypse, blowing most of his head off in the process. The gang had all posed for a group photo afterwards. Everyone looked happy, apart from Annabel who was unconscious at the time, but they'd propped her up against the bar and drawn a moustache and some spectacles on her face.

'Oh that,' said Scratch. 'That's the Dead Hunters. None of them are here right now.'

'Can I have a closer look at it?' said Dracula, holding out his hand.

Scratch unpinned the photo and handed it to him. 'You can look at it,' he said. 'But I want it back.'

Dracula ran his fingers over the photo. 'Such beauty,' he whispered. 'I have not seen a beauty such as this since my beloved Esmeralda.'

'That's Jasmine,' said Scratch. 'Everyone likes her. I've got some better pictures of her on my phone if you want to see them? When you get a cell phone of your own I'll send them onto you. But like I said before, you can't keep this photo, and to be honest you wouldn't want it. I've caught Zilas kissing it quite a few times.'

'No, not Jasmine,' said Dracula, shaking his head.

Scratch was puzzled. 'How do you even know which one is Jasmine?'

'Zilas showed me some photos of her on his phone. But I'm not interested in her. I've had a thousand women like her in my time.'

'Oh,' Scratch was surprised. 'You must mean Flake then? I wouldn't really rate your chances there either.'

Dracula continued gazing at the photo like a love-struck teenager. To Scratch's annoyance, he leaned in and kissed it.

'Goddammit!' Scratch groaned. 'Why does everyone have to kiss that photo?'

Dracula stroked the picture lovingly. 'Flake,' he cooed. 'He's gorgeous.'

Scratch frowned. '*He?* What do you mean, *he?* Flake's not a dude. You need glasses, you fuckin' idiot.'

Dracula ignored him and continued to gaze at the picture, so Scratch snatched it away from him and took another look at it. There were sticky lip smudges on the picture. But they weren't on Flake.

'Who exactly were you kissing on here?' Scratch asked.

'The one with the beautiful, fleshy neck.'

Scratch looked up from the photo and studied Dracula's face. The ancient old vampire wasn't joking.

'But that's Sanchez!' said Scratch, baffled. 'Are you out of your fucking mind?'

'Sanchez,' Dracula said, dreamily. 'Where might I find him?'

'He's back working at the Tapioca in Santa Mondega. I kicked him out of Purgatory. He's the one responsible for all that shit that fell down into Hell a few weeks back. And he's stunk out the bar up here more times than I can remember. He's a fucking liability!'

'So you're saying he's dangerous, and that he knows no fear,' said Dracula, his eyes lighting up.

'NO! I'M SAYING HE'S A DIRTY BASTARD!'

'Dirty eh?' Dracula's voice turned soft and seductive, which creeped Scratch out even more.

'When I say *dirty*, I mean disgusting and unhygienic!' Scratch snapped. 'Plus, he's already with Flake. And I don't care how awesome you are with a sword or with your fists, Flake is a proper badass. If you try and steal her man, she'll fuck you up.'

Dracula looked even more aroused. 'Oh I love a challenge,' he said. 'And I adore a bitch-fight.'

'Listen dickweed. You've just won your freedom from Hell. You can go anywhere in the world and seduce whoever you please. I promise you, if you try to seduce Sanchez Garcia, you'll bring a world of trouble down on yourself.'

'I don't care. I want him.'

Scratch leaned across the bar and grabbed the other man's hand. 'Dracula, I've arranged something for you already. As reward for your hard work, I'm giving you a million dollars and the deeds to a property in Santa Mondega. It's a brothel with at least twenty fine-looking women on its books. They're all yours. You've earned them. It's a good little business too, makes a ton of money. Trust me, once you've sampled the delights your new brothel has to offer, you'll forget all about Sanchez.'

Nothing Scratch said was getting through to Dracula. The vampire was gazing into space, dreaming of Sanchez.

'You fucking idiot.....'

Scratch stopped in the early stages of what was about to become a rant of epic proportions. Something more important had cropped up. Zilas and Einstein came back through the portal in the men's toilets. They were still dressed head to toe in black. Unlike Dracula they were still wearing their balaclavas, but even with their faces covered it was easy to tell them apart. Zilas had a hunch on his back and a wonky eye. And Einstein was wearing a pair of round spectacles outside his balaclava.

'It's all done, boss,' said Zilas. 'The cameras are all set up and concealed where no one will see them.'

'What about you, Einstein?' said Scratch.

'I am a genius,' said Einstein, without a hint of modesty. 'My work was completed exactly as you specified, obviously.'

'It is,' Zilas agreed. 'And when the job was complete, we put the necklace with the key on it back on Loomis's body.'

'Perfect,' said Scratch. 'Now for part two of this magnificent plan of mine.'

Zilas peeled off his balaclava. 'Do you think it will work?' he asked.

'It will work,' said Scratch, pouring himself another shot of vodka. 'Before Annabel passed out drunk, I made her tell me what the Bourbon Kid and Beth will be doing tomorrow morning. She says the Kid will rise early and go out for a run. And while he's away, Beth will head into the abbey to see if she can get a cup of coffee. That's when everything will fall into place.'

Twenty Six

When Beth woke up, JD was already gone. It didn't surprise her. He almost always rose before her and went out for an early morning run. She found a note from him on the bedside table confirming that he'd gone for a jog around the grounds of the abbey.

She took a quick shower and slung on a pair of jeans and a grey short-sleeved top. After a quick look in the refrigerator in the kitchen she realised she had forgotten to buy any coffee when she'd shopped for groceries the day before. So rather than sit around waiting for JD to return, she left a note on the fridge for him and headed up to the abbey to see if she could grab a coffee there.

An old black man in light blue overalls was outside the front entrance cleaning some plant pots with a brush. He had a thick grey beard and bushy grey hair, tucked in under a red cap.

'Mornin' ma'am,' he said as Beth approached. 'You must be Ruth.'

'That's right,' Beth agreed, dishonestly. 'Who might you be?'

'I'm Lenny. I do the gardening here. If you get any weeds over by the cottage, just come find me. I'll get rid of them.'

'That's very kind of you,' said Beth. 'Do you know, is there somewhere I can get a coffee in here? I bought some groceries yesterday but forgot to get any coffee.'

'Yeah, no problem. Pop on into the kitchen, it's the first door on the right. Sylvia's in there, she'll sort you out.'

'Sylvia? Is Mavis not here?'

'Nah, ma'am. It's Thursday. Mavis has the day off on Thursday, so Sylvia fills in.'

'I guess I'll see Sylvia then,' Beth said, laughing politely. 'Have a nice day. Lovely to meet you.'

'You too ma'am.'

Beth entered the abbey and walked along the main hallway towards the first door on the right. As she approached it, a woman in her late twenties with olive skin and mousy brown hair tied back in a bun walked out of it. She was wearing a blue housemaid outfit similar to the one worn by Mavis the day before.

'Hello,' she said cheerfully. 'You must be the new lady who moved into the cottage.'

'Yes, I'm Ruth. Lenny said I could get a coffee in here, is that okay?'

'Well, I'm Sylvia,' said the woman. 'And coffee is my specialty, so let me make you one. How do you like yours?'

'Just milk please, and not too much.'

'Coming right up. Have you had a look around the place yet?'

'Not really. My other half came up here briefly yesterday and met everyone.'

Sylvia's eyes grew wide with excitement. 'Have you met Master Loomis yet?' she asked.

'No, I, er....'

Sylvia pointed up to the landing on the upper floor. 'That's his private quarters up in the corner over there,' she said. 'Just knock on the door and go on in. He'll be up and about. I'll have your coffee ready when you come back down.'

'Oh, uh, okay.'

Beth wasn't really keen on the idea of wandering up the stairs to see the master of the house. But in the interests of being civilised and settling in, it was the right thing to do. JD had warned her that Loomis was a weirdo, but she reminded herself that JD thought everyone was a weirdo, so it was probably nothing to stress about.

Sylvia vanished back into the kitchen to make the coffee, so Beth headed up the main staircase to pay Master Loomis a visit. When she arrived outside his room in the corner she knocked on the door. It opened a little and made a creaking sound. A funky smell floated out from inside.

'Hello, anyone there?' Beth called out.

There was no reply so she pushed the door open a little more and peered inside. The sight that greeted her was hideous. The bed in the centre of the room had been flipped over onto its side. And right next to it, impaled on a spear was a naked, headless man. He was standing upright, propped up by the spear, which was embedded in the floor. It went up through his ass and out of a gap between his shoulders, where his head should have been. This was some proper medieval shit.

A window on the left was open and a set of curtains billowed in the wind, reaching out towards the upright corpse of the impaled man. On the floor beneath the curtains was a severed head that belonged to the impaled body. It gawped at Beth, like a fucked-up version of the *Scream* mask.

Beth screamed. She had no idea how long she screamed for, but by the time she did the sensible thing and turned away, Sylvia, the housemaid was bounding up the stairs to see what the fuss was about.

'What's the matter?' said Sylvia rounding the top of the stairs, concern written all over her face.

'It's horrible!' said Beth, steadying herself by holding onto the balcony, knowing she might throw up. The images of what she had just seen kept racing through her mind. 'Something's very wrong in there.'

Sylvia hurried over and comforted Beth, rubbing her back, recognising that she looked sick. 'Is Master Loomis okay?' she asked.

'I don't know what I just saw in there,' Beth replied. 'There's blood everywhere!'

'Blood?'

Sylvia left Beth and walked into Loomis' bedroom. She barely made it through the door before she covered her mouth as if she were about to throw up. She backed away from the room and screamed, just as Beth had done. She kept retreating until Beth grabbed her arm to stop her from falling over the balcony.

Sylvia stared wide-eyed at Beth, her whole body trembling in shock. She tried to speak but no words passed her lips.

'Are you okay?' said Beth, not knowing what else to say, because like the housemaid she was also stunned by what she had seen.

'That's Master Loomis,' said Sylvia, her bottom lip quivering. 'We need to call the police.'

The screaming of the two women had alerted Lenny the gardener. He raced into the building through the front entrance below them, and shouted up to them.

'What's all the screaming about?'

Sylvia leaned over the bannister. 'Lenny, call the police!' she yelled. 'Master Loomis has been murdered!'

Twenty Seven

Sanchez and Flake still had some work to do redecorating the interior of the Tapioca. Flake had put on a set of blue overalls and was on her hands and knees behind the bar scrubbing the floor around Sanchez's feet. He was still in his underpants because he couldn't be bothered to get dressed. There were brown stains on his undies, but where one might expect them to be skid-marks, they were actually paint stains, because he was painting the bar surface a nice cool brown colour. And at Flake's insistence he was wearing a pair of shoes because she'd gotten tired of the stench of cheese coming from his feet.

'This is really tedious,' Sanchez groaned.

'It'll be worth it in the end,' said Flake.

'It's getting chilly. Can't we close the front doors? I can feel my nipples getting hard.'

'It's best left open,' said Flake, slapping him on the shin. 'The fresh air will help the paint to dry in time for us to reopen the place tomorrow.'

Sanchez was hoping that the paint didn't dry. Even though he liked working in the bar, a grand reopening during the Lunar festival would attract a whole bunch of strangers. And Sanchez hated strangers. In the past he'd always served piss to any strangers he didn't like the look of. But seeing as how he only had one bottle of piss under the bar, he was going to have to make some more to keep up the supply.

He put his paintbrush down and grabbed an empty whisky bottle from under the bar. He flipped the lid off and held the bottle down by his crotch, and then pulled his underpants down and took aim. He was just about to pee when Flake saw his Y-fronts around his ankles and looked up.

'What the fuck are you doing?' she said angrily.

'Just taking a piss. I thought it would save time if I peed in a bottle.'

'Bullshit! I know what you're doing. You're planning on selling piss to people again aren't you? How many times have I got to tell you?'

Sanchez had his dick in his hand and the bottle was right there. 'I'm busting to go though,' he protested. 'I've already started the countdown in my head. I can't stop now.'

Flake glared at him. 'If any of that piss lands on me, you're a dead man. I already told you, no golden showers! Why don't you put the fucking bottle down and use the toilet like a normal person?'

'I would,' said Sanchez, 'But my shorts are down by my ankles and my shoelaces aren't tied.'

Flake sighed. 'Hold still a minute. I'll tie your shoelaces for you.'

'I don't think I can hold on that long,' said Sanchez, taking short breaths as the urge to pee became almost unbearable. 'I'm gonna have to pee in the bottle.'

'No you're not! This is a good time for you to learn how to hold in your bodily fluids. Maybe if you learned some self-control you wouldn't have to go so often. Now hold still while I tie your shoes.'

Sanchez knew not to mess with Flake when she was barking out orders. He could feel a sweat coming on though, because he knew if he did pee, or even let out just one drop, if it landed on Flake, she'd punch him in the nuts. He closed his eyes and did some breathing exercises while counting upwards in his head to convince his bladder that it wasn't yet time to pee.

'Are you nearly done?' he asked Flake. 'I'm ready to burst.'

'Are you okay Sanchez?'

That wasn't Flake's voice.

Sanchez opened one eye and saw Jasmine approaching the bar.

'Jasmine!' he said, opening his other eye and staring wide-eyed in panic at her because his underpants were down by his ankles.

Jasmine was wearing a white crop-top that covered almost nothing, and the smallest pair of brown shorts Sanchez had ever seen. If indeed they were shorts. They matched her skin colour perfectly, making it look like they weren't really there. And knowing Jasmine it was possible they weren't. Sanchez stared for as long as he could realistically get away with before deciding they must be shorts. At least it took his mind off the need to pee for a while.

'What are you doing?' Jasmine asked with a mischievous smile on her face.

'Nothing.'

'Are you wearing anything?'

'Yup.'

'You look like you're playing with yourself.'

'I'm not.'

'Then why do you look like you're about to shoot your load?'

'I'm doing breathing exercises.'

Jasmine didn't look convinced. 'Is Flake around?' she asked.

Flake finished tying Sanchez's shoelaces and jumped up, surprising Jasmine.

'Hey Jas! What can we do for you?'

Jasmine placed her hands on the bar and leaned over it to see what was going on. She saw Sanchez's underpants down by his ankles. And she saw everything else.

'Oh my God, *my eyes!*' she cried, stepping back. 'Should I come back in a minute?'

'Nah, it's okay,' said Flake. 'I'm finished.'

'Ugh, I don't wanna think about that,' said Jasmine.

Flake laughed. 'I was only tying up his shoelaces.'

Jasmine grimaced. 'Does he always close his eyes and pull weird faces when you do that?'

'I don't know,' Flake shrugged.

'And why are his knickers round his ankles?'

Sanchez ducked down and pulled up his underwear. 'I was about to take a pee.'

'On Flake?'

He held up his empty liquor bottle. 'No, I was gonna go in here.'

'Well don't let me stop you,' Jasmine said, rolling her eyes. 'Anyway, I came to see you, Flake. I've got two tickets for an outdoor concert that's on today. Wondered if you wanted to come with me?'

'Ooh, what concert is it?' Flake asked.

Jasmine pulled two tickets from the back of her shorts and slapped them down on a freshly painted part of the bar. 'It's this,' she said, 'It's called The Party in the Park.'

Flake snatched the tickets up before they sank into the paint. She held them up and started reading them.

Sanchez wanted to see the tickets too, but he'd just pulled his underpants open and was focussing on trying to pee into his whisky bottle. Where he'd been busting for a piss only moments earlier, suddenly now with Jasmine just a few feet away, he was getting a touch of performance anxiety. Concentration was required.

'So, do you wanna come?' said Jasmine. 'It starts in half an hour.'

'I thought you'd wanna go with Elvis,' said Flake.

Jasmine shook her head. 'Nah, him and Rex have got a secret meeting this morning with a cop lady. It's something to do with a copycat killer and I don't think Rex wanted me there. He's a little embarrassed because he got a couple of his metal fingers stuck in my ass last night.'

Sanchez's anxiety evaporated upon hearing that remark, and before he could ask Jasmine for some clarification, his dick started spraying like a fire hose. The noise of piss hitting the bottom of the whisky bottle drowned out a part of Jasmine's conversation with Flake, which came to an abrupt end anyway when Jasmine leaned over the bar to see what Sanchez was doing.

'You're really doing it?' she said. 'I was only kidding you know. Weirdo.'

'Are those new shorts?' Flake asked, in an attempt to take Jasmine's eyes off Sanchez urinating.

'Yeah,' Jasmine did a quick spin so Flake could get a good look. 'You like 'em?'

'What colour are they?'

'Funny you should ask,' said Jasmine. 'When I picked them up at the market they looked like they were see-through, but the guy that was selling them told me they adapt to your skin colour when you put them on. So I tried them on and he was right. They're exactly the same colour as my skin. How cool is that?'

'Maybe you should wear some underwear with them,' Flake suggested.

'The guy in the market said you're not supposed to. They only work if you don't wear undies. I can get you a pair if you like?'

'It's okay,' said Flake. 'We'd look silly if we both wore them.'

'That's true. Is he still peeing?'

Sanchez was close to filling the liquor bottle. 'I told you I was desperate,' he said.

Jasmine leaned over the bar to get another look. 'Holy crap, that's going to overflow in a minute!'

Flake changed the subject again by reading out what was on the concert tickets. 'I've only heard of one of these bands,' she said. 'Psychotherapist are a local group, but I've never heard of Donna Winter, Freddy Venus or the Shearing Sisters.'

'Me either,' said Jasmine, her eyes fixed on Sanchez and the piss bottle. 'A guy in the street gave me the tickets for free though. He said the concert is already sold out and the tickets are normally a hundred bucks a head.'

'And he just gave them to you?'

'Guys give me stuff all the time. He even put his phone number on the back of one of the tickets.'

Flake flipped the ticket over. 'It's covered in paint now,' she said.

Sanchez finally finished peeing when the bottle was filled almost to the top. He noticed Jasmine was still watching him. 'Do you mind?' he said. 'I need to shake it.'

Jasmine shook her head and looked away. 'So Flake, do you wanna come with me, or what?'

'Woah, hang on a minute,' said Sanchez. 'What about me?' I'm not staying here and cleaning up this place on my own while you two are off having fun at a concert.'

Fortunately, Flake sympathised. 'He's got a point,' she said. 'I can't go and leave him behind. It wouldn't be fair.'

'He can have my ticket,' said Jasmine.

'Perfect,' said Sanchez.

'No, wait a second,' said Flake. 'They're Jasmine's tickets. She should have one of them.'

Jasmine shrugged it off. 'It's not a problem. I'll get another ticket when we get there.'

'I thought you said it was sold out,' Flake reminded her.

'The doormen at the concert will let me in,' said Jasmine. 'I've never been turned away from a concert before.'

'But what if they don't?' said Flake.

'Then I'll just tie their shoelaces for them.'

Sanchez screwed the lid back on his new bottle of homebrew and placed it back down on a shelf under the bar. When he came back up he saw another person had walked into the Tapioca. It was Pete the garbage man. Pete was in his early thirties and had a good head of black hair, but he was always covered in filth because of his job.

Sanchez suspected Pete had the hots for him, so he quickly pulled up his underpants. It was one thing to have Jasmine seeing him naked, but if Pete saw the goods, Sanchez feared the garbage man's infatuation with him might go into overdrive.

'Morning Pete,' he said. 'We're not actually open yet.'

Pete stank of garbage, and the smell got worse as he approached the bar. His grey overalls and orange hi-vis vest were covered in muck and rotten food. He stopped next to Jasmine and smiled at Sanchez.

'I just wanted to know if you guys were going to the outdoor concert today?' he said.

Jasmine answered him. 'We all are. It's gonna be fun.'

'Awesome,' said Pete, smiling a horrible crooked smile at Sanchez, while running his hand through his greasy hair.

'I expect the concert will be packed out,' said Sanchez. 'So we probably won't see you.'

'Are you going dressed like that?' Pete asked, peering over the bar.

'No,' said Sanchez, grabbing his bottle of piss and holding it in front of his pants to cover up his package. 'I'll be wearing something that's hard to get into.'

'Great,' said Pete. 'Hopefully I'll see you all there?'

Jasmine tapped him on the shoulder. 'Do you like my shorts?' she asked him.

Pete looked down and his face dropped. 'Oh,' he said. 'Are you wearing those to the concert later?'

'You bet I am,' said Jasmine, giving him a twirl.

'Damn,' said Pete. 'I just bought a pair of those too. I was gonna wear them today, but I'll have to wear something different now.'

'You should go dressed as you are,' Sanchez suggested.

'I can't do that,' said Pete. 'I've got blood on my overalls. Did you hear someone was murdered in an alley down the road. A cop named Bob Muncher.'

Flake butted in. 'Bob Muncher is dead? He was in here yesterday morning, and he was looking for a murderer.'

'Well it looks like he found one,' said Pete. 'It's a good job I check the dumpsters before we empty them. I found his body in there this morning. He was a real fucking mess. Someone had gouged out his eyes, and his tongue was missing too.'

Sanchez winced. 'You must have had a real good look.'

'You can tell a lot about someone from their garbage,' said Pete, winking at Sanchez. 'Anyway, I'd best be going if I want to get to the concert on time. I hope I see you guys there.'

'Definitely,' said Jasmine. 'We'll keep an eye out for you.'

Twenty Eight

After the initial shock of seeing the decapitated body of Loomis impaled on a spear, Sylvia composed herself much quicker than Beth did. The two women were still on the landing outside Loomis' bedroom, comforting each other.

'Wait here a minute,' said Sylvia, pulling herself away from Beth. 'I'm going back in.'

Truth be told, Beth didn't want to be anywhere near Master Loomis's bedroom. 'I should go,' she said. 'My husband will be wondering where I am.'

'Don't leave me on my own!' said Sylvia. 'Just wait here a minute.'

Sylvia walked tentatively back into the bedroom. Quite why she wanted another look at what was inside was anyone's guess. Beth certainly had no intention of joining her. She needed to be as far away from the crime scene as possible.

Downstairs, Lenny the gardener was on the phone to the Police, explaining that there had been a murder. Beth definitely had to be gone before the cops came. And JD needed to know what had happened. She reached into her pocket for her phone so she could call him. Before she even typed in her access code, Sylvia rushed out of Loomis's bedroom.

'Look!' she said, excitedly, holding up a shiny object. 'I've got Loomis's key.'

There was blood on the key, but Sylvia didn't seem bothered by it. She looked like she'd just found a winning lottery ticket. She grabbed Beth's hand and pulled her towards the staircase. 'You've got to come with me,' she said.

Beth allowed herself to be dragged away from Loomis's bedroom because it meant she was closer to the exit and further from the headless dead monk.

'What's the key for?' she asked.

'I took it off the Master's necklace,' said Sylvia.

'Ugh, why would you do that?'

Sylvia didn't reply. She leapt onto the staircase and started running down the steps with Beth following behind her, struggling to keep up. When they were halfway down Sylvia held up the key and waved it in the air.

'Lenny!' she called out. 'I've got the key to the Violet room!'

Lenny brought his telephone call with the police to an abrupt end and hurried along the corridor to the bottom of the stairs. He arrived at the same time as Sylvia and Beth. He gazed wide-eyed at the key in Sylvia's hand.

'It's got blood on it,' he said.

Sylvia wiped the key clean on her apron. 'Wanna see what's in there?' she said, breathing heavily.

Beth unwrapped herself from Sylvia's side. 'You should probably put that back,' she suggested. 'I don't think you're supposed to tamper with a crime scene.'

'You don't understand,' said Sylvia. 'That room has been locked for over a hundred years. Master Loomis never let anyone go in there. He kept this key on a chain around his neck his whole life.'

Lenny nodded in agreement. 'No one's ever been in that room. Not since I've been here.'

'But the police are coming, aren't they?' said Beth, not caring a jot about what was behind the door to the Violet room.

'Exactly,' said Sylvia. 'It's now or never.'

Lenny's hands were sweating with excitement. He wiped them on his overalls and reached out to take the key from Sylvia. The housemaid pulled it away. Beth couldn't comprehend how these two employees were more concerned with a stupid key than they were with the death of their employer, who she assumed was also their friend.

Sylvia walked up to the Violet room and slid the key into the lock.

'Are you sure about this?' Beth said.

'Definitely,' said Lenny. 'This is our only chance. Once the cops show up, what do you think they're gonna do, huh? They'll go in there, and you know what cops are like, if there's anything valuable in there, they'll have it away.'

Sylvia turned the key, and the lock clicked open. She hesitated, her hand hovering over the doorknob.

'I should probably leave,' said Beth. 'You don't need me for this.'

Sylvia scowled at her. 'You can't leave,' she said. 'It's an offence to leave a crime scene before the police arrive. Besides, I need you to keep watch while we check inside this room.'

'Hurry up and open it then,' said Lenny.

Beth was somewhat bemused at how suddenly "crime scene etiquette" was important again, whereas when they'd taken the key from the corpse of Master Loomis it was seen as an irrelevance.

Sylvia pushed the door open a few inches. It was pitch dark inside. The door was obviously heavy because it took an almighty shove for her to push it wide open. But it was still too dark to see anything inside.

Sylvia stepped away from the open door, seemingly reluctant to walk into the darkness. 'Go on, Lenny,' she said. 'You go first. See if you can find some lights.'

Lenny brushed past her and walked into the Violet room. He felt around on the wall just inside the door. 'There's no light switch,' he said.

'There must be,' said Sylvia. 'Keep looking.'

Lenny disappeared into the darkness. Sylvia leaned her shoulder against the door to keep it open, giving Beth a better view of the nothingness inside.

'Maybe there's a lamp in there?' Sylvia suggested.

'How am I supposed to find it in the dark?' Lenny replied. 'It's like being blind in here.'

'Darn it!' said Sylvia. 'I'll go fetch the torch from the kitchen.'

'That's a good idea,' said Lenny, his voice echoing around the room. 'Hurry up!'

Sylvia took hold of Beth's arm. 'Can you wait here?' she said. 'I'll just be a minute.'

Before Beth could protest, Sylvia dashed along the corridor back to the kitchen. The door to the Violet room slammed shut, startling Beth momentarily. They key was still in the door, but Beth didn't want to touch it, or the doorknob, for fear of leaving a fingerprint, so she left the door closed. She reached into her pocket for her phone again and was about to call JD when Sylvia reappeared from the kitchen armed with a battery torch. She sprinted along the corridor towards Beth.

'You shut the door?' she said, angrily.

'It shut itself,' Beth replied.

The sound of police sirens approaching in the distance added a sense of urgency to everything. Beth put her phone back in her pocket, unsure what she would say to JD in front of Sylvia anyway. All she really wanted was to get the fuck out of the abbey as soon as possible.

Sylvia twisted the doorknob and opened the door again. She pushed it wide open and flicked on her torch. She shone the light into the room.

'Lenny!' she whispered. 'The cops are almost here.'

Lenny did not reply.

'I should go,' said Beth.

Sylvia reached out with her free hand and grabbed Beth by her wrist this time, while keeping the Violet room door wedged open with her foot.

'Just wait here a second until Lenny comes back out,' she said.

'Okay, but I really have to get back to my husband. He'll be wondering where I am.'

Sylvia ignored her and shone her torch around the Violet room. 'Can you see Lenny in here anywhere?' she asked. *'Lenny?'*

Even with the torch lighting up part of the room there wasn't much to see. And there was no sign of Lenny.

Beth poked her head around the door and joined Sylvia in calling out Lenny's name, in the hope of speeding things up. He still didn't answer.

Sylvia handed her the torch. 'Here, see if you can find him,' she said. 'I'll go and stall the police.'

Beth didn't like the idea of walking around in a dark room looking for a man she'd only just met.

'I really have to go,' she said.

'Yes you do,' said Sylvia.

The look on the housemaid's face changed. From one of curiosity at what might be in the room, it turned to a look of anger and aggression. She grabbed Beth by her shoulders and shoved her into the darkened room. Beth spun around just in time to see the light from the corridor disappear as Sylvia pulled the door shut.

Sylvia breathed a sigh of relief. Her mission was a success. 'Goodbye Beth Lansbury,' she said.

A short while later, two cops, a man and a woman, both in standard blue uniforms entered the abbey. The male officer, Derek Skudder had fuzzy black hair and a crap moustache. His partner, Karen Butterman was a short lady with curly ginger hair.

'You're just in time,' said Sylvia as they approached.

'What's happened?' asked Derek Skudder.

'She's inside the room, and so is the gardener, Lenny.'

Karen Butterman pulled a torch from her belt and flicked it on. 'What about the Bourbon Kid?' she asked.

'He's not here yet. When he shows up, I'll send him in too.'

'Good work,' said Skudder, smiling nervously at her. 'So you gonna let us in, or what?'

'You bet.' Sylvia twisted the knob on the door to the Violet room again and pushed it open for the two officers. The room was dark and deathly quiet. 'Have fun in there,' she said. 'And don't worry, it's empty.'

The two police officers took a moment to look inside the darkened room. Sylvia had told them the truth. It was empty. There was no sign of Beth or Lenny the gardener, or anyone else for that matter.

Derek Skudder took a deep breath and walked in first, followed by Karen Butterman. Sylvia closed the door behind them.

Twenty Nine

Sally Diamond was sitting in her office cubicle at the Santa Mondega Police station when her cell rang with a call from Special Agent Richard Williams. She answered it with a polite "Hello", but the response she received was far less cordial.

'Don't write any of this down,' said Williams.

It was an odd request. Diamond had a pen in her hand, so she put it down on the desk. Williams, to his credit, was calling her back with news about the murders she wasn't supposed to be investigating.

'Okay,' she said.

'And don't tell anyone you've spoken to me.'

'I wasn't going to.'

'Good, keep it that way. Now listen to everything I tell you, and memorise it, because the minute this call ends, I'm forgetting that we ever had this conversation. Your calls aren't recorded are they?'

'No, sir.'

Sally Diamond was excited by the covert nature of the call, while also nervous about what she was doing. She was going against the orders of her senior officer, Captain Raymond Wilson. If he found out, she could be fired. She stood up and looked over her office cubicle to see if anyone was within hearing distance. The only person close enough to hear any of her conversation was an old fart called Luther Shithouse, but he was eating the packed lunch his wife made for him every day, and Diamond knew only too well, when Shithouse was eating his lunch he didn't want to hear about anything else. It was the highlight of his day.

She sat back down while Williams continued talking like he was in a Mission: Impossible movie.

'We're not sending anyone from our department to Santa Mondega,' he continued. 'That's because you never called us, and we know nothing about your case.'

'Huh?'

'Have you heard of a bar in Santa Mondega called the Nightjar?'

'Yes, I've never been in there though. It's kinda rough.'

'Be there at eleven o'clock this morning. Sit at a table in the corner and wear a red top. Have you got a red top?'

'Yes, a sweater, but it's....'

'Two men will meet you there. You tell them everything you know about these murders. *Absolutely everything*. They will then take over the investigation. Got that?'

'Yes.' Diamond was finding it hard to resist the urge to write everything down. The pressure of knowing she had to remember it all was stressing her out more than it should. 'Richard, how will I know who the two men are? Will they be wearing something specific too?'

'No.'

'Then how will I know I'm talking to the right people?'

'You'll recognise them when you see them, and you'll shit a brick.'

'Shit a brick?'

'Take copies of all the case files with you, including the files on the victims from five years ago.'

Diamond picked up her pen and wrote down, *"Take all case files"*. 'Anything else?' she asked.

'Did you just write that down?'

'No.'

'Sally, don't call me again. We never spoke about this. From here on, you speak only with the two contacts you meet in the Nightjar.'

The line went dead. It had been a bizarre but exciting conversation. Richard Williams had been so abrupt, which was not how she remembered him from his brief deployment in Santa Mondega. She replayed his instructions over and over in her head as she drove to the Nightjar. Her heart was racing. She was breaking rules, and attending a covert meeting with a couple of secret agents. It was something she might live to regret. Bob Muncher had been killed while he was working on this case, and that should have been all the incentive she needed to back off, but something had gotten her juices flowing and she needed to follow up this lead.

The Nightjar turned out to be a good place to hold a secret meeting. When Diamond arrived at 10.55 a.m. the place was dead. There were no other customers and just one bartender, a thin, creepy looking guy in a grey shirt with a black waistcoat. He served her a glass of lime and soda, while eyeing her with suspicion the whole time. Maybe he knew she was a cop? Or maybe he was wondering why a young woman would come to a nightclub in the morning on her own with a brown folder?

She wished Richard Williams hadn't instructed her to wear something red. The red sweater she'd agreed to wear had seen better days. The sleeves were too short, so she'd rolled them up to her elbow. The only thing she could find that went well with the sweater was a black pencil skirt, which wouldn't be ideal if things turned ugly and she had to make a run for it.

She took a seat at a round table in a dark corner of the bar and put on her reading glasses so she could read through the files again.

It was 11.08 when the two men showed up. As soon as they walked in, it became obvious why Richard Williams had told her she'd shit a brick. She didn't shit anything, let alone a brick, but her stomach tightened and her whole body tensed. She recognised both of the men, even though she'd never met them before, and never expected to either. Rodeo Rex and Elvis.

Elvis was wearing a red suit with a big gold belt and a pair of gold-rimmed sunglasses. He looked around, peering over his sunglasses, and spotted Sally Diamond in the corner. He nodded and waved at her. She waved back, nervously. This was creepy, because not only did he look like Elvis Presley, he also looked exactly like a guy called Elvis who was one of the murder victims in the files she had brought with her. Likewise his buddy, Rodeo Rex, a biker with long brown hair, dressed from head to toe in denim, with muscles the size of Brussels. He too was one of the victims in her files. She even had photos of their corpses, both really messed up with their eyes and tongues ripped out. Elvis had even been stabbed about a hundred times. *How the Hell was this possible?*

Elvis sauntered over to join her, moving like he was listening to music on a set of invisible headphones, while his buddy Rex ordered some drinks from the bar.

'You must be Sally Diamond,' Elvis said, his hand outstretched.

Sally couldn't stand up, on account of how close she was to soiling her pants, but she reached across the table and shook his hand anyway.

'This is so weird,' she said.

'Is it?' said Elvis.

'Yeah, I mean, I have pictures in here.' She held up her brown folder.

Elvis pulled up a chair and sat down. 'They any good?' he asked.

'You're in them,' she spluttered. 'So is your friend.'

'Dead or alive?'

'Dead. Very much dead.'

'Yeah it's a strange story,' Elvis replied. 'We *were* dead, but now we're not. For your safety it's best that you don't know any more than that.'

'For my safety?'

'Yeah. I could tell you more about it, but then I'd have to kill you.'

'Oh.'

Rex arrived at the table with two bottles of Shitting Monkey beer. He handed one to Elvis and pulled up a seat next to him. 'Hi, I'm Rex,' he said.

'This is Sally,' said Elvis. 'I've told her all she needs to know about us.'

Rex looked surprised. 'You told her about how we did a deal with the Devil?'

Diamond wasn't sure she was hearing correctly. 'You did what?' she asked.

Elvis slapped himself on the forehead. 'Jeez, man, I didn't tell her that. I was trying not to freak her out too much.'

Diamond *was* freaked. 'I'm sorry,' she said. 'What are you talking about?'

Rex and Elvis both took a pull on their beers and glared at each other. Eventually Rex put his beer back down and responded to Diamond's question.

'Forget about it,' he said. 'It's not important.'

He eyed her brown folder. 'What's this?' he asked, reaching across the table and picking it up. He opened it and flicked through the photos, wincing occasionally. Then he handed it to Elvis who did the same. While Elvis flicked through the photos, Rex took on the role of inquisitor.

'General Calhoon tells us you've had three more murders like the ones from five years ago. Is that right?' he asked.

'I don't know a General Calhoon,' said Diamond. 'I spoke to someone else, but I can't say who. He looked into it and called me back this morning to tell me to meet you two in here.'

Rex looked at her like she was mental. 'You've got three more murders though, yes?' he said, eventually.

'It's actually just gone up to four,' Diamond replied. 'My colleague Bob Muncher was working on this case with me, but the garbage-men found him in a dumpster. His eyes and tongue were cut out, just like the others.'

Rex rubbed his chin. He looked deep in thought. 'You got any suspects lined up?' he asked.

'We've got nothing,' she replied. 'I was hoping you guys might have an idea who's behind it.'

Rex and Elvis stared blankly at each other for a few seconds. The two of them seemed to have their own language, built entirely upon shrugs, protruding bottom lips and raised eyebrows.

Eventually Elvis replied to Diamond with a shrug, a protruding bottom lip *and* some raised eyebrows. 'We don't know shit,' he said, translating the entire secret language for her in just four words.

Diamond took a sip of her drink, and when she was certain it was her turn to talk, she spilled the details of the case. 'Okay, so five years ago the killer was a guy named Archibald....' She noticed both men raise their eyebrows. 'Err, sorry, you already know that, I suppose?' she said, blushing.

Rex nodded.

Elvis put the folder down on the table. 'Somers had nothing to do with these new murders, if that's what you're thinking,' he said. 'That asshole's dead.'

'Well, I thought that myself,' said Diamond. 'Right up until I saw you two walk in here, *alive*.'

'Trust me,' said Rex. 'Somers is definitely dead. And he's living out eternity in a special level of Hell. He's one of the Devil's favourite inmates. He's not getting out ever, not even on day release.'

'You're sure of that?'

Elvis got a nod from Rex, before answering the question for her. 'Archie Somers has his mouth attached to his own asshole. He spends his days shitting into his own mouth, digesting it and then shitting it back into his mouth again. Pretty sure he's doing that for all eternity.'

'Oh.'

Both men picked up their beers and took a swig. Rex held his bottle in his gloved right hand. Sally noticed it for the first time. One hand with a glove, and one without. So while the two men were drinking, she asked a question she'd promised herself she wouldn't.

'Can I see your metal hand?'

Rex blew some beer out of his nose and slammed his bottle down on the table. 'You what?'

Elvis nudged him. 'Go on, show her.'

'I didn't mean to be rude,' said Diamond, backtracking.

'No, it's okay,' said Rex. He peeled the leather glove off his hand and revealed a fully functioning metal hand.

'Oh my God,' said Diamond. 'That's incredible! And it works just like a normal hand?'

'Yeah.' Rex held it out and wiggled his fingers for her.

She was about to touch it when she noticed something. 'Are the fingers going rusty?' she asked.

Rex pulled his hand away. 'No, that's something else.'

'Anyway,' said Elvis, changing the subject while Rex slipped his glove back on. 'Have you found anything at all that connects the victims, apart from the way they were murdered?'

'Not exactly, but according to the files, when these murders happened five years ago, Archie Somers was trying to get his hands on a precious stone called The Eye of the Moon. Rumour had it that the stone could control the orbit of the moon and make an eclipse permanent. Does that sound right to you?'

'Yeah that's about right,' said Elvis.

'So I was thinking that maybe this new killer is looking for the Eye, because there's an eclipse again on Friday.'

'That's not a bad thought,' said Rex. 'I think Flake's got the Eye now, doesn't she?'

Elvis agreed. 'She wears it on a chain around her neck, I think.'

'Who is Flake?' Diamond asked.

'A friend of ours,' said Elvis. 'We'll contact her and let her know to be careful. You got any other leads?'

Diamond shook her head. 'That's it. I'm not allowed to work on this case. The whole department has been forbidden from working on it.'

'And that's why we're here,' said Rex, taking another sip of his beer. 'So, who's stopping you from working on this?'

'The Mayor. He says nothing is to be released to the public about this until after the eclipse, if at all. It's a PR nightmare, apparently.' She reached into her jacket pocket and pulled out two plastic cards. 'I got these for you. They're fake ID passes that will get you into the coroner's office on Hanmore Street. That's where you'll find the new victims. I thought maybe you could check them out and see if the killer is doing everything exactly like Somers did.'

Elvis took the two cards and inspected them. 'These pictures look nothing like us,' he said.

'I know,' said Diamond. 'All you have to do is swipe them through a turnstile and they get you in. No one ever checks that you're using your own card, so these will be fine. I created them for you this morning, but I didn't know your names or what you looked like, so they're just people I made up.'

Elvis handed one to Rex. 'You can be Roland Chang. I'll be Clifford Alvarez.'

'*Roland Chang?*' said Rex, his voice dripping with disdain. 'I don't look anything like a *Chang.*'

'You *do* look like a Roland though,' said Elvis.

'Why would you pick these names?' Rex asked Diamond.

'It's not important,' she said, blushing again. 'When you get to the morgue, ask to see the coroner, Dr Taylor. He'll be doing the autopsies, and he'll know everything about the victims from five years ago too because he's been working there since forever.' She placed her business card down on the table. 'My number is on here if you need me.'

Rex picked it up. 'Thanks' he said. 'I'll text you my number, so you can call me if any more dead people show up.'

'One last thing,' said Diamond. 'As I said before, my colleague Bob Muncher was murdered because he was investigating this case, and as I understand it, you two were killed five years ago because you were on the killer's tail. Should I be worried that the killer might come after me?'

'Yes you should,' said Rex.

Elvis tried to offer her some reassurance. 'I wouldn't worry too much,' he said. 'Once you've been stabbed in both eyes you'll probably pass out, so you won't feel anything after that.'

Thirty

JD left Beth a note saying he'd gone for a jog, which was only partly true. He'd gone to scout out the grounds surrounding the abbey. The estate was huge, which was a promising sign because it meant there were plenty of possible escape routes. JD just needed to work out the most efficient ways to escape depending on the circumstances.

He was still undecided about what route he preferred when the sound of a police siren distracted him. He saw a cop car racing along a narrow country lane towards the abbey. His phoney jog turned into a full on sprint back to the cottage.

When he walked in through the front door into the kitchen he found a note from Beth stuck on the fridge, saying she'd gone up to the abbey for a coffee. What a disaster.

The police car had parked outside the entrance to the main building, and from the window in the bedroom at the back of the cottage JD saw two cops exit the vehicle and race inside as if there was some kind of emergency.

He texted Beth a message warning her to get out of the abbey and back to the cottage as soon as possible. He waited for a reply while he stared at the cop car outside the abbey. But Beth didn't respond to the text. JD's phone indicated that she hadn't even received it. It just floated around in that non-existent place where lost text messages go.

Fuck it.

There was only one cop car, and just two cops, which probably meant they hadn't come looking for him. But it was their bad luck that they'd stumbled upon him and Beth, because now they were going to have to die.

JD was already wearing a pair of black cargo pants and a matching vest. He scrambled through the closet in the bedroom and prepared himself for a spot of murder. He strapped on a shoulder holster, tucked his Headblaster gun in one side and a Glock pistol in the other. The final piece of the jigsaw was his long black hooded coat. He put it on and it hid the guns from sight.

He headed back into the kitchen and was a moment away from opening the door when he saw something moving outside in the graveyard. He pressed his back up against the door and peeked out of the window. A man dressed from head to toe in black was sneaking up on the cottage. And then he saw another. In a matter of seconds he'd counted four of them. They were using the gravestones as cover, sneaking from one to another as they closed in on the cottage.

JD's time on the run from the law, the undead and the Devil had prepared him for just about anything. But this was new. He had a group of Ninja assassins coming for him. What the fuck were Ninjas doing in a monastery a million miles from anywhere? Those assholes belonged in Japan, or in action movies from the 1970s. Not here, not now.

He locked the front door by sliding a deadbolt across it, then reached inside his coat and pulled out his Glock. He peeked out of the window again to see how close the assassins were. Suddenly everything became clear. At the back of the graveyard, leaning against a large angel statue was a tall black man in a red suit, with a Fedora hat, smoking a cigar. And this asshole wanted to be seen.

Scratch.

JD ducked down and scampered back into the rear bedroom. There was only one way out of the cottage now and that was through the secret tunnel. He lifted up the rug and pulled open the trapdoor in the floor. For one fleeting moment he hesitated, knowing that he was probably walking into a trap. But the tunnel was the only option. He lowered himself into it and dragged the rug back into position as he pulled the trapdoor shut.

As soon as his feet touched the ground he grabbed the torch from the wall and hurried along the tunnel, half expecting someone to jump out at him at any moment. No one did. At the end of the tunnel he ditched the torch and climbed the ladder to the top. He unlocked the manhole cover and pushed it up a few inches. There were no Ninjas in sight, just gravestones.

He crawled out of the tunnel and ducked behind a nearby gravestone. The Ninjas had already broken into the cottage and were trashing the place looking for him. But there was no sign of Scratch. JD kept low and made a break for it. He scurried over to the police car and ducked behind it.

'Psssst! JD, over here!'

The young woman who called his name was standing just inside the arched red doors at the front of the main building. JD didn't recognise her. She had olive skin and mousy brown hair tied back in a bun, and she was dressed like a housemaid. She beckoned JD towards her.

'Beth's in here,' she whispered. 'Quick!'

The maid ducked back inside the building. JD had no choice but to follow her, even though he couldn't shake the feeling that he was being led into a trap. The regular housemaid, Mavis had been replaced by this younger, better-looking version. This had Scratch's fingerprints all over it.

JD made it into the building without catching the eye of any of the Ninjas. He half expected to see Scratch waiting for him in the main corridor of the abbey. But the maid was the only person inside. She hurried along the hallway and stopped outside a door opposite the main staircase.

JD sprinted after her. 'Where's Beth?' he called out.

'She's in here,' the maid replied. She turned the knob on the door and pushed it open.

JD caught up to her and took a moment to soak in her appearance. Did she look trustworthy? Hard to tell. Gut instinct. Probably not.

'Quick,' she said, pointing into the room. 'There's no time to waste. Hide in here.'

'Who the fuck are you?' JD asked her.

'I'm Sylvia. Your friend Flake sent me to help you out. She said Scratch is coming. Beth's waiting for you in here. Quick! Go! I can hide you.'

JD checked the nameplate on the door. *The Violet room*. It was the room the previous housemaid, the even weirder one, had told him was never opened and had remained locked for about a hundred years. Everything about this situation was wrong. It all pointed to a sting, a set-up, a cunning plan arranged by Scratch. And this woman, Sylvia was claiming to be a friend of Flake's? That didn't ring true either. Flake would never send a stranger to do a job she could do herself.

'What's the name of the café Flake worked at?' he asked her.

'Tapioca.'

'Before that.'

Sylvia looked guilty as sin. JD had a pretty good internal lie detector, and this woman was full of shit.

He grabbed the front of her apron and pulled her in close so that his face was right next to hers.

'Tell me where Beth is or I'll rip your fucking fingernails out one by one,' he snarled.

Sylvia swallowed hard, her bottom lip quivered. 'She's in there,' she said. 'I promise. It's a gateway to freedom. You have to go in and close the door for it to work.'

JD reached into his jacket and pulled out his Headblaster gun. He pressed it underneath her chin. 'I don't believe you,' he said.

'You've got to hurry,' she said. 'They're coming!'

Her eyes switched to something behind him. He didn't even need to see for himself what she was looking at. The Ninjas were coming, and Scratch wouldn't be far behind.

'You're coming with me,' he said.

'No, no wait…'

He dragged Sylvia into the darkness inside the Violet room.

'No!' she cried again. 'Don't shut the door!'

JD ignored her and kicked the door shut.

Thirty One

The best thing about going to an outdoor music festival was that Sanchez got to wear his favourite blue Hawaiian shirt. Flake had also convinced him to wear a pair of khaki shorts that she thought looked good on him. In return he convinced her to wear an oversized white T-shirt from his collection. It was an old classic with the words "FUCK OFF" emblazoned across the front. It hung down almost to the knees on her skinny black jeans.

After a cab ride with Jasmine they arrived at the outdoor festival, which was situated high up on Corned Beef Hill, an area of Santa Mondega known for its grassy fields and good drainage. The idea behind having the concert there was that if it rained it wouldn't become a mud pit like so many other similar events.

Sanchez and Flake got into the event with the tickets Jasmine had provided. They left her behind at the entrance where she was befriending the security team in order to get another ticket for herself.

While Jasmine's amazing shorts kept the entire security team occupied, Sanchez managed to steal a program from a pile on a table inside the entrance. He and Flake then joined the massive crowd of people watching a grungy band performing on the main stage. The music was loud, monotonous and mostly out of tune. The lead singer, a nutcase with a skull painted on his face, was shouting along to the music, but the lyrics were incomprehensible.

A younger generation of party lovers had been drawn to the concert. They had haircuts that they would all regret later in life, and clothes with political messages on them, none of which came close to Flake's "FUCK OFF" logo.

'I think we made it just in time,' said Flake. 'How cool is this?'

The music suddenly came to an abrupt end and the crowd cheered and clapped to show their approval.

'Perfect timing,' Sanchez agreed. 'I couldn't have listened to much more of that.'

'Who's up next?' Flake asked.

Sanchez checked his program. 'It should be someone called Freddie Venus.'

'What kind of music is that?'

'I can't tell, but he's on for an hour.'

'An hour? Cool,' said Flake. 'Who's on after him?'

'Psycho the Rapist.'

'Psycho the what?'

'Rapist.' Sanchez grimaced. 'He sounds awful. I wouldn't want to meet him.'

Flake snatched Sanchez's program away from him and took a look for herself. 'You idiot. It's Psychotherapist. They're a local indie band. The lead singer is a transsexual. We've seen them before, remember?'

'Psycho the Rapist is a transsexual?'

'No it's *Psychotherapist!*' Flake shouted. 'It's one word, you moron.'

Sanchez snatched the program back and was annoyed to see that Flake was right, although it was good that Psycho the Rapist didn't actually exist. Psychotherapist didn't sound much better though.

A piercingly loud synthesiser kicked in as the next band started their set. It sent the crowd into raptures, and some idiot threw a plastic cup of beer up in the air. It landed all over Sanchez and his program.

Flake screamed, 'It's Radio Gaga! I love this song!'

Up on the main stage, a man dressed in yellow leather trousers and a Flash Gordon T-shirt was prancing around geeing up the crowd.

'That must be Freddie Venus!' said Flake.

Sanchez groaned. 'Oh, fucking hell. It's another Freddie Mercury tribute act!'

'Brilliant isn't it?' said Flake. 'I loved Queen.'

'I hope he suffers the same fate as the last Queen tribute act I saw,' said Sanchez, recalling an incident some years earlier at the *Back From The Dead* talent show in the Hotel Pasadena. On that occasion the Freddie Mercury impersonator had been eaten alive by a bunch of flesh hungry zombies. Sanchez shuddered when he thought about it. The only good thing about the whole show had been a Janis Joplin impersonator with Tourette's, who'd called the judges a bunch of shit-sniffers at one point. Just thinking about her put a smile on Sanchez's face for the first time since he'd arrived at the concert. If Janis was on the bill at this show, they'd be in for a great time.

He shook some beer off his soggy program and checked the playlist again. There were only two more acts after Freddie Venus and Psychotherapist. The Shearing Sisters were a Scissor Sisters tribute and Donna Winter was a Donna Summer impersonator.

'Hang on a minute,' Sanchez shouted to Flake over the music. 'This is a gay festival isn't it?'

'Yeah, so?'

'So I'll have people hitting on me all day,' Sanchez groaned. 'You know all gay people find me irresistible.'

Flake stopped jumping around and squeezed his hand. 'Calm down, it'll be fine. You just need to loosen up a bit.'

'You mean tighten up a bit, don't you?'

Flake laughed. 'No, just calm down, will you? These are all friendly people.'

'That's what I'm afraid of.'

'You just need a drink.'

'Fine, get me a beer.'

Flake kissed him on the cheek. 'Okay, but only if you promise to stop moaning.'

'I can't promise that.'

Flake reached into a pocket on Sanchez's shorts and pulled out his wallet. 'Wait here while I go get some drinks,' she yelled. 'Any idea what Jasmine's drinking?'

'Tap water.'

'Are you sure?'

'Positive.'

'Okay, I'll be back in a minute.'

Flake vanished into the crowd, leaving Sanchez surrounded by a group of people whose gender was hard to determine. Everyone seemed so bloody happy too. The bastards.

When "Radio Gaga" finished, Freddie Venus launched into a rendition of "The Show Must Go On". Sanchez hated the song. There was only one thing to do. He'd picked up a new hip flask on the way to the concert and now was the perfect time to fill it up. He just had to find a private place to do the deed. There was a tall black woman in a blue bikini in front of him, so he tapped her on the shoulder and shouted in her ear.

'Excuse me, do you know where the toilets are?'

'Yeah,' the woman replied in a husky voice. 'There's a bunch of portaloos over that way, bro.' She pointed at a long row of portaloos in the distance, past the crowd, on the edge of a steep slope that led all the way down to a busy road below. It crossed Sanchez's mind that there would be quite a lot of piss and shit flowing down the slope before the day was over.

'Christ, isn't there anything closer?' he groaned.

'Just whip it out and piss here,' the bikini woman replied. 'That's what I do.'

Sanchez considered what had just been said. *"Whip it out. That's what I do."* Not only was it a strange thing for a woman to say, but it was also said in a very deep voice. He glanced down and saw a large bulge in the front of the bikini bottoms. A quick look back up at the face and he realised he was talking to a man. Probably. There was a slight chance it might be a woman. And if it was, then she had a very deep voice, a moustache and a penis.

'Go on, whip it out!' the guy repeated, grinning at Sanchez.

Sanchez had no intention of "whipping it out" in front of anyone at this concert. 'Erm, I can't,' he mumbled. 'I, umm, I might need a shit.'

The man in the bikini, laughed, then shouted at someone else. 'Great shorts!'

The "someone else" he shouted at was Jasmine. She rocked up next to Sanchez and started grinding up against the dude in the bikini. 'Hey, thanks!' she said. 'Love your bikini!'

'Wanna swap?' the guy suggested.

'Sure!'

Jasmine lifted up her top, giving Sanchez an eyeful of her boobs. She had a habit of undressing without a moment's notice, and she never seemed to care where she was when she stripped off. As she pulled her top over her head, quite a few people nearby stopped and stared. But there was one man who stared right past Jasmine's tits and focussed on Sanchez instead. And because Sanchez was trying not to stare at Jasmine in case Flake saw him, he unintentionally made eye contact with the man. It was Pete, the garbage man who had a habit of sniffing through Sanchez's trash. He was wearing a rainbow coloured shirt and short shorts, and he was heading towards Sanchez with a big smile on his face

'Hey Sanchez!' he shouted as he fought his way through the crowd.

Sanchez tapped Jasmine on the arm. 'Jasmine!' he yelled over the music. She didn't seem to hear him. In a moment of unfortunate timing, the music stopped just as Sanchez yelled, 'I'M JUST GONNA GO FOR A SHIT!'

If it hadn't been for Jasmine's tits, a lot of people would have been giving Sanchez strange looks.

'Did you really need to shout that?' Jasmine asked.

Sanchez lowered his voice and did his best to maintain eye contact with Jasmine even though her tits were right in his eyeline. 'Flake will be back in a minute,' he said. 'Tell her I'll be back in a bit.'

The music started up again so Jasmine muttered some kind of acknowledgment and went back to dancing with the person in the blue bikini. It was a blessing of sorts because the two of them grinding together blocked off Pete's path to Sanchez. Sanchez made a break for it and fought his way through the crowd over to the portaloos.

As was customary at these kind of events, there were about fifty portaloos all lined up in a row. And each one had a queue outside of it, six or seven people deep. It reminded Sanchez why he didn't normally attend such events. He scanned the line of loos looking for his best option. It didn't take long to see it. At the far end of the line, right on the edge of the hill were two extra-large portaloos. A man in a wheelchair was queuing in between the two portaloos, each of which had a large DISABLED sign on it.

Perfect.

Sanchez barged his way past a bunch of women dressed as men, and men dressed as women and other people who could be a bit of both. By the time he arrived at the disabled portaloos, he'd inadvertently danced with about twenty different people. He breathed a sigh of relief and stopped behind the man in the wheelchair. The man had long hair and he was wearing a horrible green shirt and shorts. Sanchez tapped him on the shoulder.

'Hey buddy, mind if I go in before you?' he asked. 'I'm busting.'

The wheelchair man sneered at him. 'Fuck off, fatty. Get in line.' Then after looking Sanchez up and down he asked. 'Are you even disabled?'

'I've got metal legs,' Sanchez replied, forgetting that he was wearing shorts. No one normally dared to check if he really had metal legs so he'd used the excuse many times before and always gotten away with it.

'You fucking liar,' the other man hissed. 'I can see you're lying. You're a fucking fake!'

Sanchez cursed his luck. It was Flake's stupid idea for him to wear shorts. He stepped back and discreetly kicked some mud over the wheels on the man's chair to teach him a lesson.

Before things escalated too far, one of the portaloos became available. A young blonde woman, wearing cut-off jeans and a white blouse staggered out of one of them. She looked totally wasted, so Sanchez figured she'd probably made a real mess in the loo. So being second in the queue for the toilet wasn't such a bad thing after all. He nudged the guy in the wheelchair.

'Good luck in that one,' he said. 'She looks like she's had a skinful. There'll be piss all over the seat in there, I reckon.'

The man in the wheelchair glared at Sanchez. 'That's my wife!' he yelled. 'And she's got cerebral palsy, you ignorant fuck!'

'Well she probably shouldn't drink so much then,' Sanchez suggested. 'Need a push?'

'Fuck off.'

The man wheeled himself over to the portaloo, stopping briefly to chat to his wife, who then made a rude hand gesture at Sanchez. She looked bloody angry too, which was hardly surprising really, what with being married to such a miserable bastard. Evasive action was required, so Sanchez hurried up to the other disabled portaloo and knocked on the door.

'Hurry up in there, will you!' he shouted. There was no reply from within, and no splashing sounds coming through the door. Sanchez knocked again. 'Anyone in there?'

He tried the door and to his great delight it wasn't locked. He squeezed in and pulled the door shut, locking it to make sure the angry woman couldn't follow him in.

It was dark inside the portaloo, which might have bothered a lesser man, but Sanchez considered himself to be an experienced night-time urinator. He flipped open the lid on his hip flask and unzipped his fly. With the skill of a man who'd peed into a hip flask a thousand times before, he took aim and unleashed a fountain of piss into it.

Everything was going smoothly until someone started thumping on the portaloo door. Then someone else banged on the side. The portaloo started rocking back and forth. It broke Sanchez's concentration and he took a sideways step to steady himself. He trod on something soft on the floor, which knocked him off balance. He looked down, and thanks to a small sliver of light coming in through the door, he saw a man lying on the ground by his feet. There was blood all over the man's face and around his head. Sanchez leaned down to get a closer look, inadvertently peeing on the man's face. It wasn't a pretty sight. The man on the ground was dead. His tongue had been cut out and his eyes were missing.

Thirty Two

'Don't shut the door!'

Sylvia's words echoed around the room as they bounced off the walls, each of which was changing colour. The room, where once dark, blossomed into light, a strange ambient violet light that emanated from a collection of oil lamps on the walls. Violet coloured flames flickered in the lamps. The only other light in the room came from a raging hot yellow and gold fire behind a thick glass window in the wall directly opposite the door. JD had seen its like before. Down in the depths of Hell there were a vast number of incinerators used to torture and burn alive the prisoners. It was a punishment normally reserved for those who had committed crimes such as arson. Scratch loved to hear their screams as hour after hour, day after day they suffered the infinite punishment of being burned alive, brought back to life and then burned alive again.

JD took in the new surroundings in a matter of seconds. Neither the violet lamps nor the incinerator furnace were a threat. But since he had closed the door, two new people had appeared in the room. One was a policewoman with curly ginger hair. The other was Beth.

'What have you done?' Sylvia groaned.

JD ignored her. He smiled at Beth, who was obviously relieved to see him. She ran up to him and threw her arms around him.

'Oh thank God you're here,' she said. 'Do you know where we are?'

He didn't fully understand the question. Of course he knew where they were, and so should she.

'Come on, we've got to get out of here,' he said, pulling away from her and heading back to the door.

'No, wait!' Beth cried. 'It's not safe out there!'

'I know. Scratch has found us,' JD replied. 'Did you see him?'

'He's not out there. We're not in the abbey anymore. We're somewhere else.'

The policewoman chirped in. 'Beth's right,' she said. 'It's not safe. We're not where we were before. We're in some weird alternate dimension or something.'

JD pointed his gun at her. 'Who the fuck are you?'

'Officer Karen Butterman. Listen, I'm not here for you. Me and my partner Derek, we just came here to investigate the murder of the monk that runs the abbey.'

'The monk? You mean Loomis? The weirdo?' JD looked to Beth for confirmation.

She nodded. 'I saw him this morning. He's been murdered. Someone beheaded him and impaled him on a spike. It was horrific.'

'What the fuck? Who did that?'

'We don't know,' said Karen Butterman.

'I wasn't talking to you.' JD kept his focus on Beth. 'So how did you end up in here?'

Beth pointed at Sylvia. 'She pushed me in here.'

JD turned his gun on the treacherous housemaid again. 'You, what's going on in here?'

Sylvia trembled and raised her hands. 'Please don't shoot,' she said. 'I don't know anything. I'm in the dark like you.'

'Bullshit! You know exactly what's going on here.'

Beth tried to drag JD's focus away from Sylvia. 'Listen,' she said. 'I've been in here for about twenty minutes. Lenny the gardener was here when I arrived. The police showed up just after me.'

'Wait, what?' said JD, looking around the room. 'Where's Lenny the gardener then? And the other cop?'

'They went back out through that door,' Beth continued. 'But they haven't come back. We're pretty sure they're dead.'

JD headed straight for the door to see for himself. As soon as his hand settled on the doorknob, the three women screamed at him not to open the door. He opened it anyway, just enough to see out into the corridor. The others weren't kidding. Everything was different. The old corridor with the black and white tiled floor was gone, replaced by a dark corridor, dimly lit by more of the oil lamps with the violet flames. The staircase was still there, opposite the door, but it was now made of old wood, the kind that looked like it would creak every time you stepped on it. He checked along the hallway to the front entrance. Moments earlier a small army of Ninjas had been flooding into the building. They were gone too. He closed the door and turned to face the others, who all breathed a sigh of relief.

JD turned his gun on Sylvia yet again. He was certain she knew something about their predicament because she'd been terrified from the moment he dragged her into the room with him.

'You'd better start talking,' he said.

'What?'

'You know where we are. Start talking or lose some limbs.'

'I don't know what you mean,' Sylvia mumbled, her voice cracking.

'I'm gonna count to three, then I'm gonna blow one of your legs off at the knee.'

'I swear, I didn't know....'

'One.'

'I just did as I was told.'

'Two.'

'It was a man dressed in red.'

JD gritted his teeth. 'Was it Scratch?'

She nodded.

Beth grabbed her stomach. 'Oh no. Not Scratch. Not *the* Scratch?'

'Yeah, the Devil's here,' said JD. He waved his gun under Sylvia's chin. 'This cunt here is working for him. And my guess is, she's led us into some level of Hell that Scratch has arranged specially for us.'

Officer Karen Butterman raised her hand. 'Excuse me, but you're talking in riddles,' she said.

'You shut your mouth,' JD replied, without even looking at her. He glared at Sylvia instead. 'Why are you working for Scratch?' he asked. 'And what exactly have you gotten us into here?'

Beth tugged at the back of JD's coat. 'Don't take it out on her,' she said. 'We've got bigger problems. There's something evil on the other side of that door.'

JD waited for Sylvia to answer him, which she duly did while staring down at his gun, praying he wouldn't blow her head off in mid-sentence.

'Scratch never told me what was in here or how to get back. He just told me to get you both in here, and if necessary to say I knew your friend Flake. I was never supposed to be in here with you.'

JD took a step back and pointed his gun at the end of Sylvia's nose. 'What did Scratch give you in return for screwing us over?'

A solitary tear trickled down Sylvia's face. 'He said he would bring my daughter back.'

Beth stepped in. 'What happened to your daughter?' she asked, showing some genuine concern.

Sylvia lowered her head, but before she could answer, JD answered for her.

'She killed her daughter. Didn't you?'

Sylvia put her head in her hands and sobbed. 'It was a mistake.'

'Nah,' said JD. 'If you're working for Scratch, it's because you've done something fucking terrible. If any of us are gonna get out of here alive, you need to tell us everything you know. Do you understand?'

'Yes.'

'Good. Is anyone else coming through that door? Or is just gonna be us from now on?'

'I don't know!'

'Is Scratch coming in here?'

Sylvia sobbed some more. 'I'm sorry, I just don't know.'

'Then we're all gonna have to go back out through that door. Because as far as I can see, there's no other option.'

Karen Butterman cut in. 'One of us ought to wait here,' she said. 'It's possible someone could come to our rescue.'

'You're hopeful,' said JD, looking at her with contempt.

Karen shrugged. 'I'm just saying there's something out there, and I don't think I want to confront it.'

'It's true,' said Beth. 'When Derek and Lenny went out there, we heard screaming. Karen went out after them. She saw it.'

'Saw what?'

Karen shook her head. 'I don't know what it was, but it wasn't human. If you go out there, you're not coming back.'

'Well, I am going out there,' said JD. He pointed at Sylvia. 'And she's coming with me.'

Thirty Three

Rex and Elvis stopped off at a car rental place and hired an old rock band's tour bus to drive to the morgue. Tour buses had become a feature of their time working for the Devil. Whenever they left Purgatory via the portal in the men's toilets, they would invariably have to find their way back again at some point. And that often meant hiring a bus and taking turns driving it back to the Devil's Graveyard.

Rex drove the bus while Elvis sat in the passenger seat next to him, pointing out any people he saw wearing interesting costumes for the Lunar festival.

'There's a kid dressed as the thing from Saw!' Elvis yelled, nudging Rex and almost causing an accident.

'I didn't see him,' said Rex.

'It was the kid on the tricycle. Fucking brilliant costume.'

'Have you called Flake yet?' Rex asked.

'Flake? No, what for?'

'She's got the Eye of the Moon, remember? Our killer might be looking for it.'

'Oh yeah, that.' Elvis picked his cell-phone out the breast pocket on his red shirt and dialled Flake's number. After a few seconds he hung up. 'She's not answering,' he said.

'Keep trying.'

'There's no point. She's at the Gay Pride concert with Jasmine and Sanchez. You know how loud concerts get, she'll never hear her phone ringing. But at least it'll be safe there. No one's gonna gouge her eyes out in the middle of a crowd of people. Besides, we don't even know for sure if the killer is after the Eye anyway.'

'Well, let's hope this coroner, Doctor Taylor has some answers for us,' said Rex.

Rex parked the bus outside the morgue and the two men headed inside, armed with the ID cards Sally Diamond had given them.

After successfully passing through an unmanned set of turnstiles, they headed to the coroner's office to find Doctor Taylor. They found his office at the back of the building. It was a large room with a high ceiling and a serious lack of central heating. No wonder there were so many dead folks in it, it was fucking freezing. There were lots of metal tables scattered about the room, each supporting a dead body covered in a thin sheet. The bodies were in various states of examination. A tall thin man in his early forties, wearing a long white lab coat was dissecting one on a metal table in the centre of the room. He had thick shaggy brown hair that hung down over his face and flopped around as he poked, prodded and sliced the corpse. He looked up when he heard Rex and Elvis approaching, and almost immediately he clutched his chest like he was having a heart attack.

'Holy Christ!' he said, backing away and waving his scalpel in a useless criss-cross motion in front of him.

'Doctor Taylor,' said Elvis, cheerily. 'Remember us?'

Dr Taylor attempted to steady himself on a table behind him, but placed his hand on a dead man's leg, which made him even more jumpy.

'Bet you weren't expecting to see us, huh?' said Rex, as he and Elvis approached.

Doctor Taylor made a strangled cry in the back of his throat and took a halting step backwards.

'Take a minute,' said Elvis. 'We're here about the latest murders.'

'But….. but you're dead!' Taylor said clenching his fists by his sides. It looked like he was doing breathing exercises.

'You're half right,' said Elvis. 'We *were* dead. But now we're not. We just need you to answer some questions for us.'

'I….I'm not sure I can,' the doctor replied, trembling.

'Well, if you don't we're going to haunt you for the rest of your life,' said Elvis. 'I'll sing to you while you're trying to sleep at night, and Rex will watch you in the shower.'

Dr Taylor looked genuinely terrified. And Rex looked irritated by the insinuation that he'd be perving on the doctor in the shower.

'Just tell me what you want from me,' said Dr Taylor, pulling his coat tighter, as if worried that Rex was leering at him.

'We just need you to show us the corpses with the eyes and tongues ripped out,' said Rex.

'That's one right there,' said Taylor, pointing at the body he'd been working on when they walked in.

'Which one is this?' Rex asked.

'That's Mark Hasell. He came in last night.' Dr Taylor scratched his forehead like he had a nervous itch and his left leg started shaking. 'Seriously,' he said, 'what the fuck is going on? How are you both here? I did both of your autopsies on this table five years ago!'

Elvis slapped Rex on the arm. 'You're gonna have to tell him, or he's just gonna keep asking.'

'You tell him.'

'Fine.' Elvis gestured for Taylor to calm down. 'What's your first name?'

'Taylor.'

'Oh, right. So what's your surname then?'

'Taylor.'

'Your name is Taylor Taylor?'

Dr Taylor nodded. 'Yeah. I know it's stupid. I've got a twin brother called Tinker. Our parents were idiots.'

'Yeah.'

Rex closed in on Dr Taylor, cornering him next to a wall of drawers filled with even more dead people. The coroner tried to squirm out of the way, but Rex grabbed him and wrapped a friendly arm around his shoulder, pulling him away from the wall. Dr Taylor seemed to relax at the weight and warmth of Rex's arm.

'Listen, doc,' said Rex. 'This won't make a lick of sense, and if you tell anyone else about it, they'll think you've lost your mind.'

'Uh huh, I'm listening.'

'Me and Elvis, we were both murdered five years ago, just like this dude over here, but before we were murdered, we'd already made deals with the Devil, so that in the event of our deaths, we would both be brought back to life to work for Satan hunting down Hell dodgers.'

'Hell dodgers?'

'Yeah, folks who belong in Hell but have chosen to stay on earth.'

Taylor still looked confused.

'He means vampires, werewolves and stuff,' said Elvis.

'The undead?' asked Taylor.

'That's right,' said Rex, guiding Dr Taylor back over to the corpse of Mark Hasell. 'But enough about all that stuff. My friend and I need to know if these new murders are exactly the same as the murders from five years ago?'

Dr Taylor took a deep breath. 'Err, well, there are a couple of things different.'

'Good,' said Rex. 'Like what?'

'The victims from five years ago had their tongues literally ripped out of their throats and their eyes were gone completely. These latest victims have all been injected with a paralysing agent, which is new. So the killer is keeping them alive while he cuts their tongues out with a sharp instrument. Then he gouges their eyeballs out, but unlike five years ago, he's not eating them this time.'

Elvis and Rex took a moment to digest the information. 'Hold on,' said Elvis. 'The asshole that killed us, ate our eyeballs afterwards?'

'And your tongues,' said Taylor. 'At least that's what was assumed at the time, because the eyes and tongues were never found, whereas this new killer sometimes leaves the tongue and eyes at the crime scene.'

'Five years ago the killer was a cop named Archie Somers,' said Elvis. 'Did you know that, doc?'

Taylor nodded. 'It was in the news a while later.'

'Any ideas on who might want to copy him?' Rex asked.

Taylor wriggled away from Rex and dusted himself down, which was fair, considering he thought he'd had a dead guy's arm around his shoulder. 'Is it possible Archie Somers did a deal with the Devil, too?' he asked. 'I mean, if you guys—'

'Definitely not,' Rex interrupted.

Taylor paused for thought. 'Well then I've got no idea,' he said.

'Have you still got the records from five years ago,' Elvis asked.

'I've got all of them,' said Dr Taylor, 'apart from one.'

'Which one?' Rex asked.

Taylor looked around as if he was worried someone was listening, then he spoke quietly. 'One of the bodies was stolen.'

Rex frowned. 'Stolen? Which one?'

'It was the old woman. The one they called the Mystic Lady. I think her real name was—'

'Annabel,' said Elvis. 'Annabel de Frugyn.'

'Why would someone steal Annabel's body?' Rex asked.

Dr Taylor avoided eye contact and scratched his head. 'Uh, well, you see this guy came in, and he said he knew her and wanted to take her body to be buried in her home town. And you know, I was *busy as shit* that week, what with all the massacres and stuff, so I let him take the body.'

'That's not stealing,' said Rex. 'That's *you* giving a body away. How much did you make?'

Dr Taylor lowered his head. 'Five thousand bucks. Like I said, I was busy as shit. The guy made me an offer I couldn't refuse.'

'What guy?' asked Elvis.

'I don't know. I never actually saw his face.'

Elvis groaned. 'How did you not see his face?'

'It was the Lunar Festival. Everyone dresses up, don't they? This guy was wearing face-paint. He looked like the Devil.'

'Have you *seen* the Devil?' Rex asked.

'No.'

'Well he doesn't wear face paint. What did this guy look like?'

'Erm, uh, like I said, it was red face paint. And he had little horns all over his head.'

'Like Darth Maul?' said Rex.

'I don't know who that is.'

'Cunt,' Elvis muttered under his breath.

'I wonder if Annabel knows this?' said Rex, looking at Elvis, to see if he had an opinion on the matter.

Dr Taylor was confused. 'What do you mean?'

'Annabel de Frugyn,' said Rex. 'The Mystic Lady, she made the same deal with the Devil as we did. She works with us sometimes. She's good at seeing the future, fifty percent of the time.'

'Well, then I guess she might know who took her body away,' Taylor suggested.

Rex grew impatient with the direction the conversation was taking. 'Forget Annabel for a minute. Is there anything else about these latest murders that's different to five years ago?'

Taylor scratched his head. 'There is one other thing,' he said. 'Although it's something I've only realised this morning. I don't know if the cops know it yet.'

'Go on,' said Rex.

'Well, all four victims are men.'

'I reckon the cops know that,' said Elvis.

'Yes, I'm sure they do,' said Dr Taylor, not appreciating the sarcasm. 'Would you just listen a minute. The most recent victim, Bob Muncher, he's a cop. So I suspect he was killed because he tracked down the killer. But the other three victims, if I'm correct about this, they're all homosexual.'

'How do you know that?' asked Rex.

Dr Taylor shrugged. 'Two of them are very open about it.' He pointed at the corpse on the table. 'But not this one, Mark Hasell. He's happily married, but I've heard that he goes to church almost every Saturday night to confess that he's been sleeping with men.'

'So they're all fags?' said Rex.

'You can't say fags,' said Taylor.

'Why not?'

Taylor let out a deep sigh. 'Since you guys have been gone, Santa Mondega has changed a lot. The new Mayor introduced something called Political Correctness a few months back. There's a whole list of stuff you're not allowed to say anymore. And most of it involves funny names.'

'Political what?' said Rex.

'Correctness. Look, it's not that important.'

'So is it okay to say gay?' Elvis asked.

'Yes,' said Taylor. 'Listen, if you're serious about finding the killer, focus your attention on looking for someone who hates gay men. I can think of one person straight away.'

'Who's that?' asked Rex.

'A fellow doctor, a guy named Melvin Melt. Have you heard of him?'

Rex and Elvis exchanged a look.

'Yes, we've heard of him,' said Rex at the same time as Elvis said *"No we haven't."*

'So you have?' asked Dr Taylor, looking confused.

'Yes, we know who he is,' said Rex.

'But we've never met him,' Elvis added.

Taylor sighed. 'You must have heard he escaped from prison the other night. He's a killer and he's on the loose somewhere in this city.'

Elvis changed the subject. 'Can you still say queer?'

Rex stepped in front of Elvis, to prevent him from asking any further irrelevant questions. 'Okay, doc, apart from all of these victims being flyboys, is there anything else that you can think of that might link them to each other? Anything at all?'

'Sorry no. But if I'm correct with my theory about the victims being gay men, then I would think the killer might strike again this afternoon at the Gay Pride concert. Maybe you should head there.'

Rex looked at Elvis. 'Come on, let's go.'

The two men left Dr Taylor and headed back out of the building.

'Where to now then?' said Elvis, as they walked out into the street.

'I'm gonna drop you off at that Gay concert,' said Rex. 'You can go find the others and look for the killer.'

'What are you gonna do?'

'I'm going to pay a visit to Papshmir. See what he's got to say about Melvin Melt. I think he owes us an explanation.'

Thirty Four

JD opened the door of the Violet room and shoved Sylvia out into the corridor. He followed her out with his Headblaster gun drawn, ready to shoot anything that jumped out at them. Beth waited in the open doorway of the Violet room, watching the two of them proceed along the darkened corridor into the unknown. The strange violet light in the corridor reminded her of a Pink Floyd concert, without the music.

'This is a bad idea,' said Sylvia. 'We should go back.'

JD pushed her in the back. 'What are you afraid of?' he asked.

'I don't know. I just have a bad feeling. You heard the others. They said Derek and Lenny came out here. Neither of them came back.'

'Maybe they found a way out?'

'Karen said she heard them screaming.'

'If you don't shut up, they'll hear you screaming too,' said JD. 'I promise you, if there's something out here that kills people, you're gonna be the one that reasons with it.'

'Please don't make me do this. I'm scared.'

'I don't give a fuck. You see Beth back there? She's pregnant and you tricked her into this place. The Devil might forgive you for that, but I won't.'

Beth squirmed out into the corridor with them, closing the door behind her. 'I'm coming with you,' she said.

JD stopped and turned around. 'No way,' he whispered. 'You're safer in there with the cop lady.'

Beth covered her mouth and nose. 'What is that smell?' she said, grimacing.

Sylvia replied. 'It smells like rotten flesh, doesn't it?'

'Forget the smell,' said JD. 'Beth, stay in that room. I'll be back as soon as I find a way out. You'll be safer in there.'

'I won't though,' said Beth. 'What if Scratch or some of his Hell demons come through the door while you're away?'

JD thought about what she was saying. There was a very real possibility that Scratch or the Ninja people might enter the Violet room. If that happened then the corridor was probably the better place to be. *Probably.*

'Okay,' he concluded. 'But stay close to me.' He clicked his fingers at Sylvia. 'You, is there a back door out of this place?'

'I don't know. Why don't we just head out the front entrance?'

'Because that's where Scratch and the Ninjas were. For all we know, the only thing that's really changed here is the lighting.'

'The floor tiles have gone too,' Sylvia reminded him.

'It could all be a trick. Where's the rear exit?'

Sylvia looked around to get her bearings then pointed along the corridor. 'There's a second kitchen at the back of the building with a back door in it. We should head to the end of this corridor and turn right.'

'Okay, you lead, *we'll follow.*'

Sylvia moved tentatively along the corridor like she was walking through a minefield. Beth held onto JD's arm and they followed Sylvia into a darker area of the abbey. JD prodded his gun into Sylvia's back to hurry her up.

'Come on,' he said. 'We haven't got all day.'

Sylvia didn't really move any faster but she certainly breathed a lot heavier. If it were any louder it would wake the dead.

'Would you keep it down?' JD hissed at her. 'We might as well be wearing clogs, the fucking noise you're making.'

'Sorry, but I'm nervous,' she replied, before bursting into a coughing fit.

When she finished wheezing, another shove in the back from JD set her on her way again, this time quieter than before. The violet flames on the candles flickered, reminding Beth of a Haunted House ride she had been on once. A big hairy monster had come of nowhere and pounced on her. It had only been a man in a suit, of course. Her worry now was that in the darkened corridors of the abbey, the monsters might just be real.

CRUNCH!

The sound came from up ahead. 'What was that?' Beth whispered.

Sylvia replied. 'I just kicked something.'

JD put his hand across Beth's chest to stop her moving. 'Wait here a second,' he said.

'What is it?' said Beth.

'I can't see anything,' Sylvia replied. 'Have you still got that torch?'

Beth had forgotten all about the small torch Sylvia had given her earlier. It was tucked into a pocket on her jeans.

'You've got a torch?' said JD.

'I forgot I had it.'

She pulled it out and switched it on. She shone it at the floor where Sylvia was crouching. The phoney housemaid gasped and jumped back, blocking the light. JD pushed her aside and leant down to inspect the object that had scared her.

'What is it?' Beth whispered, shining the light for JD.

He picked up an object from the floor and held it up for her to see. It became clear why Sylvia was so spooked. In JD's hand was a human skull. Beth winced. The skull had smoke floating out of its mouth. JD placed it back down on the floor.

'Was that a real human skull?' Sylvia asked.

'Sssshhhh,' JD said putting his finger to his lips. 'There's something up ahead.'

They stood still. Beth held her breath and listened. Somewhere much further down the corridor something was moving. Footsteps were coming towards them, getting louder with each step.

'Should we go back?' Beth whispered.

'Keep the torch pointed straight ahead,' JD replied.

Sylvia trod on something else that made a loud crunching noise. Their attempts at sneaking around were thwarted at every turn by the bogus housemaid. She made Beth look like a master at stealth.

'Have you got a trumpet you can play as well?' Beth hissed at her.

'Sorry.'

The footsteps up ahead stopped. JD held up his hand to signal that no one should move. After a few seconds of silence, the footsteps started again, this time moving much quicker than before, coming towards them.

Sylvia called out. 'Lenny?'

JD grabbed her by her collar and pulled her towards him. He pressed his gun under her chin again. 'What the fuck is wrong with you?' he whispered.

Beth shone the torch at Sylvia's feet. The light settled on another pile of bones with smoke floating up from them. JD let go of Sylvia and lowered his gun. He crouched down and picked up part of a human ribcage, but then put it back down almost instantly.

'It's hot,' he whispered.

'Hot?' said Beth, as quietly as she could. 'Why is it hot?'

'That smell,' JD whispered, standing up. 'That's burning flesh. This poor bastard was set on fire...... recently.'

The footsteps up ahead continued to get closer all the time. Sylvia snatched Beth's torch away from her and shone it in the direction of the footsteps. It lit up a figure that was moving towards them.

'Oh my God,' she whispered. 'What the Hell is that thing?'

Thirty Five

'Hang in there Sanchez, I'm coming!'

Flake tucked her phone into a pocket on her jeans and turned away from the beer stand, knocking into a couple of people behind her. She'd been queuing for drinks for several minutes and had reached the front of the queue when Sanchez called her from a portaloo. He was panicking because a gang of angry people were rocking it from side to side while yelling along to Freddie Venus's rather impressive and rousing rendition of "We Will Rock You".

There was no quick route to get to the portaloos. The only way was through the crowd, so Flake lowered her head and started barging people aside as she fought her way across the concert site to get to Sanchez. With her elbows outstretched she knocked drinks and cigarettes out of people's hands, and caught a few shorter people in the face, so every few seconds someone shouted something at her, and none of it was complimentary. It was just as well she was wearing a T-shirt with the words "FUCK OFF" emblazoned on the front.

She was halfway across the crowd when she spotted Jasmine bouncing up and down with a group of drunken men, all singing along to "We Will Rock You". Flake made a detour and headed over to her. She grabbed Jasmine's arm and yelled over the sound of the music.

'Jas, come quick. Sanchez is in trouble!'

Jasmine stopped bouncing and looked to see who had grabbed her. 'Oh, hey, Flake. Have you seen my clothes anywhere?' she asked.

Flake hadn't noticed it before because of the suffocating crowd, but Jasmine was wearing nothing, apart from a pair of sneakers. She hadn't been wearing much when they left the Tapioca, but now even her invisible shorts were gone.

'What the Hell happened to your clothes?' Flake asked, momentarily forgetting about Sanchez's plight.

'I gave them to some guy and he ran off with them. Can you believe that?'

'Uh, no, that's so unexpected.'

'Lucky I kept my sneakers on,' said Jasmine, pointing at her footwear. 'Or I'd be totally nude.'

Flake momentarily tried to process the logic of what Jasmine was saying, but soon shook her head to rid herself of the stupid thoughts. 'Look, we gotta move. Sanchez is stuck in a disabled portaloo with a dead body, and he says there's a bunch of angry people trying to get in. They're shaking the portaloo and he's getting piss all over his clothes.'

'He's always got piss on his clothes.'

'At least he's wearing clothes.'

'Fair point. Let's go!'

Flake let Jasmine lead the way, which halved the time it took to get to the portaloos. People tended to step aside when they saw Jasmine coming, usually just to get a better look. Quite a few people were taking photos too. It all helped. The only downside was that it looked like Flake was chasing Jasmine. And because people in large crowds behave like sheep, a line of people formed behind Flake, which gave the impression that Jasmine was some kind of naked Pied Piper, without the pipe.

As they neared the portaloos it was easy to spot which one Sanchez was in. A gang of angry lunatics were rocking it back and forth and screaming obscenities.

'Over there!' Flake shouted. 'See it?'

'Shit, they look really angry,' said Jasmine, slowing down. 'What do you wanna do?'

'I'm gonna go kick someone's head in. You coming?'

Flake sprinted past Jasmine and headed for the rocking portaloo. She grabbed the first person she came across, who happened to be a blonde woman in knee-length blue jeans and a white top who was somewhat unsteady on her feet. Flake wrapped her hands around the woman's waist and pulled her away from the door.

'Hey, what are you doing?' the woman complained, unable to see who was dragging her away from the action.

Flake twisted her around so they were facing each other, then nutted her. And Flake knew how to give a good head-butt. The woman turned cross-eyed and her body shook like she was standing on a wobble board. Flake followed up the head-butt with a punch to the chin which was enough to knock the woman unconscious. She landed in a pool of mud and her eyes rolled up in her head. Flake turned back to find her next victim. A guy dressed as a pirate with a very authentic looking wooden leg from the knee down, was staring angrily at her. His left eye was covered by an eye-patch, but Flake could tell by the look in his good eye, that he was up for a scrap. His peg-leg made him easy prey. She charged at him and kicked his wooden leg out from under him. He fell onto his back, hitting his head on a rock. A quick kick in the balls put him out of the game completely.

Jasmine hung back and watched the events unfold while she analysed the situation. Her instincts were telling her something didn't look quite right. There was a guy in a wheelchair repeatedly barging into the portaloo door. An old lady wearing dark sunglasses was also hitting the portaloo with a white walking stick. And when Jasmine saw Flake kicking the one legged, half blind guy in the balls, she recognised the situation. These angry people were all handicapped and Sanchez was locked in a toilet specially designated for them. And now Flake was beating them all up.

Shit.

'Hey Flake! Wait! Stop!'

Before Jasmine could wade in and drag Flake away from the situation, someone pinched her on the ass. And whoever it was, stuck his or her thumb up her butt too, which was still sensitive from having Rex's metal digits up it for an hour the night before. She looked over her shoulder and was surprised to see there was no one there, although there were a bunch of guys standing a few feet away with their phones pointed at her.

'Hey, who grabbed my ass?' she asked, turning around to confront them, with her hands on her hips and a scowl on her face.

'I did,' said a voice.

Jasmine looked down and saw a small face staring up at her. It took a moment before she realised it was a midget. He had thick grey hair tied back in a ponytail and he was wearing a black and red striped jumper. He was grinning at her and wiggling his eyebrows up and down.

'Hey babe,' he said. 'You ever tried going midget?'

What this guy needed was a good hard kick in the balls. Jasmine duly obliged. She swung her leg hard and connected sweetly with the little man's nutsack. The kick lifted him off his feet and sent him flying through the air, squealing like a pig. He went high enough and far enough that he could have gone over a set of goalposts for three points. Eventually he landed on a crowd of people thirty metres away and knocked them over like bowling pins.

'HEY, YOU CAN'T DO THAT!' someone shouted.

'GET HER, AND HER FRIENDS!' screamed another.

A number of angry concertgoers started surging towards Jasmine. Fortunately, the group of guys who were filming her, unwittingly acted as a shield, which slowed down the angry mob just enough for Jasmine to make a break for it.

When she turned back around she saw Flake had disarmed the blind woman and was beating her with her own walking stick. Sanchez was peeping out of the door of the portaloo, cheering Flake on. Unfortunately the man in the wheelchair had his back wheels up against the portaloo door, preventing Sanchez from escaping. So, even though Jasmine didn't want to get involved in fighting with a bunch of disabled people, she had no choice but to go after the wheelchair guy. She rushed over and grabbed the handles on his chair, yanking him away from the portaloo.

'Hey!' he yelled, looking up at her, no doubt surprised by her nakedness.

Jasmine didn't have time to reason with him, so she gave his chair an almighty push that sent it rolling past the portaloos and downhill towards the road.

By now, Flake had knocked out the blind woman and Sanchez had sneaked out of the toilet and was kicking the unconscious pirate. Jasmine grabbed Flake by the arm and pointed at the crowd of angry people heading their way.

'LET'S GO!' she yelled.

Flake and Sanchez finally saw the mob of angry hippies marching towards them. They both stopped what they were doing.

'What the Hell?' said Flake.

'This way!' Jasmine yelled.

She sprinted down the slope, following in the tracks of the man in the wheelchair. Flake grabbed Sanchez and dragged him with her down the slope that rapidly turned into a hill with a stream of piss and shit floating down it. A lynch mob of about fifty angry people charged after them, baying for blood.

'Fucking hell!' said Sanchez. 'Where did all these lot come from?'

'We've upset just about everyone,' said Jasmine. 'Keep running!'

The hill was quite a monster. It carried on for almost half a mile, all the way down to a busy highway. That was no problem for Flake or Jasmine, who were both in good physical shape. But for Sanchez this was not looking good. His fitness levels had once been politely described as "sub-par". And he had no speed whatsoever. Luckily for him, the angry man in the wheelchair (who Sanchez believed was to blame for the whole sorry incident) hit a large rock that was protruding up from the ground. He bounced up out of his wheelchair and landed on his face in the stream of shit that was flowing down the hill. And, rather like Augustus Gloop in the *Charlie and the Chocolate Factory* story, he floated downriver with it, swallowing lots of it as he went.

Not wanting to let a good wheelchair go to waste, Sanchez jumped into it, settled comfortably into the seat, and rolled down the hill after Flake and Jasmine. He built up a good head of speed and it wasn't long before he pulled up alongside Flake.

'Hey baby, need a ride?' he yelled.

Flake didn't hesitate. She jumped onto Sanchez's lap and they rolled down the hill together. They soon caught up with Jasmine and found that she was on her cell phone, screaming at Elvis.

'Meet us on the highway at the foot of the hill. FUCKING HURRY!'

Sanchez whispered in Flake's ear. 'Where did she get that phone?'

'You don't want to know!' said Flake. 'Let's just hope there's some brakes on this thing, or we're going to roll into traffic!'

Thirty Six

'What the Hell is that thing?' said Sylvia.

The *thing* was walking along the darkened corridor towards her. Beth and JD were standing just behind her. The light from Sylvia's torch wasn't powerful enough to get a perfect look at what was approaching them, but one thing was certain, it wasn't Lenny the gardener, or the cop, Derek Skudder. It was a tall black shape with something white surrounding its head and neck.

'It's a nun,' said JD.

He tapped Sylvia on the shoulder. 'See if it's got a face,' he said quietly.

Beth whispered in his ear. 'Why would it not have a face?'

'Can you see a face on it?' he replied. 'Because I can't.'

Sylvia called out to the nun. 'Hello? Can you help us? We're kind of lost.'

JD took a cautious step back and pulled Beth along with him. He had his Headblaster gun concealed behind his back, ready to use it if the need arose.

He called out to the nun. 'Who is that?'

The nun-thing did not reply. She continued moving towards them. Her dress was so long it touched the floor, hiding her feet from sight, making it look like she was gliding. However, the sound of her shoes crunching on the ground was evidence enough that she was not slowing down. Sylvia took a step back, only for JD to push her closer to the incoming nun.

Sylvia shone the light up at the nun's face for a second, but then almost immediately she spun around and shone it at JD.

'It's got no face,' she squealed. 'It's got no face!'

JD snatched the torch from her and shone it down the corridor at the nun. Sylvia was correct. The nun's habit was empty. There was no face inside it.

JD handed the torch to Beth and pulled his gun from behind his back. He aimed it at the nun. 'Last chance,' he called out. 'Who are you?'

The nun ignored him again. As it came closer, Beth lit up its face. The nun had no eyes, no nose, no teeth, no hair, no lips and probably no ears either. All that was visible beneath the black cowl was a charred black oval shape, like it was wearing a balaclava with no eyeholes in it. Beth had seen some nasty undead creatures in her time, like vampires, werewolves, zombies, ghouls and even the Four

Horsemen of the Apocalypse, but this was something else, something grim, like an undead Aunt Beru dressed as a Sith Lord.

When the nun was about five metres away its face finally moved. It had a mouth after all. A small hole opened in the lower half of its face and a flicker of yellow light lit up the back of its throat.

Beth squinted to try to get a better look at it. 'What the Hell is....'

She didn't finish the sentence. JD dived on her, knocking her to the floor. A huge gust of bright yellow flames blew over their heads, missing them by inches. Sylvia wasn't so lucky. The flames engulfed her and she screamed like the brakes on a train making an emergency stop. She tried to fight the flames off by spinning around in the corridor and throwing her arms around as if she was swatting a million flies away.

JD climbed to his feet and hauled Beth up with him. 'MOVE!' he yelled.

This was their only chance. The nun was preoccupied with Sylvia. It reached out with both arms and grabbed the burning housemaid, pinning her arms to her sides. The nun pressed its face up against hers and spat more fire into her face.

JD pushed Beth back the way they had come and took aim at the nun with his Headblaster gun.

BOOM!

The circumference of the blast hit the back of Sylvia's head and the front of the nun's at the same time. True to form, the impact blew both their heads off their shoulders. A loud splat indicated that a lump of mush that was once *a pair of heads* had splatted against the wall further along the corridor. Sylvia's burning corpse collapsed to the ground and the flames turned from yellow to violet, just like the flames in the oil lamps.

The stench of burning flesh and the fumes coming from Sylvia's decaying corpse were overwhelming. Behind the flickering flames, the nun's headless body staggered back three or four steps and toppled over, landing with a thud on its back.

Beth covered her mouth and nose. Her eyes were stinging and beginning to weep. 'What should we do?' she asked.

JD lowered his gun and surveyed the crisping body of Sylvia and the smoking corpse of the nun. The violet flames on Sylvia's body were gradually petering out.

Beth tugged at his sleeve. 'JD, what should we do?' she repeated.

He still didn't respond.

She tugged his sleeve harder, to remind him she was still there.

He eventually responded, but all he said was, *'What the fuck?'*

The body of the headless nun was still moving. Not twitching or writhing in agony as one might expect. It sat bolt upright. It no longer had a head, but that wasn't stopping it from getting up. It placed its hands on the ground and lifted itself up from the floor.

JD pointed his gun at it again but didn't fire. Beth stood by his side and the two of them watched on as the headless nun stood fully upright. What happened next was unprecedented. From within the gaping hole between its shoulders, a small black shape emerged. It looked like black putty wriggling around, but it soon formed into a small oval shape that kept growing and pulsating as it enlarged.

'It's growing back,' Beth said, stating the obvious.

'No shit,' said JD. 'This is bad.'

He grabbed her hand and they turned to flee, only for both of them to stop without even taking a step.

'Oh shit,' said JD.

Their situation had gotten a lot worse. Because further down the corridor, another nun was walking towards them. It had already passed the Violet room. And it too, had a black, charred, featureless face.

Thirty Seven

Buses weren't exactly designed for racing at high speed across town. But Rex was doing his best to drive one like it was a sports car as he and Elvis raced to Corned Beef Hill in response to a call for help from Jasmine. Overtaking in a bus was difficult, and undertaking was nigh on impossible. But Rex had managed it. Elvis was alongside him at the front of the bus, pointing through the windshield at the upcoming traffic and screaming instructions.

'Mind that old lady!' Elvis yelled.

'It's okay, I saw her.'

'Watch out for that stop sign!'

'Would you shut up?' bellowed Rex, tiring of Elvis constantly pointing at stuff and saying what it was.

'This is kinda fun innit?' said Elvis. 'Bit like that movie Speed. You know the one?'

'Yeah I know it.'

'I guess I'm sorta like Keanu Reeves and you're Sandra Bullock.'

'I am not.'

'She was the one driving the bus in the film, and Keanu was standing alongside her giving orders, remember?'

'Shut up.'

'There they are!' said Elvis, pointing at the roadside up ahead. 'Move up the inside of that Station Wagon.'

Rex was glad the high-speed driving was about to come to an end, and he had a newfound respect for Sandra Bullock who'd made it look easy in Speed. And she'd been driving a bus that was primed to explode if it dropped below 50 miles per hour. Whereas Rex was speeding because Elvis had taken a phone call from Jasmine, a phone call that hadn't made a great deal of sense. The general gist of it was that Jasmine was with Flake and Sanchez, and the three of them were being chased by an angry mob. Quite who the angry mob were, and why they were angry was anyone's guess, but there was a policy among the Dead Hunters that when a member was in trouble, no matter how trivial the issue might seem, it should be reacted to as if it were a "life-or-death" matter. So breaking the speed limit in a bus was a minimum requirement.

Rex swung the bus across two lanes of traffic, almost hitting an old man on a motorbike, and causing a few other vehicles to swerve to avoid a collision. The sound of honking horns filled the air as Rex finally brought the bus to a stop at the side of the road. He breathed a sigh of relief and looked through the passenger side window for any sign of Jasmine.

'What fucking shit have they got into this time?' he asked, gobsmacked by the sight that greeted him.

Jasmine was naked, which wasn't *that* big of a surprise, but she was sprinting down a grassy hillside towards the road. Sanchez and Flake were behind her, riding along in a wheelchair that was bouncing precariously from side to side. And charging down the hill behind them was an angry mob of hippies, including a guy with no legs who was bouncing down the hill, head over torso.

'This looks bad,' said Elvis, grabbing an M16 rifle from a large sports bag on the floor.

'I bet this is Sanchez's fault,' said Rex.

'I'm not taking that bet,' said Elvis. 'Just get ready to make a quick getaway. This looks like it could get ugly.'

'It's a good job we were already on our way here. This looks fucked up.'

Elvis opened the door and stepped out onto the sidewalk. He aimed his rifle at the angry mob behind Jasmine, Sanchez and Flake.

Jasmine reached the bottom of the hill and leapt onto the sidewalk. She sprinted up to Elvis, kissed him on the cheek, said something that sounded like "Thanks honey", then jumped aboard the bus. She put her hand on Rex's shoulder and bent over to catch her breath.

'Hey Rex,' she said. 'How's it going?'

'I have no idea,' he replied, his eyes fixed on the wheelchair bouncing down the hill behind her.

Flake and Sanchez were obviously clueless about how to stop a wheelchair from rolling down a steep hill. Flake made a sensible decision and dived clear just before they reached the sidewalk. Sanchez didn't have the nerve, so instead he let nature take its course. The wheelchair flipped up when it hit the sidewalk and sent him flying into the side of the bus.

That was Elvis's cue to start shooting at the angry mob. Or, as he and Rex had done many times in their careers, he gave the crowd what was commonly known as *"The A-Team treatment"*, which is to say that he fired the M16 near the people he was shooting at, without actually hitting anyone. The plan worked exactly like it always did in *The A-Team* too. The bad guys, or in this case, the angry mob, who probably weren't bad people at all (in fact they were much more likely to be innocent victims of something terrible that Sanchez had done), stopped charging down the hill and started retreating. It wasn't exactly a success though. The ones at the front got bundled over by the ones behind, and before long everyone was in a heap on the floor, rolling in all directions with limbs entangled. It looked like a weird, rolling orgy.

When it was clear that no one was deliberately running towards the bus anymore, Elvis stopped shooting and helped Flake peel Sanchez off the sidewalk. Between them they pushed him onto the bus and then jumped aboard themselves.

Rex hit the gas and suddenly they were back in the middle of *Speed* again. And this time they had some passengers for added authenticity.

Elvis removed the ammo clip on the rifle and set it down behind Rex's seat. He barely had time to turn around when Jasmine grabbed him and gave him a big kiss.

'Thanks for coming so quick,' she said.

'No problem,' said Elvis. 'Who wants to explain to us what the fuck just happened here?' He looked Jasmine up and down. 'And how come you ended up naked again?'

'You wouldn't believe it,' she replied. 'There was this guy and he was wearing a really cool blue bikini, and I thought it would look good on me. He suggested we swap clothes, and I thought I'd struck gold because the bikini looked so nice. So I whipped my shorts and my top off and gave them to him. But then he asks if he can take some photos of me because he's a professional photographer, so I did some poses for him.'

Elvis slapped his forehead. 'Oh God, not again.'

'I know,' said Jasmine. 'He asked me to turn around and bend over, so I did and I held the pose for about twenty seconds, but when I looked back over my shoulder, he was gone.'

'Of course he was.'

'Yeah, and there were like twenty other people there taking photos of me. And I think some of them were filming.'

Elvis shook his head. 'How do you keep getting into these scrapes?'

'It's a mystery,' Jasmine replied.

'Okay,' said Elvis, looking at Flake and Sanchez. 'Which one of you clowns is going to give me a sensible answer?'

Sanchez had finally caught his breath so he offered his version of events. 'It was a nightmare,' he said. 'I found a dead body in one of the portaloos, and then suddenly all these drunk people were rocking the portaloo from side to side and trying to get in to attack me.'

'What?' Elvis shook his head. 'That doesn't make sense.'

'That's not what happened,' said Jasmine. 'He was using the disabled portaloo, and the handicapped people were annoyed about it.'

'I'm still not seeing why they were chasing you all,' said Elvis.

Flake offered some clarification. 'There was this drunken bitch banging on the door of the toilet, calling Sanchez names and stuff, so I nutted her. After that, all Hell broke loose. A guy dressed as a pirate tried to hit me, so I took him out too, and then Jasmine punted a midget into a crowd of people....'

'Wait, what?' said Elvis.

Flake ignored him and carried on with her story. 'And then she pushed a guy in a wheelchair down the hill.'

'Hey, don't make out like I was the instigator!' said Jasmine, taking offence at the way the story was told. 'You're the one who hit the blind woman with her own stick!'

'What blind woman?' said Flake, horrified by the accusation.

'The woman with the dark glasses and the white stick was blind,' said Jasmine.

Flake put her hand to her mouth as the truth dawned on her. 'Oh, *shit!'*

'Don't worry about it,' said Sanchez. 'I'd hit Stevie Wonder if I thought I could get away with it.'

'That's not all,' Jasmine continued. 'The first woman Flake head-butted had cerebral palsy!'

Elvis glared at Flake. 'You did *what?'*

Flake turned slightly pale. 'Why do you think she had cerebral palsy?' she asked Jasmine.

'Because she *had* cerebral palsy!' Jasmine replied.

'How do you even know what cerebral palsy is?' Flake asked.

'One of the hookers I worked with at the Beaver Palace had cerebral palsy, that's how I know!'

Sanchez jumped to Flake's defence. 'I have to vouch for Flake here,' he said. 'That woman was totally wasted. She was staggering all over the place. People like that are dangerous.'

Jasmine put her hands on her hips and glowered at him. 'Do you even know what cerebral palsy is?'

'It's a form of telepathy isn't it?' said Sanchez, clearly unsure of himself.

Elvis stepped in to calm things down. 'Okay, everybody, I'm getting a clearer picture now,' he said. 'It's obvious what's happened here.'

'*It is?'* said Flake.

'Yes,' Elvis replied. 'What's happened is, we've reached an all-time low. Even for *us* this is *incredibly bad.*'

'Hey!' yelled Rex. 'What do you mean *us?* Don't include me in this, or yourself. We had nothing to do with it.'

Elvis disagreed. 'I fired about fifty rounds from an M16 at a bunch of gay disabled people, and you were the getaway driver. We're all involved in this. Fuck me, wait 'till Scratch hears about it.'

'He'll love it,' said Sanchez.

'That doesn't mean that what just happened here was anything but incredibly wrong on every possible level,' Elvis pointed out. 'You know what, I'm making an executive decision here. From now on, Jasmine, Sanchez and Flake are not allowed to go anywhere together unsupervised.'

Rex agreed. 'Yeah, for now, I think we should all lay low for a while,' he said, steering the bus off the highway towards the town centre. 'I'll take Sanchez and Flake back to the Tapioca, where I suggest the pair of you open the bar up and pretend you've been working there all day. A change of clothes might be a good idea too.'

'Has anyone got any underwear I can borrow?' Jasmine asked.

'You're coming with us,' said Rex. 'Me and Elvis are looking for a serial killer. Someone's murdering people and ripping their eyes and tongues out, just like Archie Somers did before the last eclipse.'

'Hang on a sec,' said Sanchez. 'The dead guy I saw in the portaloo had no eyes or tongue.'

'Are you sure?' said Elvis.

'I'm positive,' said Sanchez. 'I accidentally peed in his eye sockets.'

Elvis groaned. 'Accidentally?'

'People were shaking the portaloo,' Sanchez reminded him. 'I can't control my aim when I'm moving around like that.'

'Was this dead guy anyone you recognised?' Elvis asked.

'Nah, I think he was Asian, and I'm not sure, but I think he only had one arm. I don't know any Asians with one arm.'

'You're sure it was a man though?' asked Flake.

'I think it was,' said Sanchez. 'But I have been fooled before.'

'Let me get this straight,' said Elvis. 'You pissed in the ocular cavities of a dead, gay Asian person with one arm?'

'He's technically blind now too,' Sanchez added.

'Christ, what a shit-storm,' Elvis groaned.

Rex slowed the bus down at a set of traffic lights. 'Yo Elvis!' he called out.

Elvis looked round just as Rex tossed a cell phone at him. The King caught it but looked bemused.

'What am I doing with your phone?' he asked.

'Call Sally Diamond,' Rex replied. 'She's gonna want to know about this new dead body. Just don't mention to her about Sanchez pissing over it.'

Thirty Eight

Nuns on both sides.

Beth squeezed JD's hand. 'What do we do?' she asked, panicking.

The answer to her question came from up above.

'Beth! Up here! Quick!'

Lenny the gardener was leaning over the balcony on the landing, waving frantically, gesturing for Beth and JD to run up the stairs. Further along the landing there was an open door behind him.

JD didn't hesitate. He pushed Beth towards the stairs and turned his gun on the nun that had crept up behind them.

BOOM!

The blast hit the nun in the chest and knocked her off her feet. She rocketed back along the corridor into the darkness, eventually landing on the floor and crashing into something.

Beth ran around the smouldering corpse of Sylvia and sprinted up the stairs towards Lenny. JD spun around to confront the nun whose head had just grown back. She was moving back towards the staircase at a much faster pace than before. The lit flame at the back of her throat became visible again as she closed in on JD. He straightened his arm and blasted off another shot from his gun. It blew the nun off her feet. She vanished into the darkness, as if yanked back by a bungee cord.

A hand grabbed JD's shoulder. He spun around, pulling another pistol from inside his coat. This time he wasn't confronted by a nun, but by Karen the ginger-haired cop. She had bailed out of the Violet room and decided to take her chances with him. In her hand she had a six-shooter pistol. It wouldn't be much use against the nuns. And seeing as how Karen looked like she was having a panic attack, she probably wouldn't be capable of firing it anyway.

'What are they?' she screeched.

'Who cares. Move!'

JD sprinted up the stairs, about ten steps behind Beth, with Karen following behind him.

Lenny was frantically waving them up. 'Quick!' he yelled, as if no one realised there was a need to hurry. 'They're getting back up.'

When Beth was almost at the top, Lenny grabbed her hand and dragged her along the landing to the open door. JD rounded the top of the stairs and chased after them with Karen several steps back, screaming the word *"Shit!"* over and over.

The four of them piled through the open door, straight into another slightly lighter room. Lenny slammed the door shut behind them and turned a key in the lock. The old gardener looked like he was about to have a heart attack. His chest was heaving and he was sucking in deep breaths.

'Where's Derek?' Karen asked.

Lenny grimaced. 'He didn't make it. One of those things set him on fire, burned him to a crisp. Didn't you hear him scream? It was awful.'

'Any idea what the deal is with those nuns?' JD asked him.

Lenny shook his head. 'No, they're everywhere. I got real lucky and found this room unlocked.' He held out his hand to JD. 'I'm Lenny by the way.'

'Good for you,' said JD, making no attempt to shake his hand.

Beth intervened. 'This is my husband, Luke,' she said. 'Thank you so much for helping us back there, Lenny. I thought we were done for.'

'You had the right idea when you decided to stay in the room downstairs,' said Lenny. 'I didn't expect you to come out. I thought I was stuck up here all on my own.'

Karen was standing with her back against the door. She'd turned a ghostly white colour. 'We're screwed,' she said. 'We're going to die here.'

Beth switched off her torch and looked around the room. It was a decent size. The walls were a cream colour, and a window allowed in a beam of moonlight from outside, but there was nothing much to see. It was filled with junk. And none of the junk looked like the kind of stuff that could be of any use. There were books and rolled up posters scattered around the floor, along with a broken oil lamp. There was an old wooden closet against the wall. Its doors were open, but there was nothing inside it apart from some old rags in the bottom.

JD reached inside his coat and pulled out some ammo for his Headblaster. 'How many of those nuns do you think there are?' he asked, reloading.

'Hundreds,' Lenny replied.

'Hundreds? Shit.' JD looked around the room and his eyes settled on the small round window. 'Is there any way we can get out through there?' he asked.

THUD! THUD! THUD!

Beth tensed up. Something outside had hammered on the door. No one moved, and thankfully, after the third knock the thudding stopped, replaced by the sound of footsteps walking away. Everyone breathed a collective sigh of relief.

'Is that door strong enough to keep them out?' Beth asked.

'They don't come in here,' said Lenny. 'They just wander the halls. They bang on the door now and again, but they never try to get in.'

JD walked over to the window and pressed his face up against it to get a look at how far the drop to the ground was. When he turned back to look at the others, Beth could tell from his face that the news wasn't good.

'What is it?' she asked.

'It's bad,' he replied.

Beth went to the window to see for herself. The night was drawing in over the abbey. Nothing had changed outside except for one thing. There were faceless nuns everywhere, just like the ones outside the door. There were too many to count and most of them were carrying flaming torches. As if recognising that they were being watched, all of them in unison stared up at the window, *at Beth*. She jumped back.

'Oh crap,' she said aloud, surprising herself. 'I think they're going to burn this place down.'

JD was picking through all the books and other items on the floor, looking for anything that might be useful. Karen was standing in a corner as far away from the door as possible, and Lenny was watching everyone, like he was desperate for someone to talk to. Beth smiled at him, which was all the invitation he needed.

'Was it Sylvia who got burned downstairs just now?' he asked her.

JD answered even though he was sifting through all the rubbish on the floor. 'Yes, and she was a phoney,' he said. 'Sent here by Scratch to trick us into going into the Violet room. She's lucky the nuns killed her. I'd have done a lot worse.'

'Who's Scratch?' Lenny asked.

'He's the Devil,' said Beth.

Lenny looked baffled. 'The Devil?'

'Yes, *the actual* Devil,' Beth replied, knowing that it wasn't going to help much.

'But why would the Devil want us all in here?' Lenny asked.

JD turned on Lenny. 'He doesn't want you at all. You're just collateral damage here, unless you're working for him too?' He eyed the gardener with suspicion. 'You're friends with Sylvia, aren't you?'

Lenny raised his hands defensively. 'She only started here a few months ago. I barely knew her. But you're saying she works for the Devil?'

JD moved his attention onto Karen. He pointed his Headblaster gun at her. 'You,' he snarled. 'Give Beth your gun.'

Karen shook her head. 'No way.'

'I won't ask again.'

'But it's all I have to protect me from those things out there,' Karen replied, nervously.

'Don't worry about them, because if you don't give Beth that gun right now, I'll blow your fuckin' face off and throw the rest of you out the window.'

Karen looked for support from one of the others. She got nothing. So reluctantly she unholstered her gun, knelt down and slid it across the floor to Beth. Beth picked it up, unsure what to do with it.

'What are we going to do now?' Karen asked, her voice giving away how disgruntled she was at having to give up her gun.

JD answered. 'Okay, listen, this is what I think is happening. If my instincts are correct, we're in what's known as, *a living Hell.*'

'A living Hell?' Lenny repeated. 'What's that supposed to mean?'

'Listen fuckhead,' JD replied. 'I've been in Hell. I know what it looks like. It's different for everyone. But what we're in right here, is someone's very personal eternal Hell.'

Karen made a high-pitched whimpering sound. 'This can't be happening to me,' she cried.

'Well, it is,' said JD. 'So get to grips with it.' He walked over to the window and looked out at the army of nuns again. 'This was all a set up,' he said, giving Beth a conciliatory smile. 'Everything that's happened since we arrived in this place, the underground tunnel, the death of the monk with the key, it was all part of an elaborate trap that led us here. Scratch arranged all of this.'

'But we can find a way out, can't we?' said Beth.

JD ran his hand through his hair. 'I hate to say it, but I think we're fucked.'

Karen wailed like a dying seal. 'What about me! I'm not supposed to be here! How do I get out?'

JD gave her a look that spoke a thousand "four-letter" words. He pointed at the door. 'You want out of this? Step outside. Those nuns will end it for you real quick. That's the only way this nightmare ends for you, or any of us.'

Thirty Nine

Rex drove like a maniac through the back streets of Santa Mondega as the gang made their escape from the fiasco at the outdoor music festival. He swung the bus around a bend on the wrong side of the road, inducing more beeping horns from other drivers.

'Jesus, man, slow down!' said Elvis.

'Did you call Sally Diamond yet?' Rex asked.

Elvis tossed Rex's phone back to him. 'She didn't answer, so I left her a message.'

The phone landed between Rex's legs and got wedged underneath him on the seat. Elvis headed back down the bus to join the others before Rex could berate him for it. Rex reached down and tried to retrieve the phone. It was hard to get a hold of it while driving. And as if he wasn't distracted enough, he heard Jasmine shouting at Flake and Sanchez in the back of the bus.

'Someone's gonna have to give me some pants!'

Rex checked his rear-view mirror to see what was going on back there. Whatever it was, it was weird. It looked like Flake and Sanchez were playing Rock, Paper, Scissors, while Jasmine and Elvis watched.

'What the fuck are you doing back there?' Rex yelled at them.

'Fucking hell!' Flake groaned. 'You can't just do scissors every time, Sanchez!'

'It worked though, didn't it?'

Rex's view from his mirror wasn't very good at all. Everything was smaller and back to front, but the outcome of the rock, paper, scissors game was that Flake had to give Jasmine her jeans, while Sanchez had to hand over his Hawaiian shirt. Elvis was overseeing the exchange.

CRASH!

Shit!

Rex had been so busy watching what was going on in the mirror he'd driven the bus into row of parked cars.

'Sorry everyone!' he called out.

It was a relief that no pedestrians had been hurt in the crash. And even more pleasing for Rex, there weren't any witnesses. None that he could see anyway. He checked his mirror again and saw that the others were on the floor in a heap. Legs, heads and asses were all over the place, reminding him of a film he'd seen many years earlier called *Society.*

'Everyone okay back there?' he asked.

'I've got my hand stuck in something,' Jasmine groaned.

Sanchez piped up. 'Someone's got their hand in my shorts!'

'It's not me,' Flake replied.

Jasmine screamed. 'OH GOD NO!"

And then Elvis waved frantically at Rex. 'Just drive! Get us out of here!'

'What exactly is going on back there?' Rex inquired.

All four voices replied in unison. 'Just drive!'

Rex reversed back out of the row of cars he'd crashed into and drove a little more sensibly for the rest of the journey. He eventually parked up outside the Tapioca and pressed a button to open the bus door.

The door hadn't even finished hissing open when Sanchez rushed past him, wearing just his shorts and shoes. His shorts were ripped at the back so Rex got a glimpse of some crumpled white underpants with brown streaks on them. Sanchez jumped onto the pavement and ran up to the Tapioca's entrance, holding his shorts up with one hand. Flake came next, but Rex grabbed her arm before she could get off the bus. She was wearing nothing but an oversized T-shirt that said "FUCK OFF" on the front. Lucky for her it was an extra-large shirt, so it came down almost to her knees.

'Flake, quick question,' said Rex.

Flake glared at him. 'This had better be important.'

'Have you still got the Eye of the Moon?'

'Seriously? Is that the best question you can come up with? Pervert!'

'No,' Rex protested. 'We've got a new serial killer in town and we think he might be after the Eye.'

'Well I don't have it. Scratch took it off me.'

'You're sure about that?'

'Of course I'm sure. Can I go now?'

'Uh yeah,' said Rex, releasing his grip on her arm. 'But be careful because this new killer we're after is ripping out people's eyes and tongues just like Archie Somers did five years ago. Back then, Somers was tying to get the Eye because it had the power to make an eclipse permanent.'

Sanchez overheard what Rex was saying and ran back to the bus. 'That's not why Somers was killing people,' he argued from the sidewalk, while holding his shorts up with one hand. 'Somers murdered all the people who borrowed that weird *book with no name* from the library. I should know, he killed my brother Thomas and his wife Audrey because they'd read it.'

Rex shouted over his shoulder. 'Yo Elvis, is that true? Somers was killing people who read The Book With No Name?'

Elvis called back from the rear of the bus. 'I remember Annabel saying it's why Somers killed her. She was the last one to ever borrow the book from the library.'

Rex turned back to Sanchez. 'Where's this book now?' he asked.

'It burned in a fire at the museum,' Sanchez replied.

'Well, we think it did,' said Flake, 'because we left it there when the fire started.'

'Funny thing about that book,' said Sanchez, jogging on the spot to keep warm. 'Even though Somers killed everyone who read it, it kept finding its way back to the library. Maybe you should check there and see if it's back?'

Rex took a moment to let Sanchez's suggestion sink in. There was nothing stupid or sarcastic about it. 'Hmm,' he said. 'That's possibly a good idea.'

'Sanchez has lots of good ideas,' said Flake.

Rex smiled at her. 'Go put some pants on. And don't forget to open up the Tapioca. Make it look like it's been open all day, yeah?'

'Oh, *now* you want us to hurry!' said Flake sarcastically.

Rex's butt started vibrating, indicating that Sally Diamond was phoning him back. 'I gotta take this,' he said, reaching down between his legs for his phone. 'Hurry up and go, and Flake, *nice T-shirt.*'

Flake poked her tongue out at him and hopped off the bus, holding her T-shirt down so it didn't blow up in the wind.

Jasmine and Elvis moved to the front of the bus to join Rex. Jasmine was wearing Flake's jeans and Sanchez's Hawaiian shirt, which meant she looked sorta cool, sorta naff, and she smelled like piss and sweat. Rex wanted to comment but he had to take the call from Sally Diamond before it was too late.

'Hi Sally,' he said.

He put his phone down on the dashboard and turned on the speaker so Elvis and Jasmine could hear.

'I'm glad you called,' Diamond replied. 'There's been another murder. I'm on my way to it now.'

'Was it at the outdoor concert?' Rex asked.

'It was. How did you know? I only just found out myself.'

Rex grimaced. 'I've just come from there,' he replied. 'One of my team saw a dead body there in a portaloo. It had its eyes and tongue ripped out, just like the others. It's possible the killer is still there at the concert.'

Diamond sounded surprised. 'So why did you leave?'

'It's complicated,' said Rex, shaking his head disapprovingly at Jasmine, who responded by raising her middle finger.

'Well I've got another lead for you,' said Diamond. 'Several people at the concert say they saw the killers.'

'Killers?' said Rex, looking at Elvis who was equally surprised. 'You mean there's more than one?'

'Apparently,' said Diamond. 'Eyewitnesses are saying it was a fat Mexican pimp and two hookers. One of the hookers was a dark-skinned woman with no clothes on, so if nothing else, *she* should be easy to spot.'

Jasmine shouted at the phone. 'Did they say she was pretty?'

Elvis put his hand over her mouth to shut her up.

'Who was that?' Diamond asked.

'That's my colleague, Jasmine. She's helping us out,' Rex replied.

'Oh, right. No, *no one* said the hookers were pretty. I mean, they're hookers, right? So they might be *pretty skanky*, but definitely not *pretty. Hahahaha!'*

Elvis had to wrestle to keep his hand pressed over Jasmine's mouth.

'I wouldn't worry about the Mexican and the hookers,' said Rex. 'We saw them. They were nothing to do with it.'

'Are you sure? We've got eyewitness saying they were beating up disabled people.'

'Trust me, Sally. It's nothing to do with our case, and the less you know about it the better.'

'Okay, but just so you know, some of the witnesses think the fat guy pissed into the victim's eye sockets.'

Rex groaned. 'Okay, we'll look into that, thanks. Anything else?'

'Uh yeah, did you get to the morgue yet?' Diamond asked.

'Yeah, me and Elvis were there half an hour ago. Your friend Dr Taylor was quite useful. He says all the victims so far are either homosexual, or bisexual, apart from Bob Muncher who was killed because he was a cop. Basically, they're all men who do it with other men. And seeing as how the latest victim was at the Gay Pride event, his theory seems to be hanging together.'

'That does make sense,' Diamond agreed. 'The first victim I found was in an alley behind a gay nightclub. Maybe you could stakeout some gay clubs?'

Rex caught sight of Elvis shaking his head to show his lack of enthusiasm for the idea, so he changed the subject. 'What was the name of this latest victim, Sally?'

'Erm, his name was..... Hassan Altabar.'

'Okay, that's good to know,' said Rex. 'We're going to make a trip to the library later to follow up a lead. It'll be worth checking all the victims library records.'

'Sounds intriguing,' said Diamond. 'Call me if you get anything.'

'Oh wait, Sally. There's one thing you can do for us. It might be nothing, but if you can look into it, it would be real useful.'

'Sure, Rex. What is it?'

'Five years ago one of the victims was Annabel de Frugyn.'

'The Mystic Lady?'

'That's her. The coroner says that her body was taken away by a relative and buried somewhere else. Can you do some digging and see if you can find out where Annabel's body went?'

'Definitely. I'll go through all the records and see what I can find.'

'Thanks Sally. Call me if you get anything.'

'Same to you. Bye Rex.'

Rex ended the call and slipped his phone into a pocket on his jeans.

'What now then?' Elvis asked, removing his hand from Jasmine's mouth.

'I'm gonna go visit Papshmir,' said Rex. 'You two should head to the city library. See if this book with no name is anywhere on the shelves, or if they've got any record of it. And check the library records for all of the victims. I think Diamond said the latest one was called Hassan Altabar, didn't she? Write it down.' He pulled a slip of paper from his breast pocket and handed it to Elvis. It had the names of the other victims on it.

'Hassan Altabar.' Elvis said it out loud so he wouldn't forget. 'Got it.'

'We need to move fast on this,' said Rex. 'We've gotta catch this killer before he strikes again. I don't want any more innocent people murdered, not while we've got a chance to stop it.'

'I agree,' said Jasmine. 'But can we get some food first? I'm pretty hungry.'

'Good idea,' said Elvis. 'I could murder a cheeseburger.'

'I was thinking of Chinese food,' said Jasmine.

Rex had visions of a million Chinese dishes running through his head. He started salivating at the thought of it. 'I'll tell you what,' he said. 'I saw a new Chinese restaurant a couple of blocks back. They're doing an offer, three-course meals for ten bucks.'

'Let's do it,' said Elvis. 'I know the place you mean. It's called Emperor Ming's and it's a short walk from Papshmir's church, so when we're done eating, you can head there. Me and Jasmine will take the bus and head across town to the library.'

Rex started up the engine on the bus and pulled out into the street. 'We mustn't take too long,' he reminded the others. 'There's a killer on the loose, remember?'

'Absolutely,' said Elvis. 'That's our top priority.'

Jasmine was tapping away on her phone. 'I've booked us a table,' she said.

'Can you order us some beers too, ready for when we get there?' Elvis asked her.

'Sure thing,' said Jasmine. 'It says here we can get three pitchers for the price of one.'

Rex's eyes lit up. 'Three for the price of one,' he said out loud. 'Shit, we may as well get six.'

'Six?' said Jasmine.

'Yeah, we'll just have to drink them real quick.'

'Done,' said Jasmine. 'I ordered a couple of bottles of wine too.'

'What for?' asked Elvis.

Jasmine shrugged. 'In case we run out of beer.'

Forty

'I don't understand this,' said Karen. 'Hell is for dead people, isn't it? And none of us are dead. Are we?'

'No we're not,' Beth assured her.

It was becoming quite claustrophobic in the upstairs room of the abbey. The walls felt like they were closing in because there was no getting away from the anxiety building in the air. Karen was openly panicking. Lenny was by the window, biting his nails, and JD was ignoring everyone while he tried to come up with a solution to their predicament. It left Beth with the unenviable task of trying to keep the others calm. She could relate to what Karen and Lenny were experiencing. She had been terrified the first time she ever saw a vampire, but since then she'd encountered just about every undead creature imaginable, and she'd even spent time in a bar with the Devil.

Lenny looked out of the window for the umpteenth time to see if the nuns with the burning torches were still loitering outside. They were.

'If this isn't Hell, it's pretty darn close,' he said.

'Think of it like this,' said Beth, trying to quieten him down before JD lost patience with him. 'If there is a Hell, then it means there must be a Heaven.'

'I wonder what people do in Heaven?' said Karen. 'I mean, what if it's boring? What if there's no alcohol? Or no TV? What do you do all day? If you spend your eternity with your relatives, they'll just get on your nerves after a few days. Mine do. Are there books?'

Rather inevitably, JD turned on her. 'You're getting on my nerves,' he said. 'And I've only known you for five minutes. So do yourself a favour and shut up.'

Lenny had moved from biting his nails to scratching his grey beard. 'This is a goddamned joke!' he said. 'There's no way this is real. This must be a secret camera show or something, mustn't it?' He pointed at JD. 'And you're an actor. I bet there's hidden cameras in here, aren't there?'

JD marched up to Lenny, grabbed him around the throat, lifted him off his feet and slammed him against the wall. He squeezed the gardener's throat. 'When I say we're in some kind of Hell,' he said in a gravelly voice. 'I fucking mean it. Now if you ain't got nuthin' helpful to say, I suggest you shut the fuck up, or get used to having a broken neck.'

Karen spoke up in defence of the gardener. 'Who do you think you are?' she said. 'We're all having a tough time with this, and you're not helping.'

JD relinquished his grip on Lenny's neck and dropped him to the floor. Lenny crouched down by the closet and rubbed his neck as he sucked in some air. Beth quickly jumped in front of Karen before JD could get his hands on her.

'His name's not really Luke,' she confessed to Karen. 'He's the Bourbon Kid. So do yourself a favour and listen to what he says. You've got one chance of getting out of this place alive, and *he's it*. So shut the fuck up unless you've got something useful to say.'

'The Bourbon Kid?' said Karen, her bottom lip quivering.

Lenny straightened up and stared at JD. 'I knew you looked familiar,' he said. 'I've seen your picture in the newspaper. If you really have seen Hell, then what is this place? Come on, you must know what's going on?'

One of the psychotic nuns out on the landing banged on the door again, which startled everyone, apart from JD, who ignored it like it hadn't even happened. He responded to Lenny's question.

'I've been thinking about this, okay. Every person who goes to Hell, goes there because of something they did. Maybe they killed someone, raped someone, abused children, started a war, whatever. But when they get to Hell, whatever they did is generally repaid back on them for all eternity. So if you stabbed someone to death, you can expect to be stabbed to death over and over in Hell. That's your punishment.'

'What's that got to do with our situation?' Karen asked.

JD remained calm. 'My first thought was that this whole thing was for me. But I've never killed a nun, and this particular scenario is full of them. Have any of you ever done anything bad to a nun, even if it was something stupid you did when you were a kid? Anyone?'

Beth shook her head. 'Not me.'

'Me either,' said Lenny.

'Nor me,' Karen chimed in.

After a short silence, Beth came up with a suggestion. 'Didn't your friend the Red Mohawk murder a nun once? I'm sure you told me that.'

'He did,' JD agreed. 'But I don't think that's it. If it's nothing to do with any of us, then it's something to do with *this place*. That dead monk, Brother Loomis, maybe he coulda done something evil?'

Karen pressed her hand against her chest. 'Oh my God,' she said. 'I know what it is.'

'So spit it out,' said JD, keen to hear her thoughts.

'Umm, well, *I think* I know,' said Karen. 'But it's not anything to do with Brother Loomis. It's to do with another monk who lived here over a hundred years ago. It's quite a well-known story locally.'

Lenny perked up. 'You mean Benedict of Assisi,' he said. 'The Mad Monk.'

'I thought Rasputin was the Mad Monk,' said Beth.

Lenny shook his head. 'No, Rasputin was a song by Boney M.'

Beth was about to continue the argument when she spotted JD subtly shaking his head at her.

Karen continued. 'Benedict lived here back in the late nineteenth century. Back then this place was a refuge for homeless women. Benedict owned it. He'd come over from Italy, and the locals all thought he was wonderful. He opened the abbey to homeless women, and women who'd been abused. In return for free accommodation all they had to do was become a nun and abstain from sins of the flesh.'

'What did he do to them?' JD asked.

'Unbeknown to any of the locals he was having sex with most of them. But that's not the horrible part. It being the nineteenth century, there wasn't much in the way of contraception. Consequently, many of the nuns became pregnant. Benedict couldn't have pregnant nuns walking around because it would have been clear evidence of what he was getting up to. So, whenever he found out one of the nuns was pregnant he would sneak into their room at night and drug them. Then he'd take them downstairs to the Violet room. Do you remember seeing the incinerator in there?'

Beth covered her mouth. 'Oh God.'

Karen nodded. 'Yep, while they were unconscious from the drugs he burned them alive in the incinerator furnace.'

'How the Hell did he get away with that?' Beth asked.

'Apparently,' said Karen, 'he told the other nuns that their pregnant sisters had gone away to another nunnery to have their children in secret.'

'But they found out he was lying, yeah?' said JD.

'Yes,' said Karen. 'And they plotted their revenge. Benedict liked a glass of wine before bed, so one night they drugged his wine. When he retired to bed, he always locked his door because he was paranoid, *obviously*. Anyway, it was the year 1896 that this happened. And on the night they drugged his wine, one brave nun hid in his closet and waited for the drug to kick in. Then as soon as he was asleep she sneaked out and let the others into his room. The nuns then dragged him from his bed and carried him downstairs to the Violet room. Then they did to *him* what he had done to their sisters. They burned him alive in the incinerator. After that, the nun who had hidden in the closet took over the manor. It stayed in her family for years until Brother Loomis inherited the place. He stopped taking in homeless people and just lived here on his own with Mavis the housemaid.'

'That's true,' said Lenny. 'Loomis never liked people. I swear if he could have done the gardening himself, he would never have let me onto the premises.'

'I can believe that,' said JD.

'What do you think?' Beth asked JD, hoping the story would mean something to him.

He took a moment to think before replying. 'I think I know what's going on here,' he said. 'Do you remember how I said Hell is a personal thing for each individual? I think we somehow stumbled into Benedict's personal Hell when we entered the Violet room. His punishment for what he did to the nuns will be an eternity of reliving the terror of being captured and burned alive by them. My guess is, those fire breathing nuns outside are the ghosts, or demons of all the pregnant women he burned alive.'

Beth clutched her stomach. The mention of pregnant women and their unborn children burning alive was a horrible thought. Her child wasn't even born yet, but it was still her child.

'How does any of this help us to get out of here though?' Lenny asked.

'I'm guessing Benedict is in this building somewhere,' said JD. 'That's how an eternal damnation works. Every time the nuns find him, they burn him alive. Then the whole thing starts up again. He hides, they find him, they burn him alive, he hides, they find him, you get the picture? That goes on forever.'

'Now that we've worked that out,' said Karen. 'I mean, now that *you've* worked that out, what do we do?'

'We find Benedict,' said JD. 'If I'm right and he's here somewhere, we could maybe hand him over to the nuns. Then maybe, *just maybe*, that'll get us out of here.'

Lenny scoffed. 'Seriously? That's your plan?' He looked at JD and realised whose plan he was mocking, and then added, 'I like it, it's a good plan.'

'I'm glad you like it,' said JD. 'Because you're coming with me to look for Benedict.'

Forty One

Scratch paced up and down in Purgatory, waiting for news of how his wonderful plan was panning out. Annabel was sitting at a table near the bar, huddled over her crystal ball looking for any information she could pass onto him. Scratch had forbidden her from drinking any more alcohol because she seemed to be developing a bit of a drink problem in recent times, which had made her even more annoying than usual.

Dracula was sitting at the bar nursing a glass of red wine. The vampire bat was wearing a thick blue jumpsuit, the kind worn by Michael Myers in the Halloween movies. Such an item never existed back in his time on earth, but Scratch had convinced him that he would like it because it could be unzipped and discarded in a matter of seconds, which was perfect for someone who had to get naked every time he transformed into a bat.

'This wine is nice,' said Dracula, staring up at the TV. 'Who's that lady up on the screen? I would very much enjoy making love to her.'

Dracula's regular announcements about whom he'd like to make love to were starting to grate on Scratch's nerves. Scratch was much more interested in what Annabel had to say, but she wasn't saying much at all. Rather than respond to Dracula's announcement that he'd like to make love to Melissa McCarthy, Scratch yelled at Annabel for what felt like the twentieth time in as many minutes.

'Have you seen anything yet, you old crone?'

'I told you before, it's all playing out exactly as you hoped,' she replied.

'Give me an update anyway. What's happening?'

The Mystic Lady pulled her cardigan tight as if she were cold, then waved her hands over her crystal ball for effect. Her bony old fingers shielded it from the light coming in through the windows, and conveniently shielded it from Scratch's view too.

'I see something,' she said. 'I see the policewoman, Karen Butterman. She's about to complete her part of the mission. She has followed your orders exactly and has convinced the Bourbon Kid and Beth that she can be trusted.'

Scratch pumped his fist. 'Perfect. Where are they all at the moment?'

'They are in a room on the upper floor, but any moment now, the Bourbon Kid and the gardener are going to leave the room to go looking for Benedict.'

Scratch could barely contain his excitement. 'This is really excellent,' he said, his pulse racing.

Dracula spoke up from the other side of the bar. 'Does this mean I can go now?'

Scratch pretended like he'd forgotten about the Count. 'Are you still here?' he said.

'Yes. I want my money and the brothel you promised me. Come on, I'm sick of sitting around drinking, I want to be out in the world, fornicating.'

'Fine, fine.' Scratch slid sideways over the bar and rocked up to the till. He typed some coordinates into the keypad. 'Your new brothel is in Santa Mondega,' he said. 'It's called the Cherry Poppins.'

'Cherry Poppins? What kind of name is that?'

'You can always rename it if you don't like it.'

Dracula drummed his fingers together in excitement. 'Good, gooooood,' he cackled. 'Because I was thinking I'd call it *Count Dracula's Palace of Love.*'

Scratch seethed. 'Listen you idiot. I picked a brothel in Santa Mondega, because that's the safest place for you to operate without the authorities finding you. But if you insist on naming the place after yourself, I promise you, people will come looking for you and you'll be back down in Hell before you know it.' He reached down below the bar and lifted up a suitcase. He placed it on the bar in front of Dracula and flipped it open. It was stuffed full of cash. 'There's exactly one million dollars in there,' he said. 'Zilas will help you settle in and take care of any administration issues for you.'

'Perfect,' said Dracula. 'Can I also have that photo you keep behind the bar?'

'The one of the Dead Hunters?'

'Yes, please.'

'No you fucking can't! I told you already. *Stay away from Sanchez.* If you go after him you'll get nothing but trouble. Be grateful for the brothel I'm giving you.'

'Oh, I'm grateful,' said Dracula. 'I'm also a highly sexual being, and I know what I like.'

Scratch pointed at the door to the men's toilets in the corner. 'Get out of my sight,' he said. 'And stay away from the Tapioca.'

Dracula closed the suitcase of money and hopped off his barstool. 'Is that it then? Can I go?' he said, his face a picture of innocence.

'Just wait a minute while I get Zilas,' said Scratch.

He reached down below the bar and grabbed a red telephone to make a call to Zilas. The hunchback answered the call straight away.

'Zilas speaking,' he said.

'Hey fuckface, get your ass up here,' said Scratch. 'Dracula is ready to move into his new brothel.'

Zilas started to reply but Scratch hung up the phone and replaced it under the bar.

'Right then, Count,' he said. 'This new brothel of yours has about twenty hookers working there, as well as a bunch of meathead bouncers and bar staff. They're all Devil worshippers, so once you show them your little trick where you transform into a bat, they'll all follow you and hang on your every word. But as I told you before, keep a low profile, because if you get killed again you'll be back down in Hell for all eternity.'

'Got it.'

'Good, now fuck off.'

Dracula took his suitcase full of money and headed to the men's toilets to wait for Zilas. He watched the TV some more while he waited and made his usual remarks about wanting to have intercourse with everyone he saw on screen. Eventually, when Scratch was at the end of his tether, Zilas showed up. The hunchback and the Count passed through the portal and were transported into a bathroom in Dracula's new brothel, the Cherry Poppins.

The bathroom in the brothel was magnificent. It had a Jacuzzi bath big enough for six or seven people to sit in. There was a set of open showers on one wall, and a toilet, which was opposite the showers.

'That's weird isn't it?' said Zilas.

'What is?'

'The toilet is just out in the open like that.'

'I don't understand. What's odd about that?'

'Well you could be having a shower and there'll be someone opposite you taking a dump and watching you shower.'

Dracula looked confused. 'Don't people do that anymore then?'

'Not usually.'

'The world has become very strange,' said Dracula, shaking his head. 'I used to love watching naked people showering while I was on the throne.'

It was Zilas's turn to be confused. 'I'm not sure what we're talking about anymore,' he said.

'It matters not,' said Dracula. 'Once we meet the fine young women that work here, I'll introduce you to the many fetishes that were popular during my time on earth.'

'Awesome,' said Zilas drying his sweaty hands on his pants. 'Let's go find the women then.'

'I've got a better idea,' said Dracula. 'Why don't you go sort out everything that needs to be sorted, have sex with as many of the hookers as you like, and I'll catch up with you later.'

'Why? Where are you going?'

'I'm off to a place called the Tapioca.'

'What for?'

'To find my true love, Sanchez Garcia.'

Zilas scratched his head. 'You really find Sanchez attractive?'

'He's like a Roman God,' Dracula replied, gazing into space and going all misty-eyed.

'I wouldn't let him use this toilet if I were you,' said Zilas. 'Especially not while people are showering.'

'Why not?'

'Because the smell that comes from his guts is strong enough to render a room full of people unconscious.'

Dracula scoffed. 'Pfft, modern people are so weak. I'll tame this Sanchez fellow with ease, and disarm him with my dashing good looks.'

Zilas groaned. 'Don't say I didn't warn you.'

Dracula licked his finger and ran his hand through his hair. He stared into a mirror next to the toilet and pretended to admire himself even though he had no reflection.

'How do I look?' he asked.

'You look like a janitor,' said Zilas.

'Perfect!' said Dracula, clearly unaware of what a janitor was. 'I'll see you when I get back with my new lover.'

'Wait!' said Zilas. 'Before you go, can you at least show everyone here your trick where you turn into a bat? Once they see that and realise I'm with you, I'll be able to takeover the running of this place.'

Dracula took his eyes off the mirror. 'Very well,' he said, reluctantly, 'but let's get it over with quickly.'

Forty Two

'This is fucking suicide,' said Lenny.

JD was too busy double-checking that both of his guns were loaded to pay any attention to Lenny's whining. His Headblaster gun was the only one that would realistically be of any use. It had three of the specially modified bullets left in it. His other gun, a Glock had about fifteen rounds in the clip.

'Beth, give me that gun,' JD said.

She handed him the pistol that had previously belonged to Karen. It was a small Beretta, easy to conceal. JD took it and turned away from Lenny and Karen, pretending to inspect it. He emptied the bullets from it and slipped them into his pocket without anyone seeing. He turned around, made a show of checking that the safety was off, and offered the gun to Lenny.

'Take this,' he said. 'But don't use it unless you have to, because as soon as one of us fires off a shot, those nuns are gonna come from all directions, so only use it as a last resort. Understand?'

Lenny accepted the gun, but he held it like an amateur who really didn't want to use it. The poor old fool looked like he was going to puke. He certainly didn't look like he was up for the challenge of scouring the abbey in search of a crazy monk who might not even be there.

'You'll be fine,' said JD. 'I'll deal with any nuns we come across. But if we end up surrounded and it's absolutely certain that we're going to die, that's when you start shooting in all directions, okay?'

Karen rubbed Lenny's arm to show some support. 'It'll be okay,' she said. 'You've only got to make it to the door at the end of the corridor, just like we talked about.'

'Yeah right,' said Lenny, scowling at her. 'But if the door is locked, or the monk we're looking for isn't in there, then we're screwed.'

'It's the same room Loomis stayed in,' said Karen. 'It stands to reason Benedict would have stayed there too. It gives the best view of the grounds.'

'If you're so sure, why don't you go?' Lenny snapped at her. 'You are a cop after all. I'm just a gardener.'

JD pushed Lenny in the chest. 'She's staying here with Beth,' he said. 'Grow a fucking pair, will you?'

Beth sneaked up behind JD and slid her arms around his waist. 'Be careful out there,' she said. 'I don't want my baby growing up without a father.'

JD twisted round to face her and stroked her hair, tucking some strands behind her ear. 'Everything's gonna be fine,' he said. 'You know me. I always come back. You ain't getting rid of me yet, I promise.'

'You're not getting rid of us either,' said Beth, glancing down at her stomach.

He could tell she was worried. Who wouldn't be? Over the course of the last six months she'd gotten better at hiding her fears and anxiety, but there was no denying it here, she was trembling in his arms.

Beth kissed him one last time, knowing that it might genuinely be the last time. She made a point of savouring the kiss, remembering how it felt, just like the first kiss they had shared all those years ago on the pier in Santa Mondega. This kiss was every bit as passionate. When it ended she kept her arms around him and left him with one final message.

'I'm not leaving this room until you come back.'

He smiled at her. In his eyes she saw the face of the boy she'd met on the pier, the optimistic young man she had planned to spend her life with. On that occasion, after their first kiss, they didn't see each other again for eighteen years.

He whispered in her ear. 'I love you Beth.'

'I love you too.'

He unholstered his Headblaster gun and headed over to the door. He leaned against it to listen for the sound of any nuns outside.

Lenny whispered to him. 'Is anyone out there?'

JD put his finger to his lips to shush the old gardener. He opened the door a little and peered out onto the landing. There were no nuns in sight.

'This is it,' he whispered, gesturing for Lenny to join him. 'Let's go find ourselves a monk.'

Lenny approached the door. His body language screamed at a desire to stay where he was rather than go through with the plan. JD sensed it, so made the decision for him. He grabbed a handful of Lenny's overalls and dragged him through the door. He shoved the gardener in the direction of the room in the corner and closed the door quietly. Lenny was in a major panic, checking left, right, straight ahead, on the floor and up above, as if he thought there might be nuns dropping down from the ceiling. He stayed close to JD like a child glued to a parent in a busy supermarket.

Although there were no nuns visible on the upper floor, there were at least three wandering the corridor below, their figures barely visible in the violet light. JD crept along the landing, making barely a sound, dragging Lenny with him. The journey to the room in the corner was a simple one that took less than ten seconds. With a sliver of moonlight coming in through the window adjacent to bedroom, JD was able to see what he was doing. He grabbed the doorknob and twisted it one way, then the other. It was locked, and while that was not unexpected, it was disappointing nonetheless.

'Is it locked?' Lenny whispered.

JD glared at him, which was the quietest way of saying, *"Shut the fuck up"*.

He tapped lightly on the door and pressed his ear against it to listen for movement inside. He heard nothing.

'Is he there?' Lenny whispered.

JD ignored him and weighed up his options. The balcony behind them was too close for him to get a decent stride in to kick the door down, which meant that the quickest way in was going to involve blasting the lock off. JD tucked his Headblaster back into a holster inside his coat and pulled out his Glock. Those nuns would flock in from all directions as soon as they heard him fire a shot. If Benedict wasn't inside the bedroom, this could turn out to be a very short mission. The monk was all they had to bargain with if the nuns cornered them.

JD lined up the barrel of the gun against the part of the door where the locking bolt ought to be.

'Wait! Lenny whispered loudly.

JD looked back at him. 'What?'

Lenny pointed at the window. 'Look! Out there!'

JD glanced over at the window. There was nothing there. He'd expected to see a face at the window or something important that warranted his attention, but whatever Lenny had seen was no longer there. There was nothing to see but the sky and some fields in the distance.

BANG!

JD felt a sharp pain in his back and chest. A splodge of blood sprayed across the wall beside the window. *His blood.* He pressed his hand against his chest and felt a patch of warm, sticky blood seeping out of a hole two inches below his collarbone. Lenny had shot him. The sneaky gardener had a second gun, one that *was* loaded, and had been concealed in his overalls the whole time.

The energy drained from JD's body as the blood pumped out of the wound in his chest. His gun slipped from his grasp and clattered onto the floor. His strength deserted him.

And then from behind him he heard Lenny say three words that hurt more than the bullet.

'Scratch says hello.'

Forty Three

Santa Mondega was quite a bizarre place. Dracula had been to some exotic locations in his lifetime, but nothing compared to this. The streets were filled with people dressed in extraordinary costumes and there was a riotous party atmosphere all around. Everyone seemed so friendly too. Everywhere he went people smiled and waved to each other and to him. Back in the fifteenth century such behaviour would have been dealt with by way of execution. But here it seemed to be considered normal.

He arrived at the Tapioca with a feeling of great optimism, excited about finally meeting Sanchez in the flesh.

A sign on a sandwich board in the street outside the Tapioca read -

"GRAND REOPENING. EVERYONE WELCOME"

Dracula accepted the invitation and entered the building. The bar area was already brimming with customers. The first person he recognised was the barmaid, Flake, who he had seen in Scratch's photo. She was wearing a tight blue T-shirt with a picture of a yellow bird on it. If what Dracula had heard was true then she was his main rival for Sanchez's affections. She was in good physical shape, but she was no match for Dracula and his magnetic sex appeal.

Flake was so busy serving customers that Dracula was sure she didn't notice him hovering in the shadows at the back of a crowd of people. Dracula scoured the bar area for any sign of Sanchez, but the tubby Mexican bartender was nowhere to be seen.

It wasn't until Flake had finished serving all of the waiting customers that Sanchez appeared. He strolled down a set of stairs behind the bar, carrying a pint of fizzing yellow liquid in his hand. He was wearing a pair of brown shorts and a white string vest. The sight of him set Dracula's heart racing. He could feel invisible love hearts floating out of his chest. The moment had to be seized, so he made his way through the crowds of drinkers and slinked up to the bar. He raised his hand.

'Over here, kind sir,' he said, smiling seductively at Sanchez.

Sanchez heard him and despite looking somewhat unenthusiastic, he strolled over to where Dracula was waiting.

'Let me guess, you're new around here,' said Sanchez.

'As a matter of fact I am. My name is Vladimir. I'm so pleased to meet you, and what a delightful establishment you have here.'

'What do you want to drink?'

Dracula ran his index finger around his lips. 'I'm not sure,' he said, coyly. 'Do you have any good red wines?'

'Nope. But it's your lucky day,' said Sanchez. 'All strangers get a complimentary free drink.' He placed the fizzy yellow pint on the bar in front of Dracula. It had a frothy head on it and quite a strong smell, one that the Count couldn't quite place.

'What is it?' Dracula asked.

'It's my special homebrew, a local delicacy. If you can down it in less than ten seconds, you win a free bowl of peanuts.'

'Peanuts eh? They sound exotic, what's in them?'

Sanchez shrugged. 'Mostly salt…. and nuts.'

'Nuts eh?' said Dracula, pursing his lips to show how full they were.

His banter wasn't getting much of a reaction from Sanchez. In fact, his romancing of the bartender wasn't going well at all. He could tell from Sanchez's expression that there was no spark of electricity between them. It had been so long since Dracula had tried to woo anyone that he'd seemingly lost his touch. Either that, or Sanchez was impervious to his charms. It was time to try a different approach.

'I like your hair,' he said, winking at Sanchez.

Sanchez picked something out of his nose and wiped it on his shorts before responding. 'Listen fuckface, do you want a free drink or not?'

Dracula eyed up the yellowy potion Sanchez was offering him. 'What flavour is it?' he asked.

'It's a secret recipe,' said Sanchez, losing patience. 'You either drink it or leave.'

'Have you ever drunk it yourself?'

Sanchez nodded. 'I drank it this morning. It was very tasty.'

If Dracula was going to win Sanchez's heart he was going to have to take the drink, even though it smelt like stale onions and baked beans, with a slight hint of curry. He picked up the pint glass and raised it up to eye level, spilling a little on his hand. It was surprisingly warm.

'Well, here's to your good health,' he said, cheerily.

'And yours,' Sanchez replied with a very enthusiastic smile. 'Down it in one, and I'll be very impressed.'

Dracula put the glass to his lips and started drinking, hoping to polish the whole pint off in one or two gulps. It had quite an acidic and bitter taste. He was barely halfway through it when he began to feel queasy. He was about to stop and take a breath when he felt Sanchez's hand on the bottom of the glass, pushing it up, forcing more of the drink down his throat.

'Keep going,' said Sanchez. 'You're almost there.'

Dracula's throat tightened, and with Sanchez pushing the glass up, he couldn't pause for breath. His stomach was pushing the last few gulps back up, but Sanchez was forcing the next few gulps down, which caused some major flooding in his throat. Dracula started choking, and with nowhere else to go, the dubious yellow liquid started spurting out of his nostrils and all down his face. He staggered back away from the bar and dropped the glass onto the floor.

Saliva was building up in his mouth and he was burning up like he was in a sauna. He clutched his stomach and bent over while he tried to catch his breath. The hot acidic liquid was burning his lungs and nose, and the taste of it was vile beyond belief.

After a heavy coughing fit, he straightened up and noticed a number of nearby drinkers laughing at him. 'What the hell was that?' he spluttered, wiping liquid from his face.

'Strong stuff innit?' said Sanchez.

An eruption of vomit surged up from Dracula's stomach towards his throat. He managed to fight it off and swallow it again, but he knew it would come back. He didn't want to embarrass himself by throwing up in front of Sanchez, so he excused himself.

'I'll be back in a minute,' he said, his face burning red.

He turned and sprinted for the exit, where he bumped into a group of young people in weird costumes who were entering the Tapioca en masse. There was no way around them, and Dracula didn't want to puke all over them, so he changed direction and headed towards a door marked, "Disabled Toilet". He burst through it and headed over to a rather unappealing white toilet that had splashes of urine all over the seat. He dropped to his knees and leaned over the toilet bowl. Normally there would be a small pool of water at the bottom of the bowl. However, in this instance there was a mountain of brown stuff at the bottom, wrapped around some twisted sheets of white toilet paper.

BLEURGH!

A huge stream of vomit burst out of his mouth into the toilet bowl, not once, not twice, not even three, four or five times, but *six times* in succession. The vomit landed on (and got mixed in with) the horrendously stinky diarrhoea and toilet paper that was already in the bowl.

When he finally finished puking he took a few deep breaths, which only made him feel worse, because of how bad the smell in the toilet was. He wiped his face clean with his hands and spat on the floor a few times. Whatever it was that Sanchez had given him to drink, it was strong stuff. Alcoholic drinks had changed a lot during Dracula's time in Hell. He pressed his hand down on the toilet seat and pushed himself up. One of the great frustrations about being a vampire was that he couldn't even check in the mirror to see how bad he looked. He just knew it would be bad. And now his hands were wet, and sticky too.

The foul taste in his mouth was getting worse, so he staggered over to a washbasin and rinsed his face with water from the tap. He swilled some water around in his mouth, but nothing seemed to rid him of the disgusting taste of Sanchez's home-brew. He grabbed some paper towels from a dispenser by the sink and wiped his face and hands dry. There were some nasty stains down the front of his blue jumpsuit too, but they wouldn't come off no matter how much he wiped them. This was a disaster. His plan to woo Sanchez had ended in humiliation and now he stank of puke and shit. There was only one thing to do. He stripped off his jumpsuit and threw it onto the floor by a waste bin filled with paper towels. As soon as he was naked he made the rapid transformation into a bat. It made him feel better straight away, although the smell from the toilet was still lingering because he hadn't flushed it.

He flew up to the ceiling above the toilet to see if he could escape through any windows. There was only one window, but it was sealed shut. The only way back out was the way he'd come in. He was about to switch back into human form so he could open the door, when suddenly it burst open anyway. He had been in such a rush to be sick that he'd forgotten to lock it. It turned out to be the first moment of good fortune he'd had all day. Sanchez walked through the door into the toilet and locked the door behind him.

Perfect.

Dracula had Sanchez all to himself in a locked room. Suddenly his plan to hook up with the bartender was back on. There was no need to try and impress him, or woo him with seductive looks and chat-up lines now. He could just do it the old fashioned way. A bite on the neck and Sanchez would be transformed into a vampire. Then the two of them could spend eternity together as lovers, just as he had imagined it.

Forty Four

JD fell to his knees. He pressed his hand on the floor and steadied himself. Blood rose up through his lungs into his mouth and spilled out onto his chin. It was hard to plan for what to do next. Questions were racing through his mind at a million miles an hour. How had he not recognised the danger? How long had Scratch been planning this? When was Lenny going to fire a second shot? And where would it hit him? In the head? The heart? And what would become of Beth? What horrors lay in store for her when this was over?

He twisted round into a seated position to face Lenny, the muscles in his legs weakening with every passing second. The timid old gardener with the bushy grey beard hadn't looked a threat. But he had a gun trained on JD's head. Smoke was floating up from the barrel, and Lenny looked awfully pleased with himself. But he didn't shoot. Instead he raised his arms aloft like he was signalling a Touchdown.

'Praise be to the Prince of Darkness,' he cried. 'My time of glory is here!'

JD's vision started to blur. He kept blinking to try and refocus. It wasn't working. He fumbled around on the floor, hoping to find the Glock pistol he had dropped. Blood was pulsing out through his chest and back, taking his strength and energy with it.

Lenny lowered his hands, his gun pointing at JD again, but instead of pulling the trigger and finishing him off, he pressed the gun underneath his own chin and said one final thing.

'I give myself to you, my Lord, so that I may live in eternal glory!'

BANG!

A splash of red burst forth from the top of his skull and he fell like a rag doll, landing flat on his back. The dumb fucker had blown his own brains out. It ought to have been a good thing. On the whole, JD had to admit it was an unexpected bonus. But now there was another problem, the small matter of the nun walking along the landing towards him. It had been coming up behind Lenny, drawn to the sound of the first shot he'd fired. It wasn't the only nun heading JD's way either. They were coming from everywhere, drawn to the source of the gunfire. Lenny might have just had a lucky escape.

JD gave up feeling around for the Glock and reached into his jacket for his Headblaster gun. He pulled it out and pressed the barrel of it against the floor, using it as a crutch to push himself up onto his knees. From there he reached out and grabbed hold of the balcony. Three more nuns were on the stairs heading up towards him, and those on the upper floor were closing in at speed. The first nun was almost upon him. Its mouth opened in readiness for unleashing a deadly burst of fire.

JD held onto the balcony and tossed his Headblaster gun over it. It clattered onto the floor below. With every last ounce of strength he had left, he threw himself over the balcony after it. The ground floor was a long way down.

SMACK!

His landing was harsh and sounded like someone belly-flopping into a swimming pool from the high board. The wooden floor had very little give in it. His right shoulder took the brunt of the impact. He felt it dislocate, like it had repositioned itself behind his head. It knocked the wind out of him and he let out a loud grunt that would make a tennis player proud.

"Get up. GET UP!"

The words, *"Get up"* were easy to say in his head. The act of actually *getting up*, was another thing altogether. His dislocated shoulder rendered his right arm useless. He reached out and grabbed the Headblaster with his left hand and lumbered to his knees to gather his bearings.

By now the nuns had all turned and were charging back down the stairs. JD crawled towards the Violet room using his left hand and his Headblaster to drag himself inch by inch to his destination. In the back of his mind he knew that if he did make it into the Violet room there was a strong chance Scratch would be waiting inside.

One of the nuns was almost at the bottom of the stairs and was set to reach JD before he made it to the Violet room. He rolled onto his side and managed to muster enough strength with his left arm to aim the Headblaster at the nun's lower body.

BOOM!

The recoil from the gun almost dislocated his other shoulder. The blast threw him back into the wall. But the shot was a success, blasting the nun's legs off at shin height. The nun toppled sideways and unbalanced the next one coming down the stairs. It caused a domino effect, knocking the nuns down, one at a time, all the way up the stairs. It would have been comical had it not been such a relief.

JD crawled the last few metres to the Violet room, arriving outside it just as the pile of nuns on the stairs began climbing to their feet. He reached up for the doorknob and twisted it. The door clicked and he pushed it open by leaning his back against it. He eased himself into the room, blood oozing from his upper body onto the floor, greasing the way for his legs to follow.

The door slammed shut again just before the nearest nun could reach it. JD sat with his back up against the door, knowing that if the nuns really wanted to get in, he wouldn't be able to stop them.

But, as was their routine, the nuns merely took turns banging on the door. It was an anxious few minutes before they moved on, continuing with their never-ending patrol of the halls in search of Benedict the evil monk.

JD reflected on the mistakes he had made. He'd gotten soft. In his younger days when he murdered for fun and was always in the thick of danger, he would have known instinctively that Lenny was working for Scratch. The image of Lenny shooting himself in the head flashed into JD's mind. It made no sense why the gardener would kill himself before killing JD. Either Lenny was a fucking idiot, or he was following Scratch's orders to the letter. And if that was the case then what did Scratch have planned next?

His thoughts returned to Beth. He was in no position to reach her. And she was alone with Karen.

He pressed his hand against the open wound in his chest, hoping to stem the flow of blood. Now that he was safe from the nuns, the adrenaline from his escape was fading. It was going to be hard to stay awake.

Forty Five

Sanchez could not believe his luck. Minutes after taking a piss into a pint glass, he'd tricked some loser in a blue jumpsuit into drinking the whole lot. The piss was so fresh it still had steam coming off it. Consequently, it came as no surprise when the loser in the jumpsuit turned and ran away, looking like he was ready to vomit.

Sanchez looked around the bar for someone to share the story with, but there wasn't anyone. The place was heaving with customers, but he barely knew any of them, and he certainly didn't know any of them well enough to tell them he'd been serving piss to the punters. It left him with only one option, he could tell Flake.

Flake was collecting empty glasses from around the bar area and wiping down tables with a wet rag. A smile broke out on Sanchez's face as he watched her bend over to wipe some mess from one of the tables. It was such a turn-on watching Flake clean tables. It was right up there with watching her cook his breakfast or iron his underpants. While gazing at her with love in his eyes, Sanchez relaxed a little more than he should have. A rumble in his stomach hinted at trouble, and before he could clench, he sneaked out a dirty fart.

Flake returned to the bar with a tray full of empty glasses. She sidled up next to Sanchez and placed them down on the bar in front of him.

'Seen any cops yet?' she asked.

'No, why?'

'You haven't forgotten already have you?'

'Oh, you mean about the disabled woman you beat up?'

'Yeah.'

Sanchez shook his head. 'No, I haven't seen any cops. You'll never guess what I just did though.'

Flake narrowed her eyes. 'Served someone piss?'

'He wasn't a regular.'

'Oh for Chrissakes, Sanchez! How many times have I got to tell you not to do that?'

'I didn't judge you when you hit that blind woman with her own stick.'

Flake clearly had no interest in reliving the fight with the blind lady. 'Who did you serve the piss to?' she demanded.

Sanchez looked around for any sign of the guy in the blue jumpsuit. He was nowhere to be seen. 'I think he's gone,' he said, standing on tiptoe to get a good look around the bar.

Flake frowned and then sniffed the air. 'What is that smell?' she asked.

'I think that might be me. All that excitement earlier has upset my stomach a bit.'

A few customers behind Flake turned up their noses and started looking around for the instigator of the foul aroma.

Flake grabbed a handful of Sanchez's vest and pulled his face up to hers. She spoke quietly so no one else would hear. 'What have you been eating?'

'Just some peanuts.'

'And?'

'A microwave curry pot.'

'And?'

'Some Jamaica cake.'

'*My* Jamaica cake?'

Sanchez squirmed. 'Yes.'

'How much of it?'

'All of it.'

Flake closed her eyes and took a few slow breaths. 'How long ago did you eat it?' she asked eventually.

'About ten minutes ago. I wasn't wasting time though. I ate it all while I was peeing into a pint glass.'

Flake's nostrils flared, a sure sign she was annoyed. 'You idiot,' she hissed. 'How on earth are you eating and peeing into a glass at the same time?'

'Well, what I did was....'

'I don't care. Look how busy we are! I can't cope with all this on my own.'

Sanchez knew what Flake getting at. On several previous occasions when he'd mixed peanuts, curry and Jamaica cake together for a light lunch, he'd ended up stuck on the toilet with a nasty case of the shits. If it happened again, and it felt like it was about to, then Flake would be working the bar on her own for about half an hour in the *not-to-distant-future*.

A young lady dressed as Wonder Woman walked up to the bar. 'Hi,' she said, smiling at Sanchez. 'Can I get a vodka and....' She suddenly turned pale and started blinking a lot.

'Are you all right?' Sanchez asked her.

Wonder Woman turned cross-eyed and fell backwards. She landed on the floor in the middle of a group of young people dressed as wizards.

Flake gasped and covered her mouth. 'Oh no, has that woman just fainted?'

A Harry Potter lookalike crouched down next to Wonder Woman and tried giving her mouth-to-mouth, but after a few seconds *he* turned cross-eyed and fainted too. He fell on top of Wonder Woman, with his head in her cleavage. That was the cue for all Hell to break loose. A man dressed as Hellboy stormed over and accused the unconscious Harry Potter of feeling up his girlfriend. A Hermione Granger lookalike smacked Hellboy on the ass with her magic wand, and then people in all kinds of bizarre costumes waded into a full blown bar fight.

Flake elbowed Sanchez in the gut. 'Look what you've done now!'

Sanchez winced in pain. 'I'm not sure you should have done that,' he said, holding his belly. 'I think you've jarred something loose.'

'For fuckssake! Get to the toilet right now,' Flake thundered. 'And be back by the time I've finished breaking up this fight.'

'Can't I stay and watch?'

'No, because you'll only cause more fights! This is all your fucking fault.'

'How is it my fault if Hellboy is fisting Harry Potter?'

'It's the stench of your farts that made those people pass out. NOW GO! And be back within twenty minutes.'

Flake hurdled over the bar and waded into the fight with the wizards. It was hard to tell what was knocking everyone out, Hellboy or the stench from Sanchez's ass.

Sanchez left the bar and ran to the disabled toilets. No one else ever used them, so by default they were usually the cleanest. He barged through the door and locked it behind him, unleashing another dirty fart that felt like it might have caused some follow-through. He leaned back against the door and wiped some sweat off his forehead. Judging by the gurgling sounds coming from his stomach and the smell emanating from his underpants, this one was going to be lethal. He frantically unbuckled his belt and rushed towards the toilet. To his great surprise, a small animal that looked like a mouse with wings, fell from the ceiling in front of him. It landed in the toilet bowl and made a light squelching sound.

Sanchez was confused as to why it didn't make a splash, so he approached the toilet with caution, keen to see what had become of the small winged creature. When he looked into the toilet bowl he saw a small bat lying in a pool of vomit and shit in the bottom, which explained why there was a squelch instead of a splash.

Sanchez shook his head. *"Disgusting,"* he thought to himself. *"Someone's puked in the toilet and not flushed it. There are some filthy people around."*

For a brief moment he wondered if the phrase "batshit crazy" had anything to do with the odd phenomenon of bats falling into shit-filled toilets. The stricken bat was lying on its back, so it was hard to tell if it was asleep or unconscious, or maybe even dead.

A gurgling from Sanchez's stomach reminded him there wasn't time to dwell on trivial matters such as the origin of the phrase "batshit crazy". Flake would need him back in the bar soon, and he knew from experience if he took too long, she'd be banging on the door.

The first thing he would have to do was flush the toilet. 'Sorry about this Mister Bat,' he said, apologetically.

Sanchez flushed the toilet and looked away as the bat started swirling around with the evil concoction in the bowl. While the flush took place, Sanchez unbuckled his shorts and pulled them down, ready to sit down on the toilet seat. There were some dodgy-looking splashes of liquid on the seat, but there was no time to wipe it clean.

When the toilet-flush had finished and most of the filth was gone, the bat was still there, floating in the water. Sanchez couldn't believe it was still alive. He wanted to hook it out, or at least wait for the cistern to refill so he could flush it again, but there wasn't time. He had no choice but to do his business on the bat.

As soon as he sat down on the toilet seat, it became evident that this was no ordinary peanut-curry-Jamaica-cake poop. It came out like a rocket, accompanied by some epic trumpeting noises. Normally Sanchez would have dropped a few sheets of toilet paper down first to lessen the effects of the splash-back, but there hadn't been time, so he was thankful the vomit-covered bat was there to take most of the impact.

Eventually, after quite a noisy, stinky and exceptionally sloppy dump that felt like it might never end, Sanchez breathed a sigh of relief and wiped some more sweat from his forehead. While he was wiping the sweat onto his vest, he noticed there was a blue jumpsuit on the floor next to a bin for the paper towels. There was a curious phenomenon based around the toilets in the Tapioca. Ever since the day the bar first opened, Sanchez had been finding weird things left behind in the toilets. Some of the more memorable items included inflatable unicorns, snorkels, mannequin hands, oven mitts, cucumbers, rubber chickens, Patrick Swayze facemasks, and many other things that he'd long since forgotten.

He stretched and yawned, then stood up and braved a look down the pan. As he expected, it was a mess. There was shit everywhere, and right in the middle of the brown mountain of slop was the face of the bat. Its eyes were open and it was looking at Sanchez with panic all over its face, as well as poop. The poor little creature was in shock.

'Hey there little fella?' said Sanchez. 'Are you okay?'

The bat did not reply. It looked optimistically at Sanchez, like it was hoping he would rescue it. Unfortunately for the bat, that was never going to happen. Sanchez reached out for the flushing lever and, out of a sense of compassion he issued a warning to the bat.

'Take a deep breath buddy, you're going round again.'

He flushed the toilet once more, and watched to see what became of the bat and the shit. It was like seeing a giant walnut whip swirling around in the loo. This time the bat went down the U bend with everything else. Sanchez sat back down on the sticky, wet seat and reached over to the wall to grab some toilet paper, but all he found was a circular piece of cardboard.

Dammit. No toilet paper. Again.

He pulled his shorts up and headed over to the paper towel dispenser. That was empty too, leaving him with no option but to wipe his ass on the discarded blue jumpsuit. It was a little rough, but with a bit of initiative Sanchez found that the sleeves and legs of the jumpsuit could be used to wipe in an efficient "canoeing" motion that really ought to be more popular with people suffering from the shits. When he eventually finished he shoved the blue and brown jumpsuit in the waste bin and headed back out to the bar.

To his surprise, the Tapioca was empty again. Flake was the only person in the bar area, and she was cleaning up.

'Where did everybody go?' Sanchez asked.

Flake glared at him. 'While you were in the shitter, someone from Health and Safety showed up and shut us down again.'

'How come? I thought we had all our permits?'

'We did, but then half our customers passed out because of the smell you made.'

'Oh.'

She threw a damp cloth at Sanchez. It landed on his face, and it was remarkably cooling. He peeled it off and was surprised to see Flake smiling at him.

'This has worked out perfectly,' she said. 'Now I can get changed and go to the Mayor's office. I was worried I'd be late, but thanks to you, I'll make it on time.'

Sanchez played it off like it was his plan all along. 'Well there you go,' he said. 'The things I do for you, eh?'

'What took you so long in there anyway? Flake asked. 'I was beginning to worry that you'd fallen into the toilet again.'

'It's the darndest thing,' Sanchez replied. 'There was a bat in the shitter. I shat all over it and flushed it away. And then there was no toilet paper, so I had to canoe myself clean with a jumpsuit I found in there.'

Flake looked bewildered. 'You flushed a bat down the toilet?'

'Yeah.'

'Have you not seen that film *Alligator?*'

'No, why?'

'I saw it when I was a kid,' Flake continued. 'I can't remember it exactly, but at the beginning someone flushed a baby alligator down the toilet. It lived in the sewer for a while afterwards, eating all the turds until it grew to an enormous size, then I think it came back up and ate the people who flushed it down the toilet.'

Sanchez swallowed hard. 'Do you think a bat could get big enough to eat a person?'

Flake shrugged. 'I dunno, probably not. But if you sleep with the light on you should be okay. Bats don't like the light.' She sniffed the air. 'You stink. I'll tell you what, you finish cleaning the tables, and I'll run you a bath while I get ready to go out.'

Forty Six

Beth and Karen had heard the gunfire, the pounding of feet on the landing outside, the loud boom of JD's gun and then the sound of the nuns rushing back downstairs. After that, nothing.

'I hate this,' said Beth. I want to know what's going on.'

Karen was standing in front of her, staring at the door. 'I think it's over,' she said.

'You think they found the monk?'

Karen turned around. She had a blank look on her face. 'My work here is over,' she said.

The last thing Beth needed was Karen acting weird. She was a cop, and cops were supposed to be cool under pressure.

'What are you talking about?' Beth asked her.

Karen looked up at the ceiling and held her arms out in a weird Christ-like pose. 'Praise be to the Prince of Darkness,' she said, her face twitching uncontrollably.

'Seriously, what are you talking about?' said Beth, backing away.

Karen stopped staring at the ceiling and lowered her gaze, focusing on Beth. The friendly cop had gone, replaced by a vacant, dead-eyed lunatic. She grinned at Beth, but also stared right through her, like only a psycho can. 'My time of glory is here,' she said.

Beth tensed up. 'Karen, calm down. It'll be okay,' she said, hoping to bring the ginger-haired policewoman back to reality.

Karen's voice went up a few levels. 'I give myself to you, my Lord!' she yelled. 'So that I may live in eternal glory!'

Beth was fraught with indecision. Clearly, Karen had gone mental. The sensible thing to do might be to attack her, but Beth didn't rate her chances of winning a fight with a cop. Karen had broad shoulders and a man's chin.

Karen zoned out into a creepy trance, and laughed, a loud horrible cackle, then she swivelled around on her feet, turning her back on Beth. She walked up to the door. Her hand reached out to open it.

'Don't do that!' Beth screamed at her.

Karen ignored her. She turned the knob and flung the door wide open, then she positioned herself in the doorway, blocking much of Beth's view of the outside.

Beth yelled at her. 'Shut the door!'

Too late. A nun appeared on the landing in front of Karen, just as Beth had feared. Its giant figure filled the doorway, and its charred black face loomed over Karen. Beth wanted to yell at the dumb cop some more, but couldn't for fear it might draw the nun's attention her way.

The nun reached out and placed its black charred hands on Karen's shoulders. It tilted its head to one side and opened its gaping black mouth. With an almighty roar it spewed a lungful of raging hot fire into Karen's face. The fire made a horrible whooshing sound and Karen's head lit up like a giant match. She screamed and tried to wriggle free from the nun's grip, but the nun was a big, strong motherfucker and had no intention of releasing her. It spat fire over her neck and shoulders, the flames spilling over onto the open door. Karen's face melted away, while the flames crackled and spread down her body.

The stench of burning flesh was horrendous, and the heat from the fire turned the room into an oven. The air in the room blurred up and everything became out of focus, and unbearably hot. Beth found it hard to breathe, and even though she was struggling to see anything, she caught sight of another nun on the landing behind the one that was barbecuing Karen.

Beth panicked and looked for somewhere to hide. There was only one place.

The closet.

Its doors were already open, so Beth jumped inside and pulled them shut. The bright light from the flames vanished, replaced by a claustrophobic darkness. Smoke trickled in through the cracks underneath the doors and floated up towards Beth's face.

Wooden closets were probably very high up on the list of "the shittiest places to hide in the event of a fire," but in Beth's current predicament it was the *only* place to hide. And the fire wasn't the only thing she had to hide from. With the door to the room open, the nuns started filtering in.

Forty Seven

The Church of the Blessed St Ursula was rarely busy during the day. Rex passed only one person on his way down the aisle in the main hall, and that was an old man sleeping off a hangover on the floor between two rows of pews.

Rex marched up to Papshmir's office and banged on the door three times. He shouted through it. 'Papshmir, are you in there? It's Rex.'

'Come on in.'

Rex pushed the door open and saw Papshmir sitting behind a desk, reading a thick hardback book. He was dressed in an official black church robe, with a silver cross hanging in front of his chest on a chain. He didn't look up as Rex walked in, preferring instead to finish a passage of the book he was so engrossed in.

'What's up, my friend?' he asked, turning the page in his book.

Rex placed both hands down on the edge of the desk and cast a long shadow over the holy man.

'Anything you wanna tell me?' he asked in a husky voice.

Pasphmir placed a bookmark between the pages of his book and closed it. He took off his reading glasses and smiled at Rex. 'Like what?' he asked.

'Like where the fuck Melvin Melt is?'

'Melt?'

'Yeah, Melt. We shoved him through the portal into your bathroom the other night, just like we agreed. So where is he now, and what's he doing?'

Papshmir looked confused. 'You shoved him into my bathroom? Are you sure?'

Rex studied the priest's face. It was hard to read, on account of Papshmir being all old and stuff. Was he playing dumb? Or was he actually an idiot?

'Me and Elvis broke Melvin Melt out of prison the other night, just like you asked,' Rex replied. 'And we transferred him into your bathroom, just like we said we would. Are you telling me you didn't see him?'

Papshmir's face finally revealed something. His eyes opened wide in horror. 'You did what? Fuck-a-duck! You left him in my bathroom without checking if I was here? You idiot! Tell me you're kidding!'

'Why the fuck would I be kidding?'

'Cunting Hell,' Papshmir stood up and walked over to a window. He stared out into the churchyard. 'You know that man's dangerous, right?' he said.

'Of course I know,' said Rex. 'I broke him out of Death Row, didn't I!'

Papshmir turned away from the window and laughed. 'Yes, that was a pretty big clue I suppose.'

Rex didn't see the funny side. 'Paps, If you didn't see him, why the fuck didn't you call me and ask where he was?'

Papshmir chewed on his bottom lip. 'Are you sure you stuck him in *my* bathroom and not someone else's?'

'I'm one hundred-fucking-percent-fucking sure it was your bathroom.'

'So where the fuck is he?'

'That's what *I'm asking you!*'

Papshmir walked back to his desk and sat down on his chair. 'Oh this is so bad,' he said, gnawing at his fingers. 'I swear to you, I never fucking saw him.'

Rex shook his finger at the priest. 'I hope you realise Paps, if Scratch finds out what we did, we're all dead, and that includes you. In fact, I'll have no qualms about lying to Scratch and telling him that you were responsible for all of it.'

'Oh, *fuck no*, don't do that!'

Rex calmed down a little. 'Paps, you know there was a guy murdered outside your church the other night, don't you?'

'There was?'

'Yes. In the early hours of the morning, a few hours after we sent Melt into your bathroom.'

'I've heard nothing about this,' said Papshmir, visibly concerned. 'Who was murdered?'

'Someone called Mark Hasell.'

Papshmir grasped the silver cross on the chain around his neck. 'Oh no. Who did it?'

'Someone who hates homosexuals.'

'Mark Hasell wasn't homosexual.'

'Well we've got several other victims who were, and a cop who was investigating the case. The killer has ripped out the eyes and tongue of all his victims.'

Papshmir looked stunned. 'No fucking way! That's like what happened five years ago!'

'Yes, it is,' said Rex. 'I remember those murders well, obviously. Now tell me, was Mark Hasell having any kind of sexual activity with men?'

Papshmir nodded. 'He was married, but he regularly came to confession and admitted to sleeping with men behind his wife's back.'

'So he *was* gay!'

'I think is the term you're looking for is bisexual.' A light suddenly went off in Papshmir's eyes. 'Hang on a minute,' he said. 'If Mark Hasell was murdered outside *here,* then why haven't the Police been to see me about it? I haven't even seen an ambulance round here.'

'Cops aren't investigating these murders,' said Rex.

'Huh?'

'The Mayor doesn't want the rest of the world hearing about it, not with the Lunar Festival in full swing.'

'The Mayor's a cunt.'

'I've never met him,' said Rex. 'But I'll take your word for it. So, my question to you is, who would be going around town murdering gay men and making it look like Archie Somers did it? And why?'

Papshmir closed his eyes. 'You think it's Melvin Melt, don't you?'

'He's right up there on my list, Paps. Now are you one hundred percent sure you haven't seen him?'

'I swear on your life, I never saw him. I've been waiting for you to show up here with him ever since I asked you to break him out of prison. I saw on the news that he'd escaped, so I was sure you had him.'

Rex walked over to a cream-coloured sofa by the wall and sat down. He took a deep breath and tried to work out what the fuck was going on.

'Are you okay?' Pasphmir asked. 'Would you like some wine?'

'No, I've just had some with my dinner, thanks,' Rex replied. 'Listen Paps, we go back a long way. In the past, I've looked after this church for you while you were away on your pilgrimages and shit.'

'And I'm grateful for that,' said Papshmir. 'Particularly the time you and Elvis saved the congregation from those vampires on that Halloween night. That was an important night for the future of Santa Mondega.'

'Yeah yeah,' said Rex. 'My point is, I feel like *you* owe *me* a favour.'

'Sure, anything.'

'Good, so answer me this, if you never saw Melvin Melt when we pushed him into your bathroom, then where do you think he would go?'

'Beats me.'

'Take a guess, Paps.'

Papshmir reached into a drawer on his desk and pulled out a pack of cigarettes. He took one out with his teeth and stared into space for a while, thinking about an answer to Rex's question

'You need a light?' Rex asked.

'Huh, no, it's okay.'

Papshmir opened his drawer again and fumbled around looking for a lighter. He eventually found one and turned away to light the cigarette. It lit up and he inhaled deep and long while he continued to ponder Rex's question. After blowing a smoke-ring up in the air he finally answered. 'My guess is, Melvin Melt would get as far away from Santa Mondega as he possibly could. I mean, why would he stay here?'

'So he could commit some more murders?' Rex suggested sarcastically.

Papshmir scrambled around in his drawer and pulled out an ashtray. He tapped some ash from his cigarette into it while he mulled things over. 'There's nothing in Melvin Melt's history to suggest he had any dislike of gay men,' he said. 'And none of his previous murders were brutal. He was just poisoning people discreetly. If you're looking for Melt for these new murders, I think you're barking up the wrong tree.'

'I thought he was murdering people who broke the Ten Commandments?' said Rex.

'That's right. But homosexuality isn't mentioned in the Ten Commandments.'

'Adultery is though.'

'Were all your murder victims adulterers then?'

Rex squeezed the arm of the sofa with his metal hand, digging hard into it. 'You're not helping much, Paps.'

'I'm very sorry about that.'

If Papshmir hadn't been a friend for so many years, Rex would have been hurling him around the room by now. But on account of their friendship, he showed some restraint.

'Okay Paps, there's one other thing you might be able to help me with. It's probably unconnected, but I'm curious about it anyway.'

'Of course, fire away,' said Papshmir.

'I was at the morgue earlier today and the guy that works there, Taylor Taylor, he says that five years ago when Somers committed all his murders, someone dressed as Darth Maul came and took the Mystic Lady's dead body away to be buried somewhere else.'

'What's Darth Maul?'

'It's a character from a movie, but that's not important. What I wanted to ask you about was the funerals. You must have done them for the victims five years ago. Did you do Annabel's, and if so, did you see her body?'

Papshmir frowned. 'Why would you want to know about that?'

'I don't. But I figure Annabel would want to know.'

Papshmir took another drag on his cigarette and thought for a second. 'I remember doing the funeral ceremonies for you and Elvis,' he said. 'But you're right, there was no funeral for Annabel. I wouldn't stress about it though. It's not unusual for someone to be transferred to another parish for his or her funeral. It happens all the time.'

'Even here, in Santa Mondega?'

'Yes. The guy that took her was probably a relative. I doubt it's anything to worry about.'

'I never said it was a guy,' said Rex.

'Huh?'

'I never said it was a guy that came and took Annabel's body away. I just said it was *someone* who looked like Darth Maul.'

'Oh,' Papshmir laughed. 'Sorry, I was just being presumptuous. Darth Maul sounds like a man's name.'

'Right.' Rex stood up. 'I'd better be on my way. Don't go anywhere, Paps, because I might be back.'

'May God be with you Rex.'

Rex left Papshmir's office and headed back through the church hall. In all the years he had known Papshmir, the preacher had never lied to him. But something was up, because Papshmir was acting strange, and everything he said sounded like bullshit. Rex just couldn't figure out why.

Forty Eight

Smoke was filtering into the closet, and bringing with it the smell of burning flesh, courtesy of Karen's smouldering corpse. A bead of sweat dripped down Beth's forehead onto her eyelid.

"I need to get out of here."

Hiding in the closet had bought Beth some valuable seconds. But once Karen's barbecued body crumpled onto the floor, it was a question of what would reach the closet first, the flames spreading from her body, or the fire-breathing nuns. Beth had no plan of escape, just a forlorn hope that someone would come to her rescue. She leaned against the back of the closet to get as far away from the incoming danger as possible. In doing so, she stepped on something by her feet. It sank into the floor and set in motion a grinding mechanism in the wall behind her.

The back of the closet turned like a revolving door. Beth moved with it and rotated a full 180' degrees before stepping off into a much cooler place with no undead nuns in it, none that she could see anyway. Her new surroundings, while preferable to the smoky closet, were covered in total darkness.

She waved her hands around and felt something soft by her side, like wool. It disconcerted her and she retracted her hand immediately, fearing she had awoken something. Nothing stirred, so she took a step forward with her hands out in front of her. They settled on a smooth surface. She moved her hands in a circular motion. It was wood. Was this another closet?

She pushed harder to try and move it, knowing that she could end up walking into a room full of fire-breathing nuns. A gentle click preceded a ray of light filtering in through a small gap, confirming that she was in some kind of closet, parallel to the one she'd been in before. She pushed the door open and poked her head out. She was in someone's bedroom. So far, no nuns.

The room looked lived in. There was a dressing table and chair opposite the closet. Elsewhere in the room there was a bed, a chest of drawers and a large window with its curtains half drawn. The last thing Beth noticed was a man standing in the corner staring at her. It startled her and she took a sharp intake of breath. The man was wearing a long brown hooded robe with a thick white string belt. He had grey hair around his ears, but he was bald on top.

Beth wanted to duck back inside the closet and hide, but it was too late for that. She stepped into the room and smiled nervously at the man. He was definitely a monk, and if he didn't turn out to be Benedict of Assisi, she was going to be mightily disappointed.

The monk looked more terrified than Beth. He clutched his chest as if he was having a heart attack. Then he held up a large metal crucifix that he was wearing on a chain around his neck, hoping it would ward Beth off. Despite being pretty fucking terrified herself, Beth raised her hands to reassure the monk that she meant him no harm.

'I'm not one of the nuns,' she said.

'Who are you?' the monk replied, breathing heavily.

'I'm Beth. Have you seen a couple of men come this way?'

'No. What men?'

'Never mind. Are you Benedict?'

The monk lowered his crucifix because his hand was trembling so much he was struggling to hold it up. 'How did you get in here?' he asked.

Beth decided to work on the assumption that this was Benedict. And that meant it was time for some serious bullshit. If she had any chance of finding out what had happened to JD then she was going to have to get this asshole out of his bedroom and into the hands of the fire-breathing nuns.

'I've been sent by God,' she announced, almost blushing, such was the magnitude of the bullshit.

'Sent by God? What witchcraft is this?' said Benedict, eyeing her with suspicion.

'There's nothing to be afraid of,' said Beth, taking a cautious step towards him. 'I'm here to help you.'

'Help me? How?'

'The nuns, they're after you, yes?'

'Have you seen them?'

'Yes.'

'They've got no faces!'

Beth nodded. 'I know, scary isn't it?'

'It's downright terrifying. Who are you?'

'I've come to help you. I'm an angel.'

Benedict's jaw dropped open. 'What?'

'God sent me to rescue you from the nuns. You're Benedict, yes?'

Benedict's shoulders relaxed and he let out a deep sigh. 'Oh praise be,' he said. 'I am Benedict. You've answered my prayers. Can you get me out of here?'

'That's what I'm here to do,' said Beth. 'But in order for your soul to be saved, you must first show that you have faith in God.'

'I do have faith,' said Benedict. He took a step towards her with his hands outstretched, like he wanted a hug. 'Just get me out of here. What *are* those things out there?'

'They're evil spirits,' said Beth. 'The ghosts of the nuns you burned alive.'

'I didn't burn them alive!'

'It's okay,' said Beth growing more confident with her bullshit. 'God admires your work greatly.'

'He does?'

'Oh yes. Those nuns deserved their fate.'

Benedict wiped his forehead with his hand and shook some sweat onto the floor. 'Those clothes you're wearing,' he said, staring at Beth's attire. 'Are those angel robes?'

'Yes, we wear futuristic clothes in Heaven, so that when we come to earth, people can see that we're different.'

'Oh, I see,' said Benedict, nodding like what Beth said made sense. 'So how do we get out of here?' he asked, his voice sounding calmer than before.

'You must prove your faith to God. Face your fears and trust in the Lord to deliver you from evil.'

'I can do that. Just show me how.'

Beth pointed at the door in the corner of the room. 'Hold up your crucifix and walk through that door.'

Benedict's eyes almost popped out of his head. 'Have you lost your mind?'

'Do you want to get out of this place or not?'

'Yes, but those nuns out there, they breathe fire.'

Beth clasped her hands together in front of her chest to add some theatrics to her performance. 'Benedict, God is asking you to show you have faith in him. Open that door and walk through it and you will be taken into the Lord's bosom.'

Bosom, great word, she thought to herself. Definitely has a Biblical sound to it.

'The Lord's bosom? You mean Heaven?'

'Yes, confront your fears, show your faith in God and you will walk through that door into the Kingdom of Heaven.'

Benedict suddenly seemed to stop falling for the bullshit. He eyed Beth with suspicion. 'If you're an angel, where are your wings?' he asked.

'My wings?' Beth needed some new lies, and fast. 'Uh, well, I don't have them yet. Only when you walk through that door into the bosom of the Lord will I get my wings. This is my trial to become a fully-fledged angel. If I cannot spare your soul, I don't get my wings.'

Benedict didn't look convinced. More bluffing was required. Beth was aware that she was already quoting some dubious facts from the film *It's a Wonderful Life*, but there was no way a monk from the 1800's would have seen the film, so she went all the way in with her bluffing.

'Did you know that every time you hear a bell ring, it means an angel has just gotten her wings?' she said.

'No, I didn't know that.'

'Well, when you walk through that door you will hear a bell ring, and I will get my wings because I will have shown you the way to Heaven. Maybe one day you will get your wings too.'

Beth was pretty impressed with herself. Considering she was making it all up as she went along, she felt like she was being quite convincing.

Benedict looked at the door, and then back at Beth, his face showing signs that he might be doubting her. 'How do I know what you're saying is true?' he asked.

'You don't. That's what faith is, believing in God without question. Make your decision now. But know that if you choose *not* to take the path I have offered you, I will leave, and you will remain here in your personal Hell for all eternity because you rejected the Lord.'

Benedict clasped his crucifix so tight that his fingers turned white. 'I don't believe you,' he said.

'Well you should. If you don't open that door, it's a matter of time before those nuns get you.'

Benedict let go of his crucifix and reached for the door. His hand teetered over the deadbolt that was keeping it locked from the inside. All he had to do was slide it aside and open the door. Beth was praying he would do it. His fingers twitched, occasionally reaching for the bolt, only to back away again a moment later.

After a few moments, the monk went completely still. He stiffened and then turned back to Beth.

'You're a liar,' he said matter-of-factly. He was calm, far too calm. His eyes shone with hunger and desire. He slunk towards Beth, untying the knot on his rope belt as he moved. 'I'm going to have to teach you a lesson.'

Forty Nine

In all his years living in Santa Mondega, Elvis had never been to the library. He couldn't even remember the last time he'd read a book. But he and Jasmine were about to enter one of the biggest and oldest buildings in the city.

The library was impressive from the outside, standing three stories high. It had a set of concrete steps leading up to the entrance. Everything was spotlessly clean, with the exception of an unpleasant black stain on the sidewalk nearby, where a Santa Claus had been burned alive a few years earlier.

'This place looks so cool,' said Jasmine as they climbed the steps to the front entrance. 'We should become members.'

'That's not a good idea,' said Elvis. 'I heard that the government keeps records of every book you ever borrow from a library. It's one of the ways they snoop on you. Before the Internet came long, they used libraries to track the records of the local perverts.'

Jasmine gasped. 'I bet Rex is a member.'

'I think he is.'

Jasmine flipped over an "OPEN" sign on the door so that it read "CLOSED", ensuring that anyone else thinking of coming in would see it and turn away. Once they were inside they headed up a set of stairs that led into a magnificent hall filled with shelves of books that went all the way up to the ceiling.

'Wow!' said Jasmine gawping at all the rows of bookshelves. 'It would take you weeks to read all these.'

'Years honey,' said Elvis. 'In fact, make that decades.'

The only person still in the library was an elderly woman sitting behind the reception desk. She was wearing a blue cardigan over a grey blouse, and she had silver hair, tied up in a bun. Like all good librarians she also had a pair of thin spectacles that she peered over the top of when anyone came in. When she saw Elvis and Jasmine walking up to her reception desk, she squinted and tensed up like she was about to have a fit.

Jasmine whispered in Elvis's ear. 'It's true then.'

'What is?'

'Sanchez told me that people who work in libraries always wear cardigans.'

'Do they?'

'That's what Sanchez says. I wonder why that is?'

'Who cares?'

'I do.'

'Then ask this woman, she'll know.'

Jasmine didn't get a chance to ask because as soon as they arrived at the reception desk, the librarian made it clear they weren't welcome.

'We close in two minutes,' she said with a fake smile.

'That's okay,' said Elvis. 'We won't be long.' He looked down at the name badge on her cardigan. 'Would you be able to help us, Rosemarie?'

'What do you want?'

'I was wondering if you have a book with no name by an anonymous author?'

Rosemarie rolled her eyes. 'Oh God,' she said wearily. 'No we don't, but we do have a book with no pages and no cover.'

'What's it about?' Elvis asked.

The librarian clenched her fists and did some slow breathing exercises to keep calm.

Jasmine whispered in Elvis's ear. 'Let me handle this.' She leaned over the desk to get into Rosemarie's personal space. 'We're looking for books by anonymous authors,' she said. 'Do you have a section for those?'

Rosemarie sighed. 'There are hundreds of books by anonymous authors. But they usually have titles. If you could give me the title of the book you're looking for, I can find it on my computer.'

'This one doesn't have a title,' Jasmine replied. 'It's special.'

'So are you,' Rosemarie muttered under her breath.

'What's that you say?'

Rosemarie sighed again, which was beginning to get on Jasmine's nerves.

'No one is stupid enough to write a book and not give it a title,' the librarian pointed out. 'If you don't know what the title is, then you're wasting your time, and mine. And it's now closing time, so I'm afraid you'll have to leave and come back tomorrow.'

'Actually, you're already closed,' said Jasmine. 'I put the CLOSED sign up in the window when we came in. It's just you and us in here.'

'I beg your pardon?'

Jasmine grabbed a fistful of Rosemarie's cardigan. She yanked the old lady forward, smashing her head on the raised part of the desk. There was an unpleasant crunch followed by a yelp of pain and a clattering noise as the librarian's glasses fell off. Jasmine pushed her back into her seat but kept hold of her cardigan.

Tears welled up in Rosemarie's eyes. 'What on earth do you think you're doing?' she asked.

'I'm giving you motivation to be less of a cunt,' Jasmine replied.

Elvis felt bad for the librarian. But the old bag had asked for it, and once Jasmine started beating someone up there was usually no stopping her.

'Rosemarie,' he said, in an unthreatening manner, 'could you please find us the library records for the people on this list?'

He handed her a slip of paper with the names of the murder victims on it. 'It's for a murder investigation.'

Rosemarie retrieved her glasses and slipped them back on. She took the piece of paper and stared at it, blinking and squinting because she had tears in her eyes. 'I knew Mark Hasell well,' she said. 'I heard he had passed away, but no one said it was murder.'

'Well it was,' said Jasmine, letting go of her cardigan. 'Everyone on that list is dead, and they've all been killed by the same person.'

Rosemarie wiped a tear from her cheek. 'Why didn't you just give me this list to start with, instead of smashing my face into the desk?'

Jasmine grabbed her cardigan and smashed her face into the desk again, harder than before. 'We'll ask the questions,' she said.

Elvis put his hand on Jasmine's shoulder. 'Maybe I should do the interrogating,' he said.

Jasmine released Rosemarie and stepped back. 'I'm sorry about that,' she said. 'I'm a little uptight. A midget sexually assaulted me earlier today, and I also had some metal fingers stuck in my butt for an hour last night, so I'm not really myself. You know how it is.'

Rosemarie nodded. 'Yeah, sure.'

Elvis took over the questioning, and spoke softly. 'We're very grateful for your help,' he said. 'And I really like your cardigan.'

'You do?' said Rosemarie, brightening up a little.

'Yeah, the way it clings to your shoulders like that, it makes you look so sophisticated.'

'That's what my granddaughter says!'

'You're a granny?' said Elvis, feigning shock. 'Noooo, surely you're not old enough?'

Rosemarie rearranged her cardigan and broke out half a smile for Elvis. 'I do go for a lot of long walks,' she said.

'I'll bet.' Elvis leaned in a little closer. 'Could you do me a kindness?'

'I suppose.'

'Great, I just need you to print off a list of each of our victims records, showing every book they've ever borrowed, then we'll be on our way.'

Rosemarie nodded. 'Of course,' she said, wiping another tear away. 'It'll just take me a minute.'

She had wheels on her chair so she rolled herself across to a computer behind her. She tapped away at the keyboard and after about ten seconds a nearby printer burst into life.

Jasmine whispered in Elvis's ear. 'What a bitch.' Then she shouted at Rosemarie. 'Hurry up! Come on, quicker.'

'Go easy on her,' said Elvis. 'She's being really helpful.'

'Did you not see the look she gave me just now when I told her about my butt?'

'No. What did she do?'

'Pffft, well, she was all judgemental, like she's never had anything stuck in her ass!'

Elvis's phone vibrated in his pocket. He checked it and saw an incoming call from Rex, so he answered it promptly.

'Hey Rex, wassup?'

'I just paid a visit to Papshmir.'

'And?'

'And he says he never saw Melvin Melt. He claims he knew nothing about Mark Hasell's murder too.'

'You believe him?'

'No. Something really fucking weird is going on and I can't figure it out. Did you have any luck at the library?'

'We're there now. The librarian is just printing off a list of all the books borrowed by the victims. She's being very helpful.'

'Is she wearing a cardigan?'

'Uh, yeah. What? Why do you ask that?'

'No reason, just a rumour I heard somewhere.'

'Look, we're gonna be a while yet. When we're done we'll meet you back at the Tapioca, okay?'

'Yep, fine. See you there. Good luck.'

Elvis slipped his phone back in his pocket just as Rosemarie swivelled round on her chair. She pointed at the printer on the side of her desk, next to a tin of pencils.

'All the records you wanted are printing off now,' she said. 'Apart from Bob Muncher. He doesn't have an account here.'

The printer churned out about six sheets of paper. Jasmine took them off the printer and handed the top three to Elvis. 'You check those, I'll check these,' she said.

'Is that all you need?' Rosemarie asked. 'Because I'd like to go home now.'

'I bet you would,' said Jasmine, giving her a feisty stare.

'We'll just be a few minutes,' said Elvis.

He started flicking through the printouts. Mark Hasell had been very active user of the library, borrowing hundreds of books. This looked like it might be quite tedious.

'Can you see a book with no name on any of your lists?' he asked Jasmine.

'What will it look like?'

'It won't have a name.'

'That's not helpful.' Jasmine ran her finger down the top sheet as she flicked through the list of books. 'These guys read a lot of shit,' she commented.

Rosemarie chirped up. 'Hassan Altabar didn't. He only ever borrowed one book according to his records. I noticed it before I printed it off.'

Jasmine flipped over to her second sheet of paper. 'I've got him here,' she said.

'Did he borrow a book with no name?' Elvis asked.

Jasmine shook her head. 'No, but the book is by an anonymous author.'

'What's it called?'

'The Gay Man's Guide To Anal Sex.'

'The Gay Man's Guide To Anal Sex?' Elvis said, disbelieving that such a title could exist.

'That's what it says here.'

Elvis scanned through his printouts to look for any sign of it. He spotted it pretty quickly. 'Fuck me, Mark Hasell borrowed that book too.'

Jasmine yelped and held up another sheet of paper. 'So did Andrew Chutney.'

'This is it,' said Elvis. 'This is the clue we've been looking for.' He clicked his fingers at Rosemarie. 'Hey, *cardigan lady,* can you look that book up on your system?'

Rosemarie returned to her computer and tapped in some information. The results came up on her screen very quickly. 'Here it is,' she said. 'Not many people have ever borrowed it.' She ran her finger down the list of people.

'Are they all on that list I gave you?' Elvis asked.

'It looks like it.'

'Where's the book now?' Jasmine asked. 'Is it here?'

'It's been out of circulation for some time,' said Rosemarie. 'The last person to borrow it never returned it. And he's the only one not on your list of victims.'

'What's his name?' Elvis asked.

'It's that fat creep from the Tapioca, Sanchez Garcia.'

Fifty

Beth had to think fast before the dirty monk disrobed. Benedict had full-on rape-eyes and he was eyeing her like a piece of meat. His nervous demeanour had gone, replaced by what was probably his true self.

Beth tried to think of something that she knew about Heaven and Angels that someone from the nineteenth century wouldn't. The answer came to her much quicker than she expected. As the monk approached her, she reached into a pocket on her jeans and pulled out her cell-phone.

'Would you like to see what Heaven looks like?' she asked him.

Benedict hesitated and stopped short of exposing himself to her. He saw the phone in her hand and the angry look in his eyes faded.

'You... you can show me Heaven?' he asked, wrapping his robe tighter.

'Here, look.'

Beth pulled up some photos on her phone. She scrolled to the picture she had taken of the pink sky on the highway in Texas. She held it up for Benedict to see.

'Here, this is one of my favourite parts of Heaven,' she said.

Benedict stared in wonderment at the picture. 'What witchcraft is this?' he asked as he retied the knot on his belt.

Beth groaned. 'Why is everything about witchcraft with you?'

Benedict pointed at her phone. 'What is this creation?'

'All angels have one of these,' Beth lied. 'Usually I use it to show non-believers what Heaven looks like. But you being a monk, I shouldn't have to show you really, should I?'

Benedict leaned in close and studied the picture on Beth's phone. 'What are those strange trees?' he asked.

'We call them pylons. They grant wishes to people.'

'They do?'

'Oh yeah. But only those who have faith in the Lord and are willing to show it.'

'So that's really Heaven?' he asked, his face lighting up.

Beth resisted the urge to say, *"No, it's Texas",* and instead said, 'It's one of the places you can visit *if* you have the courage to walk through that door.'

'It's beautiful,' said Benedict. 'But where are all the angels?'

Beth pulled the phone away and flicked through for a picture of any people who might look remotely angelic. The first photo she found was one she'd taken of Flake and Sanchez kissing on a beach a few years earlier. Flake looked fantastic in a white bikini. She showed it to Benedict.

'Here, this is a typical moment in Heaven.'

Benedict's jaw dropped. 'Wow, is she an angel?' he asked.

'She sure is. And there's plenty more like her. And you see that fat, hairy man with her? He was in a similar situation to you. He walked through his door, and now he spends eternity with a different angel every day.'

'Even though he's ugly?'

'No one is ugly in the eyes of the Lord.'

It looked like Beth was finally getting through to Benedict.

'Will I get to meet *her* in Heaven?' he asked, pointing at Flake.

'I can arrange it for you. But you have to prove that you have faith in the Lord. So go on, open the door and she's all yours.'

Benedict looked at the door, then back at the picture of Flake in her bikini, and Sanchez in his swimming trunks.

'Could you open the door for me?' he asked.

Beth wanted to slap him. 'Okay,' she said, staying calm. 'I'll open it for you, but you must walk through it.'

Benedict stepped aside. Beth tucked her phone back in her pocket and walked up to the door. The image of Karen the cop burning alive flashed into her mind, making her hesitate. Her hand teetered over the deadbolt just as Benedict's had done before. Time wasn't on her side. She had to keep up the pretence that she was an angel. Benedict had bought into it so far, the stupid, gullible born-in-the-nineteenth-century-nun-murdering-monk bastard. Beth sucked in a deep breath through her nose, hoping Benedict wouldn't see how nervous she was, then as quietly as she could, she slid the deadbolt to the side and twisted the doorknob.

'Are you ready?' she asked the monk.

His face tensed. 'I…. I'm not sure.'

'Come, stand beside me. It will be fine, I promise. God is watching.'

Benedict edged over to Beth and stood alongside her. Before he had time to change his mind and back out, she pulled the door open, using it as a shield for herself, but opening Benedict up to whatever might lay in wait outside. He stared out at the landing and a look of relief washed over him. His shoulders relaxed and he exhaled like he'd just smoked some weed after a hard day at work.

'Oh, thank God,' he whispered. 'They've gone.'

'I told you,' said Beth. She ushered him through the door. 'Go on, nothing can hurt you now.'

Benedict stepped onto the landing. Beth took a cautious step out behind him and looked around. He was right, there were no nuns in sight. Part of her wanted to call out JD's name, but it might startle Benedict and more importantly, it might attract some faceless fire-breathers. She peered over the balcony. It was hard to see much in the poor light offered by the violet oil lamps but it looked like the nuns were gone.

Benedict turned around to face her. 'Where do we go now?' he asked.

'Just head down the main stairs and you can leave through the front door,' said Beth. 'It's perfectly safe.'

'Are you sure about this?'

'Absolutely.'

Benedict chewed on his fingernails, and for a moment Beth feared he would run back into his room. She gave him a prod and pointed to the staircase. 'Remember,' she whispered. 'God is watching.'

Benedict clasped his hands together as if he was about to pray, bowed his head at Beth, which made her feel almost like a proper angel for a brief second, then he grabbed the bannister and peered over it to check the route was clear. Beth closed her eyes and prayed he didn't see any nuns down below. When she reopened her eyes he was looking at her with a relieved smile across his face.

'They've gone,' he said. 'They've really gone.'

'I told you it would be okay.'

A pair of black hands appeared on the edge of the balcony, just behind Benedict. Beth saw them out of the corner of her eye and tried not to react. The black charred face of a nun rose up behind the hands, hauling itself up from below. Before Benedict knew what was happening, the nun had hurdled over the balcony onto the landing behind him. It swooped on him, wrapping its arms around him. One arm slid around his waist, the other across his face, muffling his screams. The long black sleeves engulfed him, and the nun dragged him back towards the staircase. More nuns appeared from all directions, swarming towards him. The only part of Benedict that was still visible was the top half of his face. His eyes pleaded for help from Beth.

The nuns amassed around Benedict and lifted him above their heads like pallbearers carrying a coffin. Beth heard his cries for help. He even screamed out her name and begged her to save him. For a fleeting moment she felt awful for what she had done to him. Then she heard him call her a "lying Jezebel whore" and the guilt subsided.

While the nuns carried the terrified monk down the stairs to the Violet room, Beth ducked back inside Benedict's bedroom to wait for JD to return.

Fifty One

Elvis yanked the steering wheel on the tour bus and swung it around a corner at high speed. Jasmine was further back in a small, confined kitchen area of the bus, trying to make a call on her phone. The wild swing of the bus sent her crashing into a cupboard door.

'Motherfucker!'

'Sorry honey,' Elvis called out. 'You had any luck yet?'

Jasmine steadied herself and checked her phone. 'He's not answering!' she yelled.

'Keep calling him,' said Elvis.

Jasmine had been trying to contact Sanchez but he wasn't answering his phone, and she couldn't bear to listen to his voicemail message because it was him singing the chorus of the Lionel Ritchie song, "Hello".

'Fuck it!' said Jasmine. 'He's probably on the shitter. I'm calling Flake. She always answers.'

She pulled up Flake's number on her phone and hit CALL. The phone rang just once before Flake answered.

'Flake! It's Jasmine, listen….'

Flake interrupted her. 'Hang on, I'll be right with you.'

What followed was a bizarre series of noises coming through Jasmine's phone. She could hear Flake cursing and smashing things. There was some screaming and groaning too, and the only thing that came through clearly was Flake calling someone a *fatheaded cunt*.

'What's going on?' said Elvis. 'Did you get hold of her or what?'

'I did,' said Jasmine. 'But I think I called at a bad time. It sounds like she's in bed with Sanchez.'

'Really?'

'Yeah. No wonder he's always got the shits. You should hear this.'

'No thanks. Just interrupt her!'

Jasmine yelled Flake's name into the phone a few times, but to no avail. It wasn't until the screaming, shouting and violent noises on the other end of the line came to an end that Flake returned to the call. She was out of breath.

'Hey Jas, what's up?'

'Is Sanchez with you?'

'No, he's probably eating a pie I made for him. Why do you want him?'

'Uh, it's just that Elvis and me have been to the library and we found out that the killer we're looking for is murdering everyone who read this book….'

'Stay down you motherfucker!'

Jasmine frowned. It wasn't the response she was expecting. 'Flake, what are you doing?'

'Oh, it's a fucking nightmare,' said Flake. 'I'm at the Mayor's office, only he's not here and two assholes just jumped me. Came at me with fucking knives, bloody great big machetes! Can you believe that?'

'Shit, are you okay?'

'Oh yeah,' Flake replied, nonchalantly. 'I kicked the shit out of them. But my new shoes are ruined.'

'Those motherfuckers! Do you want me to come down there and give you a hand?'

'No, it's okay. When I'm finished with these fuckers they won't be able to walk right for a week.'

The bus swung around another corner, sending Jasmine crashing into the cupboard again and causing her to drop her phone.

Elvis yelled at her. 'JASMINE! For Chrissakes, ask her where Sanchez is!'

Jasmine scrambled around to grab her phone before it slid underneath a seat. 'Hang on!' she yelled.

When she retrieved the phone she stood up and steadied herself by holding onto the kitchen sink.

'Flake, where exactly is Sanchez at the moment?' she asked.

'Are you okay?' Flake asked.

'Yeah, I just fell over. Where's Sanchez?'

'He should be in the bath watching *Pretty Woman* while he eats his pie.'

'You have a TV in the bathroom?'

'Yeah, we bought it yesterday so Sanchez can watch *Pretty Woman* while he's in the bath.'

'That sounds awesome. I want to try it.'

'There's room for two in our bath,' Flake replied. 'But I wouldn't recommend it. Sanchez creates his own bubbles, if you know what I mean.'

The thought of sharing a bath with Sanchez made Jasmine shudder. It was bad enough that she'd already had her hand in his shorts earlier in the day when Rex crashed the bus and everyone fell over and became entangled.

'Listen Flake, because this is serious. That serial killer who's killing all the gay people, we think he's going to kill Sanchez next!'

'But Sanchez isn't gay,' said Flake. 'Is he?'

'I'll be honest Flake, I'm confused. But the librarian told us Sanchez was the last person to borrow a book called *The Gay Man's Guide to Anal Sex.* And everyone else who's borrowed it has been murdered. Sanchez is the last one alive.'

'WHAT?'

Elvis swung the bus around another corner, which caused Jasmine to head-butt the cupboard again.

Flake yelled down the phone. 'Did you call him and warn him?'

Jasmine rubbed her head, which was throbbing. 'We tried, but I guess he's in the bath because he's not answering.'

'Oh crap! Jas get there as soon as you can. Don't let anyone kill my Sanchez!'

'Don't worry, we'll be there in two minutes.'

The line went dead, which Jasmine took as a sign Flake was on her way to the Tapioca.

'What's happening?' Elvis shouted.

'Sanchez is in the bath eating Flake's pie and watching *Pretty Woman.*'

Elvis hit the brakes and the sudden stop sent Jasmine flying. She lost her footing and fell onto the floor. The G-force made her skid head-first along the aisle of the bus until she ended up by Elvis's feet.

He looked down at her, a puzzled look on his face.

'Hi there,' Jasmine said, smiling.

'Are they both at the Tapioca?' he asked.

'No, Flake's at the town hall. Sanchez is in the bath.' Jasmine sat up. 'You know he eats pie in the bath while watching *Pretty Woman.* We should try that.'

'Yeah, sounds great. So, we're still heading to the Tapioca, yes?'

'Yes.'

Jasmine stood up and steadied herself as Elvis hit the gas and carried on speeding through the streets of Santa Mondega, swerving around vehicles and pedestrians, and honking the horn at anyone who got in his way. And there were some strange people getting in his way.

'Look at all the cool costumes!' said Jasmine, pointing at all the people on the sidewalk who were dressed up for the Lunar Festival. 'Ooh look, it's Scooby Doo!'

Elvis ignored her and kept his eyes on the road.

'Is there anywhere I can get a costume?' Jasmine asked. 'I feel kinda left out.'

'You look great as you are, honey. I like you that way.'

'Awww, really?'

'Yeah.'

Jasmine was still wearing Flake's jeans and Sanchez's blue Hawaiian shirt, so she was happy that Elvis still thought she looked hot. She grabbed the back of his head and twisted it towards her to give him a passionate kiss. It took his eyes off the road, which turned out to be a costly mistake.

He pushed Jasmine away, slammed on the brakes and yelled, 'OH SHIT!'

The reason for the "OH SHIT!" became evident when Jasmine checked the road ahead.

While they had been kissing, a naked man covered in shit had climbed out of a manhole in the middle of the road. He had his back to them so he hadn't seen them coming. Elvis hit the brakes hard, but the bus didn't stop in time. It hit the naked man with great force and knocked him over. The bus bounced up and down several times as it went over him before it eventually came to a stop in the middle of the road.

'Balls!' said Elvis. 'Who the fuck was that?'

Jasmine had seen the guy they hit but wasn't entirely sure how to describe him. 'It was a guy dressed as that thing from the movie you showed me the other week,' she said.

'What movie?'

'I think it was called Dog shit.'

'Dogma? You mean Dogma?'

'Yeah that's it. He looked like the Shit Demon in Dogma.'

Elvis checked the wing mirrors for any sign of a dead pedestrian covered in faeces. 'The Shit Demon?' he said. 'You mean *the Golgothan.*'

'Golga-what?'

'Golgothan. It's a real thing. Me and Rex had a fight with a big one a few years back.'

Jasmine opened the door on the passenger side of the bus and leaned out to look for the Shit Demon. A foul smell floated into the bus, suggesting he was close.

'Fucking hell,' said Jasmine, covering her nose. 'That smells like the toilets in Purgatory.'

'Can you see the thing we hit?' Elvis asked, wincing and covering his nose.

At the back of the bus, a brown hand reached out from underneath the chassis, followed by an angry, steaming brown face.

'Hang on, I see him!' said Jasmine. 'He's under the bus, but he's crawling out. Wow! That costume is brilliant.'

Elvis got up from his seat and joined Jasmine at the door to get a better look. The Golgothan costume was shockingly authentic. The man who climbed to his feet by the side of the bus was stark naked and covered from head to toe in steaming, sloppy turds.

'He's covered himself in real shit,' said Jasmine. 'That's got to be worthy of an award.'

'He looks pissed,' said Elvis.

'I'm not surprised!' said Jasmine. 'You hit him with the bus. I'm amazed he's still alive.'

The Shit Demon pointed a big brown finger at Elvis. 'YOU!' he growled. 'YOU'LL PAY FOR THIS!'

'We're really sorry,' said Jasmine, to the Golgothan. She turned and whispered in Elvis's ear. 'I think this guy's going to kick up a stink.'

Elvis tugged at her sleeve. 'Get back,' he said. 'He's coming over here.'

The Golgothan staggered towards the front of the bus. Jasmine pulled the door shut, not least of all because of the smell. 'I feel bad for him,' she said. 'Normally I'd suck his dick to say sorry, but it's covered in poo.'

'Sometimes it's best not to apologise,' said Elvis. 'He'll ruin our bus if we're not careful.'

The Golgothan stormed up to the passenger door and banged on it.

'Fuck off!' Elvis yelled at him.

'Let's go,' said Jasmine. 'This guy looks a bit nutty.'

The Golgothan seemed to realise they were going to "hit and run" so he stormed around to the front of the bus to block their escape route. He banged on the windscreen and yelled abuse at them in some kind of ancient foreign language.

'He's got a real shitty attitude,' said Jasmine.

'I don't like this guy,' said Elvis. 'And I don't think that's a costume.'

'It's not?'

'No. That guy's just climbed out of a sewer. And he's naked. He must be fucking mental.'

Jasmine agreed. 'We can't waste time on this piece of shit. We've got to find Sanchez.'

'Fuck it!' said Elvis. 'I'm taking this bastard down.'

He slammed his foot down on the accelerator and before the Golgothan could get out of the way, the bus hit him again, knocking him over. Once more, the bus bounced up and down as the wheels rolled over the unfortunate Shit Demon.

'Holy Crap!' Jasmine cried. 'You wiped him out!'

'Serves him right.'

The bus carried on, watched by a large audience of people on both sides of the street, who were no doubt shocked by what they'd seen. Jasmine checked the wing mirror for any sign of the Golgothan.

'Can you see him?' Elvis asked.

'No,' she replied. 'But you've left some huge skid marks in the road.'

Elvis checked the mirror on his side. 'I see him,' he said. 'He's getting back up. How the fuck did he survive that?'

'Oh, I see him now!' said Jasmine.

A couple of people had stepped in to help the Shit Demon to his feet, but as soon as he was standing again he shook them off. A moment later, Jasmine saw the brown monster vanish into thin air.

'He's gone!' she said.

'Who? The Shit Demon?'

'Yeah, he just disappeared.'

Elvis checked his wing mirror. 'Where the Hell did he go?'

SPLAT!

A sloppy lump of excrement landed on the windshield. Jasmine looked around for the source of it. 'Where the fuck did that come from?' she asked, frowning.

Elvis pointed up ahead. 'I think it was that bat. Look, over there. There's a bat covered in shit.'

A small bat was flying up ahead of them. It was moving at a startling speed, zipping past all the traffic. It wasn't long before it left the bus trailing in its wake and vanished in the distance.

'Wow, that was weird,' said Jasmine. 'That Shit Demon made a really smooth transition into a bat, didn't it? I wonder if we'll ever see it again?'

'I hope not,' said Elvis, turning on the windscreen wipers. 'It survived being run down by a bus twice and transformed itself into a bat. Whatever it is, it's bad news.'

Fifty Two

Sanchez was having the time of his life in the bath. The pie Flake had made for him was a thing of beauty. Her speciality "Eight-meat" pie had once been the most popular dish in Santa Mondega when she worked at the Olé Au Lait cafe. No one knew what the eight meats were that she used in the pie, but they were all tasty, and the gravy she drowned the meat in was something to behold. Sanchez had intended to save some of the pie for Flake to eat when she returned from her rubbish meeting with the Mayor, but the damn pie was so good, he'd gotten carried away and eaten the whole thing while he washed his armpits.

The new television that was fixed to the wall over the end of the bath wasn't fully set up yet, so Sanchez didn't have many channels to choose from. He was extremely disappointed when he couldn't find *Pretty Woman* anywhere, but he'd settled for a potentially scary movie called *The Rescuers*. The film sucked him in right from the start. It had everything, a kidnapped girl, a precious diamond called the Devil's Eye that everyone was trying to get their hands on, and Sanchez's two favourite characters, the mice who set out to rescue the girl.

The film was only halfway through when he finished his pie. The tension was unbearable because there were now some alligators trying to eat the mice. There was no way Sanchez could watch the rest of the movie without more food, so he paused the film and climbed out of the bath. After a quick rubdown with a towel he put on one of Flake's bathrobes, a pink fluffy one that he had grown quite attached to, and hurried downstairs to the kitchen to look for some more food. Before he even made it to the fridge he found a dish covered in silver foil on the sideboard. There was a piece of paper on top of the foil with Sanchez's name on it. He peeled off the foil and saw a lemon meringue pie.

'Oh Flake, you're the best!' he said, sniffing the pie and savouring the smell.

He was about to go back upstairs with it when he heard some movement in the bar area. He put the lemon meringue pie back down and headed into the bar to investigate. Flake had switched off all the lights when she went out, so he couldn't see much at all. There was a weird, low-toned "woo-woo" sound repeating over and over from somewhere, but in the darkness it was hard to tell where it was coming from.

'Hello?' Sanchez called out. 'Is someone there?'

Woo-woo..... Woo-woo.

'Flake? Is that you?'

He felt his way along the bar and ventured out into the lounge area to find the source of the noise. After tripping over a chair leg and clattering into a table, he spotted the source of the woo-wooing. In the corner of the room there was a small, bright red dot of light moving back and forth across a six-inch diameter. There was something familiar about it, but he couldn't quite place it.

'Can I help you with something?' Sanchez called out.

No one answered, so he backed away towards a light switch on the wall behind him without ever taking his eye off the red light. He felt around on the wall for the switch.

Before Sanchez found the light switch the revolving red dot leapt up about two feet and moved towards him, accompanied by some heavy, clunky footsteps. As it approached, Sanchez was able to make out the outline of the person behind the red light. It finally became clear what he was looking at. This was no man, or woman for that matter. *It was a fucking Cylon.* One of the big clunky robot things from the 1970's TV show *Battlestar Galactica.* The red light glowing back and forth was the robot's laser eye. Sanchez felt like a kid again. His Christmas wish from his childhood had come true. He had a real life Cylon in the Tapioca.

'That's fucking awesome!' he said. 'Is that you, Flake?'

'I AM A CYLON,' the giant figure replied in a robotic voice just like in the TV show.

Sanchez finally found the light switch and flicked it on. The room flickered into brightness and he quickly realised that the Cylon was way too tall to be Flake. This fucker was well over six feet tall.

'Who *is* that?' Sanchez asked, confused about which of his friends had thought to wear such a legendary costume.

As the Cylon came closer, Sanchez saw the attention to detail. This was an exact replica, complete with a laser gun holstered on one hip and a sword sheathed on the other. When it was only two tables away, the Cylon unsheathed its sword and closed in on Sanchez.

'PREPARE TO DIE!' it said.

The surge of excitement from a moment earlier vanished, replaced by an urge to piss and scream. And he knew only too well, if he pissed in Flake's pink bathrobe, she'd kill him, if the Cylon didn't get him first.

'Wait a minute,' he said, holding up his hands. 'Who are you?'

The Cylon stopped and with its free hand it reached up and removed its helmet to reveal the face of a man in his mid-thirties with a nasty case of helmet-hair. Even so, Sanchez recognised him. It was Pete the garbage man.

Sanchez pressed his hand against his chest and breathed a sigh of relief. 'Pete, how did you get in here?' he asked.

Pete grinned. 'I hid in the corner cubicle in the men's toilets while Flake was locking up. I've noticed she never checks in there when she's closing the bar down.'

'I'll have to have a word with her about that,' said Sanchez. 'Great costume though. Where did you get it?'

'Domino's.'

Sanchez nodded. 'Yeah, it's good there. I got a Batman suit from there once. Lost my deposit though because it got covered in blood. Whatever you do, don't get blood on that Cylon costume.'

'I'll try not to,' said Pete, stepping closer to Sanchez, with his sword still drawn.

'What are you doing here anyway?' Sanchez asked.

'I heard Flake was going to be at the Mayor's office, and I thought this would be my best chance to get you alone.'

'Alone? For what?'

'Don't pretend you don't know.'

Sanchez had always thought Pete was a bit creepy, but he'd also always wanted to try on a Cylon helmet. The red eye on Pete's was still moving from side to side and it looked so cool. With that in mind, Sanchez decided to forget that Pete was acting weird, and made a request.

'Any chance I can have a go with your helmet?'

'I thought you'd never ask.' Pete replied, handing him the helmet. Sanchez held it in both hands and marvelled at the rotating red light. While he was busy admiring the magnificence of Pete's helmet, he left himself vulnerable to an attack. Pete prodded his sword towards Sanchez and used it to flick open his bathrobe.

Sanchez dropped the helmet and pulled his robe shut. 'What the bejeezus are you doing?' he asked, embarrassed by his bathrobe situation.

'I've seen the way you look at me,' said Pete.

'You have?' said Sanchez grimacing. 'Don't take it personally, I'm just repulsed by you, more specifically the smell of garbage, particularly the rotten fish.'

Pete ignored him. 'When you left town a while ago, I thought I'd missed my chance. But now that you're back, I don't want to pass up the opportunity of telling you how I feel.'

'How you feel about what?'

'About you.'

'Is this because I never left a tip last Christmas? Because if it is, that was Flake's fault. She's in charge of tipping.'

'What? No. It's just when I saw that book in your garbage that time....'

'What book?'

'*The Gay Man's Guide to Anal Sex.*'

'Oh, that.'

'Yeah, I saw it and I figured it was your way of saying that you liked me.'

Sanchez tried to take on board what Pete was saying. It didn't make a lot of sense. 'I throw a book in the trash, and you think that means I like you?'

Pete blushed. 'Yeah. Does it mean something else then?'

'Er, yes. Hey look, you can have it if you want it. I've got no need for it. I've already read it.'

Pete sheathed his sword and reached out, placing one of his big metallic hands on Sanchez's shoulder. 'When I found the book, I did notice you'd turned the corner of one of the pages.'

'Did I?' Sanchez replied, eyeing up Pete's hand, and hoping he was going to remove it.

'Yes, the part about Golden Showers.'

'Oh yeah,' Sanchez nodded. 'That was the best bit.'

'If you wanted, you could pee on my Cylon outfit? I'm totally up for anything like that.'

'You'll lose your refund.'

'It's okay. I didn't rent the outfit. I bought it. It's mine.'

'Well, it'll rust,' said Sanchez, taking another step back, so that his butt was touching the wall behind him. 'Besides, I'm really not into that stuff. And I'm not gay. Ask Flake.'

'But you had the book?'

'It's a long story. I didn't mean to borrow it from the library. I picked it up by accident.'

'So why didn't you return it?'

'Are you kidding? Would you return it?'

Pete paused. 'I guess not. I would have wanted to keep it too. You must be curious to try some of the stuff in it though.'

'Nope. Not at all.'

The sound of some pots and pans crashing onto the floor in the kitchen startled both men and interrupted their conversation.

'I think someone's just smashed my back door in,' said Sanchez.

'Want me to take a look?' said Pete, drawing his sword again.

The quiet patter of footsteps came from the kitchen, moving slowly towards the bar area. Either someone had broken in, or this was the surprise party Sanchez felt he'd always deserved. He really hoped there would be a stripper hiding in a big cake. But then he remembered it wasn't his birthday. Maybe it was a *"Welcome Back to Santa Mondega"* party? That was possible. He wouldn't have invited Pete though. But the Cylon outfit was a worthy reason for him to be allowed to stay.

Sanchez tightened the belt on his bathrobe, as both men stared at the open door to the kitchen area and waited for someone to appear.

'Is this a surprise party?' Sanchez asked.

'Not that I know of,' said Pete.

Sanchez shouted out. 'Who's there?'

A tall dark figure of a man appeared in the kitchen doorway behind the bar. The man stepped into the serving area and in one swift move, pressed his hand on the bar top and handsprung over it into the lounge area where Sanchez finally got a good look at him. The intruder was dressed in loose fitting black clothes, with a cape and knee-high boots, and an eye mask that covered the top half of his face. And, just like Pete, this guy had a long sword in a sheath by his side.

'For fucks sake,' Sanchez moaned. 'We're closed, you know.'

'Oh, I know,' the man replied.

Sanchez recognised the voice but couldn't quite place it, or the man's costume. 'Are you supposed to be Grover from Sesame Street?' Sanchez asked him.

'No, you fucking clown! I'm Zorro,' the man replied, unsheathing his sword. It was a long slim, shiny sword, much bigger than Pete's.

Sanchez finally identified the intruder's voice. *'Mayor Shepherd?'* he gasped. 'What are you doing here? Flake's gone to your office to meet you there, you idiot.'

The Mayor stepped around a table and a set of chairs, edging closer to Sanchez and Pete. 'I needed Flake out of the way,' he said, his eyes focussed on Sanchez. 'You're the last one.'

'The last what?'

'The last person on the list.'

'What list?'

Pete butted in. 'Oh shit! I never realised it before. But now that he's wearing the Zorro mask I can see it...... *that's Captain Fiddler!'*

'Captain who?' Sanchez asked, bewildered.

'Captain Fiddler! He's one of the models in *The Gay Man's Guide to Anal Sex.*'

Sanchez recoiled. 'What the...' And then it hit him. 'Captain Fiddler? *Eeeewwwwww!*' You'll get slaughtered by the press if they ever see what you did with that Mannequin hand on page fifty-three.'

'That's right,' said Shepherd stepping closer and swishing his sword back and forth making a Z sign. 'There's only one copy of that book in existence and I've killed everyone who could possibly identify me from it. I thought you were the last one. But it turns out you've shown it to the fucking garbage boy too. So it looks like I'm going to have to kill both of you.'

Sanchez grabbed the laser gun from the holster on Pete's Cylon costume. He pointed it at Shepherd. 'Stay back, asshole! I'm warning you, if Flake finds out you stood her up, she'll fucking kill you.'

Pete stepped in front of Sanchez to protect him and retrieved his Cylon helmet from the floor. 'Leave this to me,' he said, squaring up to the Mayor.

Shepherd scoffed. 'What the fuck are you gonna do?'

Pete unsheathed his sword again. 'You'd better leave, or I'll ram this sword up your ass. And I know how to do it too!'

'Like on page seventeen of the book!' said Sanchez.

'That's right.'

Mayor Shepherd took up an impressive fencing pose. It looked like he knew what he was doing. 'You're no match for me, garbage man,' he said. 'I'm a master swordsman. I'll cut you in half.'

Pete placed his helmet back on his head and pointed his sword at the Mayor. 'Bring it on!' he said with great confidence.

The two men lunged at each other with their swords. And so began a fight to the death.

Fifty Three

JD wriggled out of his coat and slung it aside, along with his Headblaster gun. Getting his vest off wasn't so easy, but then nothing's easy when you've been shot. He managed it, and then tore the vest in half so he could wrap it around his chest. He tied it as tight as he could to stem the flow of blood from his wound. There was a pool of blood on the floor around him. It had even seeped under the door into the corridor.

Desperate though his situation was, it bothered him more that he had no idea what would happen to Beth. Those nuns were bastards, evil fuckers, and no one was safe with them around. And then there was Karen. JD had no idea if she was working for Scratch too. Lenny had already fooled him. He should have seen it coming. In the past he would have. All the time living a normal life with Beth had made him complacent. He'd lost his edge. He had become JD, and had lost the Bourbon Kid. If by some miracle he and Beth made it out of this predicament alive, he was going back to being his old self. And Scratch would be top of his hit list. Devil or not, that piece of shit was going down.

After tying the vest tightly around his chest and back, he crawled over to the nearest corner and sat with his back up against the wall so that he could watch the door. The pain was excruciating, but he knew if he could rest for a while it would heal enough for him to start moving again. His wounds always healed quickly, thanks to the benefits of his holy blood. The blood was the only good thing he'd inherited from his father, Ishmael Taos. Another fucking monk he didn't care much for.

His eyes burned like he'd been awake for a week. He closed them, which eased the burning. He made himself a promise that he would rest his eyes for a few minutes, then try to get up.

CRASH!

JD opened his eyes. He'd been asleep. But for how long? He reached down to his ribcage for his gun. There was nothing there. He'd taken off his coat, his holsters and *damn it*, he'd left his gun by the door. The noise that had woken him was the door opening.

A group of nuns swarmed into the room, carrying a man on their shoulders, a man dressed like a monk and screaming like a bitch. The nuns carried him across the room to the incinerator furnace. More nuns marched into the room behind them. It was becoming quite the congregation.

The terrified monk fought in vain to free himself from his captors. He screamed a whole bunch of incoherent nonsense and begged for his life. When he spotted JD hiding in the corner, his eyes opened wide in desperate hope.

'Help me!' he screamed at JD.

Even if JD could have helped him, he wouldn't have. By simple deduction he worked out that the monk was Benedict, and therefore wasn't worthy of any help. Whatever the nuns had in store for him, it was well deserved. And besides, JD had enough problems of his own. He needed to get out of the Violet room, but with nuns currently streaming in through the entrance, it was impossible. He did the only thing he could, he stayed quiet in the corner and watched the nuns dish out some vigilante justice to the evil monk who'd burned them all alive after impregnating them.

One nun was much bigger than the others. She was almost seven feet tall. If there was a Mother Superior in this group, it was definitely her. She made her way over to the incinerator and flipped open the glass door with one of her charred black hands. Then she pulled on a handle and drew out a long thick slab of hot metal. The other nuns placed Benedict down on it with his feet facing the fire inside the furnace.

From his spot in the corner, JD could already feel the heat blowing out from the furnace. Scorching hot flames burned away inside the incinerator just inches away from Benedict's feet.

'NO! NOOOO! PLEASE NOOOO!' Benedict screamed. Plenty of other words came out of his mouth, like feeble claims that he wasn't the person they were looking for, and he was sorry and blah blah blah. None of it mattered a jot to the nuns. They knew who he was. They ripped off his brown robe and the Mother Superior tossed it aside. Benedict was left naked and screaming hysterically as the nuns used the belt from his robe to tie him down.

JD approved of their decision to put Benedict into the furnace feet-first. In terms of exacting a painful revenge on him, feet-first was definitely the way to go. If they'd stuck him in head-first he'd be dead much quicker. Feet first meant that he'd feel the flames burning the skin on his toes, ankles, knees, thighs and balls well before he took his last breath.

The head nun took up a position behind Benedict's head and pushed the metal slab he was tied to, easing it back into the incinerator while her sisters chanted some religious mumbo-jumbo in a language JD didn't understand. Their chants acted as the backing vocals to Benedict's high-pitched screams. The monk's feet vanished into the flames, which sent his screeching up to a whole new level. The smell of rotting, barbecued flesh wafted out of the incinerator and floated around the room. The monk's legs and torso followed his feet into the raging hot fire, and by the time his head went in he was already dead and properly roasted. JD was glad to see the big nun shut the furnace door.

The nuns continued with their chanting while they stared at the red-hot flames behind the glass door of the incinerator. There were so many of them in the room that JD could have reached out and touched a few of them, and there were a whole bunch more in the corridor outside.

When the chanting eventually stopped, the Mother Superior bowed her head at the others, which was the cue for them to start filing out of the room. As they slowly dispersed, the Mother Superior turned her head and looked JD's way. Like all of the nuns, she had no eyes, no facial features at all, so it was impossible to know what, if anything, she was thinking about the intruder who had just witnessed the execution of Benedict.

Fifty Four

Sanchez had always suspected that gay people found him irresistible, but he'd never had a gay Cylon and a masked swordsman fighting over him before. He was rooting for Pete the Cylon because even though Pete wanted to have sex with him, the dude in the Zorro costume wanted to kill him, and possibly have sex with him when he was dead.

During the early exchanges of the duel it became evident that Mayor Shepherd was the superior swordsman, but Pete's Cylon outfit offered great protection, so even though Shepherd struck a few blows, they bounced off Pete's metal arms and torso without causing any injury.

Sanchez felt like he ought to offer some support to Pete, but all he had to fight with was the plastic laser gun he'd taken from Pete's belt. He aimed it at the Mayor and pulled the trigger to see what would happen. It made a cool, "laser-sound" and the end lit up a nice pink colour, but that was all. Sanchez threw it at the Mayor but it missed him and hit Pete on the back.

'Go on, Pete!' Sanchez shouted, to show some support. 'You can do it.'

Pete's problem was obvious. The clunky metal outfit was cumbersome and made it hard for him to move. Shepherd kept dancing around him and prodding his sword into Pete's side. Sanchez was going to have to help before Pete got dizzy and fell over. Unfortunately, he was stuck in an ill-fitting pink bathrobe, so his options were limited. If he'd had his phone with him, he would have called Flake. Without that option, he had to find a weapon in the bar area. The only things of any use were the wooden chairs dotted around the tables. Sanchez had seen the Patrick Swayze movie *Road House* enough times to know he could smash one against Shepherd's back and it would probably knock him over. If that worked, then Pete could stab the Mayor in the back, or the ass.

When Mayor Shepherd's back was turned Sanchez grabbed a chair and snuck up behind him. The Mayor had Pete cornered, so there was no time to waste. Sanchez lifted the chair over his shoulder and swung it hard at the side of Shepherd's head. The Mayor saw it coming and ducked out of the way.

CLUNK!

The chair connected with the helmet on Pete's Cylon costume and knocked him off balance. The blow also made Sanchez's hands sting. He dropped the chair and backed away, shaking his hands to try and get rid of the vibrations from the chair. Shepherd seized the opportunity and lunged at Pete, thrusting his sword into the softer material on the Cylon's armpit. The blade cut through it with ease and sank into Pete's flesh. It was weird hearing a Cylon scream because it came out in a robot voice and sounded really fake and sarcastic. Blood spurted out of Pete's armpit and he staggered backwards into a wooden table. His legs gave way and he crashed through the table, ending up on his back, staring up at the ceiling. The red light on his helmet, which had been rotating back and forth slowly came to a stop, then faded out.

'PETE!' Sanchez yelled. 'Are you okay?'

'No, he's not okay,' said the masked swordsman who had cut him down. 'He's dead. And you're next.'

The Mayor turned his sword on Sanchez. In a panic, Sanchez dashed over to a table with some empty beer glasses on it, hoping to use them to fight off the psychotic council manager. He grabbed a tall glass in each hand and turned to face Shepherd who was almost upon him.

'Stay back, fuckface!' Sanchez said in his bravest voice.

Shepherd smirked at him. 'Don't worry fat boy,' he said. 'I'll make it quick, I promise.'

'You wouldn't hit a man with glasses would you?' said Sanchez, holding up the two empty beer glasses.

'No I wouldn't,' said Shepherd. 'But, I'll happily stab you in both eyes and cut your tongue out.'

Sanchez winced. 'Why do you have to do that?'

'Because that's what the vampires used to do during the Lunar festival,' said Shepherd. 'Once this year's festival is over, the murders will stop and the cops will assume it was just another vampire that killed you, and they'll close the case.'

'You're forgetting something,' said Sanchez. 'Flake will work out what's happened, and she'll make it her mission in life to destroy you!'

'Hahahahahahaha!'

'That wasn't a joke.'

'I know. But my two security guards were waiting for Flake at my office. She'll be chopped up into a thousand pieces by now.'

Sanchez hurled one of his beer glasses at Shepherd. The Mayor ducked it easily and it smashed on the floor. Before Sanchez could hurl the other glass, Shepherd lunged forward and pressed the point of his sword against the bartender's chubby neck.

'Just tell me where the book is,' said Shepherd. 'And I'll make this quick.'

'It's behind you,' said Sanchez, desperately hoping the Mayor was dumb enough to turn around and look for it.

Shepherd sighed. 'You really are a fucking....'

BANG!

A splurge of blood burst out of the side of Shepherd's Zorro mask. He wobbled on his feet, dropped his sword, turned a bit cross-eyed, and then fell sideways onto a table. The table flipped over and Shepherd fell to the floor and lay there face down, with a jet of blood spurting out of his head.

Sanchez looked around for the person who'd fired the shot.

'You okay, Sanchez?' said a croaky old voice.

A short, hunched figure in a black dress and a grey cardigan, with a smoking gun in her hand, was standing in the doorway of the disabled toilets. Sanchez recognised her straight away.

'Annabel? How did you know I was in trouble?'

'That guy's been after you for a while,' she said, walking around some broken glass on the floor. 'His name is Dracula. He's been working for Scratch, and he's infatuated with you. I came here to kill him.'

'The Mayor's real name is Dracula?' said Sanchez, puzzled.

'The Mayor?'

'Yeah.'

Annabel came closer and leaned over the body of the man she had just shot in the head. She rolled him over onto his back and peeled off his Zorro mask. 'Who the Hell is this?' she asked.

'It's Mayor Shepherd. He's been killing everyone that knew he was a model in a gay book from years ago.'

'The Gay Man's Guide to Anal Sex?'

'That's the one.'

Annabel slapped herself on her forehead. 'Shit, I thought this was Dracula!'

'What the Hell are you talking about?'

'It's a long story.'

'Well tell me it later,' said Sanchez, concerned about other, more serious matters. 'I've got to call Flake. She's in trouble.'

Annabel put her gun down on a table and approached him with her hands up, to try and calm him down. 'You're in trouble too,' she said. 'Dracula wants you as his soul-mate for all eternity.'

'Well, he'll have to get in line.'

Annabel had a reputation for being annoying and vague, and Sanchez wasn't really in the mood to listen to more of her nonsense.

However, seeing as how she'd saved his life a few moments earlier, he had to indulge her a little.

'Listen Sanchez,' she croaked. 'There's a lot going on that you don't know about. Where is everyone else?'

'I dunno. But Flake's gone to the Mayor's place and his two bodyguards are going to kill her.'

'Bodyguards?' said Annabel. 'What are you worried about then? Flake's plenty capable of kicking the shit out of a couple of bodyguards. You've got to watch out for a man named Dracula who can transform into a bat. Tell the others so that they can hunt him down and kill him. And Sanchez, Scratch mustn't know about any of this.'

'I promise I won't tell him,' said Sanchez, still unsure of what she was talking about.

'Listen carefully, Sanchez, because this is important. Scratch has.....'

Annabel had never been one to stop talking in mid-sentence, but right in the middle of telling Sanchez something that sounded like it might be important, she suddenly made a strange choking sound and blood started oozing out of her mouth.

'Are you all right?' Sanchez asked.

Annabel didn't reply. She looked down at the floor. Sanchez did the same, to see what she was looking at. That was when he saw it, the tip of a sword poking out through her chest. Annabel saw it too. They looked up into each other's eyes.

'What's happened?' said Sanchez.

Annabel didn't answer. A face appeared over her left shoulder, the face of a pale man with brown streaks of shit in his hair and on his cheeks. He grinned at Sanchez.

'I'm Dracula,' he said. 'So pleased to meet you again.'

Fifty Five

The Mother Superior was standing motionless next to the incinerator furnace, staring at JD as the other nuns filed out of the Violet room. It was an uncomfortable situation because JD was too badly injured to put up any kind of fight if she attacked him.

When the other nuns were all gone, she took two steps towards him. He readied himself for the possibility he might have to roll out of the way if she spat a mouthful of fire at him. But the nun never took another step. A bright white light filled the room, illuminating the wall behind her. JD closed his eyes and turned away to avoid the glare. A low humming sound accompanied the white light for a while until suddenly everything went dark. And cold. The humming stopped and JD was alone in the room. The nightmare was over. The fire in the incinerator disappeared along with the violet flames on the candles.

He pressed his hand against the wall and pulled himself to his feet. His strength was gradually returning. In spite of not being able to see anything, he hobbled towards the door, keeping his hand against the wall to steady himself. With his free hand he flailed around, feeling for the presence of any undead nuns. There was nothing but air. He reached the door and felt around for the doorknob. His hand settled on it and he pulled the door open. Daylight flooded into the room, and JD staggered out into the corridor.

The abbey had returned to its former self. Gone were the violet flamed candles and the dark corridors. The black and white floor tiles had returned. No one else was around. No Scratch, no Ninjas, nothing.

He trudged across the corridor to the staircase and grabbed hold of the bannister. He climbed the stairs one at a time, like a man three times his age, occasionally pausing to get his strength back.

'Beth!' he called out. 'The nuns have gone.'

Beth didn't hear him. He called her name a few more times, and still there was no response. At the top of the stairs he walked along the landing, using the balcony to steady himself. He headed for the room he had left Beth and Karen in. The doorknob turned easily and the door popped open.

'Beth?'

There was no one in the room and everything looked completely different. Where previously there had been books and rubbish strewn across the floor, now the room was bare. Even the closet was gone. He backed out of the room and looked all around the upper floor for a sign of anyone. There was no one in sight. He pressed a hand against his chest wound. It was hurting a lot more because of all the effort involved in climbing the stairs. He shuffled over to the balcony and looked down below for any sign of Beth. She was still nowhere to be seen. His next stop had to be the room in the corner by the window. There was no blood on the floor or walls outside it anymore, and no sign of Lenny's corpse either.

'BETH!'

He hobbled quicker than before. If anywhere were to provide answers it would be Benedict's room. He turned the doorknob and pushed it open. He was immediately overwhelmed by a foul smell inside the room, and the reason for it was obvious.

In the centre of the room, next to an upturned bed was a naked, headless man. The point of a spear was poking out from between his shoulders, where his head should have been. The other end of the spear was embedded in the floor. The man had been impaled on it, right up through his ass. Opposite him was an open window with a breeze blowing in through it. The floor was soaked in blood, much of which had oozed out of the decapitated head of the monk, Loomis, who JD had met once briefly the day before. Loomis's head was on the floor by the bed. But there was still no sign of Beth.

JD remembered Beth telling him about Loomis's demise, but he was surprised by the brutality of it. It was starting to make sense now though. Scratch was obviously behind all of it. And at this point JD wasn't sure what "all of it" amounted to. Or what it meant for Beth. He had to find her.

'Beth?' he whispered, to himself as much as anything. 'Where are you?'

He was almost at a loss for where to look for her, when his eyes settled on something that looked like it was there for him to find. A photograph. It was wedged between the fingers on the right hand of Loomis's decapitated body. JD approached it and with two fingers he prized the photo from the dead monk's hand. He held it up and studied it carefully. It was an old black and white photo of a woman holding hands with a young boy. The picture was taken in the grounds of the graveyard outside the abbey. A lump built up in JD's throat. The woman in the picture was Beth. She looked a little older and her hair was different, and she was wearing an old-fashioned dress. But it was undeniably her. And the boy? He was only five or six years old, and was wearing shorts and a sleeveless jumper. JD shook his head. This didn't make sense. The photo was crumpled and worn at the edges. He flipped it over in his hand and saw a note on the back, written in black ink.

JD looked again at the headless body impaled on the spear, and at the severed head on the floor.

****

Scratch was sitting on a stool, leaning against the bar in Purgatory. Zilas and Einstein were sitting on either side of him and all three of them were watching the large television screen on the wall. Purgatory was busy for a change. A group of Ninjas were in a backroom, drinking vodka and playing games like darts and pool with Jacko, the bluesman, who had granted them entry via the crossroads in the Devil's Graveyard earlier in the day. As Jacko was discovering, Ninjas were surprisingly good at darts, but they sucked at pool.

'Do you need these Ninjas yet?' Jacko called out to Scratch.

Scratch didn't reply. Instead he clapped his hands boisterously. 'BRAVO!' he shouted at the TV screen.

The show he was watching with his two sidekicks was a Purgatory exclusive. Zilas had installed a hidden CCTV camera in Brother Loomis's bedroom, so that they could watch the events in the abbey unfold on the live feed. The Bourbon Kid was on screen, standing by the decapitated body of Loomis, holding a photo in his hand. Scratch's plan was working. *It had worked.*

'This is epic,' said Scratch. 'You know, I had my doubts, but I think it could be the greatest trick I ever pulled.'

'It's *our* finest work,' said Einstein, reminding him who created the portal in the Violet room.

'Yes, of course,' said Scratch, not taking his eyes off the screen.

'Do you think he's worked it out yet?' Zilas asked, sipping on a pink cocktail.

'For sure,' said Scratch. 'He's seen the photo. Now he knows that Loomis was his son. That was a lovely touch, leaving the photo in the corpse's hand.'

'I hope he cries,' said Zilas, beaming a goofy smile.

'He won't yet,' said Scratch. 'Once he realises it's all real, he'll head straight back to the Violet room to try and get back to Beth.' He elbowed Einstein. 'You're certain the portal is dismantled?'

'Definitely. There's no way he's ever seeing Beth again. She got left behind in the year eighteen ninety-six. And according to the history books, she died in the nineteen-thirties.'

'Perfect. Annabel predicted everything correctly for once,' said Scratch. He picked a thick cigar out of the breast pocket on his suit and lit it with a match from the bar. 'Where is the old crone anyway?'

'She was here a minute ago,' said Zilas. 'Want me to go find her?'

Scratch blew a smoke ring towards the TV screen. 'No need,' he said. 'Go speak to those Ninjas out back. Tell them to finish their drinks, and sharpen their swords. It's time to finish this.'

Fifty Six

Dracula yanked his sword out of Annabel's back and licked some of her blood from the blade. Annabel's knees buckled and she fell forward. Sanchez reached out and caught her in his arms. Her head slumped into his chest. Blood trickled from her mouth onto his vest.

'Oh, fucking hell, *Annabel,*' Sanchez said, doing his best to hold her up. Behind her, the weird, naked, shit-covered vampire that had thrust the sword into her back was licking both sides of the blade, devouring Annabel's blood with great gusto.

When he was done cleaning the blade with his tongue, Dracula grinned at Sanchez. His teeth were covered in blood. It wasn't a pretty sight. Sanchez had quite a predicament on his hands. Annabel was heavy, and as the life was draining from her, she was becoming even heavier. He was tempted to drop her and make a run for it, but he decided that using her as a human shield was probably a better strategy, so he kept hold of her.

Annabel lifted her head and drooled some blood onto Sanchez's chest. 'He's come for *you,*' she spluttered.

'She's right,' said Dracula. 'Scratch said I could have you.'

'What?'

CRASH!

The front doors of the Tapioca burst open and Elvis and Jasmine stormed in, pistols drawn.

'SHOOT HIM!' Sanchez yelled at them.

Elvis and Jasmine didn't need to be told twice. They turned their guns on Dracula. The naked vampire saw what was coming and transformed into a bat immediately, giving the impression that he'd vanished. His sword clattered to the floor and he flew up to the ceiling in search of an escape route. Jasmine lowered her gun and sprinted over to Sanchez and Annabel.

Elvis called over to her. 'He's up there!'

Jasmine stopped and looked up. There was a small bat on the ceiling staring down at her. Elvis started shooting at it, and Jasmine joined in without hesitating. The two of them unloaded at the bat as it zigzagged across the ceiling looking for a way out. Sanchez lowered Annabel to the ground and rested her head on the corpse of Mayor Shepherd, so he could cover his ears to drown out the gunfire. The non-stop rat-a-tat of bullets was accompanied by the sound of furniture breaking. And after a short while the gunfire became louder because Rodeo Rex showed up. Without waiting for an invite, he joined Jasmine and Elvis shooting at the ceiling. Sanchez feared he'd end up deaf, or with a ceiling collapsing on him. When a fourth shooter arrived in the shape of Flake, it looked even more likely. Sanchez didn't even see where she came from but she had an Uzi pistol and was peppering the whole bar area with it. It was a reassuring sight. The four members of the Dead Hunters took up spots in all four corners of the bar and showered the ceiling in bullets. It reminded Sanchez of his favourite scene from *Predator*. If he could have reached the Cylon laser-gun he'd discarded on the floor earlier, he would have joined in. The noise was deafening and the gunfire was making the bar area fill up with smoke, meaning that if the bat was still around it would be impossible to see.

Eventually after a two-minute barrage, the shooting came to an end. Sanchez was left with just a ringing in his ears, and tears streaming down his face from all the smoke. Jasmine dived onto the floor next to Annabel and pressed her hand over the wound in the old woman's chest. Blood seeped through Jasmine's fingers.

'Annabel, stay awake!' she cried. 'Sanchez, what happened to her?'

'The bat fella stabbed her with a sword.'

Jasmine shouted at Flake, 'Call an ambulance!'

'I'm already on it,' Flake yelled back from behind the bar.

Elvis and Rex came over to check on Annabel. A pool of blood was leaking out onto the floor beneath her from the entry wound in her back.

'Is she gonna be okay?' Elvis asked.

'What exactly were we shooting at?' Rex inquired.

'I'm not sure,' said Elvis looking around at the carnage. 'What *did* happen here Sanchez?'

'Well,' said Sanchez. 'The Mayor turned up to kill me because I'd seen pictures of him in a book about gay sex.'

'The Gay Man's Guide!' said Elvis.

'You've read it too?' Sanchez asked.

'No, but someone was killing everyone who'd ever borrowed it from the library.'

'That was Mayor Shepherd. Pete the Cylon over there took him on in a sword fight and lost.'

The fallen Cylon was covered in dust and broken bits of furniture.

'Is he dead?' Elvis asked, frowning.

'I think so,' said Sanchez. 'After the Mayor killed Pete he came after me, but Annabel showed up and shot him. But then the naked guy covered in shit stabbed Annabel in the back. And he turned into a bat when you and Jasmine arrived and started shooting at him.'

'Who the fuck was he?' Rex asked.

'A Golgothan,' said Elvis.

Rex frowned. 'A Shit Demon?'

Sanchez had no idea what a Shit Demon was, although he had to admit it sounded awesome. 'The Shit Demon said his name was Dracula,' he said.

Elvis and Rex both looked like that meant something to them. 'You mean the Count Dracula?' they both said at the same time.

Annabel sputtered loudly, the death rattle in her lungs looming. 'Scratch freed him from Hell,' she croaked.

'To come here?' said Jasmine.

'No. Tell JD, he killed Loomis.'

It wasn't the answer anyone expected. It sounded like Annabel was hallucinating or talking about something entirely different.

'Don't talk,' said Jasmine. 'There's an ambulance on the way. You'll be okay. Just hang in there.'

Annabel swallowed a mouthful of blood and coughed again. She looked up and forced half a smile at Jasmine. 'I see green fields,' she said. 'Endless green fields that go on for miles.'

'Stay *with me*,' said Jasmine.

'I played in those fields as a child with my brother,' Annabel continued. 'In the summer we played for hours and my mom would bring us ice creams. The three of us would sit and watch the sun go down.'

'That sounds really nice,' said Jasmine, stroking Annabel's hair.

'It was the best childhood you could hope for,' Annabel spluttered, her voice weakening. 'Now all those memories will be lost.'

'No they won't,' said Jasmine. 'You're gonna be okay.'

The life was draining from Annabel's face. She looked into Jasmine's eyes. 'You wanted to know how I see the future,' she said, her voice becoming weaker with every word.

'You can tell me later. It's okay. Just rest.'

Annabel was determined to tell Jasmine something. 'I knew the future because....' She coughed up some more blood. '....because my mother told me all of it when I was younger.'

'Your mother was a psychic too?'

Annabel choked hard and sucked in a short breath of air, but then her body shuddered and went limp in Jasmine's arms.

'OH MY GOD!' Jasmine screamed.

Flake rushed over with a glass of water for Annabel. 'Here give her this,' she said.

Jasmine looked up at her. 'It's too late.'

Sanchez dried his eyes. He saw for himself that Jasmine was right. *It was too late.* The old fortune-telling crone had taken her last breath. And bled all over the floor too, which someone was going to have to clean up.

Elvis turned away and put his head in his hands. Rex covered his mouth, and Flake crouched down by Annabel's side, hoping that Jasmine was wrong and that the Mystic Lady was just resting. And deep down Sanchez had to admit that he was upset. For all Annabel's faults, like how annoying she was, how often she was wrong with her predictions, and how crusty and unwashed her cardigans were, Sanchez still liked her. She'd been a friend for a long time. He thought back to the moment many years earlier when she'd helped him and Elvis escape from the Hotel Pasadena when it sank into the pits of Hell. She'd pulled up in a stolen van and let them jump aboard. Sanchez had sat up front with Annabel for the entire journey home while Elvis was having sex with a Janis Joplin impersonator on the back seat. It was a happy memory. Janis Joplin's Tourette's had made for some good giggles as Sanchez and Annabel played a game trying to guess what names Janis would call Elvis while they were fucking.

'Something's not right,' said Jasmine.

Sanchez stopped daydreaming about happier times and saw what Jasmine was referring to. Annabel's body began to change. Right before everyone's eyes she dissolved slowly into dust, which in turn vanished into thin air. One minute Flake and Jasmine were holding her, the next they were holding nothing but air. Annabel was gone, vanished into the smoke that was engulfing the bar area.

'What's happening?' said Flake, sobbing.

Jasmine looked around at the others for an explanation. Rex grabbed Elvis who was still looking away, with his head in his hands. Both men had tears in their eyes. It was looking like everyone secretly cared about Annabel more than they had ever let on.

'She's gone,' said Rex, pointing at where Annabel once was. All that remained was the pool of blood on the floor next to the dead body of Mayor Shepherd.

'Where'd she go?' Elvis asked.

'I think I know,' said Rex. 'When you do a deal with the Devil to come back from the dead, and you then die a second time like Annabel just did, you turn to dust.'

Jasmine had tears streaming down her face. 'So where is she?' she asked.

'In a better place,' said Rex.

A buzzing noise broke the sombre mood. Rex felt his thigh. 'That's my phone,' he said. He pulled it from a pocket on his jeans and checked the display. 'It's Sally Diamond.'

'Answer it,' said Elvis. 'Tell her Mayor Shepherd was the killer.'

Rex took the call and walked to a quiet corner to share the news with Sally Diamond.

Flake ran up to Sanchez and hugged him tight, burying her head in his chest. 'I should never have left you alone while I went to the Mayor's office,' she said.

Jasmine stood up and walked over to check on Pete the Cylon. She crouched down next to him and brushed some chunks of ceiling and bits of furniture off him, then she took his helmet off. The young man inside the suit was still breathing. She shouted over to Sanchez. 'Hey Sanchez, your robot is still alive!'

'Pete?'

Jasmine cradled the Cylon's head in her arms. 'Hang in there buddy,' she said to him. 'We've got an ambulance coming.'

'Hold his hand,' said Flake. 'Keep him awake and talk to him.'

Jasmine groaned, 'Ewww, he's got a metal hand!'

Elvis put his finger to his lips to shush her because Rex was coming back.

'Hey everybody, listen up,' said Rex. 'I just got off the phone to Sally Diamond. She was looking into something for me earlier. This is really weird. When Annabel was killed five years ago, her body was taken from the morgue and buried somewhere else. Sally did some digging around and found out Annabel is buried in a monastery in Texas with her mother. And her real name isn't even Annabel de Frugyn. It's Emma Palmer.'

'Technically it's Emma Lansbury,' said a voice.

Everyone in turn looked to where the voice had come from. Standing behind the bar, surrounded by smoke was a black man with blond hair, wearing a white robe.

'That's him!' said Rex. 'That's the angel I met that time, years ago!'

'Hello Rex,' said the angel. 'It's nice to see you again.' He addressed the whole room. 'My name is Levian, and I have some news for you all.'

Fifty Seven

'Is he going to go back down to the Violet room, or what?' asked Zilas.

'Any second now,' said Scratch. 'I'm certain of it. He'll be desperate to get back to Beth.'

'Then what is he waiting for?' asked Einstein.

The three men were all leaning against the bar in Purgatory watching the TV screen, waiting anxiously for the Bourbon Kid to leave Loomis's bedroom and head back down to the Violet room. But instead, since discovering the photo of Beth with their son, the Bourbon Kid had hardly moved. He'd just been staring at a wall, deep in thought.

'He's not coming to terms with it,' Zilas jeered. 'He's going to cry.'

Einstein sniffed the air. 'What the fuck is that smell?' he said, looking around.

He had a point. A sudden foul stench had floated into Purgatory. Scratch checked behind him to see if any of the Ninjas were responsible for it. Ten of them were waiting at the back of the bar for him to give the order to go after the Bourbon Kid. But it wasn't the Ninjas who were responsible for the foul stench. Dracula had walked in through the men's toilets, naked and covered in shit.

'Where the fuck did you come from?' asked Scratch, his face lined with anger and confusion.

'I was in the Tapioca,' said Dracula.

'What were you doing there? And how the fuck did you get back through the portal?'

'It was open.'

'What do you mean it was open?'

'It was open.'

Scratch roared at him. 'Just repeating what you said before is not the appropriate way to answer a follow-up question!'

'Well, it was open,' said Dracula. 'Like I said, I was in the Tapioca. And I was going to make Sanchez fall in love with me, but that fucking fortune-teller of yours—'

'Annabel?'

'Yeah, her. She shows up, kills a masked swordsman, and then warns Sanchez about my plans for him. So I stuck a sword through her heart.'

'YOU DID WHAT?'

Jacko, who had been playing darts on his own at the back of the bar, overheard what was said and rushed over. 'Did you say you killed Annabel?' he asked, angrily.

'Calm down,' said Dracula, walking round the bar to join Scratch. 'I did it because she was telling Sanchez to keep all this stuff secret from you. That woman's been working against you.'

'YOU IDIOT!' Scratch yelled. 'She's the one who predicts the future for me. And don't come any closer. You stink! Why are you covered in shit?'

'You were right about that guy, Sanchez. I should never have gone after him. He took a shit on me and flushed me down the toilet.'

That revelation was greeted by silence.

Eventually Einstein peered over his spectacles and asked the question everyone else was thinking. 'How exactly did he shit on you and flush you down the toilet?'

'Well, I was in bat form, and I was....'

'SILENCE!' yelled Scratch. 'I DON'T CAAAAAARE!' He turned back to the television screen. The Bourbon Kid was still in Loomis's bedroom, staring at the wall behind the upturned bed.

'Zilas, did I miss anything?' Scratch asked.

'He's moving!' said Zilas.

The hunchback was right. The Bourbon Kid, who had not moved for almost a minute, turned and headed for the door.

'Switch the camera view!' said Scratch.

Zilas flicked a switch on a console he was holding and the view on the screen switched to the feed from a camera on the landing outside Loomis's bedroom.

'This is it!' Zilas exclaimed. 'He's going back to the Violet room.'

Scratch sprang into action, his excitement palpable. 'Okay, everybody get ready. We're going back through the portal.'

Dracula cleared his throat. 'Uh, boss, you know the portal is directed at the toilets in the Tapioca at the moment, right?'

'Huh? Oh, yeah. What? Why the Hell is that?' said Scratch.

'Like I told you' Dracula replied. 'Your fortune-teller did it.'

Scratch hesitated. 'When the fuck did Annabel learn how to use the portal?'

Einstein raised his hand and answered. 'She was using it to send the little fat Mexican fella to exotic toilets all around the world, remember?''

'That was her?' said Scratch, before waving a dismissive hand and moving on. 'Fuck it, I'll worry about that later.' He hopped over the bar and approached the keypad on the till so he could switch the location back to Coldworm Abbey. 'I can't believe you killed Annabel,' he muttered. 'Why couldn't you have just stayed in that brothel like I told you to?'

'I wish I had,' said Dracula, wiping some poo off his shoulder and flicking it on the floor.

Flicking turds on the floor in Purgatory was normally a serious offence, but seeing as how Scratch was in an excitable mood, he let it slide.

'Dracula, you'd better have a shower before I get back, otherwise I'm going to kill you.'

'Understood,' said Dracula.

'Hurry up boss!' said Zilas. 'The Kid is heading downstairs.'

Up on the TV screen they could see the Bourbon Kid limping back down the stairs towards the Violet room. Scratch switched the destination on the keypad and headed for the men's toilets. The group of Ninjas joined him, each of them with a sword sheathed across his back.

One of the Ninjas opened the toilet door and Scratch marched through it, straight into the downstairs washroom in Coldworm Abbey. The Ninjas slinked through the door behind him, with Zilas bringing up the rear. Scratch marched straight through the washroom and out into the main corridor of the abbey.

The Devil's timing was perfect. The Bourbon Kid hobbled off the bottom of the stairs and headed towards the Violet room. He saw Scratch appear in the corridor and it was clear from the look on his face that he was a desperate, broken man. Scratch smirked at him. Everything was working perfectly. And when Scratch's army of Ninjas flooded into the corridor behind him, the Bourbon Kid made the predictable move. He panicked and stumbled across the corridor into the Violet room.

Scratch punched the air. 'This truly is my finest work,' he said, his grin bigger than ever. He pointed along the corridor. 'Okay, go get him fellas!'

The Ninjas swarmed past Scratch, moving swiftly and majestically along the corridor to the Violet room. Zilas sidled up to Scratch.

'Did he go into the Violet room again?' he asked.

'Of course he went in. Come, let's go watch the Ninjas behead him.'

The first Ninja to arrive outside the door stood by the side of it and pushed it open a little. When nothing jumped out at him, he charged in with his sword swinging. The others stormed in after him.

Scratch had no need to rush. He strolled along the corridor to the Violet room with Zilas at his side. The hunchback was breathing heavily and giggling to himself, which was annoying and would normally have meant a slap, but Scratch was in too good a mood to bother.

They arrived at the Violet room and Scratch walked in, only to be greeted by pitch darkness. 'For fuckssake,' he moaned. 'Didn't we get some lights installed in here?'

'We did,' said Zilas, squeezing through the door behind him. The hunchback found a light switch on the wall and flicked it on.

The room lit up and Scratch saw all ten of his Ninjas standing around with their swords drawn. But there was no sign of the Bourbon Kid. Scratch scoured the room for him. There was a pool of blood in one of the corners, and more of it on the wall. There was also a thin trail of blood spots on the hardwood floor and across an Egyptian rug in the middle of the room, leading up to the incinerator on the opposite wall. But there was definitely no Bourbon Kid.

'Where the fuck is he?' Scratch asked.

Zilas shrugged. 'Maybe he didn't come in here?' he suggested.

'I saw him come in here!' Scratch ranted. He karate chopped Zilas, right on his hunch. Zilas wailed in pain and dropped to his knees.

Scratch scanned the room again. There was no way out other than the way he'd come in. All that remained in the room was Scratch, Zilas and ten useless fucking Ninjas. He thought about all the effort he'd put in to get the Ninjas, and now there was no use for them. He fumed for a while, but then an idea came to him.

'Right, you lot, show me your faces!' he bellowed at the Ninjas. 'I'm not fucking kidding. SHOW ME YOUR FACES NOW!'

Each of the Ninjas unravelled the black masking on his face. Scratch checked them all. This was a classic Bourbon Kid trick, disguising himself as someone else. But the ten faces in front of him did not include the Kid. By this point Scratch was breathing fire out of his nostrils. He had a major tantrum coming on. Zilas obviously sensed it because he stayed down on the ground holding his hands up in case Scratch hit him again. Scratch raged at him.

'I thought Einstein fixed this door so that it wouldn't travel back to the nineteenth century anymore!'

'He did,' Zilas said, nodding frantically.

'Then where the fuck is the Bourbon Kid?'

Zilas was trembling. 'He…. he came in here. You said you saw it!'

'THEN WHERE THE FUCK IS HE?'

Zilas looked around the room. His eyes settled on something and he pointed at it. 'There!' he said. 'He's in there!'

Everyone looked at where Zilas was pointing. The door to the incinerator furnace was closed. Scratch marched up to it, grabbed the handle and yanked it open and pulled out a long metal slab. He expected to see the Bourbon Kid lying on the slab, or hiding inside the incinerator. But there was nothing. Just an empty metal slab covered in sprinklings of dirt and ash.

'What the fuck is going on?' he hissed.

'Maybe he burned himself alive in order to escape?' Zilas suggested.

Scratch marched across the room and kicked Zilas in the face, knocking him over onto his back. 'Does anyone have even the slightest fucking clue where the Bourbon Kid is?' he asked through gritted teeth.

The Ninjas all looked confused, and nowhere near as cool now that their faces were visible. Scratch was livid.

He pointed at Zilas who was still writhing around in agony on the floor. 'I want every inch of this building searched,' he said. He turned on the Ninjas. 'I want you to check in every single room, every alcove, every cupboard. He's here somewhere.'

Fifty Eight

Scratch left Zilas and the Ninjas behind in Coldworm Abbey and headed back to Purgatory via the portal. The sight that greeted him didn't help his murderous mood. Jacko and Einstein were sitting at a table, smoking some of Scratch's favourite cigars and drinking Pina Coladas while watching the CCTV footage on the television.

Scratch stormed over to them and snatched the cigar from Jacko's mouth. 'Did you two idiots see where he went?' he bellowed.

Einstein took a puff on his cigar and peered over his spectacles at Scratch. 'Where *who* went?' he asked, casually.

'The Bourbon Kid!'

'He went into the Violet room just before you did. You must have seen him.'

Scratch resisted the urge to throw something at Einstein. 'Of course I saw him go in there. But when I got there, he was gone!'

'Gone where?' asked Jacko.

'IF I KNEW THE FUCKING ANSWER TO THAT, I WOULDN'T BE ASKING YOU, WOULD I?' Scratch raged. He had smoke coming out of his ears, and he was turning a nasty shade of purple.

'Pina Colada?' said Jacko, holding up his drink to see if Scratch would like a sip.

'I'll Pina Colada you in the ass in a minute!' said Scratch, well aware that what he was saying made no sense.

Einstein tried a little diplomacy. 'I can rewind this CCTV footage if you like?' he said. 'It'll prove that the Kid went into the Violet room.'

'I ALREADY KNOW HE WENT INTO THE FUCKING VIOLET ROOM. CHRIST! IS EVERYBODY HERE TRYING TO WIND ME UP TODAY, OR WHAT?'

'Do you need a hug?' Jacko asked.

Scratch glared at him and took a puff on Jacko's cigar while he tried to think. It calmed him down a little. 'Okay,' he said, blowing smoke in Einstein's face. 'Rewind the video and show me where the Kid went after he entered the Violet room.'

Einstein waved the smoke away from his face. 'I can rewind it,' he said, his eyes watering. 'But there's no camera inside the Violet room, so you won't be able to see where he went once he was inside.'

Scratch gritted his teeth. 'Why the fuck not?' he asked.

'Well, you see, Zilas put the cameras up, but it was too dark to see anything in the Violet room before I installed the new lights. And by the time I'd done that, he'd run out of cameras.'

Scratch reached over the bar and grabbed a bottle of bourbon. He threw it at Einstein who ducked out of the way. The bottle smashed on the wall, narrowly missing the television.

'Why are you angry at me?' Einstein asked.

'Because I'm the Devil and I can be angry at whoever I fucking like!' Scratch replied. 'Are you sure you shut down the portal in the Violet room like I asked you?'

'I'm positive.'

'Then how come the Bourbon Kid vanished when he went in there?'

Einstein shrugged. 'Beats me. I definitely did it though.'

A pinging sound from the back of the bar indicated that someone had come up in the elevator from Hell. Scratch spun around and saw Dracula walk out of the disabled toilets. The vampire was completely naked, but he'd had a shower because all the shit stains were gone from his skin and hair.

'Must we see your cock all the time!' Scratch complained.

'You don't have to look at it,' Dracula replied, stretching his arms as if he were tired.

Scratch leaned over the bar and grabbed the first thing he could lay his hands on, which happened to be a bag of peanuts. He hurled them at Dracula, who caught them in his right hand. He read the name on the packet.

'So *these* are peanuts?' he said. 'I've been wanting to try some of these.' He opened the packet and took one out. After studying it for a second he slipped it into his mouth. 'Hmm, salty,' he said.

'Listen Count,' said Scratch, taking another puff on his cigar. 'We've lost the Bourbon Kid. Have you got any idea where he might be?'

'I've been in the shower haven't I?' Dracula replied. 'And I didn't see him in there.'

Before Scratch could do something violent, Einstein called out to him. 'Here, I've rewound the footage for you.'

Scratch looked up at the television. Einstein had rewound the CCTV footage to the moment when the Bourbon Kid found Loomis dead in his bedroom.

Dracula walked up to Scratch's side and carried on eating peanuts while they watched the television. The footage was once again showing the moment the Bourbon Kid found the photo of Beth and his son.

'Must you eat so loudly?' Scratch hissed at Dracula who was chomping loudly on his peanuts.

Dracula pointed up at the screen. 'You know I was thinking about this,' he said. 'If Beth has gone back in time and given birth to that Loomis fella, then she must have known he was going to be murdered when he was older. So I think he knew I was coming to kill him.'

Scratch rolled his eyes. 'He obviously didn't though, did he?'

'Maybe not, but all this time travel stuff is quite a conundrum isn't it?' said Dracula. He poured out a handful of peanuts and shoved them in his mouth. 'Maybe that's why Loomis had that message written on the wall for me,' he said, with his mouth half full.

Scratch coughed some smoke up in the air. 'What message?'

Dracula pointed at the TV screen again. 'There, up on the wall. See it?'

The footage wasn't very clear but it looked like the Bourbon Kid was staring at a woven textile on the wall behind the bed. The message on it was indecipherable due to the poor footage.

'I can't see it. What does it say?' Scratch asked, frowning.

Dracula shrugged. 'I thought I told you before. It said, *"Remember my last words to you".*'

Scratch stubbed his cigar out on the back of Einstein's neck and approached the television to get a better look. 'And *what were* his last words to you?' he asked, squinting at the screen.

'Pfft, it was stupid. Just after I stabbed him in the chest, he looked at me and said, *"This isn't happening".*'

'*This isn't happening?*' Scratch continued staring at the television. 'What does that mean?'

'Damned if I know.'

On the TV, the Bourbon Kid was standing by Loomis' mutilated body, staring at the woven message on the wall.

'Oh shit!' Scratch's eyes bulged wide open. 'Dracula you idiot! It wasn't a message for you. It was a message for *him!*'

'What?'

Scratch lunged at Dracula. Normally he would have grabbed the vampire by the collar of his shirt, but seeing as how he was naked, he grabbed his dick instead. And he squeezed it real hard. 'You were spying on the Bourbon Kid yesterday weren't you?' he said.

Dracula swallowed some peanuts without chewing them, for fear of annoying Scratch any further. 'Yes. He never saw me though. I was in bat form. I watched him for half the day. You know this already.'

'So you were there when the Bourbon Kid met Loomis?'

'Yes.'

Scratch squeezed Dracula's dick and pulled the vampire closer to him so he could feel his breath on his face. 'So what did they talk about?' he asked.

'Nothing interesting. It was all just introductions. I don't think the Kid liked Loomis very much.'

Scratch spoke through gritted teeth. 'What did Loomis say to the Kid? More specifically, what was the *last* thing he said?'

Dracula looked like he was trying to do some long division in his head as he racked his brains trying to remember a pointless conversation he'd been eavesdropping on while he was in bat form. Eventually, when Scratch was close to ruining his dick forever, he remembered.

'I've got it,' he squeaked. 'He made a crap joke. He said something like, *if you love someone, you dig them a tunnel.*'

Scratch let go of Dracula's penis and took a step back. He wiped his hand on his jacket and looked up at the television again. The CCTV footage showed the Bourbon Kid leaving Loomis's room and heading downstairs to the Violet room. Scratch suddenly pieced things together.

'GODDAMMIT!!!'

Fifty Nine

Beth was sitting on the bed in Benedict's bedroom waiting for something to happen. She wasn't sure *what* she was waiting for, but something like JD showing up would do just fine. The nuns seemed to have stopped patrolling the corridors outside and the whole abbey had gone quiet. All Beth could hear was her own breathing.

Twenty minutes passed before she made the decision to unbolt the door again and venture out onto the landing.

Everything had changed.

The building was no longer bathed in the strange violet-flamed light. The abbey was bright and welcoming. Beth walked along the creaky wooden floorboards on the landing as she made her way to the stairs.

'JD?' she called out. 'Jack?'

Her own voice echoed back at her, but nothing else made a sound. She walked down the stairs to the Violet room, staying alert in case any nuns showed up. She opened the door to the Violet room and looked in. It was dark like before, so she switched on her torch and shone it around the room.

'JD?' she said, calling his name louder this time. 'JACK!'

The Violet room looked empty so she walked in and shone the torch in all four corners. Nothing. She closed the door, counted to five and then opened it again. She was still in the same place. And still alone.

She left the Violet room and walked out into the corridor again. She called out JD's name over and over, but the only reply she received was the sound of her own voice echoing back at her. She was about to embark on a search of every single room in the building when a voice finally spoke out behind her. A voice that was not familiar.

'He's gone.'

She turned around and saw a black man with blond hair, wearing a long white robe. He was carrying a brown satchel over his shoulder. Even though Beth didn't know who he was, she didn't feel threatened by his presence.

'Who are you?' she asked.

'My name is Levian,' he replied. 'I've come to clear a few things up for you. I imagine you have a lot of questions.'

'Where did you come from?'

'I am a mediator for God.'

'A what?'

'An angel.'

Beth remembered how easily she'd fooled Benedict into believing she was an angel. She didn't want to be fooled by the same trick. 'Can you prove that?' she asked.

'You want me to show you some pictures of Texas on my phone?'

Beth blushed. 'How do you know about that?'

'I have been observing everything that has happened.'

'So where is JD?"

Levian pointed at the Violet room. 'He's gone back to where you came from, the present day.'

'The present day? Then where am I?'

Levian walked over to the stairs and sat down on the third step from the bottom. He smiled at Beth and patted the step. 'Please, sit,' he said.

After all she'd been through there was no reason for Beth to be scared of a man claiming to be an angel, so she joined him on the step.

Levian patted her on the knee. 'Let me explain everything for you,' he said. 'Karen Butterman, the police officer who was with you before, she was working for Scratch.'

'I figured as much.'

'You remember the story she told you about Brother Benedict and the nuns?'

'Yes.'

'That happened in the year eighteen ninety-six,' he said. 'Benedict was a man of such evil that God stepped in, which he doesn't do very often these days. He decreed that the nuns who Benedict had murdered could come back and wreak their vengeance upon him.'

'JD said this was Benedict's personal Hell. Was that right?'

'I'm afraid not,' said Levian. 'Scratch had one of his people alter the door to the Violet room so that it would take you back to eighteen ninety-six and the event where the nuns hunted down Benedict. Do you remember Karen told you the nuns drugged Benedict, and in the middle of the night one of them came out of his closet and let the others in, so they could have their revenge?'

Beth nodded.

'That story is an urban legend,' Levian continued. 'And like all urban legends it has become distorted over time. The truth is, you were the woman who came from the closet and handed Benedict over to the nuns.'

'I was *this time*.'

'No, it was always you.'

'I don't understand.'

'Beth, you are in the year eighteen ninety-six. And Coldworm Abbey now belongs to you.' He reached into his satchel and pulled out a few sheets of paper. 'These are the deeds to the abbey. Everything as far as you can see is now owned by you.'

Beth took the paperwork from him, but didn't bother to look at it, choosing instead to set it down on the step. 'But what about JD?' she asked.

'He's gone. I'm sorry, but you will not see him again.'

'NO!' Beth didn't intend to shout, it just happened.

'This was Scratch's plan all along,' said Levian. 'When he found out that you and JD were staying in the abbey, he was excited because he knew of the abbey's tragic history. He orchestrated a plan that has culminated with you stuck in the year eighteen ninety-six. And JD back in the present day.'

'Why? Why do that?' Beth's voice was close to breaking, her eyes filling with tears as she feared what Levian was saying was true.

'This will be hard for you to hear,' he said. 'Scratch found out you were pregnant, and by the laws of his contract with JD, he is legally entitled to take any offspring JD might have and burn them in Hell as punishment for JD breaking his contract.'

Beth clutched her stomach. 'He's coming for my baby?'

'He's already done it,' said Levian. 'The reason for leaving you stuck in the past, was so that he could kill your son in the present day.'

It was lot of information to take in and Beth wasn't clear she understood. 'You've lost me. I don't understand what you're saying.'

'Your son has holy blood, like his father. As a consequence he will live much longer than most people. You remember the monk, Brother Loomis?'

'Yes.'

'*He* was your son.'

'Loomis?' The image of the decapitated, impaled body of the monk flashed into her head. 'No, that can't be! You have to send me back!'

Levian maintained his calm exterior. 'Beth, if you were to go back to the present day, Scratch would see to it that your son was murdered the moment he was born. But by staying here in the past, your son will live a much longer life.'

'This doesn't make sense, you're lying.'

Levian put his hands up and motioned for Beth to calm down. He gave her a sympathetic smile. 'Your son knew his fate, Beth. He carried the key to the Violet room around his neck for all of his life, knowing that one day he would be murdered for it.'

'But if he knew that, why would he stay here at Coldworm? He could have gone anywhere.'

'He had to sacrifice himself. He lived with the knowledge that his death is what led to you travelling back in time. If you hadn't ended up here, he would have been murdered as a baby.'

'NO!' Beth shouted again.

Levian carried on, unfazed. 'When he is older you must give him the key to the Violet room, so that he may wear it around his neck. He will ensure that no one ever enters that room until the day you and JD show up to rent the cottage. His is a sacrifice that has to be made, for his own sake and that of his twin sister.'

'Sister?'

'Your daughter is every bit as brave as her brother. Maybe more so.'

'Twins? You're saying I'm having twins?'

'Yes.'

'I can't take this in. It's too much.'

'Search your heart, Beth. You can feel the truth.'

A tear rolled down Beth's cheek. 'What happens to my girl?'

'You already know,' said Levian with a conciliatory smile. 'You've met her many times before.'

'I have?'

'She's been watching out for you for many years now, warning you of the perils that lie in wait for you, keeping you safe.'

The answer came to Beth as if she had always known it. 'Annabel?'

'That's correct.'

Levian reached into his satchel and pulled out a crystal ball. He took Beth's hand and placed the ball in it. 'When she is older, give her this,' he said. 'It's not exactly magic, but it will create a mist and some images when she waves her hands over it. But for her to truly be able to predict the future, you will have to teach her about what is to come. She will use her knowledge to help people and to spy on Scratch so that she can find out the identity of her brother's killer.'

Beth's throat tingled and more tears rolled down her cheeks. Annabel, her daughter? She wished she'd known before. It made her feel sad and happy at the same time. She had always had a soft spot for the Mystic Lady.

'Does JD know about this too?' she asked.

Levian nodded. 'He will discover the truth, but he will not have the joy that you have. You will watch your children grow. You will live with the knowledge that your children will live long, happy lives. They will be safe here with you, living in the simpler times of the past where the Devil cannot harm them.'

'But how do I explain all this to them?'

'There is no rush. I suggest you let them live normal lives for as long as possible. When they are adults and they have lived, *truly lived*, that is when you should tell them. In the meantime, make a diary of all the things you need to tell them, all the things Annabel will need, like the time and date of the assassination of Pope John Paul George.'

'I can't remember the exact time and date the Pope died. I wasn't involved in it.'

Levian smiled. 'I know. I've left you a few cheat notes in those deeds I gave you. I have also planted a few images in the crystal ball for you, as a gift. Take a look, see what you can see.'

Beth looked into the crystal ball. In the middle of the swirling white clouds she saw an image of her and JD as teenagers on the pier in Santa Mondega. She remembered it well.

'That's where we kissed for the first time,' she said, another tear rolling down her cheek.

'You met Annabel that night too,' said Levian.

Beth broke into a smile that made her cry even more. 'What will happen to her? Will Scratch find out who she is?'

Levian reached over and wiped a tear from Beth's cheek. 'When she passes, she will not be taken by the Devil. Her life has been an honourable one. You will see her again in the afterlife.'

A female voice called out from the abbey's entrance. 'Hello?'

Beth looked up. Two young women had walked into the abbey. They were dressed as nuns, but thankfully they didn't have charred faces.

'That's Trudie and Monica,' said Levian. 'They lived here under Benedict's rule, but they left when their undead sisters showed up.'

As the two women made their way tentatively along the corridor, they spotted Beth.

'Who are you?' one of them asked.

'Tell them you've been sent by God,' said Levian.

Beth groaned and looked into Levian's eyes, hoping he was kidding.

'They can't see me,' he said. 'Tell them you're taking over the abbey and you're going to make it a safe place. Those two will be your friends for life.'

Before Beth could protest, Levian winked at her and then faded away into dust, as if he were nothing more than a hologram.

274

'Is Benedict here?' one of the nuns asked, nervously.

Beth smiled at her and stood up from the step. 'He's gone forever,' she said. 'God sent me to replace him. From now on, this is going to be a safe place for people in need.'

The nuns both looked puzzled.

Beth reached into her pocket and pulled out her cell phone. 'Would you like to see what Heaven looks like?' she asked.

Sixty

Scratch sprinted back through the portal into Coldworm Abbey. He blazed right through the washroom into the corridor, and then ran even faster down to the Violet room. He burst in and found Zilas chatting with two Ninjas. As soon as they saw Scratch they acted like they were busy looking for the Bourbon Kid.

'Any news?' Zilas asked.

Scratch blanked him. His eyes settled on the Egyptian rug in the middle of the floor. He reached down and grabbed hold of the nearest corner. He yanked it up and hurled the whole rug across the room.

And there it was. In the centre of the floor. A trapdoor.

'Motherfucker!'

'Is that a trapdoor?' one of the Ninjas asked, pointing at it.

'What do you think?'

'I think it is.'

'You moron, of course it is! Lift up that hatch.'

The Ninja crouched down by the hatch and opened it up. Underneath it was a dark tunnel.

'Fucking hell!' moaned Scratch. 'How did there come to be a fucking tunnel in here?'

Zilas climbed to his feet and offered an answer to the question. 'Someone dug it, I'm guessing,' he said.

'I WAS THINKING OUT LOUD!' Scratch bellowed, his eyes burning red, steam coming from his ears. 'Stop being so fucking annoying!'

'What are you going to do then?' Zilas asked.

Scratch ignored him and barked an order at the two Ninjas. 'You two idiots get down in that tunnel, and don't come back until you've found the Bourbon Kid.'

The Ninjas climbed through the trapdoor into the tunnel and started running. Zilas peered down the hole in the floor to see where they were going.

'Where do you think that tunnel goes?' he asked Scratch.

'HOW THE FUCK SHOULD I KNOW?' Scratch raged.

'Weird isn't it?' said Zilas. 'Annabel predicted everything would work perfectly. And yet, it hasn't?'

'SHUT UP!'

Scratch spent the next five minutes kicking Zilas all around the room. It was surprisingly therapeutic, as well as enjoyable, so he made a mental note to do it more often. It would have gone on for more than five minutes, but that was how long it took for one of the Ninjas to return from the tunnel. The Ninja poked his head up through the trapdoor.

'Excuse me, Master,' he said.

'Did you find him?' Scratch asked, calmly.

'No, Master, he's gone.'

'Gone? How can he be gone? He'd been shot and he could barely walk!'

'I know, but he's gone.'

Scratch wanted to beat the Ninja to death for committing the cardinal sin of giving the same answer twice, but he needed him conscious.

'Where did the tunnel come out?' Scratch asked him.

'By the side of a road on the edge of the estate,' the Ninja replied. 'But the road is deserted. The trail of the Kid's blood ends by the road. He's gone, vanished.'

Scratch clenched his fist and gnawed on his knuckles. 'Someone's helped him escape,' he said, unnerved by the thought that someone had masterminded the escape behind his back. 'But all of the Dead Hunters are in Santa Mondega. So who the fuck could it be?'

'I have a suggestion,' said a very dazed Zilas, raising his hand.

'Go on,' said Scratch.

'I think it's someone we haven't thought of.'

'YOU FUCKING MORON!'

Scratch ranted and raged for a while, and beat on Zilas some more, before eventually sending all the Ninjas outside to look for the Bourbon Kid.

They came back an hour later with nothing.

Sixty One

The tunnel under the abbey was cold and dark, and just about wide enough for two people. JD staggered along it, with one hand against the wall to stop himself from falling. Every step was draining the life out of him. There was no telling how long the tunnel was, or where it would come out. And it was only a matter of time before Scratch discovered its existence. JD was struggling to process all the information that had come his way in the last five minutes. Beth was gone, stuck in the past. Loomis was his son. Was it all true? Or just another part of Scratch's elaborate plan? Then there was the message on the wall in Loomis's bedroom, *"Remember my last words to you"*, it had taken a while to work out what that meant. Loomis had seemed odd when JD met him, and his use of the phrase "If you love someone, you dig them a tunnel" had been bugging JD from the moment he'd said it. Finally it made sense, *probably*. As he struggled on through the tunnel the biggest question he kept asking himself was, *do I have a reason to carry on?*

It wasn't just his energy that was deserting him, his will to live was fading fast too. There didn't appear to be any light, metaphorical or otherwise, at the end of this tunnel. JD travelled about fifty metres along it before his legs gave up on him. He crumpled to the ground and tried to get his breath back. It was hard to even stay awake.

'Don't worry, I've got you!'

He heard the words whispered to him. Were they in his head? Or was someone in the tunnel with him? His vision faded in and out. Even the darkness seemed blurry. Someone slid their arms under his armpits and lifted him up.

'Don't quit on me now,' the voice said.

He couldn't see who it was, but judging by the voice it had to be a woman. She wrapped JD's arm around her shoulder and helped him along the tunnel. It was a struggle, but with the stranger's help he made it to the end.

'Can you get up the ladder?' she asked him.

'Yeah.'

JD grabbed hold of one of the metal rungs built into the wall, and with the assistance of the woman behind pushing him up he climbed to the top. He used his good arm to push open another trapdoor. Daylight flooded into the tunnel. JD poked his head out and looked around. Everything was out of focus. There was grass all around the opening. He was on the edge of the Coldworm estate, next to a road. He crawled out of the hole, aided by a few shoves from below. As soon as he was out he rolled over onto his back and lay on the grass staring up at the sky, his strength all but gone.

The woman climbed out of the hole and lifted him up by his armpits again. 'Come on,' she said, 'One last push. We're almost there.'

JD managed to get his feet under him, and the woman wrapped his arm around her shoulder again, acting as a crutch. She helped him over to a black transit van at the side of the road. When they reached the van she opened the passenger door. With her help, JD managed to climb into the passenger seat. He let his head fall back against the headrest, and closed his eyes. The woman buckled him in and ran around to the other side of the van. She jumped into the driver's seat, fired up the engine and set off down the road at high speed.

JD rolled his head to the side. Through his watery vision he soaked in the image of his rescuer. It took a while, but he soon recognised her. It was Mavis, the weird housekeeper with the sneezing and twitching issues.

'What are you doing here?' he asked.

'Annabel sent me to get you,' Mavis replied.

'Annabel?'

'Just rest up. AND LICK MY FUCKING BALLS!'

'What?'

'Sorry about that,' said Mavis. 'I'll explain…' she twitched her head violently and shouted, '*SLAG!*' before continuing like nothing had happened. 'I'll explain everything later.'

JD studied Mavis's face. Something wasn't right. He was surprised he'd never noticed it before. He reached out and grabbed a handful of her blue hair. With just the slightest pull it came off in his hand. The shock of what he'd done caused her to twitch and she almost steered the van off the road. Underneath the wig Mavis had brown hair tied back in a ponytail. And suddenly it became clear that the skin around the edge of her face wasn't real either. It was a mask. JD grabbed a piece of the loose skin and peeled it away. It distracted Mavis even more than when he'd pulled the wig off.

'GIMP LICKER!' she shouted, her shoulders shaking violently.

When the mask was off, he saw the face of a much younger woman. And she looked familiar. He'd seen her once before, a long time ago, maybe ten years or more. She was one of those people, once seen, never forgotten.

'Janis Joplin?'

'Just Janis actually,' she replied, swinging the van around a bend in the road. 'Janis Joplin was my stage name. YOU FUCKING BELLEND!'

'Bellend?'

'I'm sorry. It's my Tourette's. I've travelled a lot and picked up phrases from all over the world.'

JD closed his eyes again and pressed his hand against the bleeding wound in his chest. The realisation that he was almost out of danger was making him relax. He felt sleepy again.

'Why are you here?' he asked, unsure if he would still be awake when she answered.

'Annabel was your daughter,' said Janis. 'She asked me to come and get you. I'm sorry for all that's happened to you.'

'Annabel is my daughter?'

'Yes. And Loomis was your son. Beth had twins.'

'*Beth.*' His voice cracked. 'Is she here?'

Janis shook her head. 'I'm sorry. She's gone. She's been gone a long time. But right now.... *FUCKSTICKS!* You need to get some rest. I'll explain everything else to you later.'

JD heard nothing after the word *fucksticks*. For the next few hours while Janis drove him to a safe place, he drifted in and out of consciousness.

Sixty Two

Two days had passed since the Bourbon Kid vanished. Scratch was alone in Purgatory sitting on a stool behind the bar, drinking cognac, smoking a cigar and watching a Bill Cosby film called *Ghost Dad*. It wasn't a particularly funny film, but Scratch liked the part where Cosby took a ride in a cab driven by a devil-worshipper, who then drove the cab off a bridge, killing them both. After that, the film's portrayal of what happened to Bill Cosby in the afterlife was unrealistic to say the least.

Scratch was looking for a reason to switch the film off, when suddenly Jacko walked in through the saloon doors at the front entrance. As usual he was wearing a musty brown suit and a fedora hat, and he had a guitar strapped across his back.

'Morning boss, how's it going?' he asked, cheerfully. He took off his hat and bowed his head.

'It's going shit,' Scratch replied. 'What do you want?'

'I just came to tell you that the Ninjas are all gone. They passed through the crossroads about twenty minutes ago.'

Scratch picked up a remote control and paused the television. 'What about the Dead Hunters? Have none of them showed up yet?'

'No, I haven't seen anyone.' Jacko looked around. 'How come you're on your own?'

'I'm sulking.'

'About what?'

Scratch didn't like the idea of confiding in Jacko, but he had no one else to share his problems with, so the bluesman would have to do. 'I'm fed up,' he said. 'Annabel's gone, and it looks like she's gone to Heaven. I didn't see that coming, I can tell you.'

'I miss her,' said Jacko. 'I enjoyed her predictions.'

'So did I,' said Scratch, getting a little misty-eyed. 'Especially when she got things wrong. It made things more interesting.'

Jacko looked around. 'Where's Zilas?' he asked.

'I threw him down a bottomless fire pit.'

'What did you do that for?'

'He was getting on my nerves.'

'But he always gets on your nerves.'

Scratch blew some cigar smoke at Jacko. 'And now he's paying the price for that,' he said. 'Fucking Dracula is gone now too. Fat lot of use he was. I don't know what I was thinking letting that clown out of Hell. He killed Annabel but I still had to give him the keys to a brothel. Useless bastard.'

'Do you need a hug?'

'Fuck off.'

'Fair enough. Mind if I grab a bottle of whisky? Then I'll get out of your hair.'

Scratch reached down below the bar and grabbed a bottle of cheap whisky and a glass. He slid them across the bar to Jacko. The bluesman picked them up and walked over to a table in front of the TV.

'Is this Ghost Dad?' he asked.

'Yes,' Scratch replied, flicking to another channel.

Jacko poured himself a glass of the whisky and sat back to enjoy some television. 'Oh great,' he said. 'It's Little Nicky, you like this film.'

Scratch didn't answer. He'd spotted someone outside, walking past one of the windows at the front of the building. 'Have you let anyone through the crossroads this morning?' he asked Jacko.

'No, not a soul,' Jacko replied.

'Then who is....'

A blond-haired black man in a white robe walked through the saloon doors. 'Morning Scratch,' he said, smiling.

Scratch hated angels, and Levian was one of the more annoying ones. 'What do you want?' he asked in a hostile voice.

Levian walked up to the bar and pulled up a stool. 'Just thought I'd drop by, see how things are going,' he said. He glanced over at Jacko. 'Is that Robert Johnson?'

'Never mind him,' said Scratch. 'He's watching Little Nicky. Now what do you want?'

'I heard you had some trouble. Lost your fortune-teller.'

'What's it to you?'

'I met her yesterday up in Heaven. She's having a lovely time up there. And she's very popular, tells great stories about the stuff you get up to down here.'

'Have you come here to gloat, or can I tempt you with a shot of something?'

Levian smiled. 'I would, but I can't be tempted, remember?'

'Of course,' said Scratch. 'It must be a barrel of laughs in Heaven. What do you do all day? Paint by numbers? Watch Disney cartoons? Listen to the Osmonds?'

'All of those things,' said Levian. 'Are you having fun drinking by yourself?'

'Get fucked. What do you want?'

Levian sniffed the air. 'That smell is lingering isn't it?' he said.

'I'll ask you one last time,' said Scratch. 'What do you want?'

'I've come to give you some bad news. God says you've broken one of the sacred laws.'

'Bullshit.'

'Aren't you going to ask which one?'

'All right, which one?'

'I can't say, but I'm sure you'll work it out one day.'

'Don't be a dick. Tell me.'

Levian picked a peanut out of a bowl on the bar and flicked it at Scratch. It hit him on the cheek. The expression on Scratch's face changed drastically.

'What the fuck?' he said, wiping his face where the peanut had hit him. 'I felt that.'

'Yes you did,' said Levian. 'From this moment forth, God has decreed that you will feel pain. You might even die if someone were to, let say, I don't know..... Cut your head off? Impale you on a spike?'

Scratch chewed on his cigar and spat some on the bar-top near Levian. 'If this is because I killed that Loomis fellow, I'll have you know I had every right to do that. He was the Bourbon Kid's son. And my contract with the Kid stated that any children he had could be executed by me, without reprisal.'

Levian swivelled round on his stool and stood up to leave. 'I know all about your contract,' he said. 'Anyway, there's one last thing I need to tell you before I leave.'

'What?'

'Your people, the Dead Hunters, they work for me now.'

'How the fuck do you figure that?'

'Your contracts with them have become null and void. They will be working for me from now on, hunting down devil worshippers, and dare I say it, demons, vampires, the undead, that sort of thing. Who knows, maybe one day I'll send them after you.'

'You wouldn't dare!'

'I might not have to,' said Levian, winking at Scratch. 'Someone else might get to you first.'

'If you mean the Bourbon Kid, I'm telling you, he'll never set foot in this place again!' said Scratch, flicking some cigar ash at the angel. 'I'll close off the portal so no one can get in or out of here.' He pointed at Jacko. 'And he won't let anyone in through the crossroads, anymore, will you Jacko?'

'Absolutely not,' said Jacko, without taking his eyes off the television screen. 'No one comes through the crossroads without your permission.'

'There, see,' said Scratch, feeling triumphant. 'You tell them Dead Hunters, they won't set foot in Purgatory ever again, any of them.' He paused, then added, 'Apart from Jasmine, possibly.'

Jacko groaned. 'I'll miss Jasmine.'

'Don't worry about it,' said Scratch. 'I've got photos of her on my phone.'

'I've got those too,' said Jacko.

Levian made a salute at Scratch. 'It was nice catching up with you again,' he said. 'We should do this more often. Nice to meet you too, Mister Johnson.'

Before Jacko could even wave goodbye to Levian, the angel vanished into thin air.

'Wait!' yelled Scratch. 'What sacred law did I break? YOU ASSHOLE!'

Sixty Three

*"Here lies Ruth Palmer, a fine woman who opened up
Coldworm Abbey to homeless people and those in need.
An angel to the people of the local community, and a devoted
mother.
Rest In Peace"*

The twins, Vincent and Emma were standing in an afternoon downpour of rain, looking at their mother's grave. A large statue of an angel stood atop the gravestone, making it the obvious centrepiece of the graveyard at Coldworm Abbey.

The year was 1931, and the Palmer twins were aged thirty-five. The funeral had just taken place and they were both in their best black clothes. Vincent wore a long black coat with a hood pulled up over his head to keep off the rain. His sister Emma had a black cardigan over her dress and a woolly hat to keep her warm and counter the rain.

The funeral had been a well-attended event with almost everyone from the local community present. The bad weather had seen to it that everyone headed inside for the wake a little earlier than intended, leaving Beth's son and daughter alone at her graveside.

'I'm so glad you made it back before she died,' said Vincent.

Emma reached into a pocket on her cardigan and pulled out a crystal ball. She stared into it and saw nothing but white swirling liquid. 'I feel bad that I was away for so long,' she said. 'I was having such a great time in Mississippi. I hadn't even written her a letter in months.'

'She didn't mind,' said Vincent. 'She knew you loved to travel.'

Emma shook the crystal ball. 'Let's see if she's got a message for us?'' she said.

A white mist swirled around inside the ball, but no images showed up in the centre of it.

Vincent scoffed. 'That's never going to work. I mean, it's nice and all, but it isn't going to predict the future for you, is it?'

'You never know. It might.'

Vincent stared down at their mother's gravestone. 'You're not saying you believe any of that story she told us at the end, are you? I don't know if I even believe her real name was Beth.'

'I believe every word of it.'

Vincent sniffed and wiped some drops of rain from his nose. 'Deals with the Devil? Vampires, werewolves, time travel? It's just too far-fetched.' He clutched at the key that hung from his neck on a chain. 'If everything goes according to what she says then I'm going to end up impaled on a spike, with my head cut off.'

'It's going to happen,' said Emma. 'It's already happening.'

'What do you mean it's already happening? Don't tell me you think you've seen something in your crystal ball already,' he said, teasing her.

'Not in my crystal ball,' Emma replied. 'It's just the darndest thing. When I was in Mississippi I made a lot of friends. One of them was a musician who wants to be the best guitar player that ever lived. He says he's willing to do anything to make it happen.'

'So?'

'His name is Robert Johnson.'

Vincent stared at his sister to see if she was kidding. She wasn't. 'You're friends with Jacko already?'

'Yes. That's how I know everything she said was true. I'm going to go back to Mississippi and see if he's interested in making that deal with the Devil.'

'Are you going to tell him about all the other stuff?'

Emma nodded. 'I sure am.'

'But won't that put him off?'

'I don't think it will. After all, these things have already happened, haven't they? I think he'll go for it. Think about it, in the future he's the man who decides who gets access into the hidden part of the Devil's Graveyard. I bet he can arrange for me to get tickets to that *Back From the Dead* show mom told us about.'

Vincent lowered the hood on his coat and allowed the rain to soak into his shaggy brown hair. 'This is crazy,' he said, looking up at the sky and feeling the cold water on his face. 'Don't tell me you're going to change your name to Annabel as well?'

'I think I am. Annabel de Frugyn, it's an unusual name but I sort of like it. You know if everything mom said is true, then this is going to be great fun.'

'I'm not changing my name to Loomis.'

Emma laughed. 'Scared of having a spike rammed up your anus?'

'Fuck yes. Of course I am!'

'Look at it this way,' said Emma. 'You've got a lifetime to find a way to prevent that from happening.'

Vincent ran his hands through his wet hair and then playfully flicked some water in his sister's face. In return, she shoved him in the chest. The two of them embraced, and then with their arms entwined they headed back towards the main building.

'Do you think I can I come to Mississippi with you and meet Jacko?' Vincent asked.

Emma elbowed him in the ribs. 'Let's do it. Road trip!'

****

The same place – present day

Rex was standing in front of the angel statue in the graveyard at Coldworm Abbey. It was the last resting place of Beth Lansbury, although her gravestone named her as Ruth Palmer.

Elvis, Jasmine, Flake and Sanchez had all gone inside the abbey to get out of the rain. The five of them were there for the funeral of a man none of them had even met, Loomis Lansbury.

Rex moved across to the gravestone next to Beth's. There were several bouquets of flowers placed beneath it. Unlike Beth's grave, with its enormous angel statue, this one was unmarked. It was the last resting place of Annabel de Frugyn, or Emma Lansbury, or Emma Palmer, or the Mystic Lady. Annabel had had many names in her lifetime and Rex probably didn't even know half of them. She had been buried in the unmarked grave five years ago after being murdered by Archie Somers. It was a strange thing for Rex to get his head around. Just a few days earlier he'd seen Annabel turn to dust in Jasmine's arms.

'I'll miss you Annabel,' he said. 'At least now we all know why you got half of your predictions wrong.'

The rain was beating down hard on his Stetson hat, reminding him that it was time to go inside and join the others for the cremation of Annabel's brother, Loomis. He left Annabel's grave and walked up a path towards the abbey. He was halfway there when Elvis came out of the main entrance. The King was wearing a black suit with gold trim down the sleeves and a gold belt. He spotted Rex, and ran along the path towards him, splashing through puddles and using his hand to try and protect his quiffed hair.

'Let me guess,' said Rex. 'Sanchez has made a smell in there.'

Elvis shook his head. 'Nah man, it's not that.'

'What then?'

Elvis looked around to make sure no one was in earshot. 'I just saw something fucking weird.'

'Was it the preacher lady with the blue hair?'

'No,' said Elvis, looking around again. 'That woman is weird though. She coughed earlier and I think she called me a cunt under her breath.'

'She's a fucking lunatic,' Rex agreed. I wouldn't get too close, she looks like a spitter.'

'Forget her for a minute. This is fucking mental.'

'Can you tell me inside? I'm getting soaked out here.'

'No,' said Elvis, holding his arm out to stop Rex pushing past him. 'You know this is a closed-casket affair, right? On account of what happened to the guy.'

'Yeah, so?'

'So, I went and had a look in the coffin.'

Rex groaned. 'What is wrong with you?'

'Whaddaya mean what's wrong with me? This was the Bourbon Kid's son. I wanted to know what he looked like. Weren't you curious?'

'No. Not in the least. I've seen enough dead bodies in my time, especially fucked up ones.'

'Well I looked. And you know what I saw in there?'

Rex sighed. 'A dead body?'

'Yeah. But it wasn't Loomis Lansbury.'

'How would you know? You don't even know what Loomis looks like?'

'Damn right I don't. But I know what Melvin Melt looks like.'

'What?'

'Melvin fucking Melt.'

Rex tried to process the information. '*Melvin Melt?* What are you talking about?'

'The corpse in that coffin is Melvin Melt, the guy we broke out of prison the other night, remember?'

'Of course I fucking remember,' said Rex, before lowering his voice. 'I know who Melvin Melt is! What's he doing in there?'

'I don't know. But it's mental, isn't it?'

He had a point. It *was* mental. Rex couldn't make any sense of it. 'How the fuck can Melvin Melt be in that coffin? What's he doing all the way out here in the middle of nowhere?'

Elvis looked around again to make sure no one was within earshot. 'I don't fucking know, but I bet Papshmir does.'

Sixty Four

The eclipse in Santa Mondega had come and gone without any great incident. No massacres, no vampires, just people drinking and having a good time. And now, three days later there were still a great many people out on the streets, dressed in fun costumes. One such person was a man dressed as Cesar Romero's Joker from the 1960's Batman TV show. He was sitting at a small round table on the sidewalk outside a late night bar called Logan's Rum.

With it being almost half-past midnight, most of the local assholes had already gone home. The late, late crowd were out now, and they were generally a happy bunch.

The man in the purple Joker costume was sipping on a glass of dark rum, watching the world go by when a replica of the motorbike from the TV show Street Hawk roared down the middle of the street. Its rider wore a black leather outfit with white stripes down the arms and legs, and a crash helmet with a black visor hiding her face. The bike slowed and came to a stop outside Logan's Rum. The rider dismounted, walked over to the Joker's table and pulled up a plastic chair to sit next to him.

'I thought you weren't coming,' said the Joker.

The biker removed her helmet and placed it on the table next to the Joker's drink. She shook her long brown hair and then tied it back in a ponytail.

'You're looking good, pops,' she said, with a wry smile. 'A little pale, mind.'

The man in the Joker outfit was Father Vincent Papshmir. The woman in the biker gear was his daughter, Janis.

'Is he definitely coming?' he asked her.

'He'll be here any minute now.'

A young blond-haired waiter in a black and white uniform approached the table. 'Can I get you anything to drink, Miss?' he asked.

'BANANA JIZZ!' Janis replied, twitching her head violently.

'Excuse me?'

Papshmir intervened. 'She'd like a Banana Daiquiri, please.'

'Certainly sir, I'll be right back.'

The waiter left them and headed back inside the bar.

'How was the funeral?' Papshmir asked. 'Did you get through the ceremony without swearing?'

'I might have sworn a few times but I think I got away with it.'

'And JD? How is he?'

'He's fully recovered, but he's gone to a very dark place. I didn't like telling him that Auntie Emma was dead. That was hard.'

'But you didn't tell him about me, did you?'

'How many times are you gonna ask me that? No, I didn't tell him. He still thinks the guy who was impaled in the abbey was his son. I fucking wanted to tell him though. It felt cruel.'

'I know, but like I always told you, it has to remain a secret, because if Scratch ever finds out I'm JD's son, he'll soon find out you're my daughter. And then everything my sister and I fought so hard for will be lost.'

'I know, I know, you've told me this a million times.'

'Did he ask why you helped him?'

'Yeah, and I told him I was a friend of Annabel's, and I owed her a favour because she rescued me from the Hotel Pasadena that time.'

'And he was okay with that?'

'He'd been shot and he was coming to terms with the loss of Beth and two children that he never knew about, I don't think he gave a fuck about who I was.'

'So he doesn't suspect anything?'

The waiter returned with a Banana Daiquiri for Janis. He placed it down on the table.

'Put it on my tab, please,' said Papshmir.

'Nice ass,' said Janis as the waiter walked away. She picked up the drink and took a sip through a blue straw, then had a twitching fit, spilled some of it over Papshmir's shirt and shouted, 'TASTE'S LIKE GORILLA COCK!'

'It's nice then?' said Papshmir, drying himself off with a handkerchief.

A few people passing by stared at Janis, wondering what the fuss was about, but both she and her father were used to being stared at. She'd been a potty-mouth since a very young age and Papshmir had helped her to feel normal by swearing a lot himself, so she didn't feel like a nutcase.

'I can't believe it actually worked,' said Papshmir. 'Emma and I came up with that plan not long after our mother died. It's been a lifetime's work. And it's almost done.' He paused a moment, then asked, 'Did Melvin Melt give you any problems?'

Janis pulled a pack of cigarettes out of her pocket. She drew one out with her teeth, sucked on it and it lit up on its own. She took a drag and exhaled before answering her father's question.

'Melvin Melt,' she said, smiling. 'That poor cunt was impaled on a fucking spike, right up through his asshole.' Her head twitched and she shouted 'GINGER DILDO, JIZZ FACE!' and accidentally spilled some more of her drink over her father.

'You know, I shudder when I think about that,' said Papshmir. 'It could have been me on the end of that spike.'

'It wasn't really a spike,' said Janis. 'It was wide, *fucking wide*, more of a spear really. Must have really destroyed his FANNY!'

'But Melt did everything you asked?'

Janis took another drag on her cigarette. 'Oh, yeah, I made it clear I'd fucking kill him if he didn't. He got everything right, right down to the last detail. I made absolutely certain he told JD that stupid line about digging tunnels for people you love. I almost feel bad for him that he had his butt violated so bad a few hours later.'

'He deserved it, trust me.'

'Oh yeah, I mean *fuck him*, right. The piece of DONKEY CUNT!'

Papshmir smiled. 'You know I got to see your Auntie Emma one last time the other night. She was in the Tapioca when I went to see Elvis and Rex about the prison break.'

'How was she?'

'We didn't speak much. Couldn't really, with everyone there. It's the first time I've seen her since she was murdered. I'm so glad, because otherwise my last memory of her would have been collecting her mutilated body from the morgue five years ago.'

'She was a fucking legend,' said Janis, raising her glass. 'To Annabel de Frugyn, the Mystic....' Janis twitched and sneered as she fought hard to avoid blurting out any further donkey insults. To Papshmir's relief she held it together, and after a five second delay, she added the word, "Lady" to the end of her sentence.

Papshmir wiped some Banana Daiquiri off his face and smiled. 'It's great to have you back, Janis.'

'It's good to be back,' she replied. 'You know, I was thinking, since I got to meet all the Dead Hunters at the funeral, even though I was in disguise I got on well with all of them.'

'Don't say it!'

'Say what?'

'I know what you're thinking, and the answer is no.'

Janis blew some smoke towards her father. 'I'm old enough to make my own decisions you know,' she said. 'And besides, they're working for Levian now.'

'You are not becoming a Dead Hunter.'

Janis grinned. 'Elvis still looks good.'

'He does,' Papshmir agreed. 'But you know he's with Jasmine these days, so you've missed your chance.'

'Did you know she was a hooker?'

Papshmir nodded and took a sip of his rum. 'She was also in a porno with Sanchez once.'

Janis pulled a face like she'd just bitten into a raw lemon. 'That sounds horrific!'

The loud roar of an engine drowned out Papshmir's response. A black Ford Mustang cruised down the street towards them.

'Here it comes,' Papshmir said.

Janis moved her chair around so she could get a better view. The Mustang parked up on the opposite side of the road, right outside a brothel called the Cherry Poppins.

'I wish we could go in and watch this,' said Papshmir.

Sixty Five

It was half past midnight on a Saturday night and the Cherry Poppins brothel in Santa Mondega was at its busiest. Drunken men with nowhere better to go were drinking in the lounge bar looking for a suitable lady to go upstairs with. All twenty rooms on the upper floors were in use, and judging by the number of men waiting their turn in the bar, it was going to be a long night for the hookers who worked in the establishment.

The men in the bar could be split into two categories. The regulars, most of whom were married and came in on their own. They usually drank in the lounge bar and waited until their favourite hooker became available. Then there were the bachelor parties. They sat around at tables, making lots of noise and drinking themselves stupid. None of them paid any attention to a man who entered the establishment wearing a long black coat with the hood pulled up over his head. He ordered a glass of bourbon from the bar, insisted the bartender fill it to the top, placed a ten-dollar bill down on the bar and downed the drink in one. It was the beginning of the last night in the history of the Cherry Poppins brothel.

The hooded man walked over to a jukebox, dropped a dime in the slot and selected the song "Aisha" by Death in Vegas. It came on loud and drowned out every conversation in the bar. A few angry glances were thrown his way. He ignored them and headed for the staircase at the back of the bar. The hooded man was the Bourbon Kid, the biggest mass murderer in the history of Santa Mondega. Underneath his coat he had an arsenal of weapons strapped to him, and enough ammunition to kill everyone in the Cherry Poppins at least six times.

'Hey buddy!' the bartender called out. 'You can't go up there on your own. You gotta book a slot first!'

The Bourbon Kid ignored him and carried on up the stairs. The bartender gestured to a bouncer, a big burly man named Morgan, with a rough beard and muscles upon muscles that were on show through a white T-shirt. Every week there'd be at least one idiot who tried going upstairs without a hooker accompanying him. And Morgan had always brought them crashing back down to earth.

The Bourbon Kid was halfway up the stairs when Morgan bounded up behind him and placed a hand on his shoulder.

'You can't go up there,' the bouncer said.

It was the catalyst for the slaughter that followed. The Kid grabbed Morgan's hand, removed it from his shoulder and crushed

293

every bone in it. He then opened his coat, pulled out a sawed-off shotgun, pressed it under the bouncer's chin and blasted the brains out of his head. Blood sprayed up onto the ceiling and the walls. Morgan's body wobbled for a moment then fell backwards and bounced down the stairs, ending up at the bottom in the kind of position only the women upstairs could normally achieve.

For those drinking in the lounge bar, the murder of the bouncer came as a complete shock. And before anyone had reacted, the Kid was at the top of the stairs. He took a left turn into a corridor with a hardwood floor and doors on either side. The Death in Vegas song drowned out the sound of people having sex inside the rooms as it boomed out of the loud speakers dotted intermittently along the walls of the corridor.

The Bourbon Kid opened the first door he came to and walked in, shotgun ready. He was greeted by the sight of a fat, naked and very hairy drunken man dancing a jig in front of a busty, naked, blonde hooker who was sitting on a bed clapping enthusiastically at his performance. The hooker saw the Kid first, his shotgun aimed at her naked client. She screamed, alerting the dancing customer to their intruder. Mister "Fat-naked-and-hairy" didn't appreciate the interruption to his private time and didn't seem to notice the sawed-off shotgun aimed at his low-hanging scrotum.

'What the fuck are you doing?' he growled.

The Bourbon Kid replied in a low gravelly voice. 'Where is he?'

'Where's who?'

BOOM!

The impact of the shotgun blast blew the fat guy off his feet. He crashed into the wall ten feet behind him, blood pissing out from a fleshy mess where his scrotum once was. He grabbed at the injured area and writhed around on the ground, looking for his testicles and screaming for all he was worth, which wasn't much.

A second shotgun blast ended his screaming. It turned his face inside out, making a mess all over a set of green curtains behind him. The Kid turned his gun on the blonde hooker on the bed.

'Where *is* he?' he asked her.

She stopped screaming for just long enough to look puzzled and ask, *'Who?'*

'You know who.'

'No, I don't, I....'

BOOM!

The hooker's head turned to red goo and splatted across the wall behind her. Her torso stayed upright and did a strange, uncoordinated wiggle-dance, while a fountain of blood gushed out of the hole between her shoulders, redecorating the room in claret. The Kid left the room before the hooker's body collapsed onto the bed.

Back in the corridor, other people had heard the gunfire and began vacating their rooms. Another naked hooker, a slim brunette, burst out of the next door along and stopped in her tracks when she saw the hooded gunman standing before her. Her client, another fat white guy with an abundance of hair on his chest and back, followed her out of the room, wearing nothing but a pair of sweat-stained blue underpants.

The brunette put her hands on her hips and stared angrily at the Kid. 'What the fuck have you done?'

BOOM!

The impact of the blast blew the brunette's stomach apart and knocked her off her feet. She crashed back into Mr Blue Knickers. The fat guy lost his footing and ended up on the floor on his back, with the bloodied remains of a hooker painted on his chest.

More hookers and customers piled out of the rooms along the corridor, blissfully unaware of what they were walking into. When they saw the mess the Kid had made of the brunette, the Cherry Poppins was suddenly rocking to the screams of a bunch of very panicked people. JD stood over the fat guy in the blue underpants and fired off another shot, blowing his face off and changing the colour of the floor.

Among the fleeing bodies sprinting along the corridor in the opposite direction was a wiry, balding white guy in his fifties known as O'Connor, who was naked apart from a pair of socks. O'Connor knew the place better than most, so he headed straight for a fire escape that was tucked around a corner out of range of the gunfire. He kicked the fire door open with the intention of fleeing naked into the night.

But there was no way out through the fire door. Standing on the other side of it was Elvis. The hitman was decked out in a red suit, with a double-barrelled shotgun in his hands.

'Goin' somewhere?' Elvis asked.

'Wh...'

BOOM!

The blast from Elvis's shotgun blew O'Connor back into a crowd of people who'd taken the same wrong turn as him. O'Connor's blood and guts spurted out through his back and sprayed into the faces and bodies of the fools who'd followed him. A short bald guy at the front of the fleeing mob took the brunt of it, swallowing a big chunk of

O'Connor's intestines and falling over onto a group of people behind him. They dropped like dominoes, sprayed in the remains of what was once a man named O'Connor.

The sound of a machine gun rat-a-tatting in the bar below was an indicator that Rex and Jasmine had arrived on the premises. No one was getting out of this place alive.

A hooker dressed in black lingerie wriggled free of the bundle of bodies underneath O'Connor's innards. She tried a different survival tactic. She faced up to the Bourbon Kid and raised her hands in the air.

'Where is he?' the Kid asked her, his gun aimed at her throat.

'You mean the vampire man?' she said, her whole body trembling.

'That's right.'

She pointed along the corridor. 'Last room on the left.'

By way of thanks for her cooperation, the Bourbon Kid showed her some mercy and made her death quick. He fired a shot into her throat. The blast took her neck out and made her head drop down onto her shoulders. Her knees buckled, and as she fell forwards her head dropped off behind her and bounced down the corridor behind a group of naked people who were running for their lives.

Elvis came around the corner and pointed his gun down at the face of the short bald guy on the floor beneath O'Connor. The man couldn't even plead for his life because he had a mouthful of O'Connor's lunch. Elvis hesitated for a second, as if considering a moment of mercy.

The Bourbon Kid took the initiative and did the job for him.

BOOM!

The bald guy's head splattered into a million tiny pieces.

Twelve more people were murdered on the way to Dracula's room. Elvis walked behind the Kid, checking the corpses of the devil-worshipping hookers and their clients, making sure they were dead and not carrying any weapons.

The Kid stopped outside the last door on the left. He took a step back and kicked it hard, knocking the door off its hinges. It crashed onto the floor inside the room and almost immediately a small bat flew out into the corridor. It didn't get far. The Kid made a sharp "duck and fire" move, pointing his sleeve up at the ceiling and firing a silver dart out of a small contraption concealed on his wrist. The dart hit the bat in the neck. It stopped flapping its wings and dropped to the floor with an almighty thud, where it transformed back into the naked and bleeding figure of Dracula. Elvis kicked the vampire in the ribs, turning him over onto his back. There was a silver dart poking out of Dracula's neck. Blood pulsed out of the wound.

'You're in big fuckin' trouble,' said Elvis.

Dracula panicked and chose to plead for his life rather than fight. 'Please, please, listen!' he begged, looking at both men, hoping one of them would be merciful. 'I didn't know. I just did what I was told to do.'

BOOM!

Dracula's dick and balls vanished, turned into a red spray that squelched all over the carpet behind him, seeping into his ass crack, and also onto the toes of Elvis's shoes.

The Bourbon Kid stood over his stricken victim and lowered his hood, revealing his blood-speckled face, unshaven and murderous.

Dracula was trying to hold his ass together with one hand, while he held up his other hand to beg for mercy. 'I'll give you anything you want,' he squealed.

JD grabbed a clump of Dracula's hair and hauled him to his feet.

'When I'm done with you,' he said in a deep, gravelly voice. 'You'll find yourself back in Hell. When you get there, be sure you tell Scratch, *I'm coming for him next.*'

The End (maybe....)

Printed in Great Britain
by Amazon

14504043R10171